Mercenary of the Gods

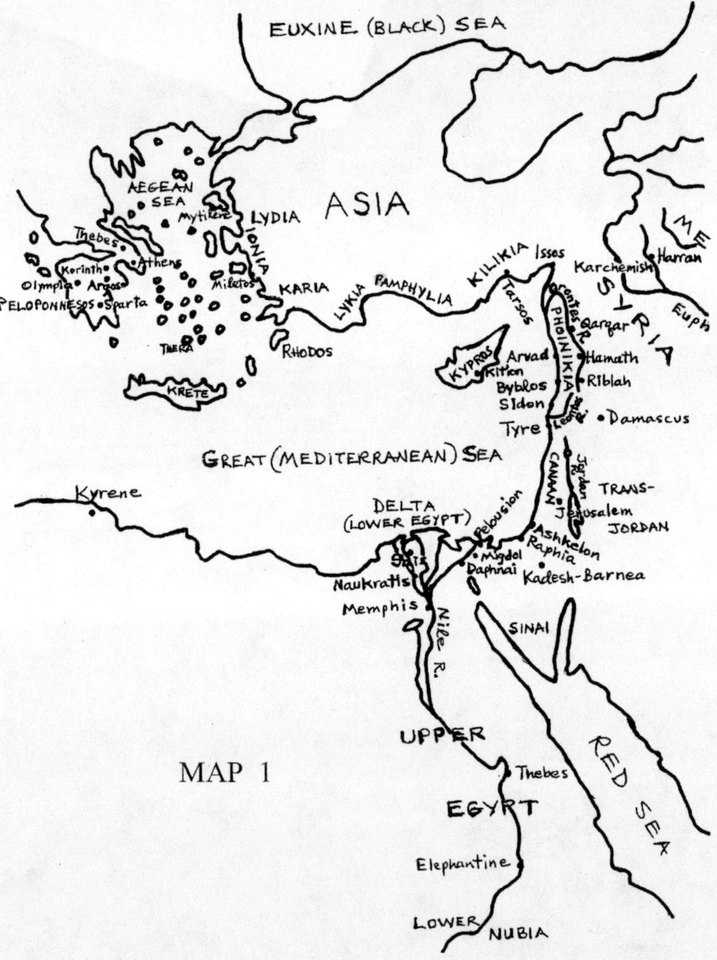
EUXINE (BLACK) SEA
ASIA
AEGEAN SEA
Mytilene
LYDIA
IONIA
Thebes
Athens
Korinth
Olympia
Argos
Miletos
KARIA
PELOPONNESOS
Sparta
THERA
RHODOS
KRETE
LYKIA
PAMPHYLIA
KILIKIA
Issos
Tarsos
Karchemish
Harran
SYRIA
Euph
Orontes R.
PHOINIKIA
Qarqar
KYPROS
Kition
Arvad
Hamath
Riblah
Byblos
Sidon
Tyre
Damascus
GREAT (MEDITERRANEAN) SEA
CANAAN
Jordan R.
TRANS-
JORDAN
Jerusalem
Kyrene
DELTA
(LOWER EGYPT)
Pelousion
Ashkelon
Raphia
Migdol
Daphnai
Kadesh-Barnea
Sais
Naukratis
Memphis
Nile R.
SINAI
UPPER
Thebes
EGYPT
RED SEA
Elephantine
LOWER
NUBIA

MAP 1

EASTERN MEDITERRANEAN AREA AND NEARBY LANDS

Mercenary of the Gods

Memoirs of a Greek in Service to Judah and Egypt

Jack Cargill

Regina Books
Claremont, California

Book design by Regina Books
Cover illustration by Scot J. Wittman

ISBN 1-930053-31-2

Regina Books

Post Office Box 280
Claremont, California 91711
Tel: (909) 624-8466 / Fax (909) 626-1345

Manufactured in the United States of America

For Shelley

Whose support at every stage was the strongest and most helpful

PREFACE

The seventh and sixth centuries Before the Common Era constituted a period of intense change and excitement in the lands around the eastern Mediterranean. Greek writers and artists, inspired by the epics of Homer and by the older civilizations to the east and south, were launching their Lyric Age in poetry, "Orientalizing" their plastic arts, and infusing their Egyptian-inspired sculptures with the enigmatic Archaic Smile. Political turmoil within the young city-states was producing broadened concepts of citizenship, even if a phase of tyranny was sometimes necessary in bringing about the transition. Greeks moved about in all directions—exiles, traders, explorers, colonists, mercenaries. All these converging stimuli were encouraging new ideas, new points of view, new ways of thinking. Philosophy, science, and rationalism were a-borning, especially among the Ionian Greeks of western Asia Minor.

Beginning just before and extending through these same centuries, Egypt saw dynasties rise and fall, experienced external conquest twice, and produced its last important native ruling dynasty of god-kings. The Kushites of Nubia subjugated and ruled both Upper and Lower Egypt, finally to be displaced not by local uprisings but by the invading Assyrians, who made Egypt for a time in the seventh century their most distant province. But then their appointees/vassals/puppets, the petty kings of Sais in the western Delta, emerged as their replacement, and the Saites even began to rekindle long-forgotten dreams of a western-Asiatic Egyptian Empire.

The Assyrians rose to their imperial height, incorporated all of Syria and most of Palestine, even briefly (as already said) Egypt, then just as precipitously declined, crumbled, and disappeared from the world scene. Their Babylonian, Chaldaean supersessors dominated affairs for little longer than the reign of their greatest king, Nebuchadnezzar II (604-562 BCE). Looming just over the temporal horizon were the golden ages of Persia and of Greece.

Hardly noticeable among all these mighty players were the small Hebrew-speaking kingdoms of Israel and Judah, the former eventually absorbed by, the latter tributary to, Assyria. Yet here, in Judah after the fall of Israel, was being launched in this seventh-sixth-century period a movement that would in its effects and impact dwarf all the accomplishments of all these great powers. Even to the present day, it has not yet been resolved whether Judah's intolerant monotheism and its equally intolerant daughter traditions will ultimately triumph over, yield to, or find some way to live with the rationalism of the Greeks and their inheritors. No period of human history could be more worthy of writing about than this one, the period in which, while empires rose and fell, both monotheism and rationalism were launched.

Yet how write about it? To do the period justice in a detailed, all-inclusive historical study is more than I feel able to do. In any case, I find it much more intriguing, and more reader-friendly, to write a book showing how most, if not all, of these momentous developments might plausibly impinge upon a single human life. Whose life? The chosen central character or narrator would have to be someone who lived a long time, traveled widely, and interacted with people of many different cultures. Rather than wracking my brain trying to find a sufficiently-attested real person, why not simply create such a character/narrator? The reader, in on the deal from the beginning, will realize that what my narrator reports having seen and heard are either events otherwise attested in actual sources (cited and/or discussed in my editorial notes), or fictional developments within his own life that I have created to increase verisimilitude and

readability (and these of course will have no source notes). My narrator's opinions, evaluations, and comments may be taken essentially as my own, allowing again for a certain amount of distancing out of considerations of verisimilitude.

Such a narrator, although a created persona, need not be entirely fictional. Better to borrow the identity of someone historically attested who has some of the necessary qualities, yet who is not documented in such detail as to put undue restrictions on my invention of other aspects of his personality or numerous details of his life story. Herodotos as narrator might have worked nicely, but he lived a century and a half too late to be situated within the seventh-sixth-century events I want to incorporate into my narrative. His predecessor as wanderer and commentator, Hekataios of Miletos, would be temporally closer, but is still a bit late. I definitely want a Greek, for the rationalist-critical angle, and it must be one attested in a cross-cultural Near Eastern context. The poet Alkaios, contemporary of Sappho on Lesbos, had a brother, Antimenidas, who served as a mercenary with the Babylonians under Nebuchadnezzar. Antimenidas could work as my narrator, but given my preference to emphasize developments in Judah and Egypt, I can more easily bring him in as a character in someone else's story.

The person who ultimately turns out to be most suitable is someone whose only attestation reveals—in his own words, not in some other writer's reportage—not only something about his deeds but also about his mental outlook. Archon son of Amoibichos, polis unknown, writer of a five-line inscription (in a Dorian dialect but an Ionian alphabet) carved on the leg of a statue of Ramses II at Abu Simbel, might reasonably be seen as consciously parodying the genre his text exemplifies. He concludes his "official report" about Psammetichos II's 593 BCE expedition into Nubia by announcing his own co-authorship with "Axe son of Nobody"—presumably the instrument with which he had cut the letters on the statue. Here is a clear-eyed, whimsical observer, one who will not be taken in by royal propaganda or religious hocus-pocus!

Taking a cue from his inscription's alphabet, I make my Archon an Ionian—and if an Ionian, why not make him from Miletos, fountainhead of the Ionian Enlightenment, the beginning of Greek rationalism? Let him be, then, the first and earliest of the glorious cadre that otherwise begins with Thales (of the traditional Seven Sages of Greece), includes the above-mentioned Hekataios, and inspires the Dorian-Karian Herodotos to write his *Histories* in the Ionian dialect. Nor is there any need to rush Archon from Ionia directly to Egypt for his service with the Saite kings. Why not allow him a prior stint in the army of Judah, whose employment of *Kittiyim* (Greeks, Islanders, Westerners) as mercenaries during this period is attested? Thus he can be present at the dawn of state-sponsored intolerant monotheism under King Josiah (640-609 BCE), and his time spent in Judahite service can be an incentive for his later Egyptian commanders to select him whenever troops are sent to provide Egyptian support for Judah during its periods of rebellion from the Babylonians. He can therefore plausibly be in Judah at the time of the two Chaldaean sieges of Jerusalem (597 and 587-6 BCE), the second of which culminates in the destruction of the city and its temple and the taking of deportees to Babylonia.

Everywhere he goes, my Archon keeps his eyes and ears open and his wits about him, and works at communicating in the local languages. His path crosses those of many historically-attested persons, from fellow Greeks such as Antimenidas and his own brother Python (named on another Abu Simbel inscription) to the prophet Jeremiah and his scribe Baruch. "Archon of Miletos" personalizes a period dazzling in its political, military, and religious complexity, and in the process hopefully makes it more accessible to the reader.

The reader is perfectly free to treat this book as a "historical novel"—albeit one severely lacking in graphic sex, gory battle details, and chatty "filler"—simply by reading the text and ignoring the endnotes and other editorial material. Conversely, the reader conversant with, or interested in, scholarly issues of biblical, ancient Greek, and ancient Near Eastern history can follow the historical events narrated in the text and consult the ancient sources and reports of modern controversies in the endnotes, essentially disregarding the details of my narrator's mostly-fictional "life story". If I have any model in this genre-bending work, it is the *Histories* of Herodotos, who presents because of their intrinsically interesting qualities many tales whose veracity he doubts or even flatly denies, yet who is extremely serious about getting his fundamental facts right and in reaching valid over-all conclusions. Before Herodotos labeled his opus, no such genre as "history" existed; his work would have been no less worth reading if he had labeled it something else.

ACKNOWLEDGMENTS

This project has gone through changes of genre, re-writings, updatings, and title changes since I began writing it in spring of 2001, near the end of a semester of sabbatical leave provided by Rutgers University, for which I am grateful. Twice I have had occasion to offer presentations about ongoing work on the project: at a panel honoring my dissertation director, Raphael Sealey, at the University of California, Berkeley, in summer of 2002; and at a guest lecture organized by Marsha McCoy at Fairfield University in Connecticut in spring of 2004. Both times, the enthusiastic reaction of my audience (mostly colleagues and former graduate-school classmates at the former, mostly undergraduate students at the latter) was very encouraging to me. So also have I been encouraged by the discussions of various chapters and parts of chapters that I have presented to my monthly writers' group, Writers Anonymous NJ. Teaching my undergraduate courses in "Early Greece" and "Ancient Near East" has helped me clarify issues for myself; especially helpful was my undergraduate seminar, "The Age of Jeremiah"—and the students enrolled in it.

My cousin Bob Cargill has been a staunch supporter of the book from the beginning, and the largely self-taught rationalism and critical thinking of my daughter Elena are never-ending sources of satisfaction and delight for me. My frequent lunchtime companions both at the "Reserved" table in the Faculty Dining Room and at the Rutgers Club have been constantly encouraging and interested. Several Rutgers History Department colleagues and friends such as David Panisnick and Dick Holland have further encouraged me. Fellow ancient historians too numerous to name, both in discussions at the annual meetings of the Association of Ancient Historians and in personal conversations and e-mails, have done much to keep up my spirits and energy in the face of publishing difficulties. I have received particular encouragement at key moments from Frank Frost, Erich Gruen, Israel Finkelstein, Richard D. Burns, Jennifer Roberts, Carol Thomas, and Waldemar Heckel.

Finally, I offer a word of gratitude to the handful of employees of literary agencies and publishers who were kinder and more encouraging than the conveyance of negative news required them to be. In an era of publishing when stamping unopened envelopes "Return to Sender" constitutes communication, and at a time when works not viewed as potential blockbusters—and their authors—tend to be treated with disdain, it is heartening to see that some publishing professionals retain their empathy and humanity.

Contents

Part II: IN SERVICE TO THE SAITE KINGS OF EGYPT

Editorial Materials:

Maps & Sources

All seven maps are hand-drawn by the author, including invariably elements from more than one published map. See "Controversies, Conventions, Sources, Abbreviations" section (between text and endnotes) or relevant chapter's notes for authors and full titles of works abbreviated here.

Prologue

"Archon, have you heard? Nebuchadnezzar is approaching Egypt with an army!" was the cry of one of my neighbors here in Daphnai, just a few months ago. Still king in Babylon, now for almost forty years! He's not as old as I am—I'm about to turn seventy-five—but he must be fairly close.[1] I remember when he was only the crown-prince, the untried commander-in-chief of the new Chaldaean kingdom in Babylonia that was just finishing off the mighty Assyrians. He defeated Necho king of Egypt at Karchemish on the western bend of the Euphrates, when the Pharaoh was trying to help the rag-tag and remnant of the Assyrians, seven years after their capital, Nineveh, had fallen and their last king had fled westward.

I fought on the losing Egyptian side in that campaign, but I had already encountered Necho four years before Karchemish. I was at that time—indeed, had been for quite a few years already—a mercenary under King Josiah of Judah. He foolishly tried to intercept the Egyptian army at Megiddo on its northward march, and paid for his foolishness with his life. Josiah was a man always oblivious of the real world, caught up in his religious fantasies and his mad belief that his single god would somehow protect him and his kingdom.

The kingdom didn't last much longer than he did. I was back again in Judah—by then having been in Egyptian service for several years—in the brief reign of Josiah's grandson Jehoiachin, when Nebuchadnezzar carried the young king and most of his family off to Babylon. And I was there again when the Chaldaeans came back to Jerusalem, about ten years later, to finish the job. Jehoiachin's uncle, a son of

Josiah, had been put on the throne by Nebuchadnezzar, who gave him the name of Zedekiah. He had later renounced his allegiance to his Babylonian masters, mistakenly relying on Egyptian help.

The adage that Egypt is a "broken reed" that "pricks and pierces the hand of whoever leans on it"[2] was certainly apt at that time, as I must admit, despite serving then as a soldier in the Egyptian army. Whereas Jehoiachin had been treated rather kindly—I have even heard that he's still alive, and well provided for by his captors[3]—Zedekiah, a rebel caught in the act, was treated mercilessly. There were more deportations, the city was destroyed, and the kingdom of Judah soon ceased to exist.

What a lot of ancient memory the advance of Nebuchadnezzar stirred up in me! He came west again, after all these years, involving himself in a conflict between rival claimants to the throne of Egypt. I was, of course, not expected to fight on either side, given my age. I rode out the conflict on the little plot of land near the delta that I had bought when I retired from service, where I have lived for a good many years, surrounded mostly by other demobilized *alloglossoi*, mercenaries of "foreign tongues"—fellow Greeks, Karians, Lykians, Lydians—even some Judahites.

Within the last few years, I had decided to write down my recollections of these tumultuous years, before all my other fellow soldiers went the way of my late brother and these events were forgotten forever. Well, not precisely *forgotten*. These eastern kings maintain annals that preserve at least their own version of what happened on campaigns, and all kinds of everyday documents exist here in Egypt on papyrus and in Babylonia (I am told) on clay tablets. I can read a little bit of the popular script used here, the kind we Greeks call "demotic", but of course both the Egyptian sacred writing and the wedge-shaped writing of the Chaldaeans and Assyrians are totally inaccessible to me.

I suppose it's a fact that I have spent most of my adult life serving one god or others as a mercenary soldier—whether Yahweh of Judah or the incarnate-god Pharaohs of Egypt, not to mention their whole Egyptian pantheon. But what gave me my strongest incentive to write was that I knew that partisans of Josiah's cultic reforms were beginning to write their version of events and developments among the Judahites. I know very well that whatever they might ultimately produce would be as culticly and theologically preoccupied as the program of the king they so much admired. A bit of Ionian critical thinking might be more useful to future generations, especially since I was an eyewitness to many of the events of Josiah's reign and later, and I had learned enough of the local language to hear stories about earlier kings and foreign invasions. I was also, by the time I was becoming seriously ready to begin constructing my narrative, in possession of several important written sources, whose acquisition I will explain in due course.

Who better to write this account than a Greek from Miletos, where my younger fellow-citizen Thales is acquiring a reputation as the most brilliant thinker in the entire world? Fifteen or twenty years ago, he actually predicted an eclipse of the sun. And he gave credit not to any kind of magic or to the intervention of some god, but simply to human reason applied to observation of the positions and movements of the planets.[4] I never knew him personally, since Thales was still a youth when I left Miletos as a very young man, but I'll wager that we shared some of the same excellent teachers. And I will likewise wager that he won't be the last great and famous thinker produced by Miletos![5]

I myself do not aspire to be counted among these, of course. A reader looking for literary skill or brilliance of description will be disappointed with this work. I merely try to discuss my own times, and report my own experiences and observations, as accurately and clearly as I can. It seems to me that the events through which I have lived are fascinating in themselves, and do not require much embellishment in the telling.[6]

Part I

In Service to Josiah of Judah

MAP 2

WESTERN ASIA (MINOR) AND OFFSHORE ISLANDS

1. MILETOS

I am Archon son of Amoibichos, an Ionian Greek of the great and ancient city of Miletos, on the western coast of Asia. Ours is a beautiful city, with bays forming three harbors along the seaward side of a promontory and an even bigger bay to the east that is formed by the promontory itself. The island of Lade lies offshore to the northwest; our hinterland is watered by the river Maiandros. We have our fine buildings and sacred precincts of Athena and Apollo Delphinios, but the city's greatest temple is not in the city at all, but in the separate sanctuary of Apollo at Didyma, some eighty-five stades down our coastal road. No one knows how long this spot has been regarded as sacred, probably since before the Greeks ever arrived in the area, but the temple has been rebuilt and enlarged more than once. I am told that since my departure from Miletos a truly magnificent structure has been emerging at Didyma, one almost 175 cubits long and having over a hundred columns, in double rows all around. The Ionians in Ephesos and on the island of Samos have been building great temples too, it is said, as if we are in a sort of pan-Ionian competition![1]

Homer's *Iliad* says the Karians ruled our city and fought on the Trojan side in the great war against the invading Achaians, but Homer also mentions a Miletos on Krete whose heroes fought on the Greek side, so maybe it was settlers from there who gave our city its name. Finally, of course, the Ionians took it over, led by Neleus the son of Kodros, king of Athens; they killed the Karians they found there, and proceeded to marry their widows. Miletos became the most populous and most prosperous of all the cities of Ionia, and sent out many colonies.[2]

I was born about ten years after the wild Kimmerians, from the deep interior of Asia, south of the Euxine Sea, swooped down and looted everything in Sardis, the chief city of Lydia, except the high citadel, and also sacked some of the Ionian cities. I was always told that Ephesos survived at that time because its chief goddess, Artemis, sent a plague upon the Kimmerians, causing them to retreat back to their territory, far to the north and east.[3] Miletos, being south of Ephesos, was accordingly also spared.

My father Amoibichos was the holder of considerable land in the hinterland, *chora*, of the city, and an important voice in the council within it. Our family was prosperous, and my brother Python and I could look forward to exercising positions of leadership in our *polis*.[4] I never really knew my mother, since she died while bearing my brother Python when I was barely a year old myself. As it turned out, however, the slave-woman who brought up my brother and me had a vital impact on my understanding and on the course my life would take. She was from the region of Philistia, the town of Ashkelon, and her name was Delilah.[5]

Slaves, like mercenaries, are often made rather than born. Such was certainly the case with our Philistine servant Delilah. She had been of a freeborn family, properly betrothed and recently married, when her husband was killed and she was captured by Skythian raiders from north of the Euxine Sea. They had swept down as far as the border of Egypt, where the first King Psammetichos had threatened or persuaded or bribed them not to invade his kingdom. Returning northward, some of them had plundered Ashkelon's temple of Ishtar—there were stories told among the Greeks about how the goddess had therefore struck them with the curse of impotence.[6] Others sallied into the town itself, killing men and seizing women as prizes of war. My father had bought her from a Phoinikian slave-trader to whom the Skythians had sold her, intending that she would provide household assistance to his young wife. He did not realize at the time that she would soon replace her in the roles of both mother and wife, or at least favored and well-treated concubine.

Her intelligence had become immediately obvious from the rapid way she learned Greek, even to the point—my father was really an unusually indulgent man—of managing to read and write a little of it, repeating an effort she had previously made in her own language and script.[7] The script, I would discover once I began my own education, was indeed not so very different from that used by us Ionians. It turned out that both our peoples had acquired it from the Phoinikians, who had developed a simplified way of writing to assist them in their far-flung trading ventures. Even the names of the letters were essentially the same, as was their sequence: Aleph and Alpha, Beth and Beta, Gimel and Gamma, and so on.[8]

Later I would learn that Delilah's language was called "Canaanite". Canaan is an old Egyptian term for a region at the eastern end of the great sea, sometimes also called *Palaistine*.[9] The Phoinikians were just a subset of the Canaanites, named *Phoinikioi*, "Purple Men", by the Greeks because of their export of the valuable purple dye they harvested from the shellfish in their coastal waters west of Mount Lebanon. I would further discover that Hebrew, the language spoken in Judah, was very closely related, essentially a dialect of Canaanite, and was written in the same script. All we Greeks had done was to turn the letters and write them left-to-right, instead of the right-to-left order employed in Canaan. In addition we had designated a few of the signs—all representing consonantal sounds in the Phoinikian "alphabet"—to represent vowel sounds.[10] This seems to me to be a great improvement in simplicity, but compared to the leap made in devising an alphabet of some twenty-odd consonants to replace the hundreds of signs needed to write the scripts of Egypt, Assyria, or Babylonia, the Greek contribution was a very small step indeed.

"We speak Canaanite now, but my people are not really Canaanites", Delilah surprised me one day by saying. "Long, long ago, we came from Kaphtor—the big island you Greeks call Krete".[11]

"What?" I said. "Do you mean that you Philistines are *Greeks?*" To myself I was thinking how odd it was that both Philistines and Milesians might claim ancestors from Krete!

"It is possible", she replied, "or maybe the Greeks took over Krete after my people departed from it. Still, I recall seeing once in Ashkelon, in a coffin in an accidentally-exposed grave, a pot that was painted in a style almost exactly like the ancient vase your father keeps among his treasures".

I knew the vase to which she referred, of course, a beautiful kráter about half a cubit high, decorated with a painting of a duck turning its head over its back. It was my father's most treasured heirloom, bought from someone who claimed he had rescued it from the ruins of a very old house in the southwest sector of Miletos, though he would not reveal the precise spot, no doubt in hopes of making further profit from his looting. He averred that it dated from the heroic age, from the very period of the Trojan War itself.[12]

What was fascinating to me, an inquisitive and ever-questioning youth, was the way that people defined and redefined themselves, or refused to redefine themselves despite obvious changes over centuries. And the similarity in the two ceramic pieces might indeed indicate that some bits of memory could survive accurately over long periods of time, even when nothing had been written down. This would be a matter I would ponder much during my sojourn in Judah, a place beset by "memories" of far-distant times that were sometimes believable and sometimes utterly fantastic.

"Greeks in Philistia are not so far-fetched", Delilah laughed. "Greeks are to be found in all the eastern and southern kingdoms—traders, artisans, soldiers, adventurers. Why, less than a hundred years ago, a Greek—at least probably a Greek, since the name given to him in the story, Yamani, seems to be just a version of *Yawani*, 'Ionian'—seized power in one of our Philistine cities, Ashdod, and defied the Assyrian king Sargon. Unfortunately for him, he relied on the support of Egypt, which was at that time under the control of the Kushites of Nubia. When the revolt failed and he fled to Egypt for protection, the Kushite Pharaoh sent him to Sargon in chains!"[13]

Thus before I had ever heard of the "broken reed" image, I had in my memory an actual example of the behavior that had led to its invention. I would have occasion to remember this story again, when I myself became a Greek soldier-adventurer in these kingdoms. Then as now, Egypt incites the small nations against the great powers of the Tigris-Euphrates valley, but leaves them in the lurch when the mighty eastern armies march in bent on punishing rebels. I would also see at close hand the damage done to Delilah's own city of Ashkelon by the conquering Chaldaean Nebuchadnezzar of Babylon.

Delilah found me, in contrast to my more conventional brother Python, an avid listener to her tales about the Philistine past. I marveled that a woman had been allowed to pick up so much from the men's conversations, but apparently her own menfolk had found her just as engaging and worthy of serious talk as the males of my family found her. Although she was a slave, my father's concubine, and almost twenty years my senior, as I approached the year of "ephebic" training in arms that would mark my transition to adult citizen status,[14] I was more than a little in love with her. She sensed this, found it amusing, and handled it with a delicacy that prevented any problem from ever arising. Though lots of women, including a couple of wives, have passed through my long life, I think of no one with greater affection and respect than our Philistine slave Delilah.

She was my first source of information on the kingdoms of Israel and (my future employer) Judah, which had both been neighbors to the Philistines, at least as long as Israel existed. Sometime a few years before the rise and fall of "Yamani", the Assyrians had conquered and absorbed Israel, destroying its capital, Samaria. The king who finished the city off was that same Sargon, though his predecessor had begun the siege.[15] A later Assyrian king, Sennacherib, would not be quite so thorough during his invasion of Judah in reaction to a revolt led by King Hezekiah, an event I will describe in much more detail later on.[16]

Unfortunately, incursions and loss of lands were not restricted to kingdoms in the region of Canaan. Within a couple of years of the completion of ephebic training by myself and my brother (his of course came one year after mine), the territory of Miletos itself became subject to attacks by the Lydians. I was told later that these invasions lasted twelve years, ending under King Alyattes. The Lydians knew they could never take the city itself by siege, so they planned a slow process of starving the Milesians into submission. Each year they would attack the *chora*, cutting down olive and fruit trees and burning the grain crops in the fields. Insidiously, they would leave all the landowners' houses and outbuildings untouched, realizing that this would lure us into coming back and planting again. Then they would return in the next campaigning season and repeat the devastation. Naturally we came out to fight them a couple of times, but we were beaten in these battles, one of them in the plain of the Maiandros.

Ultimately, during the twelfth invasion, the fire from the burning field crops spread to a temple of Athena in the countryside, at a place called Assesos, and burned it to the ground. Upon returning to Sardis, Alyattes came down with a mysterious illness, and he sent to Apollo's oracle at Delphoi to ask what he must do to recover his health. The priestess there, the Pythia, told him that he would get no oracle at all until he had rebuilt Athena's temple. By this time, thanks to the continuing crisis, a tyrant had arisen in Miletos. This man, Thrasyboulos, found out about the Pythia's response to the inquiry of Alyattes. Forewarned that envoys would be coming to negotiate a truce for the purpose of rebuilding the temple, Thrasyboulos commandeered all public and private supplies of grain and wine, and staged a great show of abundance and merriment in the city for the envoys' benefit, giving them the impression—duly conveyed to their king—that Miletos had hardly suffered at all from the twelve years of Lydian incursions. Having expected merely a truce to be followed by the resumption of hostilities and imminent victory, Alyattes instead ended up granting the Milesians a treaty of alliance on equal terms. Then he proceeded to build not one, but two, new temples to Athena Assesia. It is said also that he soon recovered his health—a development that many of course credited to Athena, with Apollo's concurrence.

These machinations of Thrasyboulos, however, came too late to benefit my family. Our extensive lands had been directly in the invaders' path; and my father Amoibichos had died fighting in the battle in the Maiandros plain, which had happened early in the twelve years of the war.[17] Python and I had managed to survive the battle, but it seemed at the time impossible to provide a living for ourselves from lands constantly subject to attack. Moreover, the raiders who had killed our father had carried off as a prize of war his concubine, our beloved Delilah. We had no idea where they had taken her, or whether she was even alive. At best, she would be sold again as a slave, perhaps in some far-distant place. It was unlikely—especially as she was now approaching forty years old and had proven entirely infertile—that she would find another master so kindly disposed toward her as Amoibichos had been, or such appreciative "sons" in a new master's house. Python and I had little reason to stay on in Miletos, to be constantly reminded of everything we had lost.

Like all who could count themselves among the aristocrats, the so-called "beautiful and good", *kaloi k'agathoi*, we had been trained in arms. Therefore we decided to seek our fortune—or at least our sustenance—as mercenaries. Every king of the east was eager at that time, indeed is still eager now, to hire Greek soldiers, whose armament and tactics make them superior to the archers who dominate their armies. Karians and other nearby Asian peoples, who fight in similar ways, are also highly prized; mercenary armies tend to include some of all of us. Python opted to stay in western Asia, seeking military employment in the wars between the kingdoms and city-states of the region. I would not see him again for many years.

In my many conversations with Delilah, unlike Python, who lacked my fascination with such matters, I had picked up a smattering of Canaanite and the rudiments of reading and writing it, so it seemed logical for me to seek employment in an area where this knowledge might be of some use. Therefore I managed to get aboard a ship heading eastward along the Asian coast and then southward down the eastern shore of the Great Sea.

My brother and I were only two of many who fell victim to the external invasions and internal political upheavals that in our youth plagued many of the Ionian and Aiolian cities, on the offshore islands as well as on the mainland. I'm particularly conscious that another troubled place was the Aiolian island of Lesbos, thanks to encounters I had both at Naukratis in the Egyptian delta and in Judah when Jerusalem was under siege, which I will describe at appropriate places in my story.[18]

2. JOURNEY TO JERUSALEM

The Ionian coast of western Asia abounded in fine harbors. It was much the same after we rounded the point of the Knidos peninsula and proceeded between the island of Rhodos and the mainland, following the coasts of Lykia and Pamphylia. Kilikia, the easternmost portion of this southern coast of Asia, where the Tauros mountain range came right down to the sea, was so pocketed and punctuated with coves and inlets that it had long been infested with pirates who practiced their art on the many traders who frequented these waters. I was not unduly alarmed about pirates, since our ship and crew were Phoinikian, and Phoinikians were the finest seamen on the Great Sea. Indeed, at one point a suspicious-looking craft did launch itself from a beach near a cave on shore, but our sailors outdistanced it so easily that it soon turned back to lurk in wait for slower prey.[25] Passing the opening of a broad, deep bay, we headed southward along the coast of northern Syria, soon passing the mouth of the river Orontes (I use the Greek names for the rivers along this coast, not knowing the local names). Most of the Syrians, or Aramaeans, as they call themselves, dwelt inland, although we saw some impressive ruins along the shore.[2]

We had all along been putting in at night to get some food and sleep, but we did not break our journey for anything more than overnight until we reached that part of the seaboard that our Phoinikian crew recognized as their homeland. The Phoinikian cities lay along the coast, at the edge of a narrow plain with the Lebanon range rising behind. Beyond those mountains, I later discovered, was a deep valley, the one through which the Orontes flowed northward until it circled to the west and entered the sea.

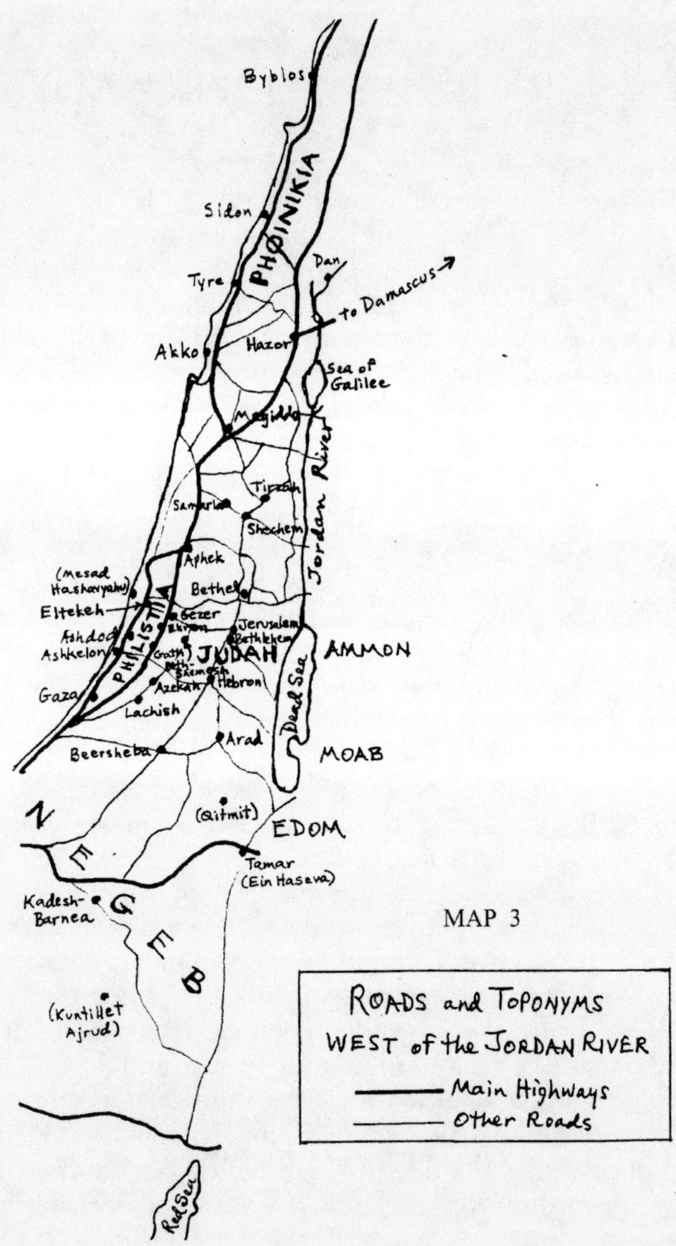
Byblos
PHOINIKIA
Sidon
Tyre
Dan
to Damascus
Akko
Hazor
Sea of Galilee
Megiddo
Jordan River
Samaria
Tirzah
Shechem
Aphek
(Mesad Hashavyahu)
Bethel
Elteke
Gezer
Jerusalem
Bethlehem
Ashdod
Ashkelon
PHILISTIA
Gath
JUDAH
AMMON
Hebron
Azekah
Gaza
Lachish
Dead Sea
Arad
Beersheba
MOAB
(Qitmit)
EDOM
NEGEB
Tamar
(Ein Haseva)
Kadesh-Barnea
(Kuntillet Ajrud)
Red Sea
ROADS and TOPONYMS
WEST of the JORDAN RIVER
Main Highways
Other Roads

MAP 3

A second mountain range, the Anti-Lebanon, rose on the other side of this deep valley, and beyond that Syria was mostly desert, with occasional oases, until one came to the great Euphrates River.

Byblos warranted a stay of several days, and gave me my first look at a Phoinikian city. The most striking thing about Byblos was its age-old connections with Egypt, which went back literally for centuries. Manufacturing of carved ivory objects and other art products was a very important industry in Byblos, and the artworks produced were decidedly "Egyptian-style"—a fact that was pointed out to me at the time of my visit, and made abundantly clear during my later sojourn in Egypt. Byblos had long been the chief port for the export of the magnificent timber harvested from the Lebanon range—everyone in the civilized world has heard of the famous "cedars of Lebanon"—and had been from time immemorial Egypt's chief supplier of wood. In return, the Egyptians had sent the Byblians their fine writing material, scrolls made of pressed-together strips from the papyrus plant that grew in the Nile. The name of the town shows up in the Greeks' word for scroll or book, *biblion*, since Byblos became the Greeks' main source for papyrus.[3]

Good anchorages were not so numerous along this coast as they were to the west and north. The Phoinikians had therefore often established their chief cities at places facing offshore islands, letting the islands function as breakwaters and protection from winds for their ships. This had been true of Arvad north of Byblos, and was the case at Sidon, the next stop along our coastal journey, and at Tyre.[4] "Old Tyre", the mainland portion of the city, was extremely ancient, but all the most important structures, including a large temple to the Tyrian god Melkart (whom we Greeks usually equate with Herakles), were located on the island, which was in effect the city's citadel or *akropolis*. The island seemed to be virtually impregnable, and I was not overly surprised to be told later that Nebuchadnezzar's siege of Tyre—which had rebelled at the same time as Zedekiah of Judah—had lasted for thirteen years![5] Being the southernmost of the Phoinikian cities, Tyre was the one that had been most involved in trade with the kingdoms of Israel and Judah. A Tyrian princess had even married Ahab son of Omri, king of Israel. I would hear more about this queen, Jezebel, during my stay in Judah. The comments were far from friendly.[6]

Akko was the only really good harbor along the entire coast, at the northern end of a large bay formed by the jutting out into the sea, some distance to the south, of the chief peak of the Carmel range. Here I took my leave of the Phoinikian ship and crew, who were continuing on to Egypt. Akko was not a Phoinikian city. It was in fact a city of the now-defunct kingdom of Israel, during the time of Ahab's dynasty and its successors. It had then been ruled directly by the Assyrians, as a part of their province of Samaria (or Samarina), but at the time of my stop there, the Egyptians were nominally in charge.

At Akko I shared a jug of the cheapest available local wine with a sweet-faced young prostitute I met in a tavern, and I was pleased to see that I could understand her language, Hebrew, when she spoke slowly enough. Having moved to the port from Judah, which had no coastline and consequently no sailors, she was something of a favorite for any Judahites passing through Akko. When I told her I was seeking employment as a mercenary, she passed on to me some gossip she had heard from a countryman among her clients. King Josiah of Judah, she reported, had recently spread word of his urgent need for non-Judahite troops. I wondered why his need should take that form in particular—the girl, Deborah, had no idea why—but I did not waste my time long in wondering.[7] I was in need of some pay and provisions, so I decided to set out for Jerusalem in Judah. Soon I acquired a rather run-down mount for the overland journey. In fact it was an ass, a donkey, since horses were a luxury well beyond my capability at this time. Given the terrain I would soon encounter, it turned out to be a happy choice. Deborah was also kind enough to put me in contact with some traveling companions and guides, three merchants from Jerusalem—more clients of hers, of course—who were on the verge of returning home. Amused at finding a displaced Ionian who could even halfway understand their language, they were happy to take me along. They did not provide me with much information, however, about my intended employer Josiah, or about the recent activities that had seemingly made him desirous of hiring foreign soldiers.

A beautiful vista confronted us as we set out from Akko, the broad and fertile Valley, or Plain, of Jezreel.[8] Its width was essentially the breadth of the bay between Akko and Mount Carmel, and it followed the Carmel range in angling across all of Canaan, northwest to southeast, from the sea to the region's eastern border, the Jordan River. It was spring when we set out, shortly before the grain harvest, so the valley was lush with barley and wheat as far as the eye could see. North of this plain I could make out the hills of the region known as Galilee. The Carmel range that formed the southern limit of the plain of Jezreel was an offshoot of what were called the highlands or hill country of Ephraim, somewhat lower than those of Galilee. Some 180 stades southeastward along the floor of the valley from Akko, the main road cut back rather sharply toward the southwest, as if angling back to the sea.

Standing guard, figuratively and quite literally, over this turn in the highway was the massive flat-topped hill of Megiddo, with its multiple fortified gateway facing north, toward Carmel. This was a place that had been occupied for thousands of years. Numerous battles had been fought at "Mount Megiddo" (*Har-Megiddon* in one Hebrew version, whence its Greek name, Armageddon), and many more would obviously be fought here in the future. I suppose that Necho's later brushing aside of Josiah would be counted as one such battle. The frequency of battles at this location is because, with Carmel coming right down to the sea and blocking movement directly up the coast, Megiddo controls the main pass through its range. No army can go from Egypt to Syria, or in the opposite direction, without being menaced by anyone who has been able to garrison the fortress here.[9] European Greeks, Dorians from the Peloponnesos, tell me that the mountain called Akrokorinth occupies a similarly commanding position there, controlling military movements in an out of the Peloponnesos.[10]

The pass, which was very narrow where it entered the mountain chain near Megiddo, had widened a bit by the time we reached the village of Aruna, and shortly afterward the road through the pass linked up with the road that would follow the coast all the way to Egypt, the one the Egyptians called "the Way of the Sea". After going along it only sixty-five stades or so, however, we had to cut sharply back eastward, in the direction of what was left of the former Israelite capital of Samaria. Thus we left the main highway for a secondary and quite inferior track that penetrated into the heart of the hill country of Ephraim. Although the walls of Samaria were so severely damaged as to make the city itself indefensible, and the former citadel had been destroyed, the country around was not depopulated. People seemed to be busy about normal agricultural pursuits, and few houses appeared to be unoccupied.

"So these are the Israelites?" I asked my traveling companions, puzzled since I had been told that the Assyrian king Sargon had transported them away into the hinterlands of his empire.

"No, no", the most talkative of the merchants, whose name was Pelatiah, answered me, "these are foreigners brought in by the Assyrians to replace the Israelites who were taken away. They speak their own languages and worship their own gods".[11]

Certainly I could not yet trust my "ear" for Hebrew, but it seemed to me that I overheard a good many of the local population speaking in a language surprisingly close to that spoken by my companions. I saw no point in entering into an argument with Pelatiah or the others on this matter, however; presumably they knew more about what had happened in this region than I did. I did not yet realize how susceptible to royal and cultic "guidance" the memories of people living in states dominated by kings and priests could be. The politics of my Greek native city had not prepared me for it. But I was eventually to learn.

The next population center was Shechem, situated in a pass between two heights known as Mount Gerizim and Mount Ebal. Whereas Samaria was still a fairly new city at the time of its sack by the Assyrians, having been built by Omri the father of Ahab specifically to be his dynasty's capital,[12] Shechem was a site of hoary antiquity.[13] Like Samaria, however, it was in a destroyed (though not abandoned) condition.

All of the sites through which we had passed so far were nominally within the Assyrian province of Samaria, but no Assyrian presence was anywhere to be seen. If the Egyptians were acting as their Assyrian allies' agents, their control was no more obvious. The kings ruling from Sais in the western delta had begun as vassals, even puppets, of the Assyrians, during the brief period—some fifty years before this time—when the Assyrians had actually ruled Egypt, having driven the Kushite Pharaohs back to their native territory in Nubia. As Assyrian influence in the west had weakened, due to continuing problems in the eastern provinces of the empire, the Egyptians, as "junior partners", had become more and more the recognized sovereign power in what had once, long before, been their own imperial province of Canaan. But at this time it was hard to see that any empire, or kingdom, was effectively in charge in Ephraim.

Consequently I would not be surprised when, shortly after I entered his service, Josiah of Judah made so bold as to lead an expedition into the territory of what had once been the kingdom of Israel, attempting to establish his authority within it. His presumption in later encountering Necho at Megiddo represented a continuation of that same policy of self-assertion. By swatting him like an annoying fly, Necho revealed the actual extent of the power underlying Josiah's grandiose claims—he was merely a pipsqueak opportunist seeking to profit from a period of temporary weakness or preoccupation among the great powers.

No further sizable Ephraimite towns lay directly along our road, which now bore due south toward Jerusalem, some 270 stades from Shechem. Off the road to our left (east) were the remains of cult centers that had once been important in Israel, Shiloh and the former royal shrine at Bethel, a name meaning "House of God". The latter was still operating as a place of sacrifice at this time; I would see it again soon enough, in company with Josiah.

Not much beyond Bethel we traversed the narrow territory of Benjamin, long incorporated into the kingdom of Judah. Passing the villages of Mizpah (on our right) and Ramah and Anathoth (on our left), we then entered the hill country of Judah proper. It was comparable in altitude with that of Ephraim, although seemingly drier. The vegetation was more sparse and scrubby, even in this most propitious time of the year, not long after the spring rains which mark the end of the winter rainy season. In the summer, which I was later to discover became steadily more rainless the farther south you travel in these central highlands, much of Judah was to be barely more hospitable than a rocky wilderness.

But it was still the beautiful part of the year as we approached Jerusalem, and the city itself was quite a resplendent sight.[14] It was immediately obvious from a distance that the capital of Judah was far larger than any town we had seen in what had once been Israel. I thought it might even have rivaled in size my own Miletos, though the appearance of a mountain city is very different from that of a great seaport. Although we approached Jerusalem from the north, we would enter the city through its main gate, on the east. The northernmost and highest part of the capital was given over to the large complex of palace and temple. The oldest part of the city (locally known as the "City of David", eponym of the dynasty that had ruled here for centuries) was a fairly long and narrow "peninsula" extending southward from this high complex, surrounded by valleys of varying width, depth, and steepness on west, south, and east. Actually, the northern portion of this "peninsula" was really sort of a saddle between the earliest-inhabited southern portion and the high royal-sacred area. Occupation and use had apparently proceeded south-to-north and uphill by stages: first the City of David, then the saddle area (the "Ophel") or most of it, then the high palace-temple area.

Within the past century, however, the city had been enlarged to take in an expanding population, so that now the comparatively shallow valley to the west of the City of David, as well as another ridge to the west of that valley itself, had been incorporated into an expanded system of city walls. This region as a whole was known as the New Town. Some of the people of Jerusalem were apparently now calling the fairly recently incorporated western hill "Mount Zion", although I had also heard it said that David had once occupied the "Fortress of Zion" in the oldest part of his city. Perhaps the toponym had shifted its meaning over the years, or was just then undergoing a shift. Additional expansion had occurred along the eastern edge of the City of David. Although the earlier wall high up the hillside had not been demolished, a second wall more-or-less paralleling it had been built farther down the slope of the Kidron Valley, seemingly to incorporate within the city's fortifications its only water source, a huge spring known as "Gusher" (*Gihon*, in Hebrew), which was further protected by massive towers immediately adjacent to the city gate through which we entered. These expansions were attributed to King Hezekiah, as was the digging of a long and circuitous tunnel from the Gihon spring to the Pool of Siloam, which conveyed water from the eastern slope of the City of David to its western slope, and a considerable distance southward beneath its length. It was a marvelous work; nothing comparable had yet been undertaken by the Greeks.

The valley at the southern tip of the City of David was called Hinnom, or Ben- (son of) Hinnom. Within it was a locale called Topheth, of which I will say more later. The road by which we reached the eastern gate ran along the Kidron Valley, to the east of which was to be seen the Mount of Olives, covered in the trees for which it was named. In clearings among those trees I could see several sanctuaries or "high places" (what we Greeks would call *temene*) dedicated to various gods, the primary gods of nations with whom Judah had been in friendly relations. These were still in operation at that time, as we entered the city; I could see columns of sacrificial smoke. Not for long.

The great temple of Yahweh, Judah's chief god, was clearly visible from outside the city, standing as it did on the highest point within the walls.[15] It was large, though not even half as large as the recently-built temple of Apollo at Didyma, probably seventy cubits long as compared with Didyma's 175 or so. It was narrower in proportion to its length than most Greek temples, the main structure itself being only some twenty cubits wide—despite its height of about thirty cubits. The proportion was improved (at least in Greek eyes) by the addition of side-chambers or storage areas along the outsides of both side walls, though these were not as high as the building itself. In the portions of the temple walls that were visible above the side-chambers, I could see that large logs had been inserted in about every third course of masonry blocks. Someone later explained to me that this was often done in large buildings to minimize the effects of earthquakes, which are frequent in this part of the world. The Greeks might be wise to adopt this technique, as our area is also earthquake-prone, and in fact Greek temples have been known to be destroyed by earthquakes.

There was no Greek-style colonnade, but only two free-standing pillars at the front (eastern) end of the temple. These, including their ornate capitals, were made not of stone but of bronze. A very large sacrificial altar could be seen, placed, as in Greek sanctuaries, outside and in front of the temple itself. A large open courtyard surrounded the temple, creating an area suitable for gathering a large crowd, as Josiah had recently done for purposes I will soon describe. Within the courtyard, or courtyards—there may have been some sort of low partition dividing the area up, it was difficult to tell from a distance—I could see various outbuildings, as well as certain cultic paraphernalia that I could see must be bronze, from the sun's rays reflecting off the indistinctly-visible items. Later I would find out that these included several large water basins for ritual washing, most importantly the largest one, known as the great bronze sea—fully ten cubits in diameter, and mounted on the backs of twelve bronze oxen facing outward, three in each direction. Had we arrived a short time earlier, we would also have seen a quadriga, a horses-and-chariot group that some earlier king of Judah had dedicated to Yahweh.[16]

Having come to Jerusalem not through the territory of Judah itself, but almost entirely through what had once been the kingdom of Israel, I had not seen any real signs of recent damage and destruction at places along our route. Jerusalem was barely inside the northern boundary of Judah, which lay just south of Bethel. We had seen ancient ruins, and also places in ruins since the Assyrian destruction of Israel, just over a hundred years previously. But of Assyrian devastation in Judah itself we had not yet seen anything, nor had the destruction that would soon be brought on rural Judah by Josiah himself occurred yet. However, the anticipation of that destruction, it turned out, was the main reason I was here.

3. JOSIAH'S REVOLUTION

Naturally, being an obvious foreigner, I was stopped at the city gate and asked to explain my business there. The guards were surprised that an Ionian could make some effort to converse with them in a language related to their own, though they handled my assertion that I had come seeking mercenary service as a routine matter. Employment of foreign mercenaries was longstanding practice in Judah, going back, I was later told, to the days of King David, who supposedly had ruled in Jerusalem more than three hundred years earlier.[1] Josiah claimed him as his direct ancestor[2]—indeed, as would soon be evident to me, he fancied himself virtually "a second David" who was going to reestablish the larger and more powerful kingdom the Judahites believed that David had once ruled.[3] I was escorted to the army's headquarters, located on the Ophel, below the upper complex of temple and palace, a very short trip from the gate I had entered, passing through only a small portion of the city.

Even in this brief journey, and despite my still very rudimentary ability to understand the local speech, I could see signs of agitation and unease. Groups of people were arguing among themselves, or being harangued by characters I would soon come to know as "prophets". Such men—even occasionally women, I would later learn—claimed a direct connection with Yahweh or some other god and asserted that the words they spoke were actually the god's words. Interestingly, sometimes more than one prophet would be engaged in these street discussions, usually making claims that contradicted their rivals' statements. Shouting matches occurred, with each red-faced participant prefacing his pronouncements with "Hear now the word of Yahweh!" or "Yahweh says this!" or something similar.

The subject-matter of these controversies in the streets seemed to be almost exclusively the recent activities of King Josiah. Words of opposition and calls for caution were confronted with pronouncements of praise and support for the king. Sometimes his admirers referred to him by a word I did not know: "Messiah!" Clearly it had a very positive implication for those who used it, but their opponents treated the employment of the word, as applied to Josiah, with especial horror—as if misuse of such a term might call down the Evil Eye on everyone involved in the discussion. Later I discovered that the word was the equivalent of the Greek *christos*, "anointed one", a term that was literally applicable to any king of Judah, since anointing with oil was part of the coronation ceremony. But in some prophetic circles it was given rather a mystical implication—some sort of present or future "savior" (Greek *soter*) of the people of Yahweh. I began to question the soldiers escorting me about what had prompted all this turmoil, but I was told that I should save my questions for the commander, the man to whom they were taking me.

At military headquarters, I met him, Benaiah son of Elhanan by name, a tallish, dignified soldier with a graying beard. Much to my delight and surprise, he spoke some Greek, thanks to his long involvement with leading foreign troops. After I learned more of the local traditions, I would realize how wonderfully appropriate his name was, since supposedly an officer named Benaiah had commanded the "Cherethites and Pelethites" for King David, that is, the Kretan and Philistine mercenaries.[4]

Benaiah—the current one, not his Davidic namesake—would prove to be an invaluable source of information for me, and not only because of our ability to converse in my language. Initially, of course, he limited himself simply to providing answers to my many questions. Once a certain level of trust had been established between us, it soon became evident that he was no partisan of the program he—and now I—had been called upon to defend and implement. He had an old soldier's somewhat jaundiced perspective on the events going on around him—loyal to his king and paymaster, but undeceived by royal rhetoric or nationalistic or religious enthusiasm. A military man, he dealt in power and in facts, and the fact was that the kingdom of Judah was not very powerful.

Many times I would thank whatever gods might be interested—Apollo, or the soldier's god Ares, or even (not to give offense to the local powers) Yahweh—for providing me with a commander who was sane and sensible, in a time and place that turned out to be filled with mad zealotry. Once he was killed, I lost no time in taking my services elsewhere. But those are events I will discuss in their proper turn. Initially, I just needed to know what my assignment was and, relatedly, what was going on that was prompting the visible unrest?

As I was told by Benaiah and as I pieced together from other informants over the next few days, these are the important events that had occurred in Jerusalem during the year prior to my arrival, year eighteen of the reign of Josiah, king of Judah.[5]

The king had sent his secretary Shaphan to confer at the temple of Yahweh with the chief priest there, Hilkiah, about payment out of state funds for craftsmen and materials involved in repair work on the temple. The priest had given Shaphan a large scroll to be delivered to the king, claiming to have found it in the temple during the process of overseeing the repairs. I would hear this famous scroll referred to many times in the next few years, variously called the "Book of the Law", the "Book of the Covenant", the "Law of Yahweh", or the "Law of Moses"—Moses being the prophet who supposedly had received and written down this law from Yahweh many centuries earlier, long before the time of David and the founding of the kingdom. I never actually saw the document itself, of course, since it was kept within the temple precinct, and certainly not made available to inquisitive Ionians.

When Shaphan read the scroll aloud in the king's presence, it is said that the king tore his clothes, which is a sign of mourning or great distress among the Judahites. I suppose that a king can afford to be so prodigal. None of the women, slave or free, in a Greek household would have taken kindly to such destruction of garments painstakingly woven in long hours of difficult work! Then Josiah is supposed to have said—I am of course getting this all third- or fourth-hand and after the fact, so the king's exact wording should not be expected—"Yahweh's furious wrath has been kindled against us because our ancestors disobeyed the word of Yahweh by not doing what this book says they ought to have done!" Next, he insisted that it was immediately necessary to "consult Yahweh" about what to do in response to the finding of the scroll. That phrase, in practical terms, meant to go and ask some recognized prophet of Yahweh.

Hearing of these events after the fact, I can have no certain idea about just *who* was involved in play-acting in the scene just described. It is obvious that the fundamental cultic regulations of a kingdom do not just disappear for several centuries in the national temple next door to the royal palace, with no one even being aware of their existence, and then turn up perfectly preserved and intact, with contents that are exactly in tune with the plans and wishes of the court and priesthood! Some have told me that Josiah had already, before the "finding" of the law scroll, manifested some zeal toward cult centralization and "purification". If so, the planting of the scroll may have been at his instructions, and his reaction to hearing it read—torn garments and all—a carefully-staged show of "spontaneity" for the benefit of any courtiers present who were not in on the plot.

My own suspicion is that Josiah was *not* in on it, but that the scene was engineered by a cabal of priests and royal officials—certainly including Hilkiah and Shaphan, and presumably several others—and that the earnest young king was among the many who were taken in. He was, after all, only twenty-six years old at the time, and he had been under the tutelage and guidance of courtiers and priests ever since his sudden accession at age eight. A palace coup had killed his father, Amon, no older at the time than Josiah was now, but a counter-coup had slaughtered Amon's murderers and put the boy Josiah on the throne. These events were talked about only very vaguely; the full facts were certainly not generally known. It was said that Josiah had been installed as king by the "people of the land".[6] Any Greek familiar with the multiple and contradictory ways our own politicians use the word "people" (*demos*) must be immediately suspicious. Whatever appearance may be given to it, whatever stories may be later told about it, a coup is always the accomplishment of some band of oligarchs. And if this is true in the comparatively open political order that prevails in most Greek states, how much more must it be true in a small backwater kingdom with a powerful class of priests closely associated with the royal court? Moreover, Josiah just did not seem to be devious enough to have set everything up. The way he later died, challenging with Judah's small army the greatly superior forces of Pharaoh Necho, showed his lack of sophistication. I know. I was there.

It will not surprise my readers to hear that the five-man committee sent to "consult Yahweh" included the priest Hilkiah and the secretary Shaphan. Nor will surprise be experienced at the court connection of the prophet, or rather prophetess, consulted. She was Huldah, wife of Shallum, keeper of the royal wardrobe. What exactly her words—I mean Yahweh's words!—were to the royal emissaries I do not know, but they prompted, or encouraged, or ratified Josiah's plans to launch a major cultic and national revolution.

The first public act of this revolution was the organizing of a mass meeting in the courtyard of the temple, at which the king had the entire scroll of the law read out to the assembled populace of Jerusalem and anyone else who happened to be in the city from the smaller towns of Judah. Then the king, standing on a dais before the temple, "bound himself"—this is the way it was told to me—"by the covenant before Yahweh, to follow Yahweh, to keep his commandments, decrees, and laws with all his heart and soul, and to carry out the terms of the covenant as written in this book". In response, it was said, "all the people" likewise pledged their allegiance to the covenant with Yahweh.

The word "covenant" which I have used several times may be confusing. It is essentially the equivalent of a treaty, although not the sort of treaty of equal alliance (*symmachia*) common between Greek cities, but rather the sort of unequal, sovereign-and-vassal treaty that the Assyrian monarchs imposed on the weaker kings whom they forced into subservience. In this particular treaty or covenant, however, the overlord was no human sovereign, but Yahweh, the god of Judah, and unswerving obedience to the law prescribed was the condition of the Judahites' participation in the covenant.

The scroll purported to be the actual law that Moses himself had written, miraculously preserved all these centuries. When I say "law" (*nomos*) in Greek, of course I am only seeking an approximate equivalent for the Hebrew term *Torah*, which perhaps means something closer to "teaching" or "instruction". It was apparently largely cultic law—as indeed many Greek lawcodes tend also to be—that is, rules and regulations regarding proper religious rituals, although some rules for fair and equitable treatment of fellow countrymen were included as well.

It was evident that Judah had never before been given a comprehensive code of law, so the one "found" by Hilkiah and promulgated by Josiah might very well be called in Greek *Proteronomia* or "first system of laws". Two elements of this "Proteronomy"[7] were particularly salient, and provocative of opposition. First, the new-found law code, and the policies of Josiah, had declared that *only* Yahweh was to be worshiped, and that all other gods were in fact false gods, mere idols and phantoms, Yahweh being the one and only actual god who existed or had ever existed! Judah's cult and its religion were henceforth to be, as we Greeks would say, *monotheistic*. Aside from the sole and exclusive worship of Yahweh, all other elements and aspects of the traditional, hundreds-of-years-old religion of Judah were defined as illegitimate, alien, and foreign. Secondly, Yahweh was to be worshiped only in very precisely limited and defined ways, and only in specific, designated places—all sacrifice and most ceremonies being restricted exclusively to the temple of Yahweh in Jerusalem, and permitted nowhere else.[8] Practices redefined as non- or insufficiently "Yahwistic" (to make up a Greek-style adjective) were to be rooted out mercilessly and destroyed, and the full power of the state and the cultic establishment was to be brought to bear to enforce the changes decreed.

Before my arrival, Josiah had already "purified" worship within the temple itself. As a Greek, I would not have been expected or even allowed to participate in any of the destruction wrought there, since the place was and is off-limits to foreigners. But the king's actions were well publicized, so I and everyone else in Jerusalem knew what had been done. Josiah had had all the cult objects made for "Baal, Asherah, and the whole array of heaven" (my informant's phrase) removed and taken to the Kidron Valley east of the city, where they had been burned. An object called a "sacred pole" had been treated in the same way, but its ashes had been thrown, for some reason, over the common burial ground in the valley, the local potter's field. Within the temple precinct—I'm not sure whether this was in the temple itself, or only in the outbuildings associated with it—a house of male "sacred prostitutes" had been torn down, and the women there who were said to have woven veils for the goddess Asherah were also expelled. Altars built by earlier kings of Judah, both on the roof of the temple itself and in its courtyard, the latter put there by Josiah's grandfather Manasseh, were broken into pieces, and the pieces were dumped into the Kidron valley. Before the entrance to the temple had stood a statue of horses that earlier kings had dedicated to the sun; this too Josiah had destroyed, as well as the chariot of the sun-god himself. The second phase of the revolution was about to begin, which would involve the destruction of cultic precincts of all types in the neighborhood of Jerusalem and throughout Judah.

I have been describing the essentials of this religious upheaval rather matter-of-factly, but any Greek reader will instantly grasp how breathtakingly revolutionary it actually was. Attributing these new and unprecedented policies to the "original" law of "Moses" was a rhetorical stroke of genius. What was actually rampant innovation was presented as a return to the primeval, correct way of doing things.[9] That a city or a state or a people should have a primary god is of course the rule almost everywhere. Apollo is obviously our chief deity in Miletos, comparable to Artemis of Ephesos, Hera on Samos and at Argos, Athena in her namesake city of Athens, Zeus at Olympia, Apollo again at Delphoi and on Delos, etcetera. The same rule applies among the large and small kingdoms here in the south and east. Moab has its Chemosh, Ammon its Milkom, Sidon its Astarte, and then there is Marduk of Babylon and Asshur of the Assyrians; Egypt's Amun-Re is actually a composite to two gods, but nowadays they are generally conceived of as one. Yahweh of Judah—and of Israel, until that kingdom was destroyed and absorbed by the Assyrians—has all along been just such another national primary god. And the Judahites (and Israelites) have always worshiped many other gods alongside, or conceived of as subordinates to, their primary god—again, just as we Greeks and all the other easterners do.[10] Miletos, for example, has precincts sacred to Athena as well as to Apollo.

Now it is obvious, just from this description of what Josiah had destroyed within the immediate area of the temple and in the temple itself, that the notion of "monotheism" with Yahweh as the only god was a very new proposition for the king and the Judahite state to assert. It was even a new thing for the priests in charge of the national cult to assert. The efforts of some partisans of the reform later to insist that all the above-described "abominations" (Josiah's supporters liked this word, and used it a lot!) were imposed on an unwilling city and nation by the unprecedentedly-evil Manasseh[11] were completely unconvincing to anyone who actually lived through the revolution. Over and over, as I would see when I was directly involved in helping to carry Josiah's program into the Judahite countryside, defenders of local sanctuaries and practices proclaimed the great antiquity of the objects and customs that were being destroyed. They insisted that their cultic observances had dated from long before the fifty-five year reign of Manasseh, which had immediately preceded the scant two years of his son Amon and the reign of his grandson Josiah.[12]

But Josiah and his supporters did not simply invent their "Yahwistic monotheism" out of whole cloth. I soon understood that the idea of Yahweh as the only god for Judah and Israel, and apparently even of Yahweh of the only god of the entire universe, had been around for a long time in certain circles within Judah and also within the northern kingdom while it had existed. These circles were primarily prophetic, that is, associated with certain well-known givers of prophetic oracles and pronouncements attributed to Yahweh and with the "brotherhoods" or "schools" who recalled their memories and their sayings.

Until fairly recently, those recollections had been orally maintained, but within the past century more and more prophetic sayings had come to be written down and circulated in textual form, while still also being recited from memory. Collections existed of the sayings attributed to Amos of Tekoa, to Hosea son of Beeri, to Micah of Moresheth, to Isaiah ben Amoz, and attributed to some others whose names I do not recall. Jeremiah of Anathoth, who began his career as a prophet during the years of Josiah's revolution and would continue to issue oracles until after the final destruction of Jerusalem and the kingdom, very consciously made sure that his prophecies would reach written form immediately. Rather than relying on the memory of any disciples he might attract, he simply employed the services of a scribe, Baruch son of Neraiah, to write his words down just as he pronounced them in Yahweh's name. I will have personal recollections of Jeremiah, and of Baruch, to report in their proper place, and Baruch's collection of oracles and stories associated with Jeremiah has been invaluable to me in constructing my narrative.

Josiah was apparently not the first *king* to be influenced by the notion that Yahweh was the sole god. At least it was generally believed—and certainly treated as an important precedent by supporters of Josiah's reform—that King Hezekiah, father of Manasseh and thus Josiah's great-grandfather, who had ruled some eighty or more years prior to the current religious upheaval, had accepted the proposition that Yahweh was the only god. Perhaps he had been influenced by Isaiah, who had lived and prophesied during his reign, and had had several consultations with the king about national policies, according to what my informants told me.[13]

Certainly, Hezekiah was cited by Josiah as precedent and justification for the other major aspect of his reform, the centralization of all sacrificial cultic activities in the temple of Yahweh in Jerusalem. I would be directly involved in this phase of the revolution, since there was no inhibition about allowing foreigners, even Greek mercenary soldiers, to set foot in small-town and rural sanctuaries. These had already been defined by the king and the Jerusalem temple priests as illegitimate, impure, and non-Judahite.

Before describing the subsequent stages in Josiah's revolution, throughout Judah and even beyond the borders of the kingdom, probably I need to give my readers some background, both on the events of the hundred years or so that had elapsed since the fall of the kingdom of Israel and on the cultic and religious traditions that had existed among the people of Judah, or at least as much of these as I was able to discover. At every point, I have tried to discount interpretations that seem to my Ionian mind to partake of excessive credulousness, and have sought to find, or suggest, interpretations that are compatible with human reason. Every people has its gods and credits them with various interventions in human lives—a child unexpectedly cured after being given up for dead, an overweening tyrant brought down at seemingly the height of his power, an unexpected victory by an apparently weaker army—but the overwhelmingly intrusive nature of divine activity, in the minds of these easterners (not just the Judahites, all of them!) is decidedly ungreek. I will try to produce a narrative that Greeks will find intelligible. This is not easy to do, when virtually all of your informants share in a deity-dominated view of the world and of human activities and events.

4. ISRAEL AND JUDAH

Judah in the time of Josiah was a very small kingdom.[1] Its eastern boundary was formed by the deep rift valley through which the Jordan River flowed southward into the so-called Dead Sea or Salt Sea, a very large stagnant and smelly lake in which no creature could live, with salt content so high that a swimmer would have found it virtually impossible to sink. Toward its southern end, I later discovered, asphalt or bitumen bubbled up in the already-foul waters, and was gathered for use in caulking or as masonry cement. The southern limits of the kingdom (not that Josiah felt bound to observe borders!) did not quite reach the southern end of this sea, whose long axis ran north-to-south, so that the Jordan and the Dead Sea together constituted its entire eastern boundary. To the west, Judah did not have a coastline on the Great Sea at any point, the coastal plain being occupied by the various Philistine cities and their territories. The foothills known as the Shephelah essentially marked the westward extent of the kingdom, although the valley of Beersheba, at the southern end of these hills, was also within it. The central part of the kingdom, the highlands or hill country of Judah, merged into barren, rocky desert as it approached the Dead Sea. The northern boundary was little beyond the capital city of Jerusalem. Thus the entire kingdom was only about 315 stades by 540 stades. It was not only small, but poor, and it was bypassed by the main highways through the area, which either followed the seacoast or went along the opposite, eastern, side of the Dead Sea. Probably its very insignificance and remoteness had saved Judah from direct absorption into the Assyrian empire, although it had, like all the other small states in the region, been compelled to pay tribute.

Israel, until the Assyrians put an end to its independent existence, had been a much richer and larger kingdom, as well as being, to its own misfortune, cut by international trade routes and closer to the Assyrian heartland. Israel had controlled the northern portion of the central highlands of Canaan, the mountainous area of Galilee, and the large and fertile Plain of Jezreel between them, as well as certain territories on the eastern side of the Jordan. Israel had had its own seacoast, including the great bay at the north end of which sat Akko, and its territory had abutted that of the Phoinikian cities, the closest being Tyre. With its lush fields, forested hills, access to the Great Sea and to the large fresh-water lake known as the Sea of Galilee, in every way Israel had been a desirable target for conquest.

The two kingdoms had existed simultaneously for a couple of centuries, apparently sometimes friendly and sometimes at odds with each other. Lists of rulers of both kingdoms must have existed and have been accessible to some within the court and temple, since the sequences of kings and a fairly clear understanding of how their respective reigns overlapped seemed to be widespread in Jerusalem. The royal dynasty in Judah was known as the "house of David", and was apparently referred to in this way by neighboring peoples.[2] In like manner, foreigners—including the Assyrians themselves—had tended to call the rulers of Israel the "house of Omri", although in Judah more was said about Omri's son Ahab, he of the Phoinikian wife, who was remembered with particular hostility.[3]

One thing that always confused me was that it was consistently claimed that David—and his son Solomon after him—had ruled not only Judah, but Israel as well, and that their composite kingdom had indeed been known as "Israel".[4] It supposedly had split shortly after Solomon's death into its northern and southern constituents. Why the breakaway portion with its upstart and illegitimate dynasty would be allowed to claim the name that had earlier denoted the undivided kingdom, while the portion that retained the capital city and the legitimate royal dynasty should be called by the name of only one of what had supposedly been twelve "Israelite" tribes was decidedly unclear to me. Moreover, there were tales of a shadowy figure named Saul, king of Israel, who was said to have been supplanted by David. If he was not simply a fictional character, created to be a foil to the heroic David, he may be a clue to indicate that Israel as a kingdom was older than, or at least as old as, Judah. Whether the two kingdoms had ever actually been united, I don't know. Certainly Josiah's partisans, and the Judahites in general, believed they had been. Prophetic oracles seemed to use "Israel" and "Judah" almost interchangeably, unless they were specifically condemning something about the northern kingdom, and Judahites were commonly included when the "children of Israel" were referred to.

My pure speculation on this matter, as an outsider lately come on the scene, is that the peoples of Israel and Judah had always been conscious of being closely related—speakers of very similar dialects of Hebrew, worshipers of the same primary god, their royal houses even at times intermarried. The rulers and people of Judah witnessed the destruction of Israel, a process taking several years and leading to the flight of many Israelites southward into Judah to escape the invading Assyrians, bringing with them many oral and maybe even some written traditions about their nation, their forefathers, etcetera. Menaced by the same invading Assyrians, King Hezekiah of Judah perhaps came to think of himself as the protector and preserver of the traditions of both peoples. Obviously his descendant Josiah did, and one passion to which the king sought to appeal was the hope of "reuniting David's kingdom".

Citizens of Greek cities usually regard themselves, truly or falsely, as descendants of some common ancestor, or from the several sons of such an ancestor, such as the eponyms of the Ionian or Dorian tribes. I know that some of the Spartans, including both of the two royal families, regard themselves as descended from the sons of Herakles.[5] The situation was much the same in Judah, where the kingdom was named for the ancestor of its main tribe; the small region of Benjamin that was incorporated within the kingdom was supposedly named for a brother of Judah. The northern kingdom was apparently named for "Israel" the patriarch himself, father to twelve brothers (including Judah and Benjamin) who became the ancestors of tribes. Ephraim, the northern tribe whose territory had constituted the central highlands, was supposedly named for the son of Benjamin's brother Joseph. The Israelites who were deported by the Assyrian Sargon were remembered in Judah as the "ten lost tribes".[6] How many of these traditions were based on truth and how many were pure fiction is probably impossible to tell, so ingrained and elaborated the beliefs had become.

It is clear that the Judahites regarded themselves as being the special favorites of their god, Yahweh, and apparently the Israelites had so regarded themselves as well. One heard the Judahites—or Israelites, since, as I have said, the terms seemed sometimes to be used interchangeably—being referred to as the "chosen people" of Yahweh. In the popular understanding, I am sure that such an expression had always only meant what it had meant elsewhere: a people or nation had a principal god, and that god looked out for the interests of that people. We Ionians, being Athenian colonists, have seen sanctuaries whose inscribed boundary stones identify them as *temene* sacred to "Athena protectress of Athens".[7] But other peoples seek Athena's protection, and Athenians also venerate other gods. Certain prophets in Israel and Judah, however, seem to have interpreted the notion of "Yahweh's chosen people" in a much more exclusive and limited way. Yahweh and Israel or Judah were depicted as father and child, or, very strikingly in the imagery of the prophet Hosea, as husband and wife. Neither side was to have any other allegiance.

No great leap in thought was necessary to get from the belief in such a sort of relationship to the idea of the "covenant" that had appeared in the scroll of the law "found" in the temple in Josiah's eighteenth year. The only really new element was *conditionality* of a very rigid kind. Judah would continue to be the favored people of Yahweh *if and only if* its king and cultic personnel and people behaved in certain precisely-prescribed ways. I know that it was said in Jerusalem in Josiah's time that Hezekiah, many years earlier, had invoked a covenant made with Yahweh by "Moses", but no written document said to have recorded that covenant had been brought forward until the time of Josiah. Since I am virtually certain that the scroll was a forgery designed to justify the reforms Josiah undertook, I have to assume that in the time of Hezekiah it did not yet exist. Once it had been "discovered" and attributed to "Moses", of course, it became desirable to insert anachronistic references to "covenants" into the traditions of Judah and Israel. So a covenant was said to have been made by Yahweh with "Abraham", the ancestor, according to at least some of the old traditions, of the patriarch "Israel", promising that his descendants would always possess the land of Canaan—including the territory of the lost northern kingdom of Israel. Similarly, a covenant was said to have been made with David, promising that a descendant of his would always sit on the throne in Jerusalem.[8] All this fit in quite nicely with Josiah's program. But why the conditionality? Why not just a promise, a reassurance, of divine blessing upon king and people?

Partly, I suspect, it was an effort—maybe even in a certain sense an honest one—to make the widespread belief that Judah and Israel constituted Yahweh's chosen, favored people compatible with the disastrous fate of the northern kingdom. Yahweh chose and blessed Israel, but the evil behavior of the Israelite kings and people—notably the favor shown by Ahab to the cults supported by his Tyrian wife Jezebel—had caused Yahweh to punish Israel, using Assyria as his unwitting tool. No doubt Hezekiah had said—and probably even believed—something along these lines in justifying his cultic reforms when he defied the Assyrian king Sennacherib. The fact that Jerusalem was not taken during Sennacherib's otherwise devastating invasion of Judah could be seen from the vantage-point of later times as an indication that Hezekiah had been more "righteous", more in step with Yahweh's wishes, than the kings of Israel had been. Still, Hezekiah's success had been only partial. Jerusalem was spared, but much of Judah had been ravaged—I would see some of the still-visible scars very soon—and some Judahite territory had been ceded by the Assyrians to certain Philistine vassals who had remained loyal to the empire.[9] Moreover, Israel was still lost to the Davidic dynasty. Hezekiah, who could not even protect much of Judah, had certainly done nothing to regain control of Israel.

Josiah had bigger ambitions. Confronting a weakened Assyria, he intended to accomplish far more than Hezekiah had ever dreamed of, to "restore" not only a pristine "Mosaic" cult (utterly under the domination of the king and the priests of Jerusalem) but also the "Davidic empire", including the northern kingdom. If he hoped to accomplish so much more than Hezekiah, his reform must be just so much more extensive, uncompromising, and complete than Hezekiah's had been. With his newly-found written law for justification, he intended to revolutionize Judahite cultic practices and revitalize national life. He would be the new David of the purified chosen nation.

The ideas underlying the revolution of Josiah's time must have been brewing throughout the eighty years or so since Hezekiah had confronted Sennacherib, if not indeed from the fall of Samaria itself, some twenty years prior to that. Given the "find-spot" of the law scroll, some faction within the temple priesthood in Jerusalem was obviously a major element in the coalition bent on redefining the kingdom's cult and way of life. Various prophets, despite their occasional criticisms of priestly practices, were probably active too, or else their words were selectively adopted and publicized by the reformers. And since the rigid centralization of authority the reform envisioned would greatly strengthen the position of king and court, I assume a group among the courtiers must have been involved as well. Exactly when the writing down, within these circles, of ancient national and tribal traditions, of prophetic utterances, and of congenially-interpreted accounts of events that had occurred within the reigns of various kings, had begun, I am unable to say. At the time of Josiah, much within each of these categories remained available only in oral memory. Early or late, much of what finally got written down was creative fiction, anyway!

The process of writing things down, and of re-explaining events that contradicted expectations, certainly continued after the reign of Josiah—at the very minimum, his own disastrous end had somehow to be explained away, since he had raised hopes so high among partisans of the revolution. The last time I was in Judah, which was during Nebuchadnezzar's second siege of Jerusalem, around twenty years ago, I was already hearing it said that when Josiah had consulted the prophetess Huldah, she had predicted the fall of the city, but had consoled the king by stating that—because of his personal righteousness—he himself would not live to see it happen.[10] Absolutely no such thing was suggested in Jerusalem at the time when Josiah was beginning his reform! Indeed, such an expectation would have rendered the whole project useless—why reform a cult and a nation that is already foredoomed? Here and there I have perhaps dismissed Josiah as over-zealous or even "mad" in the ferocity of his beliefs, but he was not so totally insane as to engage in a vast program that he was convinced in advance could not possibly succeed!

If factions among the priests, prophets, and courtiers were, as I have just said, "in on the plot", it is equally clear that other factions within each of these groups were not. The presence within the temple precinct of the "abominations" that Josiah had destroyed just before my arrival in Jerusalem must necessarily indicate the willingness of some priests—perhaps even of most of them—to provide space for such objects, images, and persons (even the male cult prostitutes, for example) within the kingdom's holiest place. Perhaps the high priest Hilkiah, by his "finding" of the scroll of the law, was in fact finding a way to establish his own precedence over a majority of priests who defied his authority! Like priests, like courtiers, I assume. Both groups came from the same restricted circle of families, and were very much intermarried. For every pro-reform courtier such as the secretary Shaphan, there must have been others less inclined to innovation, or opposed to it. The clothes-tearing scene I have described may well have been intended to bring these over to support of the movement. Certainly the prophets were not all of one mind. Rival would-be spokesmen for Yahweh routinely counseled opposite policies, and this process would continue and intensify throughout the career of Jeremiah after the time of Josiah, and be manifested even among the exiles in Babylonia. Nor were all Judahite prophets prophets of *Yahweh*. A major aspect of the revolution was to establish in the minds of the populace that Yahweh was the only god, but that was *not* the general belief in pre-Josianic Judah. Other gods had cults, had shrines, and had prophets, and this had been the norm for hundreds of years.

I described Josiah as "confronting a weakened Assyria", and the weakening of Assyria during the time he was king in Judah is a demonstrable fact, although the major disasters befell the Assyrian capitals of Ashur and Nineveh only several years after his "finding" of the law. Perhaps more importantly, Josiah was confronting a strengthened Egypt, an Egypt that under the Saite kings was bent on reasserting its ancient domination of Canaan. That Josiah grossly underestimated Egyptian strength would become evident from the way that he died, but it is clear that to some extent he defined his national program as anti-Egyptian, not anti-Assyrian, in contrast to what Hezekiah's policy had been. Egypt had in fact been Hezekiah's ally, although the "broken reed" had proved as unreliable as ever. This situation may explain the way that Egypt became the focus both of many prophetic oracles and of many national myths and legends that were being circulated, and at least beginning to be written down, in Judah in Josiah's time.

A legend very frequently invoked in that period held that the "children of Israel" had long ago, because of famine, journeyed from Canaan to Egypt, had settled and stayed there for hundreds of years, had been enslaved by the Egyptians, and then had miraculously been shown the "way out" (the Greek would be *exodos*, like the passageway from the orchestra to one or another side of a theater) by that same Moses I have already mentioned. This was said to have happened before he received the law from Yahweh—the same law, written upon the very same scroll, that Hilkiah had supposedly "found" in the temple, now hundreds of additional years later. Having received the law and assurance of divine support, the "Israelites" then proceeded to invade and recapture Canaan, which their ancestors had so long before abandoned.

Now the question of whether the Israelites—or Judahites—were invaders and conquerors, or had arisen within the region by somehow differentiating themselves from the other Canaanites, no one without a knowledge of those long-bygone days can really answer, and such knowledge is not now available.[11] The Philistines too were thought to have been invaders, perhaps even at around the same time, and my youthful discussion about the two similar vases with our slave Delilah had showed me that *this* tradition, at least, might be true. But of course I knew of no way to discover what "early Israelite" pottery might have looked like, nor would I have had any idea of who any external people might be, with whose pottery to compare it, in the way that Philistine and very old Greek pottery could be compared. Based on the legend itself, it would be reasonable to suppose that the long-captive "Israelites" would, by the time of their *exodos*, have made Egyptian-style pottery, I should think!

But frankly I found the sojourn of the entire nation in Egypt for hundreds of years very difficult to believe. It seemed to me much more likely that "slavery in Egypt" was a sort of metaphor for subjugation to Egypt *right there in Canaan*. That is, it could have represented either a vague recollection among the peoples of Canaan (Judahites and Israelites included) of the centuries of Egyptian imperial rule[12]—something about which I was to become fairly well informed during my subsequent years in Egyptian service—or it may have been simply a way of alluding to the current resurgence of Egyptian power in the area, with the Saites filling the vacuum created by the Assyrians' withdrawal. Or maybe the tradition of a "sojourn in Egypt" in some sense represented *both* these periods of Egyptian dominance. Josiah's foolhardy gesture of challenging Necho at Megiddo seems to have shown his determination not to be controlled by the Egyptians, and the legend of the *exodos*—which included Yahweh's destruction by miraculous means of an Egyptian army pursuing the "Israelites" northeastward—fit in perfectly with his program of national self-assertion.

Certain practices do seem to have been particularly associated with the Judahites and, I assume, with the Israelites when their kingdom existed, whether or not they were prescribed by the new-found law code. I am not sure exactly what was specified and what was not—it was a long document, and one that, as I have already said, I never actually saw. Certainly the eating of pork was treated as taboo by the Judahites whom I observed. The *Odyssey*'s swineherd Eumaios would not be considered such an admirable character in Judah as he is among Homer's Greek audience! How unique this particular prejudice was to Judah I cannot say. The Egyptians definitely have some ambivalence toward pork, and some contempt toward swineherds, but the eating of pork is not unknown among them.[13] I think some of the desert Arab tribes avoid eating pork, but then the barren area in which they roam is hardly conducive to the herding of pigs! Nor is most of Judah, for that matter.

One striking Judahite custom that most Greeks find appalling is what is called "circumcision", that is, "cutting around" the foreskin of the penis in order to remove the foreskin. But this custom, however strange we Greeks might think it, is definitely not restricted to the Judahites. The practice exists also among the Edomites, Ammonites, Moabites, and at least some of the desert Arabs, of the nearby peoples. I know this mostly from report, since there were no public bathhouses in Judah when I was there, nor did I think it proper, or safe, to examine too closely soldiers who had stopped to piss while on the march! Presumably all of these peoples, including the Judahites, acquired the custom from the Egyptians, who occupied Canaan for so long. That circumcision is an Egyptian practice I can indeed report from autopsy. Unlike the peoples of *Palaistine* and points east (the Assyrians and Babylonians, for example), who cover themselves up with long garments and feel an absolute horror of nudity, the Egyptians actually seem to realize that they live in a hot country, and dress accordingly, which is to say minimally. The Kushites of Nubia practice circumcision as well, but Nubia and Egypt have been in close connection for so long that it is impossible to say which of them learned the practice from the other.[14]

Customs that were already characteristic of the Judahites, or even exclusive to them, were not the primary focus of Josiah and his revolution. He was bent on eradicating practices that the Judahites shared with many peoples, as part of his process of making his nation newly unique and distinctive. Having begun by destroying several manifestations of traditional cult within the temple complex itself, he was now about to take his revolution throughout the kingdom and beyond.

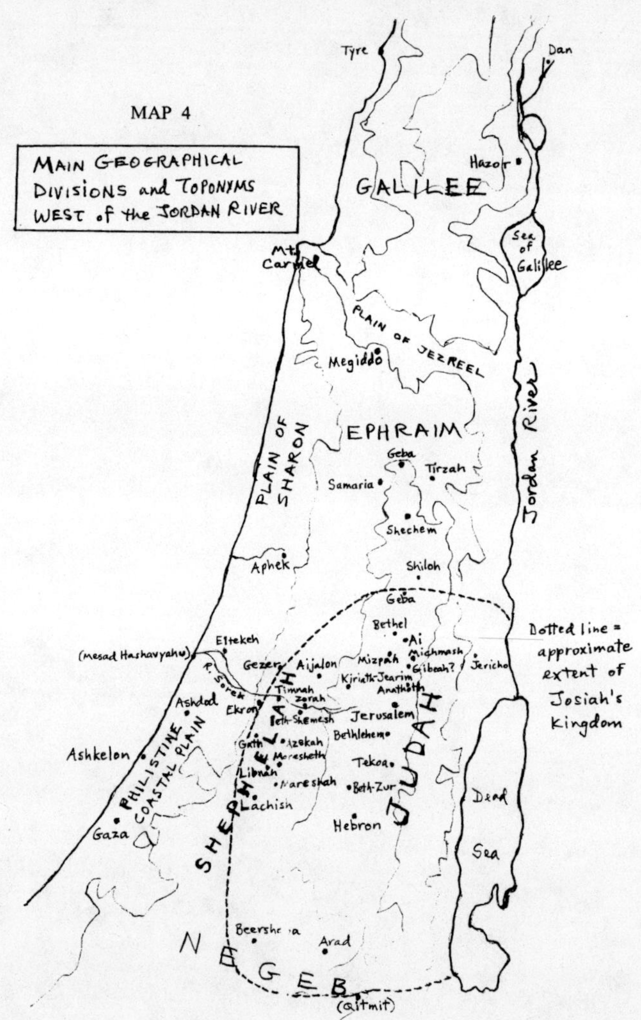
MAP 4
MAIN GEOGRAPHICAL DIVISIONS and TOPONYMS WEST of the JORDAN RIVER
Tyre
Dan
Hazor
GALILEE
Sea of Galilee
Mt. Carmel
PLAIN OF JEZREEL
Megiddo
Jordan River
EPHRAIM
PLAIN OF SHARON
Geba
Tirzah
Samaria
Shechem
Aphek
Shiloh
Geba
Bethel
Ai
Michmash
Dotted line = approximate extent of Josiah's Kingdom
Eltekeh
(mesad Hashavyahu)
Gezer
Aijalon
Mizpah
Gibeah?
Jericho
R. Sorek
Kiriath-Jearim
Anathoth
Timnah
Zorah
Ashdod
Ekron
Beth-Shemesh
Jerusalem
Bethlehem
Ashkelon
Gath
Azekah
Moresheth
Libnah
Mareshah
Tekoa
Beth-Zur
PHILISTINE COASTAL PLAIN
SHEPHELAH
JUDAH
Dead Sea
Lachish
Hebron
Gaza
Arad
NEGEB
(Qitmit)

5. IN THE STEPS OF SENNACHERIB

Benaiah, my commander, assigned me to a barracks within the New Town in Jerusalem, and I began to get to know my fellow mercenaries. They included a couple of other Ionians, a few Greeks from Kypros—along with other Kypriots of Phoinikian background, since the island had cities of both peoples—a handful of others from western and southern Asia, and representatives from several of the nearby peoples: Ammonites, Moabites, Edomites, Arabs, Philistines. Benaiah communicated with this polyglot assemblage primarily in Hebrew, but he was a considerable linguist who managed to sprinkle in a good many terms from several of our languages as needed. In any case, as I have already said, the languages of most of the peoples in the area were fairly closely related. I was a bit more able to communicate than most of the other westerners at first, but a soldier mostly has simple things to do that can be simply described, or can even be communicated largely without words.

I had barely gotten settled in Jerusalem when we were ordered to march out on our first assignment. We were to take Josiah's revolution to the foothills of western Judah, the region known as the Shephelah.[1] The Hebrew word means something like "lowlands", although the region was, as I would soon see, full of rolling hills. I suppose that from the standpoint of the highlands of Judah, the Shephelah was indeed comparatively "low", but it was considerably higher than the flat coastal plan which lay beyond it. Between the central highlands and the foothills was sort of a depression running north-and-south, which made it undesirable (especially since we were in no hurry) to march due west from the capital. Several river valleys did descend from the high plateau of Judah, through this depression, into the Shephelah, but these streambeds tended to be mostly narrow, steep, and winding. We followed the easiest of these routes, and the northernmost, the Aijalon Valley, and thus traveled east-to-west through a curved route bending northward, passing initially through some of the same region of Benjamin that I had encountered on my trip from Akko. We entered the Shephelah at its north end and then worked our way southward.

Here we were surrounded by reminders of the great invasion of Sennacherib, when he had come to punish the rebel Hezekiah some eighty years earlier.[2] The Assyrian too had passed through these foothills, going from north to south, although he had begun in the west rather than (like our troop) coming from the east. He had first compelled Hezekiah's Philistine allies in Ashkelon to surrender and replace their king with one more to his liking; next he defeated the relieving force from Egypt, led by the Kushite Pharaoh, at Eltekeh on the Way of the Sea.[3] Then he advanced up the valley of the Sorek River past Philistine Ekron, eastward to Timnah and Beth-Shemesh, then followed the road south to Azekah, Libnah, and the largest and most important of the cities of the Shephelah, Lachish. Among other still-identifiable places struck, either by the main army or by detachments sent off from the main line of march, were towns such as Philistine Gath (which Hezekiah had earlier seized)[4] and Mareshah.

Some of the cities of this region had changed hands between the Judahites and the Philistines of the coastal plain, sometimes more than once. In addition to his alliance with Ashkelon, Hezekiah had encroached on some Philistine territory. Besides taking over Gath, for a while he had held Padi the king of Ekron as his prisoner in Jerusalem, while a puppet friendly to his rebellion was installed in power. In the aftermath of the Assyrian invasion, Sennacherib had awarded some Judahite territory to his own Philistine allies in Ashdod and Gaza and—having reinstalled the king Hezekiah had deposed—Ekron. Later, Hezekiah's son Manasseh had been rewarded for his long period as a loyal Assyrian vassal by having some (not all) of the confiscated territory in the Shephelah returned.[5]

To say that some territory had been regained by the time of Josiah is not to say that most of the lost *cities* of the Shephelah had been restored. Many cities—the number I often heard was over forty fortified towns!—had been destroyed by Sennacherib's army. Some, especially the larger ones, had been rebuilt and resettled, but a good many still stood in ruins. The prophet Micah, a contemporary of Hezekiah who had come from the Shephelah town of Moresheth, had produced an oracle about the destruction in the Shephelah that was still being quoted in Judah during my time there, but several of the towns he had named no longer existed.[6] Sometimes even the connection between placename and town remains had been lost, so that often only anonymous ruins were to be seen along our line of march.

Timnah, some forty-five stades east of Ekron, on a mound overlooking a bend in the brook or river Sorek, was one of the towns that had been rebuilt after its destruction by Sennacherib. A few traces of that destruction were still to be seen. The structure at the city gate, for example, seemed to have replaced a larger one that Sennacherib had dismantled; some of the earlier foundations were visible below the later gate. Some pieces of large broken storage jars would have seemed meaningless to me, until I saw identical jars, with the same phrase, "belonging to the king" (*lamelech*), stamped on their handles, at other Shephelah locations. The jars had apparently once held provisions for the garrison troops Hezekiah had stationed at key fortified places in hopes of resisting the Assyrian invasion. I was also surprised to find current—not ancient—Greek pottery in use in Timnah, presumably brought there through trade. Later I would discover firsthand the nearby source of such pottery.

Timnah, in border territory, had been Philistine both before and after it had been Judahite, at least according to legends I heard about a mythical hero of the tribe of Dan called Samson. The stories that were told of his superhuman deeds in fighting the Philistines, here and at other places nearby, made him sound to me like no one so much as our own Greek hero and demigod Herakles. Timnah had supposedly been the home of his Philistine wife. During the period when Timnah had been reoccupied by the Philistines under Assyrian sponsorship, it seems that a large industry for the pressing of olives for oil had been established there, since numerous oil-presses were visible. Plastered vats were cut into floors, and into them was channeled the oil from olives in large wicker baskets that were pressed down upon by huge wooden beams on which were hung heavy stone weights.[7] Ekron had been the center of an even larger-scale olive oil industry, also under Assyrian hegemony.[8] With the weakening of Assyrian authority, the regional olive oil industry was becoming an increasingly valuable resource of the kings of Judah, a process that had already begun under the philo-Assyrian Manasseh, which Josiah would intensify. Even if Timnah was nominally under Assyrian control, or under the control of Assyrian vassals, Josiah had felt strong enough to send us foreign troops in to accomplish his plans here. For the time being, his estimate of the situation proved correct. The only opposition we encountered was local, nor was there—as yet—much of that.

Our instructions were to close down every place of sacrifice to any god—Yahweh included—and to eliminate every physical manifestation of cultic activity in the towns and territories we entered. Josiah's reform, following the line of the scroll of the law that had turned up in the temple in Jerusalem, not only restricted all sacrificial activity to that one locale, but also partook of what we Greeks would call "aniconism" (*aneikonismos*)—a radical and total hostility to any images, whether painted, sculpted, or formed from clay. Certain desert Arab tribes, I was later told, shared in this rejection of depictions, and it may be that the Judahites in the southern desert area known as the Negeb had picked up the idea from them. Not only were images of gods—or of Josiah's one god, Yahweh—forbidden, but even images of any kind of living creature!

This was of course all but unbelievable for a Greek like myself. It seemed to derive from a kind of simple-minded concern that worshipers would actually be misled into believing that a carved or sculpted or painted image representing a god was the god himself! Surely no Ionian had ever seen the cult statues of Apollo at Didyma, or of Artemis at Ephesos, or of Hera at Samos, as anything but metaphors for the deities they represented, made as beautiful as possible by our artists so as to honor the gods and goddesses. And not to produce images of beautiful youths and maidens, or even of fine running horses, noble hunting dogs, powerful bulls, stately stags, or any other creature—why, it almost destroys the very notion of beauty! The partisans of Josiah's revolution, with their hostility to all art, showed themselves to be what we Greeks call *barbaroi*—not merely "foreigners" but uncultured foreigners. My later employers, the Egyptians, took an attitude toward images much closer to that of us Greeks, although their images were decidedly more stylized than ours; I actually found their exoticism rather appealing.

When I stigmatize the aniconism of Josiah's partisans, I emphatically do not criticize the Judahites in general. It was very clear that the great majority of them wanted no part of the king's craziness! Unfortunately, however, the man who was out to destroy their traditional religious practices was our employer. When they resisted us, we reluctantly employed force. It soon became clear why Josiah had been eager to hire foreign troops. Better to let the Judahites vent their initial hate and resentment upon the *goyim*—a word meaning "foreigners", with pretty much the same implications as the Greek *barbaroi*—rather than on their king and his Judahite officials. Once the people of Judah had been bludgeoned into accepting the radical alteration in their worship and way of life, they would soon be convinced by incessant government-sponsored rhetoric that the new practice constituted their own "belief" and had actually been their "traditional, ancestral way". Then there would be no further need for non-Judahite enforcers.[9] Indeed, in retrospect, I can see that there was a built-in contradiction in our use from the beginning, because the revolution was fundamentally anti-foreign in every way, designed to drive a wedge between the Judahites (or "Israelites", as they liked to call themselves) and all other peoples. But much of what was now being defined as "foreign" was in reality not foreign at all, but was Judahite (and probably Israelite!) practice from time immemorial.

Being now away from the capital, and able, at least to some extent, to understand some of the outcry from the rural victims of the king's program, I was increasingly able to see that the "reform" of Hezekiah, offered by Josiah's partisans as a parallel and precedent for their revolution, had been far less radical and disruptive. The earlier king seemingly did not share Josiah's extreme aniconism, since some of the jars stamped "belonging to the king" bore not only the four Hebrew letters of that term but were also stamped with images of creatures—Egyptian-style scarab beetles.[10] It may well be that Hezekiah had shut down local cultic sites, but it was manifest in several places I later visited that he had not *destroyed* them. Hezekiah's activities had been about *centralization*, about concentrating all of the nation's resources, including its population, into Jerusalem and certain well-supplied and fortified regional centers, in hopes of resisting the invasion of the mighty

Assyrian army. In the Shephelah, destruction by the Assyrians themselves had been so widespread that it could easily have been believed that Hezekiah had wiped out cultic facilities, but elsewhere—in southern regions of Judah, into which Sennacherib did not penetrate—I would soon see that sacrificial precincts, even actual temples, in royal district centers had not been destroyed, and had operated continually. Until now.

Here in Timnah, given its position in a Philistine-Judahite border region, it was easy and natural to define many cultic artifacts as "foreign", that is, Philistine. This description certainly fit the mold-made female figurines that we destroyed in some quantity. Whom or what did they represent? Asherah? Some Philistine goddess who might perhaps have been ultimately a Greek goddess—recalling my conversations with Delilah—Artemis or maybe Aphrodite? Resistance to the destruction we wrought was not strong at Timnah, probably because we were only now beginning our mission. We hit the local priests and elders by surprise, showing up unexpectedly in their town with our demands that they turn in all images for destruction and get out of their "high places" and other sacred precincts to allow us to desanctify and physically destroy them. With minimal resistance, requiring only one or two well-placed blows for the quelling, they quickly complied. As we progressed through the Shephelah and beyond, however, knowledge of our assignment spread rapidly by word of mouth, and resistance and resentment became ever more outspoken. The same levels of destruction came to require higher levels of physical violence. My own feelings had begun as simple cynicism: "Fine, if the king is willing to pay us for enforcing his foolishness, what do we care? It's all just silliness on both sides, and he's paying our wages, which puts us on his side, rather than theirs!" But I experienced a growing distaste at being expected to break heads to force compliance with a program that so few seemed willingly to support.

Benaiah sent off a small detachment to wreak the prescribed havoc in whatever was left of nearby Zorah, supposedly the birthplace of Samson, while the main body of us continued eastward along the road, the brook Sorek close beside us on our left. We traversed a distance about the same as that between Ekron and Timnah, until we arrived at Beth-Shemesh. I should say that we arrived at the spot, high on the south bank of the brook Sorek, that had once been Beth-Shemesh. Zorah was clearly visible across the valley and so was Timnah, if we looked westward, downstream. Between Zorah and Beth-Shemesh the river was bridged, and the road southward or southwestward to Lachish ran right beside the ruins we were approaching. Here again, Sennacherib had destroyed the town, and it had not been rebuilt. Doubtless the Assyrians were the ones who had broken up the several *lamelech* jars we saw and had destroyed the massive two-chambered gate on the northern side of the city.

In the middle of a plastered city square that lay just inside that gate was the opening of a vertical shaft that turned out to lead into a very large underground municipal cistern. Pressing an extremely reluctant Moabite, who happened to be the smallest of our troop, into service, we lowered him, with a lamp, down the shaft on ropes into the now quite dry cistern. We hoped he might chance upon some booty, some gold or silver tossed down there in expectation of retrieving it after the invaders had departed. He found nothing but various broken pots, but amazed us with his report of the huge size of the well-plastered cistern. It was shaped like the Greek letter *chi*, with each of its four arms radiating outward for about 15 cubits, and six or seven cubits deep; two of the arms were around four cubits wide, the other two about half that. The entire strangely-shaped cavern had been cut into the soft limestone bedrock, then roofed over with stone and plaster, and could obviously have held enough water to supply the town during a siege. It seemed odd, however, that the only way to get the water would have been by lowering buckets down the shaft in the town square.

Near the western edge of the square, one of our Karians noticed a pile of dirt and broken pottery that appeared to have been dumped there with some purpose in mind. By digging into it just a bit, we uncovered a couple of stone steps. Without proceeding further, we were able to guess that here had been a stairway leading down to one of the cistern's four arms, which citizens of Beth-Shemesh—or their serving-women—could have descended to fetch water in jugs. Who had plugged up the town's main access to water? I suspected that in this case the Assyrians were not the culprits, since it would have been immaterial to them whether the place was habitable after their departure or not. More likely, I thought, were the Philistines. We were still in the border district here, but getting closer to the heartland of Judah as we moved farther east. Perhaps the Philistines in Timnah or Ekron, uncertain that they would be able to hold Beth-Shemesh themselves, preferred an abandoned site to a town occupied by Judahites, so they drove off whatever squatters had settled in around the reservoir and sealed up its entrance. This would particularly have made sense if the town was within territory that the Assyrians had required their Philistine vassals to cede back to Manasseh as part of his reward for loyalty. It would not have been the first or the last time that a dependent ally, forced by its hegemon to give territory to its local rival, had made an effort to render the ceded territory as valueless as possible.[11]

Beyond the bit of exploring that we had taken upon ourselves, we had very little to do here. Only isolated farmhouses were occupied. We flashed a few swords and terrorized a few farmers' families, confiscating various household gods and chopping them up before their horrified faces. Since our band of mercenaries, even subdivided for forays into other villages, virtually outnumbered the men able to bear arms in the immediate vicinity, the resistance we encountered was purely verbal. "*Goyim*!" and other unfriendly labels were spat at us, but the insults were carefully *not* directed at King Josiah, whose agents we were. Where kings rule, only those who believe themselves to speak the words of gods—prophets, I mean—dare to voice criticism or disapproval. So recently had I come from Ionia, and I was already a part of this oppressive system.

Some of the farmhouses we encountered here and elsewhere were obviously extremely old, probably built centuries earlier and constantly refurbished and repaired by succeeding generations within the family groups that occupied them. The oldest ones we saw had thick stone walls around the outside of the first floor, sometimes extended to form an open courtyard in front. The house proper would be divided by interior walls or rows of columns (thick wooden poles set on stone bases) usually into four definable areas—not exactly four "rooms", unless the lines of columns were somehow connected together to form barriers that functioned much like walls. A wide room usually ran all the way across the rear of the house, separated by an interior wall with a door, and the remainder of the house was often divided into three long "rooms" by two rows of columns. These columns, along with any interior walls, supported a ceiling of branches laid across large beams, with mud and plaster smoothed over this platform to create a floor for a second story. Its layout generally repeated that of the first, though the walls at this level tended to be built of mud bricks rather than stone. Finally came another ceiling, this one carefully maintained since it also constituted the roof, which both kept off the winter rains and provided a cooler place for the family's sleeping mats on hot nights. Living quarters were on the second level, with the ground level reserved for cooking, penning domestic livestock, and housing large storage jars with the family's supplies (especially in the large rear room).[12]

In searching such houses—we did not ransack them unless we encountered resistance—we occasionally came upon a simple family shrine in an interior room. Any images we discovered within such shrines were confiscated and destroyed, as I have said. Sometimes the household cult did not employ actual "images", but only carefully chosen stones, merely smoothed or not worked at all, that apparently symbolized gods—I'm sure that sometimes the god symbolized was none other than Yahweh himself. But even an uncarved standing stone was not sufficiently aniconic to please Josiah; these too had to be smashed and broken. Sometimes a flat stone was set in front of a standing stone, thus seemingly serving a "deity" as an "altar", and we did indeed encounter incense being burned on such primitive altars.

Just as often as there was one standing stone, there were *two* standing stones, and in such cases invariably the stone to the viewer's left was taller, while the one to the right was usually wider and shorter. Members of my company who had served in this region longer than I had instantly recognized such pairs of stones as symbolizing Yahweh and his consort Asherah. Simple cultic sites of this type were not found only within houses. Many of the installations on "high places", that is, hilltops, took this form, and such *temene* were to be seen even deep in the southern desert. I suspect, in fact, that they were ultimately a desert type of installation that had only later been brought into the more populated areas. They accorded well with the tendency toward aniconism that I have already connected with the desert.

At Azekah and Libnah and other places along the road that we were now following southward, we continued to add our devastation to that wrought by Sennacherib—and possibly also by Hezekiah, as he had closed down cultic sites and herded the population into garrisoned strongholds in preparation for meeting the invaders. Subsidiary parties continued to be sent to small sites off the road, and I was myself detailed to such a party for approaching Mareshah, which was about thirty-five stades northeast of our eventual rendezvous point at Lachish. At Mareshah we encountered something surprising. There were signs of habitation—cooking fires still smoldering, houses well-stocked with food, animals safely within their enclosures—but where were the people?

Soon we discovered the natural phenomenon that had saved their ancestors from Sennacherib and would—they hoped—save them from the king's soldiers now. Not that we were bent on doing anyone personal damage, and in fact their abandonment of their homes gave us a free hand to do the sort of damage we *were* there to do! Having destroyed their shrines and images, both in the abandoned houses and on the nearby hilltops, we began a desultory search for the populace, if only to tell them they could return home now. At the base of a hill that had borne a "high place", one of our troop discovered a cave entrance concealed behind some bushes. We cautiously entered, and were amazed at the way the cave opened up and appeared to go on for stades and stades in several directions. Apparently the rock in this region has a fairly hard crust, but at a short distance beneath the surface it becomes chalky and quite soft. Digging out caves is very easy, and the entire area is honeycombed with them. When enemies approach, the local people simply disappear underground—their galleries are always well stocked with supplies and water. It was not worth our while to search for the villagers hiding within the convoluted network of tunnels; making the effort was only likely to get us lost. So we exited where we had entered and moved on, leaving the cave-people of Mareshah unscathed except for the damage we had done to their shrines.[13]

Finally we approached the last stop in our foray into the Shephelah, the partially-reconstructed former metropolis of the area, Lachish. Rebuilding had begun under Manasseh and was continuing under Josiah, although it was clear from the debris and ruined buildings that the city destroyed by Sennacherib had been much larger and more impressive. It must have rivaled Jerusalem itself in size and population. I could get a fair idea of the appearance of the earlier city and its fortifications by surveying what was still standing, from a low hill to the west of the city's higher mound. The double walls—the lower one still fairly high up the mound, connected by a smooth-stone glacis with the inner wall—were pierced by a double gate complex at the southwest corner. This had been rebuilt in somewhat less imposing fashion than before, to judge by the massive stone blocks in the lower levels of the outer gate, which had apparently been left standing by Sennacherib, and seemed somewhat out-of-scale with the structures now above them. The ruins of a very large building complex, doubtless the residence of the regional governor during Hezekiah's time, were visible at the highest point on the mound. Much of the huge earthen ramp that Sennacherib had built for his siege machines, which had followed the line of the road leading up to the gates from the south, was of course still in place, but enough of it had been cleared to reopen the road and make the refortified gateway again accessible.[14]

We passed through the outer gateway and assembled in a large open court, which led to the right and uphill to the inner gateway. One of the towers of the gate complex constituted a guard-room. The Judahite soldiers stationed there, aware of our mission, waved us on through. They were happy to have the unpleasant and unwelcome duty of destroying the city's longstanding cultic facilities left to a band of despised foreign mercenaries—less hostility would be directed toward *them,* in consequence. Our first stop within the city was its temple of Yahweh, reconstructed by Manasseh to replace the temple looted and destroyed by his Assyrian masters. The priests there, about to lose their jobs and their income, stirred up a mob to resist us, but our superior armament eventually overcame the insurgents. I don't think anyone was killed, but some nasty blows were exchanged, and one priest was severely injured when he flung himself on one of our Greek Kypriot soldiers. We closed the structure down and dismantled its altar, destroying the cult statues to the various gods who had shared the temple with Yahweh. Then we issued our usual orders to the local populace to turn in all its cultic figurines and statues and all its sacrificial paraphernalia—or else have their houses thoroughly searched and rummaged. Most of the residents grumblingly complied; the others bore the consequences. After the altercation at the temple, we were not much in the mood for opposition, so our searches were more destructive than usual, more careless of breakage.

After a day spent thus in the restored town, we carried our mission of destruction outside, despoiling the nearby high places and descending on individual farmhouses. The first phase of our part in Josiah's program was completed. Other units had been sent elsewhere within the kingdom, and we would soon have further assignments, but for now we were to return to Jerusalem by the main roads—east from Lachish to Hebron, then north to the capital.

Later, from a Greek who had served with the Babylonian army when it pillaged Sennacherib's palace at Nineveh, I would discover that the king had taken such pride in his successful siege of Lachish that he had devoted an entire large room in his palace to a series of relief carvings depicting the siege, the fall of the city, the impaling of certain resisters, and the carrying away of much booty and numerous captives. My informant—whom you shall meet in due time, readers—said that the sculptures showed Sennacherib himself seated on a throne viewing the procession of prisoners and booty.[15]

6. CONSOLIDATION IN THE CAPITAL

We had only been away from Jerusalem for a matter of weeks, but on our return it was already possible to see Josiah's revolution taking firm hold in the city. This was not particularly surprising, since the royal administration and the temple hierarchy were quite firmly in control there, able not only to suppress dissent immediately, but also to dispense a steady flow of pro-revolution rhetoric. Prophets of Yahweh who were unfriendly to the movement still spoke out occasionally, but their voices were muted and overwhelmed by those of court-and-temple-approved prophets such as Jeremiah and Zephaniah. The latter claimed a Hezekiah among his ancestors; I don't know whether that person was the king or just someone bearing the same name, but Zephaniah's hearers were impressed by the apparent royal connection.[1] Prophets of other gods were not only shouted down, but beaten up and run out of town. I am not even sure that all of them escaped with their lives, and if they did, their good fortune might have proved temporary, as the zeal and ferocity of Josiah's movement fed on its early successes. Our foray into the Shephelah was counted among those successes, so our band of foreign mercenaries was accorded some grudging respect by the king's advisors, despite the awkwardness involved in employing our help in a militantly nationalistic movement.

In the ensuing days of barracks life, with nothing much to do since local law-enforcement (whether political or cultic) was in native hands, I was able sometimes to wander about the city observing and listening. Benaiah did not insist on

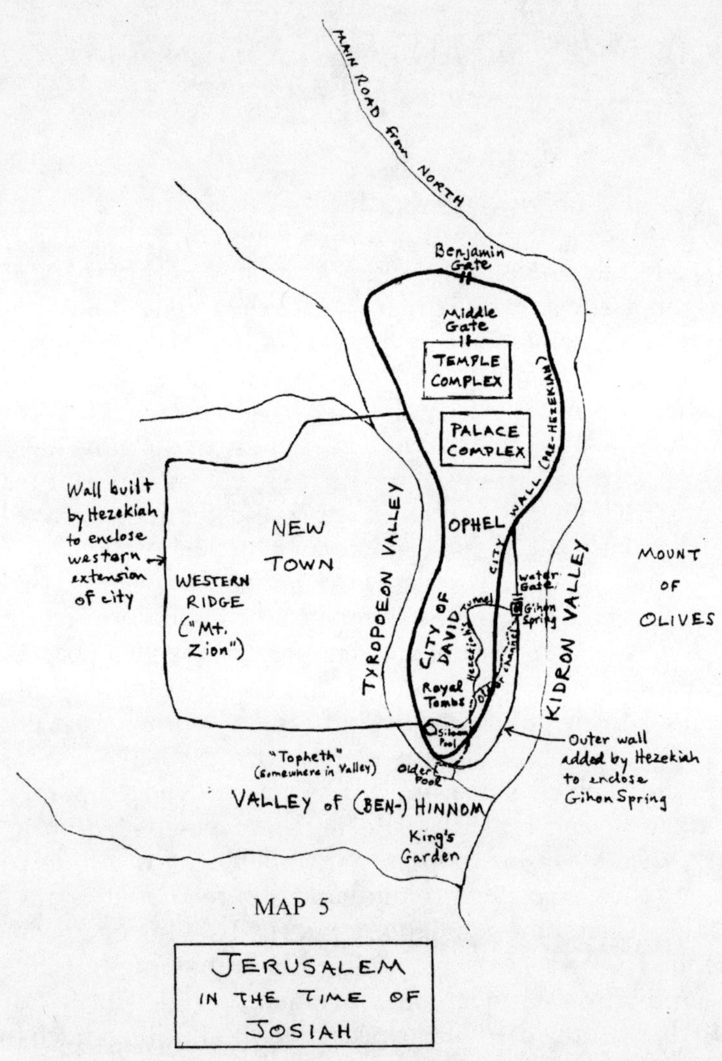

MAP 5

JERUSALEM IN THE TIME OF JOSIAH

our maintaining military garb when off duty, sensing—perceptive, experienced commander that he was—that we would encounter less hostility if we were less obviously foreign. Sometimes he even accompanied me, as he had become an important mentor to me during the course of our expedition in the western foothills. I found it easier to converse, of course, with the Greek-speakers among our company, but they had little to teach me, being almost as new on the scene as I was. Nor did any of them seem particularly curious about the events going on around us, whereas Benaiah, an older man and a Judahite, had a mind that worked much more like mine did: he wanted and needed to understand things, and he could have been a pure Ionian for skepticism. He counted me, despite my youth, among his most reliable soldiers, and he appreciated my insatiable curiosity about the revolution and everything that had led up to it. On my part, I plied him for as much information as possible, which he was happy to supply.

One thing he enabled me to understand—not easy for a Greek who found himself plunged into the fiery middle of the revolution, with angry people screaming all around—was the more socially benevolent motivations that coexisted with the nativistic and iconoclastic aspects of the movement. To understand those, I needed more background than I could gain from mere observation. With Benaiah's help and encouragement, I was able to acquire some knowledge to clarify what I had been seeing. The physical damage done to cities and countryside by the invading Assyrian army had been amply evident during our journey through the western foothills, but the social damage was not so readily comprehended, by anyone unaware of events prior to the invasion.[2]

The fall of Samaria had apparently had a huge impact in Judah, in several ways. First, it had produced streams of refugees that the kingdom of Judah had had to absorb somehow. Secondly, it had made Judah a tributary state directly bordering on the Assyrian Empire, no longer buffered by the territory of Israel; any Assyrian force assigned to take punitive action toward Judah had merely to cross its own border to enter the kingdom. Thirdly, and probably most importantly, the fall of Samaria raised serious issues for the very religious-minded Judahites, especially the prophetic faction that believed that Yahweh was the *only* god. Israel's destruction cried out for explanation and for justification. How could Yahweh have allowed the blood-thirsty Assyrians to destroy a nation of the chosen people? For those unwilling to countenance the proposition that the god Asshur had simply proved stronger than Yahweh—which was of course the Assyrian line—it had to be assumed that Yahweh had allowed, indeed intended, the disaster to happen. If that were so, and if Yahweh were a just god—another thing that was strongly believed—then Samaria and Israel must have *deserved* destruction, that is, the destruction had come as punishment, with Assyria merely serving as Yahweh's agent.

Punishment for what? Certainly the Yahweh-alone faction emphasized religious and cultic "crimes", worshiping other gods in addition to Yahweh and worshiping Yahweh in inappropriate ways, for instance by employing images. But other crimes, ones more intelligible to my Ionian mind, were also cited. Great disparities of wealth had arisen in Israel, and great oppression of the poor by the rich. The sayings of the prophet Amos, in particular, dwelt on such abuses in impressive detail and with genuine humanitarian passion:

> They hate the man who teaches justice at the city gate
> and detest anyone who declares the truth.
> For trampling on the poor man
> and for extorting levies on his wheat:
> although you have built houses of dressed stone,
> you will not live in them;
> although you have planted pleasant vineyards,

you will not drink wine from them:
for I know how many your crimes are
and how outrageous your sins,
you oppressors of the upright, who hold people to ransom
and thrust the poor aside at the gates.[3]

Subjugation to Assyria—the kingdom had been tributary long before it was absorbed—exacerbated these conditions. Mere participation in the international economy of the empire had required farmers to emphasize exportable crops for trade such as wine grapes and olives, rather than subsistence crops for feeding their families. Over and above the impact of this centrally-imposed agricultural innovation was the necessity to produce a surplus in order to meet the Assyrians' demands for tribute.

The tributary state of Judah in the days of Hezekiah suffered essentially from the same problems as had plagued Israel before its fall. When Sargon, who had completed the siege of Samaria and deported the Israelites, was unexpectedly killed in battle against foes to the north and east of the Assyrian heartland,[4] and his son Sennacherib had to engage in considerable internal strife to secure the throne for himself, Hezekiah must have concluded that he could alleviate many of Judah's ills by breaking away from the empire. He accordingly withheld tribute, and his gamble looked good for about four years, which is how much time elapsed before Sennacherib consolidated his position and brought his army westward. Meanwhile, Hezekiah prepared to resist the invasion he knew must come at some point. As I have already mentioned, he repaired the walls of Jerusalem and added further walls to enclose newer areas of the city, swelled by refugees from the north and no doubt also now by others fleeing from the countryside of Judah; he also safeguarded the city's water supply with his new pool and tunnel.[5] He established fortified centers—Lachish, as we had seen, had been one such, for example—and stationed garrisons in them, with supplies organized centrally, as indicated by the *lamelech* jars for provisions we had observed.

The closing down of local cult sites by Hezekiah has to be seen as part of his general policy of centralization and consolidation. There was in his time no "scroll of the law" to demand that all sacrifice be restricted to one single spot (interpreted as the temple in Jerusalem), and in fact—as we mercenaries would see quite clearly in our next excursion into the Judahite countryside—Hezekiah had not closed down cultic installations, even actual temples, in his garrison towns and regional centers. *State* shrines continued to operate, while local cults were suppressed. A key aspect of centralization, of putting all power in the hands of the king and the Jerusalem establishment, had been breaking the power of local leaders—tribal and clan elders, town aristocracies, local priests. Doing this had made it easier to persuade the farmers and townspeople to withdraw to the fortified centers and to Jerusalem itself, where some measure of protection from Assyria's wrath could be provided for them. I wonder if any Greek leader will ever dare to attempt such a drastic strategy—bringing his state's entire population into one or a few fortified centers while allowing the enemy to ravage his entire countryside and destroy his smaller towns, hoping to wait out the invasion until the foe withdraws in frustration? The technique might be possible for an island city, or a coastal city with a fortified port and a large navy,[6] but Hezekiah lacked these advantages, so his attempt was even bolder—and seemingly involved an underestimation of his enemy's strength.

For all the current praise of Hezekiah by those who likened Josiah's measures to his, Hezekiah's revolt had failed disastrously. Sennacherib had taken town after town, throughout the Shephelah and in the region just north of Jerusalem,[7] and he had deported thousands of Judahites and taken away considerable territory, all in addition to levying a crippling tribute on the rebel, so high, it was said, that the king had been forced to strip the gold from the doors of the temple in paying it.[8] For the last fifteen years or so of Hezekiah's reign, he was a loyal tribute-paying vassal of Assyria, and that was the policy he had passed on to his son Manasseh. If the policy of centralization continued in force, this would largely have been because Judah at that time consisted of little more than Jerusalem and its immediate environs. As to efforts to stamp out non-Yahwistic worship, I think it is doubtful that Hezekiah had ever made any such efforts at all. Certainly some of the altars and statuary to other gods that Josiah had recently destroyed within the temple precinct itself had been attributed to kings *before* Hezekiah,[9] so he manifestly had not destroyed the paraphernalia of other cults even in the place where his power was unchallenged, the very temple of Jerusalem, in effect the royal chapel!

Jerusalem survived, perhaps because a plague struck the army of Sennacherib as it was laying siege. The story told in Jerusalem while I was there was that "the angel of Yahweh" had killed 185,000 Assyrian soldiers in one night in their camp.[10] I disregard the huge number; all sides grossly exaggerate their triumphs, here in the east as well as back home in Ionia. Plagues are always attributed to gods, and it is obvious from things I have already reported that similar stories have been told among the Greeks. A bizarre tale I later heard at a temple in the Egyptian delta (despite its being connected with the wrong Egyptian king) told of Sennacherib—he was mentioned by name, the priests insisted—having been turned away from the borders of Egypt when his army was attacked at night by a huge horde of field mice. Supposedly the rodents had chewed away all the quivers, bowstrings, and shield-handles, causing the suddenly-defenseless army to withdraw in panic. If mice are associated with plague, as would appear to be the case from the Homeric connection of the Mouse-god Apollo with pestilence, the Egyptian priests' story, offered in explanation of a statue of a king holding a mouse in his hand, may have represented a garbled memory of how Sennacherib, having defeated the Egyptian army at Eltekeh in Canaan, was hit by plague and was unable to follow up his victory by invading Egypt.[11]

But what a desperate situation prevailed in what was left of Judah! The Shephelah had been the primary grain-producing region of the kingdom, and now much of it belonged to various Philistine kings: Mitinti of Ashdod, Sillibel of Gaza, and Padi of Ekron. The last of these was the very king whom Hezekiah had deposed and held captive until Sennacherib had forced his restoration. How was Judah even to feed itself? The solution, probably adopted under Hezekiah in his later years and intensified during the long reign of his son Manasseh, was the cultivation of marginal areas to the east and south of Jerusalem, areas up to that time regarded as essentially barren desert. With painstaking care and very close husbanding of water resources, a process involving the construction of many new cisterns to hold what little rain fell in these areas, it had proved possible to coax crops of barley and other grains out of the reluctant earth. Most farming efforts had to be devoted, however, to producing the products—wine and oil—required by the Assyrian empire's international economy.[12]

It must have been particularly galling to the Judahites to see the bulk of their olive crop taken to Philistine Ekron for processing (whether the olive presses of Timnah had been in Philistine or Judahite hands during any given period was difficult to tell). Achish, the son and successor of Padi of Ekron, in gratitude for his prosperity, dedicated a large temple to his protective goddess. I managed actually to visit the temple once and read its dedicatory inscription in Philistine Canaanite. The goddess, perhaps Asherah, seemingly was not named. Rather, I was almost certain that she was referred to by a term transliterated from the Greek *Potnia*, "Mistress", used sometimes in describing Artemis as "Mistress of Wild Animals", *Potnia Therion*. Perhaps I was misreading the inscription, however; one letter in the word seemed rather doubtful, maybe incompletely cut.[13]

Even when the devastated areas of Judah were partially rebuilt and resettled after the Assyrians' withdrawal, the centralization that had marked Hezekiah's revolt continued. After all, most of the surviving, undeported population of the kingdom was at that time clustered in and immediately around Jerusalem. Repopulation of the countryside and towns, therefore, would have been from Jerusalem, and the returnees—many of whom would have been going not to their original homes but to other places in Judah—would have thought of themselves as subjects of Jerusalem and its royal and cultic establishment. Only gradually would a sense of local traditions have re-emerged and the power of local and tribal and clan leadership have been reasserted. The long decades of peace under Manasseh had encouraged such a return to "normal", and he apparently had seen it as being advantageous to the central government not to interfere with local cultic practices. Whatever disruption Hezekiah's closing of local high places had caused had been reversed—not by fiat of Manasseh and his administration, but simply by allowing local customs to reestablish themselves without interference.

It might be said that there had been *some* cultic interference, in the sense that worship of the gods of imperial Assyria had been encouraged as a routine condition of vassalage. Josiah later would make much of this policy of his grandfather, although there was nothing unusual about it, nor had it given offense to many Judahites. They had always worshiped many gods in addition to their special god Yahweh, so restoring the cults of the few Assyrian deities Hezekiah had briefly disestablished would have had little impact. More important had been the social and economic interference of the royal administration. Where Hezekiah had been a reluctant and rebellious vassal, Manasseh had been an enthusiastic one, and one bent on profiting from the imperial system. Agriculture and trade in Judah became ever more centralized and regulated, and then there was always the matter of raising the necessary tribute payment every year. The economic crunch had been eased somewhat when, in reward for his long-time loyalty, Manasseh had had some of the territories returned that had been given to the Philistines. He had also been permitted to get Judah involved in the lucrative trade in spices carried largely by Arab caravans in the deserts to the south. Certain rest-stops at oases and fortifications in the Negeb seem to have been in Judahite control during the time of Manasseh; the "border" in the south remained rather fuzzy even in the time of Josiah, as I would soon see for myself. A measure of prosperity returned, but it was a prosperity restricted largely to the wealthier portions of the population, and mostly to the wealthy of the capital.

Hezekiah had revolted during an apparent period of Assyrian weakness that had proved illusory (or at least temporary), and national independence had probably been his primary goal. The weakening of Assyria that Josiah and his courtiers saw was *not* illusory; the empire actually was in its death throes, and this was evident to almost everyone. So Josiah more or less simply assumed that Judah was already independent, in effect, and thought in terms of geographical expansion of his kingdom. Moreover, he and his advisors, for all their emphasis on ritual and cultic matters, did show some genuine concern for alleviating some of the social ills that had afflicted Judah during the period of Assyrian domination. The law code attributed to Moses had a good many provisions that were not cultic in nature at all, but indicated concerns to ease the sufferings of the poor, widows, orphans, even resident aliens and indentured servants. Many aspects of the law code would have been quite congenial to a Greek law-giver, and would have made him, as its promulgator, a "friend to the *demos*". Asserting divine—in reality priestly and royal—sanction for benevolent social measures and rules to promote justice and peace within the kingdom seemed eminently worthwhile, especially in this part of the world, where no governments partook even slightly of popular control or limitation. Any thorough-going legal or social or economic reform here must inevitably have been imposed by royal and priestly authority and must have claimed divine sanction.[14]

In my skeptical Ionian eyes, the aspects of his revolution that appeared most to motivate Josiah—eliminating the worship of all gods except one, restricting all sacrifice to one single place, emphasizing and increasing the differences between Judahites and other peoples—seemed unnecessary and really undesirable accretions. Having myself no allegiance to the dispossessed gods and their cultic personnel, I would continue to assist in dispossessing them, even though I felt distaste for the force to which we sometimes had to resort. Nor did I have any more regard for the single god and the exclusive priesthood we were supporting than for the gods and priests we were suppressing. Josiah had at least made our tasks a bit easier and less distasteful by lately adopting a policy that priests who had been officiating at shrines and high places dedicated to Yahweh would be allowed to relocate to Jerusalem and would be fed from the revenues of the temple priesthood there, although they would cease to perform any priestly duties.[15] This policy development was designed to—and did—have the effect of undercutting opposition to the reform from one of the key elements of local leadership. Had this policy been in effect earlier, it might have saved a priest at Lachish some blows!

Before our band of mercenaries was dispatched again into the countryside—this time heading south rather than west—the king decided to make use of us in the near neighborhood of Jerusalem itself. We were sent to the southern end of the Mount of Olives, which faced Jerusalem from the east, across the Kidron valley. There were located the large and elaborate high places at which sacrifices were offered to

Astarte of Sidon, Chemosh of Moab, and Milkom of Ammon. These shrines, which I had noticed at the time of my first arrival in the valley, had supposedly been established by King Solomon, son of David, to honor the gods of some of his foreign wives. Now these cults, which by Josiah's own reckoning had been operating within sight of the city for three hundred years—and certainly had not been interfered with by Hezekiah, since their attribution to Solomon made them obviously royal shrines—were denounced as "foreign" and non-Judahite. We were set to breaking up the altars and destroying all the cultic images, polluting and rendering unsanctified all the cultic precincts.[16] Too bad for the priests of these extremely ancient Judahite—but non-Yahwist—high places: nobody offered *them* a share of the bread of the priests of Yahweh's temple!

The last act of destruction to which we were assigned in the vicinity of Jerusalem was one I found actually quite congenial. We were ordered to desanctify and generally destroy the cult site known as Topheth, located in the valley of Ben-Hinnom, south of the City of David. This had been the place where a horrifying rite had been enacted, one that pretty clearly showed the savagery of the religious beliefs and behavior prevalent in this part of the barbarian world. Some parents actually convinced themselves that their gods required them to kill their eldest child by burning the baby boy or girl to death with fire![17] The phenomenon was known as "Molech worship", and sometimes it seemed that the deity involved was named Molech or Moloch, but I am unclear on the details. The consonants of the term—which is all that most of the peoples in this part of the world, even the Egyptians, show when they write—are the same as the word for "king"; I recalled the storage jars stamped *lamelech*. Perhaps some anonymous king of the gods was referred to, the name being too horrible to mention. Or maybe the god who was worshiped in this terrifying manner was Yahweh himself!

Certain kings of Judah—Manasseh, of course, since all things evil were attributed to him, truly or falsely, but others as well—were said to have passed their own sons through the fire for Molech.[18] Whatever god was associated with such practices, I was glad, even eager, to assist in destroying and closing down his precinct. While it is true that we Greeks sometimes expose children, it is usually the reluctant act of a poor family that cannot afford to feed another child, and we tend to lie to ourselves by saying that perhaps some childless family rescued and brought up the child we were forced to abandon. Presumably such abandoned Greek children usually starve to death, or are killed by animals, although a lucky few baby girls may be snatched by owners of brothels and reared to be slave-prostitutes. In any case, we do not directly kill the children, especially not by the excruciatingly painful means of fire, and we do not do it in seeking any kind of divine blessing for ourselves or our other children. When Josiah decreed an end to Molech-worship, he had this Ionian enthusiastically on his side!

Knowing more about the revolution associated with the law code "found" in the temple, I had experienced all the positive and negative feelings about it that I have described, sometimes alternating or sequentially, sometimes simultaneously. I was still generally willing to do my job. There were definite positive aspects of the reform, measures that would benefit any state or any people. That being clearly the case, the Judahites would be no worse off, I decided, by being restricted to a single god, or by being made to perform their sacrificial rites exclusively in one location. Judah was a very small country, after all, and Jerusalem was no great distance from any point within it.[19] So if Josiah wanted more rural shrines closed down and desanctified, I was still up to the task. Enthusiasm was not required of me, only obedience to orders, and the man issuing my orders—Benaiah—was no more a zealot than I was, so I did not expect to find undue blood on my hands. Nor did I, so long as my orders came from him.

7. INTO THE SOUTHERN DESERT

We retraced the route of our return from the Shephelah, going this time south from Jerusalem to Hebron, but instead of taking the road west from there to Lachish, we now angled southwest to Beersheba. En route to Hebron, we made sallies to do our customary damage at places we had neglected during our first pass through the Judahite Hill Country—Bethlehem, Tekoa (home town of the prophet Amos, although he had done his prophesying in the northern kingdom), Beth-Zur, and other towns. I don't remember the names of all of them, including one place near Hebron where I saw a quite striking gravestone whose inscription Benaiah helped me read. Above a somewhat stylized carving of a hand—the hand of Yahweh, I assumed, since it extended downward from the sky—was the epitaph, saying "Uriyahu, the Prince; this is his inscription. May Uriyahu be blessed by Yahweh, for from his enemies he has saved him by his Asherah".[1] This old gravestone was obviously neither monotheistic nor aniconic, but desecrating graves had not yet become part of Josiah's program (or perhaps was not part of his program in Judah itself), so we left the slab alone. Funereal *cults*, however, that is rites and sacrifices at gravesides, were among the cults we were instructed to suppress, since the veneration that peasants and villagers had customarily shown for their clan ancestors had now been defined as "worshiping the dead" or divination through the dead. Such practices were now to be eliminated, along with reliance on what partisans of the reform called "spirit-guides and mediums".[2]

Our swath of destruction and disruption continued through all the towns and villages on or near the road to Beersheba, the primary town of the valley that merged the southern end of the Shephelah into the southern desert known as the Negeb (the word in some Hebrew expressions means "south"). Everywhere we encountered high places and household shrines, and we destroyed literally hundreds of clay images. Probably the most common type of all was what might be called a "pillar figurine", generally about a span, or perhaps a span and two fingers, in height. The body was simply a clay cylinder, spread into a flange at the bottom so it would stand upright, but then separately molded head and arms and exaggerated breasts were added to the pillar—the breasts so large that they actually rested on the arms for support.[3] Perhaps these statuettes represented a fertility goddess—Astarte?—although the emphasis seemed more on lactation than on procreation.

Asherah might be a better guess. She had apparently once been a full-fledged goddess, and the consort of Yahweh, but as Yahweh had absorbed the characteristics of more and more deities—El, Baal, and others—and the cry in some circles for the exclusive worship of Yahweh had grown, depictions of Asherah had seemingly become more and more stylized. Increasingly she was represented less as a goddess (that is, as a woman in form) and more abstractly, as a sacred tree or even as what the reformers denounced as a "sacred pole". The pillar figurines we found and destroyed—who knows how many hundreds we missed!—may have represented a sort of halfway or compromise stage between a normal human figure and a completely symbolic representation. Phrasing such as we had found on the gravestone just described seemed to indicate that Asherah had come to be thought of as some sort of instrument or go-between employed by Yahweh, perhaps something like the "angel" that had supposedly destroyed the army of Sennnacherib, rather than as an independent deity. Or maybe even the in-between status of Asherah was only an earlier, pre-Josianic, version of the official line, tending toward the monotheism he demanded unconditionally. Perhaps the women mostly still saw Asherah as an agent in herself, and were devoted especially to her. That might explain the numerical predominance of such female figurines among the household gods we confiscated and destroyed; no doubt wives tended to dominate ritual life within the households.[4] Not that male figurines were entirely lacking; the most common type of male image consisted of a stylized horse and rider—probably Yahweh as warrior or as rider of the storm-clouds.[5]

Beersheba was the southernmost large city of Judah, that is of the area firmly under Jerusalem's control. It represented sort of an oasis in a valley already tending toward the dryness of the desert beyond (the "Beer-" of the town's name meant "well", although there was some uncertainty about the meaning of the remainder). Here, it appeared, developments in the time of Hezekiah had at least partially anticipated our work. Blocks from what must have been quite a large stone altar had been built into a fortification wall. Perhaps the Judahite troops Hezekiah had stationed in Beersheba, fearful at hearing of the progress of Sennacherib, moving in their direction through the Shephelah, had strengthened their fortifications with every available hewn stone—a precaution that seemingly had proved unnecessary when he had apparently turned from Lachish to move against Jerusalem itself.[6] I could tell that the stones were from an altar because some of them bore the customary "horns" that marked the corners of the upper sacrificial surface of many altars in Judah. Some of the stones also showed traces of burning on their surfaces. We had encountered several smaller, monolithic, altars of the same type in our forays already, but the dismantled example at Beersheba was much larger. When assembled, it must have measured three or more cubits in each dimension, to judge by the size of the stones reused in the wall. One block had incised on it the figure of a serpent.[7]

So we were saved the job of dismantling the town's main altar, and contented ourselves with the usual despoiling of household shrines and nearby high places, including one known as the High Place of the Gates, at the gate of Joshua, governor of the city, to the left of the main city entry.[8] One type of implement I have not yet mentioned in discussing our work elsewhere (although examples had indeed turned up in several places) was the terra-cotta cult-stand with a flat top for the offering of incense. Some of these were quite plain, others elaborately molded and decorated with figures human and animal, "windows", and various vegetation. Snakes—compare the serpent on the dismantled Beersheba altar—were quite common among their decorations.[9] Just another form of grist for the grinding, crunching mill of Josiah's revolution! We foreign mercenaries, millstones in his machine, departed Beersheba and headed eastward toward Arad.[10]

Arad was not a city, but a fortress built at the highest point on a sort of bowl-shaped hill, in its northeastern part. Apparently there had once been a city on the lower western part of the hilltop, but of it there remained only a mound with occasional visible stones. Between the ruined town and the fort was a depression, at the bottom of which was a deep well, the water source for the fortress in this dry landscape. It was not a protected source, like Jerusalem's Gihon spring, but was exposed and at a considerable distance—I estimated almost 250 cubits—from the western side of the fortifications. The citadel, which had supposedly been established by Solomon, had been damaged and rebuilt several times. During one of these rebuildings, long ago, a channel, less than a cubit wide, had been cut that ran under the outer revetment wall (separated from the massive main fortification wall by a sloping rampart), under the rampart, under the wall, and into cisterns (two of them, I was told, though they were of course invisible, being well underground) beneath the center of the fort.

Water had to be laboriously carried from the well to the opening of this channel, in order to fill the cisterns and provide the fort with a safe water supply in case of attack. Obviously there could be no replenishment of the supply while the fort was under siege, which may help explain why it had been so often taken and re-taken. Control in this desert region had tended to alternate between the Judahites and the Edomites who had moved into the region from the east, sometimes in alliance with enemies of Judah and sometimes simply taking advantage, on their own initiative, when Judah was under attack from other quarters. It was to be destroyed and rebuilt yet again one more time while the kingdom of Judah continued in existence, prior to another destruction at the time of Nebuchadnezzar's second siege of Jerusalem, when the area would pass definitively into Edomite control.

We entered the fort through the large two-towered gate on its eastern side, having been told in advance that there was within the fortifications a long-established temple of Yahweh, which we were ordered to close down. We quickly spotted the *temenos* ahead and to our right, in the northwestern corner of the fort. Entering the walled precinct at its southwest corner, we could see the wide temple structure itself stretching across the entire back portion of the area, but there was no altar in front, which we knew to be a normal feature of temples. Eshiyahu, one of the local priests—they had lived in small rooms adjacent to the precinct—was coerced into explaining why. Hezekiah had indeed halted sacrifice in this place, although he had not closed the temple itself. There was in fact an altar, quite a large one, reportedly five cubits square, the priest said, in this courtyard, but it had been covered over with earth, along with paraphernalia that had been used in sacrifice upon it. "Someday", he said, "when kings cease to misunderstand the will of Yahweh, someone will dig our altar back up and reinstitute sacrifice there!" Rather the opposite, we told Eshiyahu. We were here not to restore the altar but to shut down the temple also; he and his fellow priests would be fed from Jerusalem temple revenues if they relocated to the capital, but there would be no more cultic activity in this fortress.

We proceeded to the temple. Its wide main room, called in Hebrew the *hekhal,* we entered through a door that was a bit to the left of center (some phase of rebuilding had enlarged the structure on the right side, apparently, without a corresponding enlargement on the left). Within it were low benches, plastered, on which had been placed various offerings. Directly across from the outer doorway, and thus also now slightly off-center, was the entrance to the interior part of the shrine, the so-called "holy of holies" or *debir*. It was not a room of comparable size to the *hekhal,* but merely a squarish niche, something over two cubits in width and depth, elevated slightly above the main room. Flanking the two steps at its entrance were limestone incense altars, the one on the left somewhat larger. Within, on a low platform at the rear, stood two stones, called *masseboth* in Hebrew, singular *massebah* (the Greek would be *stelai* and *stele*). As elsewhere, the taller one stood on the left; it was apparently associated with the larger of the two incense altars. Undoubtedly they represented, as was usual, Yahweh and Asherah.

Deciding, in this long-venerated place, to follow the precedent Hezekiah had set with his treatment of the altar, we merely laid the offending altars and standing stones on their sides and covered them up with dirt, although we removed and destroyed all the iconic votive offerings we found on the benches within the temple. Issuing instructions to the commander of the fort to build over the area that the temple and its courtyard had occupied, so that it could no longer be devoted to cultic uses, Benaiah was prepared to lead us back to Jerusalem, with stops along the way to carry out our general instructions as occasion should arise.

But as we were preparing to exit through the fortress gate, we were met by a delegation just arriving from the capital. Whereas we infantrymen had slogged through our long journey on foot, this party was mounted—on horses, not on the inferior sort of steed that had originally taken me to Jerusalem. It had been not only the status of their leader that warranted this privilege, we would soon see, but also deliberate haste to intercept us before we had begun our northward return march. The leader was immediately evident from his expensive garments, in contrast to the soldiers' gear worn by his military escort. Presenting our commander Benaiah with his signet ring for identification, he announced: "I am Asaiah, minister to King Josiah, bearing new orders to you directly from the king himself". The ring confirmed his statement. On its small red stone was carved "Belonging to Asayahu, servant of the king". Theophoric names such as his—the last part invoked Yahweh—existed simultaneously during this period in longer and shorter forms. The shorter forms, those ending simply in "-yah" or "-iah", were probably originally characteristic of Yahwistic families in the northern kingdom; the longer "-yahu" form was traditional Judahite orthography. I tend in my narrative to use the shorter forms, but to transliterate directly the longer forms I saw in inscriptions. I could not avoid noticing that the signet worn by this insider of a program of militant aniconism bore, in addition to his name and title, a nicely-carved image of a galloping horse. I would soon discover that hypocrisy was the least of his character flaws.

The announcement of new orders was puzzling to us, since we were already at the fortified place farthest to the southeast within the kingdom, and had already visited the southwesternmost, at Beersheba. Were we about to be asked to engage in some higher level of destruction while on our way back to Jerusalem? Were such instructions sufficiently important to require a high courtier as emissary, with a military escort? Asaiah was such a high courtier. He had been one of the three officials who had accompanied the priest Hilkiah and the secretary Shaphan to consult the prophetess Huldah at the time of the "finding" of the scroll of the law. That is to say, he was definitely one of the court faction that had been "in on the plot" of planting the recently-written scroll in the temple; he was among those at the very heart of the revolution. To say that his faction "spoke for the king" may have been actually to reverse matters; perhaps it actually dictated what the king said, or at least carefully led him to say the kinds of things it wished him to say.[11]

"The king has decided", Asaiah announced, "to extend his reform into the Negeb, to destroy the shrines and high places there". Benaiah was astounded. "That is outside the territory of Judah", he protested. "You are asking us to invade the Edomites' lands—maybe provoking a war in doing so".

"Who are the accursed Edomites to us?" thundered Asaiah. "Thieves and assassins, they seized our land during the time of our weakness, during the vile Manasseh's subservience to Assyria. Now Yahweh directs his servant Josiah to reclaim our people's heritage. David and Solomon ruled the entire Negeb. Their descendant Josiah, with Yahweh's blessing, shall do so as well!"

Benaiah refrained from saying what he and I were both thinking: "This is madness". Instead, he simply pointed out that our few mercenaries could not possibly do the job. If the king wished to declare war, he suggested, the king should organize and lead an army in an invasion of Edomite territory. As part of the army, we would of course loyally participate, but we could not take on the entire burden ourselves.

Asaiah was unsympathetic. "The Edomites are little better than desert nomads, mere raiders and scavengers unable to stand before a disciplined corps of any size. I myself and this cavalry squad with me will accompany you and provide support. They will not dare to oppose us, and if they do, with Yahweh's help, we will slaughter them!"

There was no arguing with him, especially since he unquestionably spoke with the authority of the king, so we were forced to acquiesce, and just to hope that the element of surprise would save our minuscule invading party from destruction. Obviously, the Edomites expected no such act of open aggression, so they would have made no effort yet to counteract it. Perhaps we could get in and get out before they put together an organized army to crush us. Asaiah left behind one of his young cavalrymen, Eliashib by name, to make sure that the construction we mercenaries had mandated should actually be carried out, and to make sure that the garrison at Arad would be prepared in the event the Edomites should counterattack—we would certainly need to take refuge here, if they did, and if any of us were left alive to do so. The rest of us, Asaiah included, set out at once, heading south into the heart of the Negeb.

I had heard of the Edomites immediately upon my arrival in Judah some months earlier. The pronouncements of various prophets, constantly quoted by the brotherhoods associated with each of them, were filled with dire condemnations of the Edomites, a people whose homeland lay on a high plateau east of what was called the Arabah, the depression that continued the line of the Jordan River and Dead Sea southward to the tip of the eastern gulf of the Red Sea. Their kingdom lay south of that of the Moabites, who lived directly east of the Dead Sea. I refrain from quoting any of the anti-Edomite oracles[12] for fear I will confuse ones I had heard by this time with ones created or expanded and added to later, when the destruction of the kingdom of Judah by the Babylonians allowed the Edomites to take over great portions of the Negeb, and even to move northward as far as Hebron, with no reasonable prospect that the defeated Judahites would ever be able to dislodge them.[13]

The Judahites' hostility toward the Edomites was affected—sometimes in the direction of moderation, sometimes in that of increased bitterness—by their general belief that the peoples were closely akin. Supposedly, the patriarchal eponym Israel, at an early time in his life when he was called by his original name of "Jacob", was the brother of "Esau", who was thought of as the ancestor of the Edomites.[14] The periods of quarrelling and reconciliation that alternated in the stories told about these brothers perhaps reflected the periods of friendliness and hostility between the two nations that were said to be descended from them. Whether the Edomites considered themselves kin to the Judahites, I cannot say; I heard only the Judahite version of the tradition.

What was certain was that the Edomites had long coveted the Negeb, and that whenever Judah was weak, they made incursions into the region. They would control parts of it for a time, then be forced to retreat back across the Arabah during periods of Judahite strength. I have already mentioned that at times they had even taken over the fortress at Arad, for example. The Negeb had been to some extent "up for grabs" ever since the devastation of Judah during the reign of Hezekiah, although Manasseh's policy of cooperation with the Assyrians had allowed some Judahite resurgence in the area, with the rebuilding of some forts. Still the region was largely, as Benaiah had pointed out to Asaiah, beyond the recognized boundaries of the kingdom of Judah, and the Edomites' claims there were as strong as, or stronger than, those of the Judahites. There was some truth, to be sure, in the unstated presupposition of Josiah and his courtiers that control in the Negeb was to be determined largely by the sword. But we mercenaries were not happy at being given the responsibility for wielding that sword, especially since we feared being outnumbered and overwhelmed in any encounter.

We passed unopposed through a considerable distance beyond what might have been thought of as the frontier, and without encountering any Edomite settlements. We destroyed a few isolated high places and knocked down a few standing stones, though not many. Later, in Egyptian service, I would discover in my travels back and forth between Egypt and Judah that the great majority of desert shrines were in the *southern* Negeb and on what is called the peninsula of Sinai. At that time, of course, it was no longer my job to destroy such ancient installations, and I left them alone. As far as I know, they are still standing, as many of them had already been for centuries—neither the invading Babylonians nor anyone else shared in the mad destructiveness of Josiah and his revolutionaries.[15]

After a journey of about 225 stades almost due south from Arad, we came upon a flat-topped low hill overlooking a valley to the west (I remain ignorant of toponyms in this waterless wilderness).[16] We never saw its inhabitants; they had fled, probably seeing our approach from afar. But it soon became clear that here was indeed an Edomite holy place—the completely un-Judahite nature of the ceramic pieces they had left behind showed this beyond any doubt. Such pieces had showed up occasionally in some of the cultic sites we had despoiled in the past few months, but here they were not just isolated oddities, but the entire assemblage, with no native Judahite admixture.

One fascinating piece, just under two spans long, was a winged sphinx with a human head, its wings pointing directly upward over its back. Several human-shaped figurines were to be seen. Individual facial features seemed usually to have been molded separately and then added onto the heads of the figures, often creating strikingly asymmetrical faces. A warrior statue clutched a dagger that proved to be a separable piece. One stick-like man not much above a span in height appeared to be kneeling in prayer within a high place defined on three sides by low stone walls. An even lower wall created a lopsided circular enclosure, within which was a lustral basin some two cubits across that was coated with plaster inside and out, along with a small altar and a pit dug into the rock, perhaps for the catching of sacrificial blood.

In the same enclosure in which we found the kneeling-man figure we also discovered several cult stands—including a very striking wheel-made example with interesting human facial features added and decorated in red and black paint, and a rather amazing ceramic head with some kind of three-horned headgear and a large knob, painted black, projecting from the very top of the head. North of these low-walled enclosures was the temple proper, odd in its form in that all three of its rooms opened directly in front, while the rooms were not themselves connected; the entranceway to the middle room was more elaborate than those of the others. A podium about two cubits in height was built into each of the three rooms, and on each of these stood more statues and cult vessels. A further complex to the north repeated some of the same features.

Egged on with gleeful enthusiasm by Asaiah, who pressed his cavalry escort into helping us, we set about destroying the fascinatingly exotic figures he could see only as "abominations", set up by invaders in what he called the national territory of "Israel" (the reader will recall that Judahites tended to call their country by that name when they were thinking in expansionist terms). By knocking down the roof of the temple, we acquired enough wood—it must have been tremendously difficult to haul it in to build the temple we were now destroying—to set fire to the place and burn it down. Just about everything ceramic—hundreds of objects!—we broke up and scattered about the site. Our courtier zealot seemed immensely pleased with this dubious accomplishment, and encouraged by the lack of opposition we had encountered, indeed by the complete lack of people. He insisted that we must now push deeper into the Negeb, and in fact must now swing eastward, toward the Arabah in the direction of the Edomite homeland, as well as penetrating farther south.

We encountered, and desecrated, a few more Edomite cult sites, but our next important stop was about 245 stades southeast of the hilltop site just described. This place had a name, or at least Asaiah declared that it had a name—Tamar, the "Tamar in the desert" at which Solomon was said to have built fortifications.[17] Indeed, there were fortifications present that looked both old and impressive—probably 150 cubits square—but in a damaged state, and undefended. Not far from the northernmost corner of the abandoned fortress, outside the walls, however, there was a cultic *temenos* that appeared to be very much in use. The four or five priests present fled when they saw us coming, all but the one who appeared to be the oldest and was probably the chief priest. Asaiah sent his cavalry after the others, but we were here on the edge of the broken, rocky country of the Arabah depression, within sight of the hills of Edom on the other side. Men on foot, who knew the area and had a head start, were able to elude pursuers on horseback to whom the region was unknown and threatening, so our men came back empty-handed, much to Asaiah's displeasure.

He interrogated the old priest brutally, with many slaps and shouted insults. Hebrew and Edomite were similar enough languages that some degree of understanding could have been possible, if the questioner had been bent on learning something, rather than primarily on intimidating and degrading his prisoner. Finally tiring of the game, he turned to one of his recently-returned and now-dismounted soldiers and gave the order: "Kill him!" The cavalryman, who was young (all of them were) and obviously inexperienced at the brutalities of war, seemed about to ask "Why?" but apparently he concluded that there would be no use in asking. He drew his sword and dispatched the dazed old man. Asaiah was not finished with his insults, even of the dead. "Rip that signet ring off his hand", he ordered another young soldier. "It symbolizes his office as an idol-worshiper. No such office shall exist from now on, *here in Israel*!" Grabbing the ring from the soldier so roughly that the signet stone popped out of its setting, he flung both stone and ring aside into the sand in different directions. Then he assigned a detail—this time from among us foreign mercenaries—to dispose of the body. I was almost relieved to be chosen, since the burial detail at least took me away for a while from the presence of our power-mad royal official. This was the first time I had been within a breath of killing him, and hang the consequences; it would not be the last. I wish I had done it that day.

Fortunately, I would be given some time to cool down. Asaiah decided to take his cavalry escort and scour the nearby countryside for any Edomites he could find, while leaving the mercenaries at the ruined fort with the assignment of dismantling the cultic site and destroying all its images. We were all, from Benaiah on down, disinclined to comply, despite our fear of the consequences. It had been crazy enough to go around within Judah destroying Judahite shrines on the orders of the king, but at least they had been in a sense *his* shrines, to do with as he wished; the king was, after all, the undisputed head of the national cult. But here at Tamar (if that is really where we were—we only had Asaiah's word for it) we were at a site that was very obviously Edomite, not Judahite, and practically on the edge of the Arabah, in territory not controlled by Judah for a long time, if ever. Dozens of vessels and images—mostly of clay, although a few were of carved stone, along with seven small limestone altars—sat on the flat surfaces within the open shrine or temple alongside the old wall (it was as if stone benches formed three sides of an enclosure, which lacked a fourth side). We had been willing to destroy a great many more similar objects at that other shrine recently, but the mindless murder we had just witnessed had given us more grounds for resisting compliance with the man issuing us our orders.

Moreover, the objects, now that they seemed less strange, since this was the second large group of them we had encountered, had a sort of haunting beauty that made me, at least, not want to destroy them. Why not just dig a pit and bury them, as we had buried the elements of the shrine at Arad? I made bold to broach the idea with Benaiah and, slightly to my surprise, he agreed. A real soldier, a combat veteran, he recognized the posturing of our courtier, and knew him for the coward he was. "Hurry", he said, "and get the pit dug and the things covered up before Asaiah returns. I doubt that he will check to see whether I'm telling the truth when I say we broke up the objects before we buried them. Once we complete that task, then we can dismantle the shrine itself, whether by then he's back or not". So several of us set immediately to digging a good-sized pit to the left side of the shrine. It took a while, but finally we were ready to lay all the cult objects carefully within it.

Some of them were quite striking indeed. One cult stand for burning incense strongly resembled a fat old woman with wide-set eyes, holding a bowl (for the incense) with her right arm. Another, with a bell-shaped base, had along the bottom edge of its incense-bowl a row of perforated triangles, with a ceramic pomegranate hanging from each triangle. I was also determined to rescue the signet ring of the murdered priest and bury it in the pit with the ceramic and stone objects. Pretty soon I was able to find the grayish round stone on which the seal was carved, but I could not locate the ring itself. With Benaiah's help, I was able to puzzle out the consonants of the mirror-image inscription: "Belonging to M-s-k-t son of V-h-z-m". Since none of us had heard the priest's name pronounced, and we had no knowledge of Edomite names, the consonantal skeleton was all we could hope to know. The very skillful carving below the priest's name on the stone showed two standing male figures in long robes with a horned altar between them, perhaps a priest and a worshiper making a votive offering to the Edomite god, who (I would later learn) was named Qos. I was just about to put the signet in the pit and begin filling it in when, unexpectedly soon, Asaiah and the horsemen reappeared. Apparently they had given up their project as hopeless, having found no Edomites in the vicinity.

When the exalted "servant of the king" saw the unbroken vessels lying in our not-yet-filled-in pit, he flew into a rage. "I must have been mad", he fumed—he was right enough on that score—"to trust Greeks and other foreigners, idolators all, to deal properly with these Edomite abominations! They were to be smashed, destroyed, not given some kind of honorable burial like a beloved kinsman!" Then he ordered several of us to pry some large stone blocks out of the walls of the old fort, and to carry those blocks over to our pit and drop them—from head height—onto the vessels in it. So instead of a protective coverlet of earth, our ceramic treasures got a rough blanket of stones, and doubtless every last one of them was smashed, presumably never to be reassembled. As for the signet, I surreptitiously threw it away again, not daring to be caught with it.[18]

There was, however, one surprising consequence of this confrontation. Having lost patience with us, and seeing nothing more to expect us to do in the area (something else his search for fugitives had revealed), he decided to order us to return to Jerusalem immediately, with the spiteful promise that our half-hearted commitment to the great cause of the king would be duly noted in official circles. He forgot, or simply ignored, the fact that we had not yet even begun to dismantle the shrine itself, a task we had put off while working on our pit. The cult place was still standing, although not in use, I have been told, when the fort was rebuilt on a smaller scale a few years later, either by Josiah or by one of his successors. Fortunately also, we were able to make our journey back to the capital without Asaiah's uncongenial company. He and his mounted soldiers could not bear to travel slowly enough to match our walking pace, and not even an official as unreasonable as Asaiah could expect us to march fast enough to keep up with horsemen. When we stopped at Arad briefly to rest, we saw that Eliashib had not rejoined his cavalry mates on their return trip, but was still there making the arrangements he had been charged with making. It was just as well that he took care with the fortress, since he would be stationed there again later, as its commander, and in fact would meet his death there. But those events were still many years away. Nor did I know yet of Eliashib's ancestral connection with Arad.

By the time we reached Jerusalem, several days after Asaiah did, the courtier had become somewhat mollified in his attitude toward us. We had not, after all, actually disobeyed any direct orders or openly defied his authority, and it was perhaps expecting too much to look for genuine "Israelite" Yahwistic zeal in benighted *goyim* who had been brought up worshiping legions of false gods. So no punishment was forthcoming, and the awkwardness of the incident at "Tamar" was more or less officially forgotten. I had not forgotten, however, the murder of the priest that Asaiah had ordered; I vowed to avoid him forever hence, if at all possible. Unfortunately, it did not prove to be possible.

This was because across-the-border adventurism was now very much the "bright new idea" in Jerusalem—and largely because of the "success" our band of mercenaries had had in the land of the Edomites, much advertised and exaggerated by Asaiah as a means of enhancing his own reputation and influence. Prophets were not now content with shouting oracles against the Edomites. Zephaniah was proclaiming the coming judgment of Yahweh upon the Philistines: "For Gaza will be abandoned and Ashkelon reduced to ruins; Ashdod will be driven out in broad daylight and Ekron uprooted. Disaster to the members of the coastal league, to the nation of the Cherethites!" he proclaimed in the streets.[19] His followers parroted the phrases until they stuck in my memory and I can report them now, so many years later, even though his prophecies were not among the ones I would later accumulate in written versions. Zephaniah also proclaimed doom on Nineveh and Assyria—proving soon a true prophet on that score, at least—and on the Kushites (somewhat anachronistically, since they had not ruled in Egypt for quite a while).[20]

One person who listened avidly and excitedly to such expressions of zealotry was King Josiah. Now the time seemed propitious for what he expected to be his crowning achievement. He would take his revolution not merely into the almost-uninhabited southern desert, but into the heartland of Israel. He would purify the cult there, and then he would reunite David's shattered kingdom! Our services were about to be required again, and this time the king himself would lead us.

8. BETHEL AND BEYOND

"Too long has Israel been under the control of *goyim* brought in by the Assyrians, with their false priests!" This was the battle cry heard from the palace, as Josiah's expedition into the territory of the former northern kingdom was being organized.[1] Benaiah informed us that our foreign mercenaries would be among the troops the king would lead, goyim versus goyim in the eyes of the makers of the revolution. It was only a matter of days before we mustered in Jerusalem to set out northward.

Although I had been in Judah for some months by this time, I had not actually seen King Josiah in the flesh. Eastern kings, I realized, were not like Greek magistrates. They kept themselves apart and surrounded by flatterers, to shelter them from opposition and to maintain a superstitious mystery about them, the better to elicit obedience from the mass of the people, all of whom had been nurtured in a tradition of revering royalty. Now he finally appeared, mounted on a fine black horse, as the army was set to depart.

What a small, insignificant-looking man he was! Although he was well into his mid-twenties, his beard was still almost as thin and scraggly as an ephebe's might have been; by appearance, he could have easily been eighteen or nineteen years of age. Nor were his mannerisms and speech such as would dispel this suspicion. For all his undoubtedly genuine zealotry, he seemed greatly concerned to please the priests and courtiers who constituted his inner circle, all of whom were his elders. They had apparently been controlling him since his accession as a child, and were still largely doing so, despite his eighteen years as ruler. Unfortunately, among the officers accompanying the king on the expedition, Asaiah was to be included—a reward for his "accomplishments" in the Edomite lands.

A short distance north of Jerusalem, the road forked into parallel tracks that veered to either side of Bethel, then reunited a bit north of Bethel and continued again as a single road. In my descent from Akko, I had followed the western track along the watershed of the hills, but now we took the eastern road that swung close to Anathoth, Gibeah, and Michmash—towns in the path of devastation the prophet Isaiah had attributed to Sennacherib at the time of his approach to Jerusalem. Bethel was accordingly a bit off our road and to the left. Nearby and close to the road lay the impressive mound of ruins marking a city destroyed so long ago that the mound was simply named Ai, "Ruin".[2]

Bethel had been the location of one of the two chief temples of the kingdom of Israel. The other, far to the north at Dan, may have once been equally important in Israelite eyes, but it did not preoccupy the Judahites like the much closer Bethel sanctuary did. Both were said to have been founded by King Jeroboam when he supposedly broke away from Solomon's son Rehoboam to establish the northern kingdom. Legend further held that the patriarch Abraham had built an altar at Bethel, long before either kingdom existed, but this may have been only a story made up to strengthen Judahite claims to Israel's chief shrine. It was said in Jerusalem that the idolatrous Jeroboam had set up two golden "calves", one in each place, and he was said to have proclaimed of each: "Here is your god, Israel, who brought you out of Egypt!" Tellers of wilder versions of the story even had Jeroboam also fashioning statues of "satyrs" to be worshiped as well.[3]

What would a skeptical foreigner have made of such tales? At the very least, the supposed "calves" must have been bulls. By now, when I write this, I have learned of bull cults on Krete and in Egypt, and the obvious power and strength of the bull makes him a natural image for a mighty god;

the Canaanite chief god, El, I also know by now, was often symbolized by a bull.[4] So I assume that Jeroboam's bulls (not calves) symbolized the mighty Yahweh. Official aniconism, the reader will recall, was a new development even in Josiah's Judah, and certainly would not have existed in Israel hundreds of years earlier. Of course, images made of gold tend to disappear when countries are conquered, so there was no gold bull—or calf!—at Bethel when our army arrived there. There was a functioning shrine, however, dedicated to Yahweh—though not exclusively, as the Jerusalem temple had not been, until very recently.

The priests had run away before our arrival. Bethel was close enough to Jerusalem that they had received ample warning of Josiah's expedition. His attitude toward the northern priesthood was also no secret, and it had caused the priests—how very rightly no one can testify better than I!—to fear for their lives, so they had left their temple and altar unattended, and had fled to the villages around Samaria. The official line within the Jerusalem temple priesthood was that all legitimate priests were members of the tribe descended from Levi, one of the twelve sons of "Israel", and that the high priests, the only ones permitted actually to enter certain areas of the temple, were descended from a single Levite family, that of Aaron, the brother of Moses. It was asserted that the priests of the northern kingdom had never been Levites, but had been appointed by the Israelite kings (beginning with Jeroboam) from any families they wished. All the Levites had supposedly fled south to Judah at the time of the secession. I had even heard it said that Jeroboam would appoint anybody a priest who showed up with a bull and seven rams to be sacrificed at his shrines![5]

With great enthusiasm, Josiah personally directed the destruction of the high place and altar at Bethel, long the chief rival of the temple in Jerusalem; he burned the sacred pole or Asherah there as well. Some people asserted later that he poured over the ruined cult site at Bethel the ashes of the non-Yahwist cult objects from the Jerusalem temple that he had burned, but I did not see any such action, so I suspect the story is mere embroidery. More ominous was what happened just *before* the altar at Bethel was destroyed. Josiah saw slabs marking certain old family tombs on a nearby hillside. In a moment of what he no doubt thought of as inspiration, he immediately directed a couple of soldiers to break into some of the tombs and gather bones from them. These grisly remains he placed on the altar while it was still standing, and proceeded to burn them—thereby desecrating the spot beyond hope of its ever being reconsecrated. There was some murmuring among the soldiers, including the Judahites, at this extreme insult to the dead, but Josiah was, as I have already said, opposed to any cults of ancestors. I thought at the time that he also simply regarded the former kingdom of Israel as so irredeemably sinful that no outrage against it could be inappropriate.

"What is that monument I see?" asked the king, with reference to the most ornate of the gravestones among the nearby tombs. Several of the local townspeople had gathered to watch the soldiers from Judah demolish their ancient holy place. One of them was inspired now to a feat of sycophancy that I would have thought would be transparent even to Josiah. But no, the king lapped it up as divinely-inspired truth. The man said that the monument marked the grave of a "man of God" who had come up from Judah and confronted King Jeroboam when he was holding a great feast at the altar of Bethel, and had prophesied that a son was to be born to the house of David, *Josiah by name*—that is correct, he did not even shrink from plugging into his story the name of the king he was flattering!—who will burn human bones on this altar and will slaughter the priests of the high places of Israel in their own sanctuaries.

There was much more nonsense along the same lines: it was predicted that the altar (presumably not the same one standing there now!) would spontaneously burst apart, which it obligingly did; the king was given a leprous hand by the man of God, then cured of it upon entreating him; the man of God was killed by a lion on his way back to Judah, then buried in this tomb which had belonged to a prophet of Bethel, who was himself later buried in the same tomb. Suddenly the respecter of the dead, Josiah proclaimed: "Let him rest, and let no one disturb his bones!" So one large tomb escaped desecration. I wonder whether the motivation of the story-teller had really been mere sycophancy; if so, he gained nothing. Perhaps the ornate gravestone had marked the tomb of his own family or clan. If that were the case, he had found a clever way to safeguard the cult of his own ancestors—were they maybe prophets of Bethel?[6]

It was highly unfortunate, however, that the story-teller had quite unnecessarily thrown in the "prediction" about Josiah slaughtering the priests of the high places in their own sanctuaries. Although no priests had tarried at Bethel to become victims of that policy, it turned out that such would be the royal practice at the remaining high places in Israel, and not all of their priests had had the wisdom to flee. I did not know whether Josiah was heeding the just-made-up prophecy, or had already been influenced by suggestions from hard-liners such as Asaiah, who had had no qualms about killing Edomite priests. To my horror and shame, I soon found myself an instrument of this murderous program. Israelite cults were "foreign", therefore Israelite priests were "foreigners", therefore they were entitled to no protection and no consideration. They were enemies to be exterminated.

So numerous were the places we still had to visit—whether towns or mere settlements around the ruins of cities that had been destroyed—that Josiah now decided to split up his army into several divisions, so that we would be able to descend upon several sites simultaneously. The splitting up probably contributed to the fact that priests were subsequently caught at several places. Perhaps rumors of troops advancing elsewhere had lulled them into believing that their own sanctuaries were not in immediately danger. The greatest misfortune from my own standpoint was that the "king's servant" who had been set over my own unit of foreign mercenaries was none other than the hated Asaiah, on the basis that he had worked effectively with us before! We had been given the "honor" of suppressing the cult at the settlement built on the site of Samaria itself, the former Israelite capital.

I had passed by Samaria on my initial journey to Judah, but now I examined the remains of it much more closely. What had apparently been originally a rather small hilltop had been hugely enlarged by surrounding it with massive walls (in some places still standing, at a height of six cubits or more), then filling the space behind the walls with earth and rubble, thus creating a platform for the royal palace and other buildings. Only remnants of the destroyed palace complex remained, but I picked up a few pieces of carved ivory, with decorations that looked Egyptian or Phoinikian, and I was astounded to find part of a carved stone column capital with volutes on it that, I thought, looked very much like capitals I had seen in Aiolia, north of my native Ionia, on a brief visit during my boyhood.[7]

Unfortunately for all concerned, at the high place of Samaria we chanced upon two priests who had not learned of our approach in time to flee—or who perhaps had trusted that Yahweh would save them from the revolution of Josiah! Not having been informed that Josiah and his chief ministers, upon splitting up the army, had agreed that the policy henceforth would be to execute any "alien" priests who were caught at their high places, we were dumbfounded to hear Asaiah announce that the two priests were to be slaughtered on their own altar before the altar itself was desecrated by burning human bones upon it and then demolished.

Somehow Asaiah had found out that I had been the one behind the troop's attempt to bury the Edomite cultic vessels unbroken at "Tamar". He immediately looked directly in my eyes and thundered: "You! Ionian! You kill the old one. Now!" My commander Benaiah attempted to intervene, saying that no such thing, since the beginning of the reform, had ever been done to their fellow countrymen. "I see no fellow countrymen", sneered the king's minister. I see only the offspring of the foreign dogs the kings of Assyria settled on land Yahweh gave to us. Either your Greek will kill this Babylonian—or whatever he is!—or your Greek will be executed for refusing to obey orders. And as his commander, it will be your duty to carry out the execution".

I could not saddle my friend Benaiah with that responsibility and—I might as well confess it—I did not want to die (I was not much beyond twenty years old at the time). So I consoled myself with whatever lies I could. The priest was old and might die soon anyway. Somebody else would do it if I didn't. Even the assertion that he could and should have shown sense and fled. Saying in the best Hebrew I could muster "I'm sorry, old man", but not having the effrontery to ask his forgiveness, I took his arm and bent him backward over his own altar. He looked me unflinchingly in the eye and said kindly: "I do not blame you, my son. The mad king of Judah is behind this. Yahweh will punish him. Do the deed quickly". I obeyed him, the tears flowing so copiously that I was surprised to find my sword-thrust so accurate. His pain no doubt was intense, but it was brief; his blood flooded the altar and splashed on my legs. I tried to pray to all the gods to forgive me. All except Yahweh. At the time I put some of the blame on him for all the evil that was being done in his name. Now he seems to me just like the others, all products of men's vivid and vicious imaginations. It is men who kill and men who—on rarer occasions—spare. It is madmen who glory in it, and attribute their deeds to the will of the gods, or of a single god.

"Now the other one, Greek!" roared Asaiah, gleefully, enjoying my pain—and Benaiah's—as much as he had enjoyed the priest's death.

This was too much for my commander. "No!" he ordered me, "Put up your sword. If the King's Servant wishes any more blood shed on this altar, he will have to shed it himself". Then turning to Asaiah: "My men will do no more of your murdering for you".

The courtier seethed with barely-controlled fury. "That defiance would have cost you your life", he told Benaiah, "if you were not a fellow Israelite. You have commanded these foreign vermin too long. You have begun to think like them. I believe, on my advice, the king will soon relieve you of your command. But as you would spare your precious goyim their duty of supporting their king and master, I will this time do as you suggest. I'll kill this idolatrous alien priest myself, with pleasure!" He unsheathed his sword and roughly grabbed the arm of the other priest, who was younger than the first, but still a man of forty years or so.

Without thinking at all, I found myself now screaming "No! Enough! Damn you, if you proceed with this murder, you'll answer to me. Maybe the innocent blood you have put on my hands will be washed away, at least a little bit, if I spill your own foul guts on that altar!" Benaiah tried to hold me back, realizing that my words had probably already pronounced my own death warrant. I myself was beyond caring. I was willing to die for the privilege of ridding the world of Asaiah. I swung my sword and struck him a fierce blow at the base of his neck. He fell like a slaughtered calf.[8]

I dropped my sword and did not resist when several of my comrades grabbed and held me. Benaiah stood silently for a while, thinking. Then he reached a decision of terrifying boldness. It is still, after all these years, hard for me to believe that he risked everything for a foreigner he had known for only a few months, and put his life in the hands of other foreigners he knew even less well. Of course I assume that some of his motives were also personal: he had hated Asaiah as much as I had, and had been threatened by him. There was no question of regretting his death; the only issue was how to mitigate the possible consequences of it. "Priest!" he said, turning to the man my impulsive act had saved, "Go find me some kind of old sword near the sanctuary here, and bring it, quickly!" Then he saw a young woman, weeping, leaning against one of the walls of the enclosure of the cult place, and ordered her to bring water. Both sword and water appeared very soon, as both the priest and the girl were in mortal fear of these violent men, most of whom spoke their language with difficulty if at all.

"Dip the old sword in this man's wound", he said, gesturing toward the body of Asaiah, "then put it in the hand of the dead priest. And dip the slain man's sword in the priest's blood, and put his sword back in his hand. Wash the altar, wash off the sword of this Greek here—and his legs". The priest performed the required movements with the swords and wounds, the woman did the washing, sobbing quietly all the while.

"This is what happened", Benaiah announced. "The courtier here came at the old priest to kill him, following some plan known to him but not to any of my soldiers. But the old man had had a sword concealed in the shrine, and he surprised the King's Servant by defending himself. By chance, they struck each other simultaneous fatal blows, before anybody could intervene. No other priest was found at the high place. The bodies will be preserved in their present condition until we can send a rider, on Asaiah's horse and bearing his signet ring, to apprise the king of this tragic event and request an emissary to come and verify the story and give us further instructions. Is there anyone here who disagrees with this summary of what just happened?" Silence from all the mercenaries. "Priest, why are you still here? Get out of here as fast as you can, and hide as deep as you can until the king's expedition passes".

Then to the woman: "I don't know how much you saw, but your continued weeping alarms me. Is there reason for me to suppose that I can trust you to back up our story? Who were these priests to you? If the one spared is your father, we might count on your gratitude, but then why so much crying? So I must assume that your connection was with the old priest, the slain one. Is that correct?"

"He was my grandfather and my only guardian; my father died long ago and I have no brothers, and no dowry for a husband. Now I have no one, and no idea what I am to do", said the girl, who must have been about seventeen years old. Seeing me slump visibly at hearing that I had deprived her of her only protection in life, she completely surprised me by turning and addressing me directly.

"Ionian", she said, "I saw everything, including the pain that you suffered from what you were forced to do, and I heard my grandfather say he did not blame you. Therefore neither do I blame you, and I will choose to think of you more as his willing avenger than as his unwilling slayer. The man responsible for his death lies next to him now. I will support every word of your commander's story".

I was touched beyond measure. Even if Benaiah's ploy had failed and my deed had been found out, I would have gone to my grave rejoicing in her kindness. Nothing I could ever do could repay her for either the wrong I had done her or the kindness she had shown to me. I was ashamed to raise my face to hers, but I felt I must at least try to thank her. "Young woman–" I began, but she cut off my reply by saying: "I am Tirzah, daughter of Zelophehad, son of Machir; my grandfather, the priest, was Machir. I have already told you that you do not need to ask my forgiveness. I bear you no malice".

"May I, then, Tirzah, at least offer you some assistance? My mercenary's pay has not allowed me to accumulate enough to provide you with a dowry, but all that I have so far I will willingly give to you, to help you survive at least for a while. Perhaps some man of your people will see your excellent qualities—your kindness, your beauty (this was no exaggeration; the girl was exquisite, with her dark curly hair and dark eyes)—and wed you without a dowry", I said.

"My people", said Tirzah, this time with some passion, her weeping now done, "is the people Israel, for all that these Judahites disparage us as 'Samaritans' and claim we are all foreigners imported by the Assyrians. That is only the story they use to justify seizing our land. My father named me for the city that was the capital of Israel before Samaria was built; our family was already living here when it was still the capital".[9]

I was silent, stunned. How many lies had I, and everyone in Jerusalem and Judah, been told to justify the ambitious project of Josiah and his courtiers and priests? I recalled now what the old priest—no, let me call him by his proper name—what Tirzah's grandfather Machir had said to me with reference to Josiah: "*Yahweh* will punish him". Yet Asaiah had called all priests in this territory idolators, and my traveling companions when I had first passed this way had said that everyone here came from another place and worshiped foreign gods. Yahweh was not worshiped *alone* and *aniconically* in what had once been the northern kingdom, that was true. But I had already seen very clearly that such statements were equally true of Judah, until Josiah and his supporters had recently decreed otherwise, "finding" support for their revolution in their supposed law of Moses!

Seeing me silent and in deep thought, Tirzah spoke again: "What is your name, Ionian? And how do you come to speak our language fairly passably, although you are still apparently quite young?"

I told her, "Archon son of Amoibichos, from Miletos", and then rather embarrassedly revealed that my tutor in the languages of Canaan had been a Philistine woman of Ashkelon. I expected some kind of negative reaction, the sort I had experienced from just about everyone in this part of the world except the wise and tolerant Benaiah. Tirzah surprised me again.

"A Philistine?" she said. "Oh, that explains the funny way you pronounce certain words. Not everyone in Canaan, whatever Josiah king of Judah may have told you, is hostile to foreigners. It is true that the Assyrians took away most of the rich and powerful of Israel, and some skilled workers they wanted to employ, but probably eight of every ten Israelites were left in place.[10] What good would a devastated, unproductive province have been to Assyria? The people from Babylonia and other parts of the land of the two rivers who were brought in to replace the deportees have merged by now into the vast majority surrounding them, and they are Israelites like the rest of us—it has been a hundred years, after all! We don't mind being called 'Samaritans' if it simply means people of the province of Samaria, but we have always been Israelites and worshipers of Yahweh. The kings of Judah and the priests of Jerusalem have resented us and have wanted to take us over—they even claim that long ago we *were* once ruled from Jerusalem!—and Josiah is just the most recent in a long line of power-seekers".

It seemed to be my fate to encounter exceptional women. Obviously Machir had taken great pains to teach his granddaughter many things. At this point my thoughts were taking a surprising—even quite crazy—turn, considering that I had myself killed her beloved grandfather. I no longer just wanted to help Tirzah, from a feeling of guilt and responsibility. I wanted her with me. Her lack of dowry meant nothing to me; no landowner's daughter was going to marry a mercenary anyway. And she had said she did not hate foreigners. So, amazed at my own temerity, I asked her to step aside with me, away from my comrades, and actually broached the subject: "Tirzah, you have no one now, I know only too well, to my sorrow and shame. I cannot dower you, as I have already said, and I am still willing simply to give you my accumulated savings and move on, wishing you well and probably never seeing you again. But if you would prefer my protection and could endure my company, knowing what you know, I will willingly and joyfully, as soon as possible, marry you by whatever ceremony is possible between us".

To my surprise and delight, she consented. Life is not easy for a woman alone in this world, so I do not flatter myself that she considered me any sort of perfect match. But there was, in a strange way, a kind of blood bond between us already, and we both experienced its power. When we departed from the sanctuary, I left her some provisions and some shekels of silver, and promised to come back for her as soon as this hated expedition was completed.

I was able to carry on this prolonged conversation with my—I suppose one might say—"betrothed" because our troop was hanging around, waiting for our messenger to return from his mission to the king. Much to our surprise, Josiah had accepted the story at face value, and did not even send anyone to verify the details, merely gave instructions that Asaiah's body should be sent to Jerusalem for burial; he retained his servant's signet ring, probably with the intention of returning it to his family. We dutifully sent off the body, detailing a Karian to lead the courtier's horse southward with the corpse draped over it. Then we buried Machir, putting the old sword in the tomb with him, just in case anyone should ever question our story; maybe we could strengthen our case by digging him up!

The expedition did not last much longer. Geba, just north of Samaria, was the only additional place our band visited, and we made very sure, by sending a peasant running ahead to warn all the priests to flee, and then by approaching as noisily as possible, that we would encounter only inanimate objects on which to turn our swords. Josiah would later boast that he had imposed his reform "from Geba to Beersheba", encouraging the interpretation that he was fully in control of everything south of the Geba our mercenaries pillaged. But his actual royal sphere of influence probably extended only to another Geba, which was just a short distance north of Bethel![11]

Although we were able to spare the life of the younger priest, and our troop committed no further homicides in Josiah's name, the same was not true of all the divisions of his army. In fact, our story about the old priest defending himself with a sword seemed to increase Josiah's ferocity against any priests he himself encountered. He would have his parties sneak up stealthily so as not to frighten anyone away, then mercilessly slaughter any high place priests he was able to seize. Apparently the same procedure was followed by the other divisions, so that the glorious mission to reclaim Israel for Yahweh was in general a murderous bloodbath.[12] And it was little more than a raid, with no real military or administrative presence established. We came in, did our damage, then retreated back to Judah. A sham, a pretense, a lie, the entire enterprise! But of course that was not the way Josiah's admirers told it, and they were the ones with the power to tell the official story and control what would be remembered. I even heard it said that priests at high places in *Judah* now began to be slaughtered, but I did not personally see that happen.[13]

In any case, I had had my fill of Josiah and his revolution. Besides, most of the dirty work was done by now. But since I had taken on the responsibility of supporting Tirzah, I needed a continuing income, so I did not simply seek to leave the army or to leave the country. Instead, I asked Benaiah to help me find a garrison post as far from

Jerusalem as possible, in hopes that if I had to use a sword or spear on anybody it would be soldiers, not priests. He was able to find me such a station, on the coast, and I soon moved there, taking Tirzah along. In that remote but exposed locale (a situation I shall explain) we dwelt happily for several years, while events transpired in the wider world that would ultimately destroy both Josiah and his kingdom. Next I will summarize both our personal lives together and those momentous events, until fate should bring me to the same place as Josiah again, one final time, at Megiddo.

9. ON THE EDGE OF EVENTS

Judah lacked, as I have said, access to the sea, and King Josiah's plans for increasing the kingdom's power and status came up against this hard fact. Despite the encouragement of well-wisher prophets, he lacked the power to conquer the Philistine cities and thus annex territory to connect Judah with the coast. On the other hand, the weakness and well-nigh invisibility of the Philistines' hegemon, Assyria, during this period is a factor I have also noted, nor were the Egyptians active in the area with much frequency. Consequently, Josiah's advisors suggested that it might at least be possible to seize and fortify a spot on the coast. What was needed was one from which easy escape routes into Judah existed, should a large army appear on the Way of the Sea, either coming up from Egypt or coming down from Assyria.

The king's wish to distance himself from non-Judahite elements, now that the chief destructive phases of his revolution were completed, made Benaiah's foreign mercenaries the ideal troops to be stationed at such a location. We would have constituted a first line of defense against an invading army, and, assuming we could get out, a means of warning the main armed forces of the kingdom. Conversely, even if a band such as ours should have been trapped and slaughtered, our destruction would have bought some time, and we would not have been considered much of a loss in court or temple circles. So we would serve our purpose, whether we lived or died, and those outcomes were equally immaterial to our paymasters.

A location at the mouth of the brook Sorek, downstream from Eltekeh on the coast road, had seemed advantageous.

From there it was possible to flee either southeast, directly up the valley of the Sorek past Ekron and Timnah to the Beth-Shemesh area, or to veer more directly eastward along the main road by Gezer and Aijalon—the route we had taken on our earlier march into the Shephelah. So we were dispatched to the site, which, being uninhabited, as yet had no name. We called it simply "the fort"; whether it has acquired a more precise name since my departure I do not know.[1] Along with us mercenaries were sent out a certain number of conscripted laborers—Judahites—to do the actual constructing of the fort and a number of mud-brick dwellings, and then to farm the nearby countryside to provide food for the soldiers and for themselves. The construction did not take long, and soon we were moved in. Once the building had been done, the conscripted laborers were sent home and usually only brought back for planting and harvest; most of the time we soldiers had the place to ourselves.[2]

Garrison troops in areas of limited danger are customarily allowed to maintain a degree of domestic life, so I had little trouble in fetching Tirzah from the area of Samaria to come share my humble house at the fort. This was my first taste of "marital" life. When I was at Samaria retrieving her, we had gone through a type of ceremony, presided over by the priest in hiding whose life I had saved from Asaiah, though I doubt that the efficacy of the rites would have been accepted either in Jerusalem or in Miletos. It was indeed my first experience of domesticity in any form since my brother and I had left Miletos upon the death of our father and the abduction of Delilah, now close to a year earlier. The life emphatically agreed with me. My intelligent and lovely Tirzah was a wonderful companion and helper. Soon I was able almost to forget the bloody deed that had been the beginning of our association, which was something of which we never spoke.

It was an unexpected benefit to have my entire troop stationed here on the coast with me, when the best I had hoped for was to be assigned alone to some remote post, where I would have to learn to communicate with everyone from scratch. Especially congenial was the continuing presence of Benaiah, who now frequently joined Tirzah and me for evening meals and long conversations. He was a widower who had never remarried, a man accustomed to the loneliness of command—a quality that had no doubt been heightened by his longtime assignment commanding non-native troops. Having found in me a kindred spirit and now in Tirzah a sharer of his own language who could help him in communicating with me, he became a sort of honored favorite "uncle" in our young household, if not indeed a replacement for the father each of us had lost prematurely.

Several years at the seaside fort ensued, not marked by enough momentous events to warrant my reporting them in detail.[3] Periodically occurred the march of an Egyptian army up the Way of the Sea, bringing aid to the beleaguered Assyrians. Forewarned in each case, we quickly evacuated the fort and retreated into the protective interior of Judah, taking our respective dependents along with us, and passing on the warning that the army of Judah should be in readiness. The Egyptians never bothered to pursue us, or even to pillage the temporarily-abandoned fort. Once they had passed by, we returned until their next appearance, which might be a year or two later. Tirzah bore me a daughter whom we named Mahlah (a family name, she said) and, two years later, a son I insisted on naming Benaiah, for his "great-uncle", who was honored and highly pleased by the gesture. Unfortunately, the boy was sickly and died within a year of his birth. Tirzah seemed to be unable to conceive again after bearing him, although my passion for her gave her innumerable further chances. We consoled ourselves that our charming little Mahlah, the image of her beautiful mother, was prospering and in excellent health.

Being on the coast, our fortress was occasionally visited by traders' ships, and I was able periodically to acquire both news and artifacts from Greece. A surprising amount of Greek pottery was to be seen in the soldiers' homes in this place, and not just in those of us who were Asian or Kypriot Greeks; its beauty and quality made it a favorite among many of the mercenaries, as well as the native laborers. Our community even occasionally acted as middlemen in sending some of it up the Sorek valley to the Philistine and Judahite towns south and east of us.[4] No news reached me of my brother Python, however, and of course none of our captured servant and surrogate mother Delilah. I did hear of other Greeks—Ionians, Aiolians, and Dorians—who had left our homeland seeking mercenary service and had ended up far to the east or south of where I was. Some of them I would later encounter in person, including members of quite well known and aristocratic families.

The biggest "event" in Jerusalem during our sojourn at the fort had occurred just as it was being constructed. Josiah had celebrated the "success" of his revolution by organizing a huge festival known as the "Passover". This ceremony was said to have commemorated a particular miracle performed by Yahweh at the time of the *exodos* led by Moses. Supposedly Yahweh's angel of death had struck Egypt to force the stubborn Pharaoh to allow the Israelites' departure, killing the firstborn of every household, including Pharaoh's, and—just for good measure—even the firstborn of the flocks and herds, but the houses of the Israelites had been "passed over" and spared this calamity. The usual conflicting stories had arisen, saying either that this was the first time such a ceremony had ever been celebrated in Jerusalem or that the observation had been anticipated by Hezekiah. Either way, Josiah gained credit, whether as the very first king to follow the letter of the recently-discovered law of Moses, or else as the rightful heir of the great Hezekiah, revered for his defiance of the hated Assyrians.

Reports that reached us on the coast varied as to the scale and magnificence of Josiah's Passover ceremony. Some said that the king and his courtiers contributed huge numbers of bullocks, goats, and sheep on behalf of the common people who gathered from all over Judah for the ceremony. Unlike many sacrifices at the temple, which involved burning the victim entirely—what we Greeks would call a *holocaust*—on the understanding that Yahweh received it in the smoke, the animals dedicated at the Passover were cooked and then consumed by the assembled worshipers, more on the order of a public sacrifice in a Greek city. Wine too flowed freely, so it was a joyous festival, and the ceremonies continued for a full seven days.

Some informants told us that during the period the only bread that was consumed was of the unleavened variety, but I recall hearing at other times that there was a separate festival of unleavened bread. Perhaps the two were now combined, or maybe only later combined, into a single annual ceremony. It was said that the scroll of law found in the temple specified several annual festivals to be celebrated at the central temple, supposedly a long-standing rule that had been ignored until this year. It was still the eighteenth year of Josiah, just at the very end, most of it having been occupied by the activities I have described.[5] I inferred that his regnal years were counted from his actual accession day, not from the beginning of the calendar year in which he was crowned.

Certainly the Passover ceremonies were popular with the Judahite population—sumptuous feasting provided by the state generally is—and encouraged many to accept, if not actively to support, the cultic revolution whose triumph those ceremonies were celebrating. The flood of pro-revolution rhetoric continued, from court and priesthood and prophets (some of these may have been on the state payroll, but others no doubt expressed their support quite sincerely). Outwardly, at least, it appeared that the movement had achieved entire success. No sacrifices, no rites of any kind, directed toward praising or propitiating any gods other than Yahweh were to be seen anywhere. No cult statues or icons—not even any that symbolized Yahweh—were visible. Everyone who talked openly talked a monotheistic, aniconic, Yahwistic line. Royal and priestly agents made sure this was true.

There was also some genuine effort by the central state to afford some protection to the poor and weak (widows, orphans, even slaves). Such a policy had the additional beneficial effect, from the standpoint of the king and his supporters, of further undermining the power of local leaders, clan officials, heads of families, and elders. More and more, the individual Judahite could seek justice, or mercy, only from the centralized state. With no local cults, no resort to his ancestors either through graveside rituals or through mediums and necromancers, he had no one to turn to during times of distress except the king and the temple priesthood.

When the central administration was seen as benevolent, such overriding of local leadership—even subordinate members of the state establishment—could be a genuine consolation and aid to the oppressed. At some point during the next few years, my commander Benaiah told me of a complaint he had seen, lodged by one of the Judahite laborers working near our fort, presumably written for him by some scribe. It had been written in ink on a potsherd (*ostrakon,* we say in Greek)—papyrus was far too expensive and rare for simple everyday documents, while broken pottery was everywhere. The man complained that his overseer (identified by name) had confiscated his outer garment at the time of harvest, apparently in punishment for some alleged wrongdoing. He denied his guilt, called upon his co-workers to witness in his behalf, and petitioned a higher official to force the local overseer to return the garment.

How the case finally turned out, Benaiah had not discovered; someone he knew in the state hierarchy had merely showed him the ostrakon. But it was clear in any case that the laborer had some hope of success in his petition, or he would not have taken the trouble, and probably incurred the expense, of employing a scribe. It is always of benefit to the poor and disadvantaged to have a written code of law. Otherwise, those in charge tend to make up any rules they like. Later on, I would hear from mercenaries who had served in Babylonia and Assyria that detailed codes of law, promulgated by kings claiming divine authority, were a very old and established custom—some such codes were said to have been written down more than a thousand years ago! So Judah was receiving a written law code none too soon, even if its subject matter was heavily cultic, and even if it received its primary sanction by being fictitiously attributed to the legendary Moses. Although I was horrified by certain aspects of Josiah's revolution, and mystified by others (why would anybody care about some of the things that exercised him?), I certainly approved of the idea of written law, and of state intervention against local oppression. Josiah's Proteronomy—first giving of law—was not all bad, despite the damage it had done to me and mine.[6]

As the revolution in Judah moved from crisis mode into its period of consolidation, life for minimally-occupied mercenaries became rather easy. I had time to spend with Tirzah and our daughter. My Samaritan wife was a mine of information on past events in Israel, both before and after the Assyrian takeover. I was surprised to find, for example, that Judah had become an Assyrian vassal even before the fall of Israel. King Ahaz, father of the great anti-Assyrian rebel Hezekiah, had voluntarily sought alliance with Tiglath-pileser the Assyrian king, because Israel and the Aramaeans of Damascus were menacing Jerusalem. Earlier than that—more than two hundred years before our own time—Israel had been a leader in an anti-Assyrian coalition, under the powerful dynasty of Omri and Ahab. They were the kings who had constructed Samaria as their capital and had engaged in vast building projects elsewhere within the kingdom—producing, for example, many of the most impressive structures still visible at Megiddo and at Hazor, far to the north, above the Sea of Galilee. It was no wonder that the Assyrians had called the Israelite royal line the house of Omri and the whole country Omri-land.[7]

From merchants moving along the Way of the Sea and occasionally from sailors who briefly beached their ships near our fort, I heard stories of things that were going on in Assyria, Babylonia, and Egypt. Supplementing these reports with information I was later able to garner, I have by now, as I write, a passable understanding of events within the territories occupied by the great powers in the eight decades since Sennacherib had invaded Judah. I will briefly describe the earlier developments as a prelude to reporting on events during the reign of Josiah, events that would change the face of this entire part of the world, which had for centuries been dominated by the Assyrian Empire—whether other nations served it, resisted it, or were incorporated by it.[8]

Sennacherib, after his invasion of Judah, had returned to Assyria and built up his magnificent palace at Nineveh—the one with the entire room devoted to reliefs of the siege of Lachish. He never returned to the west, being preoccupied with controlling Babylonia and nearby Elam. It was even said that Sennacherib had destroyed the city of Babylon, some ten or a dozen years after his destruction of Lachish. That report may have been overstated, since Babylon was obviously a thriving city during my time. Sennacherib's son Esarhaddon was supposed to have rebuilt it, but perhaps the city was only pillaged and damaged, not entirely destroyed, by his father. Esarhaddon, a younger son, had emerged as king after two of his older brothers had conspired to slay Sennacherib, and had then fled and been hunted down. To hear the story told in Judah, one would have assumed that the king's assassination had occurred immediately after his return home, perhaps as a divine judgment on him for having invaded Judah and having menaced Jerusalem. In reality, it had taken place a full twenty years later.[9]

After succeeding his father, Esarhaddon had ruled for some eleven or twelve years, and had continued to be concerned with Babylonia, but more of that later. The really interesting aspect of his reign was Assyria's relationship with Egypt. During the reign of Sargon of Assyria (Sennacherib's father), the one who had completed the siege of Samaria and had deported many Israelites, power in Egypt had been seized by the Kushites or Nubians—the people Greeks call *Aithiopes*, "burnt faces", because of the darkness of their skin. Having lived in close contact with the Egyptians for hundreds, even thousands, of years, the Kushites had interacted with them in many ways—invading, being invaded, admiring, learning from, being conquered, gaining freedom, etcetera. Having myself accompanied an Egyptian expedition into Nubia, I will have more later to report on the country and its people. At this point, suffice it to say that the Kushites ruled Egypt for about fifty years. It was a Kushite ruler who returned Yamani of Ashdod[10] to Sargon in chains; it was a Kushite king who was defeated by Sennacherib at Eltekeh when he invaded Judah; and it was a Kushite king who was attacked when Esarhaddon invaded Egypt, twice, late in his reign.

This last king, Taharqa, had fought off the initial invasion, but he was driven out of the old Egyptian capital, Memphis, near the head of the delta, by Esarhaddon's second expedition. Still, when Esarhaddon unexpectedly died on his way to Egypt a third time, Taharqa retook Memphis. It had required an invasion by the next Assyrian king, Ashurbanipal, to dislodge him, forcing him to flee to the capital of Upper Egypt, Thebes. Taharqa's nephew and successor had been driven out of Thebes (the city was sacked) and back to Nubia by yet another expedition led by Ashurbanipal, ending the Nubian dynasty's rule in Egypt—although the Nubian kingdom very much continued in existence, and is operating today, I can testify from personal experience. Since the Nubian dynasty's heyday corresponded to so much of their own period of travail, it is not surprising to hear Israelite and Judahite speakers—prophets, for example—refer to Egypt and Kush, or the kings of Egypt and Kush, more or less interchangeably. The Kushite kings had pursued traditional Egyptian objectives in the region of Canaan, encouraging resistance to imperial powers that encroached on the region from the east or north. But as an ally to actual rebels, such as Hezekiah of Judah, they had proved just as surely a "broken reed" as their Egyptian predecessors had been—and their successors would be!

Those successors were the present dynasty, the Saites, rulers from Sais in the western delta. When the Assyrians had proved unable to govern Egypt themselves—Ashurbanipal too had had his troubles in Babylonia, despite the fact that his younger brother was originally ruling there as his viceroy—they had made the current ruler in Sais, one of several local kinglets, into their vassal or puppet king of Egypt. This was the first Psammetichos, not the one under whom I served, who was his grandson; Necho was king between them. Whether or not the Assyrians had been happy to see the Saites achieve independence, they had accepted it, and the two powers had been in effect allies, whatever the actual treaty status between them might have been. As the Assyrians became weaker and weaker, especially after the death of Ashurbanipal—an event that occurred some ten years or more after Josiah had become king in Judah—the Egyptians more and more thought of themselves as hegemonic rulers in their old province of Canaan, even if they did not often intervene directly. Usually, when they marched through the area during the time of Josiah, it was on an expedition to assist the disintegrating Assyrians. They were, as I have already said, generally content to pass through without doing any appreciable damage, if not challenged or hindered in their passage. Their path did not even take them through the territory of the kingdom of Judah, anyway, since the coastal area through which the main road passed was Philistine country, until one exited the pass through the Carmel range at Megiddo and entered the Assyrian province of Samaria.

Ashurbanipal had suppressed a revolt led by his brother, and some years of peace had ensued in Babylonia, but upon his death—or that of his appointed governor, reports differ—a new power had begun to emerge in the southern part of the Tigris-Euphrates basin. The region had always been home to a diversity of peoples (*ethnoi*), and the group that now came to prominence for the first time were the current rulers, the Chaldaeans. Their leader was Nabopolassar, the first Chaldaean to hold power firmly in Babylonia (although others had briefly seized the throne in earlier periods, it was said). Struggling against both the Assyrians and other local pretenders, Nabopolassar proclaimed himself king, managed in about ten years of fighting to get his claim generally accepted, then ruled undisputedly for ten or eleven additional years. During this last period he took the offensive against the Assyrians, invading their territory repeatedly.

Alarmed at the rise of this aggressive new power, the first Psammetichos had sent a reinforcing army deep into Assyrian territory along the Euphrates, and Nabopolassar's initial invasion had been repulsed by the allied forces. But at this point other groups also entered the conflict—the Medes and perhaps others from beyond the Zagros Mountains that rise east of the Tigris. Operating at first independently and then in alliance with Nabopolassar's Chaldaeans, they steadily hammered away at the Assyrian heartland. Nineveh survived an initial Median attack, but the former capital, Asshur, fell to them soon afterward. Two years later, in what I recall as the twenty-eighth year of Josiah, the combined Medes and Chaldaeans captured and sacked Nineveh, forcing the last king of Assyria to flee westward and take refuge in the fortified city of Harran. Here again, their Egyptian allies attempted to assist the struggling Assyrians, with expeditions led by Psammetichos and then, at the very beginning of his reign, by his son Necho. By the time Necho became involved, Harran had already fallen, and the remnants of the Assyrians were scattered in the far western reaches of the empire, mostly taking refuge in the fortress of Karchemish on the Euphrates.[11]

During the period when the ever-increasing discomfiture of Assyria was evident to all and much talked about, there had been giddy exhileration in Judah. With Assyria sickening unto death and Egypt not intervening actively in local affairs, the appearance—for those seeing short-sightedly, as most people in general and certainly all over-focused zealots tend to see—was that Judah was about to be free of great-power interference at last, and free to re-take the lost territory of Israel, in the bargain. Prophets denounced all trust in foreign alliances:

> What is the good of going to Egypt now
> to drink the water of the Nile?
> What is the good of going to Assyria
> to drink the water of the River?

—asked Jeremiah, the latter reference being to the Euphrates.[12] Judah had no need for mortal allies. Judah had Yahweh.

Among those listening intently to such counsels was King Josiah. Although his earlier strike into Israel had been obviously a mere raid to those of us who had participated in it, he seemingly thought of himself now as the ruler of Israel. Hearing that Necho, the recently crowned Pharaoh, was on his way up to the Euphrates, Josiah vowed to deny the Egyptian passage through "his" territory, and planned to intercept him at the obvious place (given his insane presupposition), Megiddo.

10. ARMAGEDDON AND AFTER

Harran had fallen in the preceding year. When word reached Jerusalem that the new Pharaoh, Necho, was beginning his northward march, intending to relieve the Assyrians besieged at Karchemish, my unit was sent orders to proceed directly to Megiddo through the Carmel-range pass and begin organizing a line of defense near the city. The main army of Judah, led by the king, would rendezvous with us after making a more difficult march, going directly north through the central highlands, avoiding the coast road and the pass for fear of encountering the invading Egyptians prematurely.[1]

On earlier occasions, with Egyptian armies coming up the coastal road, after we and our women and children had withdrawn into the heartland of Judah for safety, we had been pleased to find on our return that our fortification and homes had been left completely undisturbed, as I have already said; not a goat or sheep had been taken. Now the situation was totally different. We mercenaries were being moved, not inland for protection, but northward for the purpose of fighting. The urgency of the situation provided us no time to escort our dependents to positions of safety, and in any case there would be no army present in Judah to protect them, since that army would be where we were—at Megiddo. We were going to have to gamble the lives of our families on the Egyptians' record of having left our abandoned settlement alone when they had passed through heretofore.

It was a scary situation, although we were given no choice except to take the risk. I hugged and kissed Tirzah and our daughter Mahlah with especial warmth, holding each of them so overlong that my wife could sense my fear. The fear was even more evident when I told her at unaccustomed length how much her gentleness and kindness had meant to me, and how greatly I loved her. I promised to avoid unnecessary risk-taking in any fighting that might occur, and to return to her as soon as possible. Benaiah stopped by our house to embrace and reassure her also. Then we were off, up the Way of the Sea, to be followed not many days afterward by the army of Necho of Egypt.

Shortly after our arrival at Megiddo, Josiah and his troops showed up, a considerable army, but nothing compared to what a major power like Egypt could put in the field. Barricaded atop *Har-Megiddon,* we could have withstood a siege by a larger army, of course, but we were not there to protect Megiddo. Josiah intended to deny passage of the Egyptian army to the Euphrates. To do that, we would have to do battle with that army in the field, in the plain at Megiddo. It was a task our small numbers made hopeless, as any but a one-track-minded religious zealot would have easily seen. The more competent commanders, Benaiah among them, thought only in terms of limiting our losses, each specifically determined to minimize losses among his own men. But some commanders were themselves revolutionaries who believed Josiah and his rhetoric about Yahweh defending their cause, regardless of the odds. These were sufficiently numerous to make it certain that there would be a battle of some kind. Our best hope was that it would be only a brief skirmish, because the Egyptians would be eager to move on.

After a couple of days of nervously waiting, we finally spotted a small band of horsemen emerging from the pass. These were messengers sent by Necho, and his words for Josiah—which had been translated into Hebrew—were read out loudly enough to be heard by many stationed near the king. I was not personally so near, but Benaiah and others repeated the words to me with sufficient agreement that

I am sure of the gist of the message, if not its exact wording:

> Why be concerned about me, king of Judah? I have not come today to attack you; my quarrel is with another dynasty. God has commanded me to move quickly, so keep well clear of the god who is with me!

I assume that the god to whom Necho referred was Amun of Thebes, or perhaps the composite Amun-Re, incorporating the sun god of the city we Greeks call Heliopolis. Josiah replied with a message of defiance, invoking his own god, Yahweh, so the Pharaoh's effort to avoid a battle was wasted. Very soon the army of Egypt, chariots and infantry, began filing through the pass and taking up positions in the plain opposite our vastly outnumbered army.

I could see that Necho's army also included Greeks (and Karians, Lydians, and other Asians and islanders), recognizing them from the armor and weapons borne by some of the infantry. I did not realize at the time how soon I would myself be one of their number! It was not the spear-wielding foot-soldiers who slew Josiah, however, but the archers. Foolishly making himself a target in his royal chariot, he was hit by several shafts, fairly early in the engagement. To the retainers surrounding him he cried, "Take me away; I am badly wounded". They lifted him out of his chariot and transferred him to another, less ornate but faster, and sent him off immediately toward Jerusalem. I later heard that he lingered until shortly after his arrival, then died in his capital city. Whether that was true, or just another story with the purpose of making all things revolve around Jerusalem, I do not know. Certainly he was buried with traditional rites in the tomb that had been prepared for him among his royal ancestors. Some later said that the prophet Jeremiah himself wrote a lamentation for his death, although I never actually heard it, if so.[2]

The obviously-fatal wounding of Judah's king essentially ended the battle, as the Judahite forces fled in disarray—some through the pass that had just been vacated by the enemy, some by the highland route into Judah, some even north into Galilee, apparently just in hopes of hiding out until Necho's army had departed. Unfortunately, the battle did not end soon enough to prevent what was for me a real disaster—unlike the death of Josiah, who had asked for his fate, if anyone ever had! Although the archers had determined the outcome of the skirmish by hitting Josiah, there had been some degree of clash between the rival infantries. I personally escaped with no more than a rather nasty scratch on my shield arm—someone had come at me from my left side, and I had not turned quite quickly enough to get my shield entirely in front of his thrust.

My mentor and second father Benaiah was not so lucky. Not that he was killed treacherously, or taken by surprise. Rather, the Egyptian soldier who slew him was the biggest man I had ever seen, a giant I could not imagine anyone matching up to, one-on-one. Although I could only estimate his size from a distance across the battlefield, I would say he must have been closer to five cubits tall than to four! By the time I had dispatched my own attackers and run to try to give aid to my commander, it was too late. He was already dead; I never even got to bid him farewell. As commander for many years of Greek-style heavy infantry, Benaiah himself had adopted our "hoplite" equipment, but against the incredible strength of the giant, it had proved no more efficacious than the wicker shields many of the Egyptian soldiers used. The giant's spear-thrust had gone right through his thick shield and his breastplate. Later, with bitter irony, I recalled the reputation of Benaiah's namesake, David's champion, famed for slaying a huge Egyptian warrior.[3] This was a cruel turning of the tables against my friend!

Benaiah's slayer had disappeared into the melee before I could make any attempt to avenge my friend, and in short order the battle was over, anyway. Necho had lost no time in moving his army out—Josiah had been a mere distraction for him, and he was already concentrating again on his real mission, bringing aid to his Assyrian allies at Karchemish. Soon, therefore, the field at Megiddo was empty except for the dead and some few stragglers like myself. No one seemed to be issuing any commands, as it was every man for himself, now that the battle was over and the kingdom itself had been left leaderless. My fellow mercenaries were among those who had fled. I commandeered a horse—a riderless one was not difficult to come by, in the aftermath of the battle—and laid the corpse of Benaiah over it. I would take him back to the fort for burial. Tirzah, at least, would join me in mourning for him, I thought.

In reality, it would be the mourning that soon increased, not the number of mourners. As I turned off the Way of the Sea to lead my sad burden down to the fort at the water's edge, I saw, to my horror, that the place had *not* been left undisturbed this time, as it had been on other occasions. Dead livestock littered the fields, and smoke rose from several locations where it had no business to be. As I drew closer, I saw that one of the smoking ruins was my own small house! Leaving the horse with my slain commander on it behind, I sprinted to the door, only to have my worst fears confirmed. There, among the burned roof-beams and furniture, were the charred bodies of Tirzah and Mahlah! They were recognizable, there was no doubt as to identification that could have allowed me even a glimmer of hope. But the damage was severe enough to make it unclear exactly what had killed them—whether they had perished in the fire itself or had been dead before the fire partly consumed them and, if so, what had killed them.

What other mistreatment either or both of them might have suffered before death was also indeterminable. Was this rape? Murder? Both? Or merely the unfortunate consequence of being burned out and not escaping the blaze in time? Equally uncertain was the issue of *who* had done it? I searched the area—apparently I was the first returnee among the mercenaries—and discovered that the other homes and families had been treated the same way; there were no survivors. Several possible perpetrators of these deeds of horror occurred to me. Had it been the Egyptian army, advancing through the area after my own troop had been sent to Megiddo? Or some contingent of fleeing Judahites, venting their anger at the loss of their king and the destruction of their nationalistic hopes on the families of foreigners? Or a band of Philistines from nearby Ekron, determined to punish the Judahites for setting up a fortress in "their" territory, seizing the opportunity provided by the departure of the fighting men to attack the defenseless? Or even pirates, dashing in to pillage and burn the undefended seaside settlement? I had been left without even the solace of knowing whom to hate.

One by one, most of my compatriots drifted back, to confront the same horror I had confronted (mercifully, not all of them had families). Each of us dealt with the remains of our own household, and communally we buried Benaiah with proper ceremonies. Then we discussed among us what it would be best to do, in our present leaderless state. As the one who had generally been recognized as the closest confidant of our former commander, I was chosen as acting or temporary commander, for the purpose of leading the troop to Jerusalem and inquiring as to our future duties and future commander. We all assumed he must be a Judahite, though none of us entertained any hopes that he would be a man such as Benaiah had been, so exactly appropriate for the post. Some openly expressed their hope or expectation of seeking service elsewhere, but we decided to stay together at least until we reached the capital and discovered what the new king and his advisors had planned for us.

The new king was Shallum, an adult son, age 23, but not the eldest son of Josiah, who had been given the throne-name of Jehoahaz. We were told that he had been chosen by—here's that eyebrow-raising phrase again!—"the people of the land" (*am ha-aretz*)—just as Josiah himself had supposedly been chosen. It was not difficult to guess that the same "people" who had engineered the choice of Josiah had also chosen this particular son, whose mother came from Libnah in the Shephelah, with the expectation that he would continue to support their revolution.[4] He would last three months, that is, until the return to the area of Necho, on his way back to Egypt.

Meanwhile, the foreign mercenaries were informed of the name of their new commander. He would be Elnathan son of Achbor, a younger and less experienced man than Benaiah had been. More importantly, rather than being a man of Benaiah's open-mindedness, *xenophilia,* and pragmatism, the new commander was a zealot for the revolution. His father had been, like Asaiah, one of the courtiers who had accompanied Hilkiah and Shaphan on their mission to the prophetess Huldah.[5] The movement, despite Josiah's death—and much worse, as my description of events of later years will make clear—was not going to die out in one generation, but was to be perpetuated by younger believers. Now I began very concretely to formulate plans for getting out of Judah as soon as possible. Truly I had no reasons left to stay: my family had been murdered, my commander and mentor had fallen in battle, and the state-sponsored xenophobic, iconoclastic, monotheistic revolution showed no signs of letting up or making much accommodation to reality.

Necho's base of operations in the region was Riblah in Syria, south of Hamath and upriver from it on the road that ran alongside the northward-flowing Orontes. Having proved unsuccessful in defending what little was left of Assyrian authority, he had left a garrison at Karchemish and was now encamped at Riblah, when Jehoahaz voluntarily appeared before him and offered obeisance to his sovereignty. This was a recognition of political necessity. The Assyrians were now completely out of the picture, and with the Babylonian army never having yet come beyond the Euphrates, the only major power operating along the eastern coast of the Great Sea was Egypt.

Whatever its motivation, the gesture was not enough to mollify the Saite ruler for the presumption of the Judahite "people" in choosing a king without his approval. Perhaps mostly to make it clear that Judah, formerly Assyria's vassal, was now quite definitely the vassal of Egypt, Necho deposed Jehoahaz, loaded him with chains, and took him to Egypt.[6] Soon in Jerusalem a lament would be circulating, attributed to Jeremiah:

> Do not weep for the man who is dead,
> do not raise the dirge for him.
> Weep rather for the one who has gone away,
> since he will never come back,
> never see his native land again.[7]

This would prove to be true prophecy, since Jehoahaz did in fact die in Egypt.

In place of the deposed king, Necho designated another son of Josiah—two years older—whose name was Eliakim. He was given the throne-name of Jehoiakim.[8] I found it interesting that the Egyptian king by this change replaced a name theophoric in the Canaanite god El with a Yahweh-bearing name. Perhaps this had been a conciliatory gesture toward the court and priesthood in Jerusalem, who had presumably been the ones to suggest the name to him—why would one Hebrew name intrinsically mean more to him than another? It may also have been significant that the new king's mother, a different wife of Josiah, was from Rumah, north of the Valley of Jezreel, deep into what had formerly been the kingdom of Israel. Josiah's marriage had perhaps represented his territorial claims to this northern area, but it is possible that Necho's choice of the son indicated his hope for getting a vassal who might, through his mother's influence, have been less affected by extreme Judahite xenophobia.[9]

Not that the newly-appointed vassal king was allowed to lose sight of the fact that he was a vassal! Necho imposed a tribute of one hundred silver talents and ten gold talents on Judah, which Jehoiakim was obliged to raise by levying a new tax. Interestingly, the new law code probably influenced the way this tax was collected; each Judahite head of household was taxed "according to his means".[10] At least the benevolent aspects of Josiah's revolution seemed to be surviving also, along with the destructive ones![11]

Elnathan had led us mercenaries up to Riblah for the conference with Necho, as part of the escort for the then-king Jehoahaz. He had made some congenial contacts with the escort of the Saite king, and this fact made him a logical choice to lead a party on a diplomatic mission to Egypt quite early in the reign of the Pharaoh's appointee, Jehoiakim. The circumstances that brought about this mission—in which I participated—are interesting, and they reveal much about the institution of prophecy and the unwritten rules that governed it in Judah during this time.

Jeremiah of Anathoth had been one of the most vocal and effective advocates of the revolution led by King Josiah, indeed had been advocating the kind of "reforms" the king undertook several years before the king himself began fully displaying his reforming zeal. With Josiah now dead, Jeremiah took up the line that only obedience to the law that had been "found" in the temple could save Jerusalem from imminent destruction. Early in the reign of Jehoiakim, he stood in the court of the temple and harangued all who came in from the towns of Judah:

> Yahweh says this: If you will not listen to me and follow my law which I have given you, and pay attention to the

> words of my servants the prophets whom I have never tired of sending to you, although you never paid attention, I shall treat this temple as I treated Shiloh, and make this city a curse for all the nations of the world!

Many, even among the leaders of the revolution, regarded such pronouncements as dangerous, even treasonous, to say that the capital city might warrant the fate of an Israelite shrine destroyed long before even Bethel had been established as a royal sanctuary! Clearly the fates of Samaria and Bethel were implicit in such a threat: an unrepentant Jerusalem would be triply doomed.

Jeremiah was given a sort of impromptu public trial before the courtiers, who assembled at the entry of the New Gate to the temple. Rival prophets and even some priests shouted that he deserved to die for having prophesied against the city. Jeremiah answered them fearlessly. I can report here with some precision, although I was not present at the temple gate, because Jeremiah had had his scribe Baruch write down a full account of these events, and I eventually acquired a copy of it. Jeremiah's reply had been:

> Yahweh himself sent me to prophesy against this temple and this city all the things you have heard. So now amend your behavior and actions, listen to the voice of Yahweh your god, and Yahweh will relent about the disaster that he has decreed for you. For myself, I am, as you see, in your hands. Do whatever you please or think right with me.

Now Jeremiah found defenders among the courtiers who had been gathered to judge him, and certain elders even cited the parallel case of the prophet Micah of Moresheth, who had actually predicted the destruction of Jerusalem in the days of Hezekiah—and had not been punished even though his prophecy had proved incorrect! Rather, it was proclaimed, Hezekiah and the people of Jerusalem at that time had saved themselves by heeding the warnings of Micah, and Yahweh had relented of his intent to allow Sennacherib the Assyrian to destroy the city. Jeremiah too escaped punishment. Nor did it hurt his cause that he had a powerful protector in Ahikam, son of Josiah's secretary Shaphan, the very man who had brought the scroll of the law to the king.[12]

What was significant for me personally was the different kind of behavior exhibited by another prophet of doom at around the same time. This was Uriah son of Shemaiah, from Kiriath-Jearim, who essentially said in the name of Yahweh exactly the same kinds of things Jeremiah said. But when Jehoiakim sought to apprehend him, Uriah had not, like Jeremiah (and Micah, eighty-odd years earlier), stood his ground. Instead, he had taken fright and fled to Egypt. That action had fatally undermined his prophetic authority, by proving that he himself did not fully believe in Yahweh's protection, so the accuracy or inaccuracy of his prediction of future events had become irrelevant. Micah, for his steadfastness, had remained a "true" prophet despite the fact that the destruction he had predicted did *not* occur. Uriah, conversely, was by definition a "false" prophet and worthy of death, although ultimately the destruction of Jerusalem that he predicted actually did take place. Jehoiakim appointed Elnathan to go to Egypt to secure the return of Uriah for execution.[13] I was among the escort sent to accompany Elnathan. He would return without me.

11. THROUGH THE DESERT TO THE DELTA

Probably from a desire to avoid the Philistines, who seemed newly assertive after the death of the expansionist Josiah, the advisors of Jehoiakim did not send Elnathan's contingent to Egypt along the coastal road, the Way of the Sea. Instead, we were sent along a more southerly, inland route. From Jerusalem we went through Hebron to Beersheba, then followed the somewhat meandering road through the Negeb to the large oasis at Kadesh-Barnea, a place where many caravan trails converged. Although it was outside any defensible borders of Judah, claims of control here had not been lacking, as in the Edomite areas to the east which I had visited earlier. Several kings of Judah had built fortifications at this place, most recently (I think) Manasseh. Stories told in Jerusalem about the *exodos* from Egypt under Moses had the exiles dwelling at Kadesh-Barnea for many years—something that might have been possible for a small band of nomads, but clearly could not have been done by an entire nation on the move.[1]

While we paused for a few days at the oasis, Elnathan, with a zealot's mindfulness of his sacred mission, sent parties from his escort on forays out into the desert, instructing them to seek local cult places to despoil. I was put in charge of one such party. Unbeknownst to my commander, I had already determined to bolt from Judahite service once we reached Egypt. Never having had any real enthusiasm for the destructiveness of Josiah's revolution, I certainly had no reason to pursue the policy with any passion now, since I did not expect to return for any punishment my dereliction might incur. I was much more interested in observing and learning than in destruction, and the handful of mercenaries serving under me were happy to be spared the effort and potential opposition, so they had no reason to bear tales back to Elnathan about my "inefficiency" as a revolutionary.

As we followed the desert trails, I was amazed at the number of standing stones (*masseboth*) we encountered, scattered all around this bleak landscape, some simply in isolated groups of two or three stones, others apparently associated with mounds that I took to be burials, others in what appeared to be primitive "high places" or open-air cultic precincts. Almost invariably, when a group had three stones, the tallest was in the middle, with a shorter stone on each side. When only two stones were present, the one on the viewer's left was virtually always the taller and narrower one. I was usually fairly sure about the direction for viewing, because such groups of stones tended to have a flat stone seemingly serving as an altar in front of them—almost always in a direction that I could tell from the sun was east. So my observation of aniconic standing stones in the desert confirmed what I had seen earlier in cultic sites in the Shephelah and elsewhere, and made me even more certain that the use of such stones had originated in the desert.[2]

Not too many stades south of Kadesh-Barnea, we came upon a fortified hilltop rest-stop for caravans. If I learned of any name for the place, I do not recall it.[3] I was too distracted by my fascination with what I saw there in the entranceway to the fortifications. On both sides of the passage, which was itself plastered, were plastered rooms featuring low benches on which sat numerous votive offerings. Behind the benches were storage areas filled with older votives that had been removed to make room for more recent ones. The offerings themselves were less interesting than what was inscribed or painted on them. Fortunately I had by now learned enough to read Hebrew inscriptions pretty well, even without the help of my lamented mentor Benaiah. One large stone bowl bore an inscription saying "Belonging to Obadiah son of Adnah; may he be blessed by Yahweh".

Even more interesting was a large pottery storage jar, one of several, which bore the graffito "I bless you by Yahweh of Samaria and by his Asherah"; under this were drawings of several strange figures. Two looked distinctly bovine (bull and cow?), although the sexual characteristics of the smaller figure on the right were ambiguous to me. Upwards and to the right of both of them was a distinctly female figure, seated on a lion—or lion-shaped throne—and playing a harp. Elsewhere on the same jar was a drawing of a stylized tree (the tree of life?), itself atop a very clearly drawn lion, with horned creatures (ibexes?) feeding on its leaves, one on either side. Which drawing—or drawings—depicted the goddess Asherah? The smaller bovine figure? The harpist? The stylized tree? In addition there were inscribed or painted texts on other votives that referred to El and to Ba'al.[4]

Here was very clear evidence of non-monotheistic worship at this gateway shrine, not to mention an explicit connection of Yahweh with the destroyed capital of Israel, Samaria, rather than with Jerusalem and its temple. This was definitely the sort of thing that my men and I had been ordered to destroy. We didn't bother. We went back to Elnathan at Kadesh and I lyingly reported that we had eliminated all traces of "alien practices" encountered on our side-journey. He had no reason to distrust my report, and I expected to be long-gone before he discovered the lie, if he ever did. Now the entire contingent continued on toward Egypt, joining, a bit to the southwest of the oasis, the desert path the Judahites called the Way of Shur.

If it had been doubtful that a large multitude could have stayed at the oasis of Kadesh for any long period of time, it was even more doubtful that a gigantic group could have survived at all in the blasted wilderness through which we now passed. The main road along the coast was clearly the only possible route across this desert for any large body of people, anything the size of an army or larger. It was no wonder that stories told in Jerusalem about the supposed wandering in the wilderness of the escapees with Moses included assertions that Yahweh had provided them with food in miraculous ways![5] Fortunately, we were a small band, mounted, and well supplied, so we made the unpleasant journey with comparative ease. Fairly soon we reached the line of forts that marked the frontier of Egypt proper.

The forts, which began in the north at Pelousion on the seacoast, linked up with a series of lakes that descended fairly close to the gulf of the Red Sea that lay west of the peninsula of Sinai, which we had just crossed. About halfway between the coast and the gulf was Lake Timsah, by which the desert road to Judah ran. From the lake to the city of Boubastis on the easternmost (Pelousiac) branch of the Nile River, our road followed a valley or dry river bed. Along this very route, Pharaoh Necho would later attempt to dig his canal connecting the Nile with the chain of lakes and the gulf, a project that would finally be abandoned after much loss of life caused by the brutal working conditions.[6]

The great Nile River, after flowing mostly in a single channel for many days' journey from the land of Kush in the far south, divides into several major channels in the broad plain near the sea, into which it empties by several mouths named for the cities by which they flow.[7] This whole downstream region is known as Lower Egypt, and Greeks call it the delta because it is shaped like that letter. The entire remainder of the Nile valley, all the way to Kush, is known as Upper Egypt.

Many Egyptian place-names are almost impossible to pronounce or write in Greek script. Fortunately for my readers, Greeks have by now become so well acquainted with Egypt (*Aigyptos* is in fact the country's Greek designation; the natives call it *Kemet*) that many places are commonly known by alternative Greek names. I will therefore in general use these, sometimes supplying the native forms in addition (at least the ones that seem fairly pronounceable!), and the Hebrew forms where I know them. Upper Egypt, for example, was called *Pathros* by speakers of Hebrew. I did not, of course, know my way around Egypt at all, when I first arrived here from Judah. It was by living and traveling here for many years that I developed an understanding of the geography of "the Two Lands". That phrase was a common way of referring to Upper and Lower Egypt, a division that was symbolized in many ways—including the king's titles and his double crown—and rooted in many centuries of national experience. The current residence of the king was at Sais (the Egyptians call it *Sau*) in the delta, on one of the western branches of the Nile, but other delta cities had in the past served as the capital. So had several cities in Upper Egypt. The most important was Thebes in the distant south, the Greek name for *Wast* or *Waset*, known in Judah as *No-Amon*, or "City of Amun"—named for the god whose greatest temple-complex was located there. The oldest capital was Memphis (*Mennufer*), called *Noph* in Hebrew, which was just slightly upriver from the point of the delta.[8]

The ancient royal residences still carried religious and ceremonial significance. Although kings were no longer buried in the elaborate necropoleis near Memphis or Thebes, Saite kings, for example, made offerings and repairs and additions to temples at both places. Nor had the goddess of Sais, Neith, supplanted Ptah of Memphis, Amun of Thebes, or Re of Heliopolis in the religious consciousness of Egyptians. Greeks tended to equate these deities with Athena, Hephaistos, Zeus, and Helios, respectively, but the equations clearly were rather arbitrary.[9] Indeed, as I have already said, the tendency was to combine Amun and Re into one chief god, Amun-Re, and it was the combination that most closely matched the Greeks' notions of Zeus.

As among the Hellenes, every Egyptian city had its patron deity, and there was a great abundance of gods in Egypt. Even gods with recognized Greek counterparts were often depicted as having the heads of various animals on human bodies. What to me as a Greek was merely amusing would have, I was sure, completely horrified my Judahite employers. Amun, at least, like a Greek god, was always depicted in entirely human form, although that too would have been unacceptable to my zealous aniconic paymasters.

Elnathan and his followers, myself included, were met and questioned at the fortress where our road crossed the border. The Egyptians had interpreters not only for our Hebrew-speaking commander, but for Greek speakers as well, so I was among those questioned. This fact enabled me also to do a bit of questioning back, abetted by the fact that Elnathan knew much less Greek than Benaiah had, so that he could not really understand my conversation. I discovered that quite near Sais, to which our mission was to be escorted, was a place called Naukratis that had many Greek inhabitants, mostly traders. I determined that somehow I would find my way to Naukratis and take refuge among my countrymen there.

It was not the time of the annual inundation when we arrived, a fact which actually made it rather *more* difficult to get from Boubastis on the Pelousiac branch of the Nile to Sais (or Naukratis!) in the western Delta. When the Nile rises, around the time of the summer solstice, the entire delta becomes practically a giant lake, with the cities for islands, so going from one to another by boat at that time is quite easy. The water was low now, so the flat region was a confusing network of Nile branches, canals, marshes, and paths that required much zigzagging and backtracking. Moreover, although Sais and Naukratis were both in the western part of the delta, they were not on the same Nile branch, but on two different ones. I would not be able simply to "jump ship" from a boat heading for Sais in order to reach Naukratis. Even though the cities were close to each other—separated only by some ninety stades—I would have to make my escape overland, and on foot, since we would be leaving our horses behind when we first embarked at Boubastis.[10] I decided it would be best to go on to Sais with the group, then try to get lost in the capital and slip away toward Naukratis while my commander was busy negotiating with the Egyptians about our official business, the recall of the prophet Uriah for execution.

Our circuitous boat trip did eventually get us to Sais, with its great temple to the goddess Neith and the royal palace, and I had no great difficulty in giving my companions the slip. I had not let any of them in on my plans, since I thought I would have a better chance of getting away alone, and I assumed—correctly, it turned out—that Elnathan would be less concerned to retrieve one disappearing Ionian than he would be if he had lost several of the troops in his charge. He could always claim that one soldier had died through some sickness or accident, a story that would be less believable if told to explain the disappearance of more men.

Although my overland (or over-swamp!) walking journey was short, it was still quite harrowing, thanks to the peculiar forms of animal life I encountered, particularly the hooded snake called in Greek the *ouraios* (cobra or asp) and the monstrous lizard called the *krokodeilos*. Fortunately, I managed to see each such creature before it saw me, and thus to avoid it. Stumbling, wet and muddy, into the familiar-looking *agora* of Naukratis, I was delighted to hear people talking nearby in the dialect of my beloved Ionia. Interrupting the conversation—my appearance alone was an interruption, once I had been noticed—I described myself as a Milesian suppliant seeking refuge. My elation was boundless when I was told that there was among the sanctuaries in Naukratis one dedicated to Apollo that had been established by traders from Miletos!

Asking and receiving directions to the cult place, I was happy to leave nearly half of the silver I had received in my latest wages from Judah as an offering, and to take up a suppliant's position at the altar of Apollo.[11] Recalling the scenes I had witnessed—and participated in—at altars in and near Judah, I almost wept for joy. I don't know whether I still believed that Apollo or any god would protect me, but at least I felt no fear that officials of the cult of Zeus or Hera—or Amun or Isis—would come up and kill me for the presumption of visiting Apollo's shrine. In fact I soon felt free to leave the sanctuary and move about in Naukratis, in which Greeks were permitted to come and go as they pleased, unimpeded by the few Egyptians who chanced to be present to engage in trade with them.

After a few weeks, I heard from a trader who had visited the capital that the embassy from Judah had departed with its prisoner. Elnathan had obviously made no serious effort to find me, doubtless happy to bid good-bye and good riddance to one more foreigner. I heard later that Uriah was executed in Jerusalem, and his body was thrown into the potter's field in the Kidron valley.[12] My service as a mercenary for the kingdom of Judah—or perhaps I should say for Yahweh, which is no doubt how my paymasters had regarded my job—was at an end.

On the other had, I was far from finished with the kingdom of Judah. My intention, soon realized, was to enlist as a mercenary in Egyptian service, and Judah was, after all, very much within the Egyptian sphere of influence. It was a place to which contingents of Egyptian troops—including foreign mercenaries, especially those who could understand the local language—might be sent at any time. Moreover, even within Egypt itself I would later encounter many refugees from Judah, as the growing power of Babylon eventually overwhelmed their homeland. The last time I would see the prophet Jeremiah himself, in fact, was in Egypt![13]

But many years would intervene before that occasion. Until then, I would follow Jeremiah's continuing career in Jerusalem from a distance and with a kind of bemused fascination. The prophet seemed to me as much a madman as Josiah had seemed. Unlike Josiah, however, he clearly had no personal ambitions whatever, and his courage and absolute honesty could not be doubted. I was able to bring my knowledge of his activities up to date during my intermittent periods of being stationed in Judah as a mercenary, henceforth in the employ of gods other than Yahweh.

Part II

In Service to the Saite Kings of Egypt

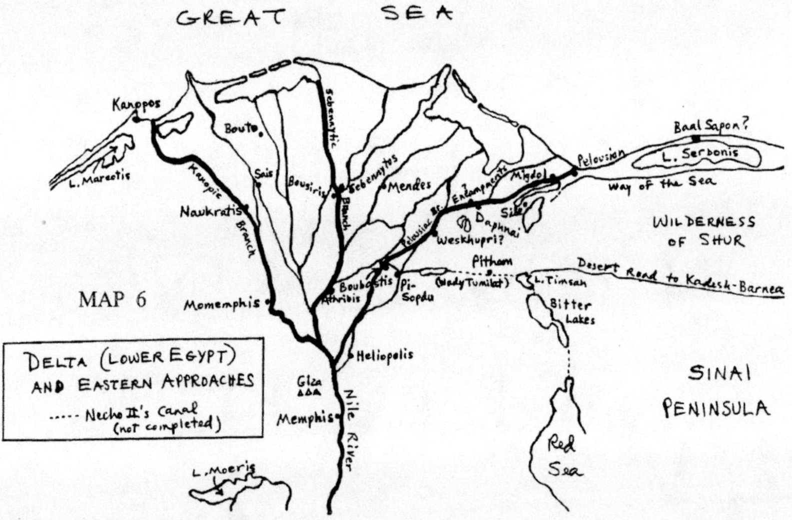
GREAT SEA
Kanopos
L. Mareotis
Boute
Sais
Bousiris
Sebennytic
Sebennytos
Mendes
Kanopic Branch
Naukratis
Branch
Pelousiac Br.
Encampments
Migdol
Pelousion
Baal Sapon?
L. Serbonis
Way of the Sea
Daphnai
Sile
Weskhupri?
WILDERNESS OF SHUR
Pithom
Desert Road to Kadesh-Barnea
L. Timsah
(Wady Tumilat)
Boubastis
Athribis
Pi-Sopdu
Bitter Lakes
Momemphis
Heliopolis
Giza
Memphis
Nile River
L. Moeris
Red Sea
SINAI PENINSULA
DELTA (LOWER EGYPT) AND EASTERN APPROACHES
----- Necho II's Canal (not completed)
MAP 6

12. NAUKRATIS

Probably someday another Greek—perhaps a Milesian, even—will visit Egypt with the time and resources to describe the whole amazing country in detail.[1] It is indeed a place of wonders! Time I certainly have had, since I reached Egypt in my early thirties and I write this recollection over forty years later. But I arrived as a suppliant and soon became a soldier, and I had little liberty or wherewithal to wander about, and certainly no high connections to grant me entry everywhere. The friends I made among the Egyptians tended to be soldiers, or ex-soldiers, though even among military men my closer associations were usually with foreigners, especially other Greeks. Some officers—Egyptians—looked kindly on my curiosity about their land and its customs, as did some of the government-provided translators who assisted Greek soldiers and merchants, so I did have some useful sources of information. But primarily I can report only what I saw, and my interpretation of things seen is subject to errors from not knowing the background or causes of the phenomena observed. Given these limitations, I will not attempt any overall descriptive treatment of Egypt or Egyptian customs, but will simply comment on things as they enter my narrative of events.

Naukratis[2] was not quite, or not yet, a full-scale Greek *polis*. Since it existed for trade, there certainly was an open market area or *agora*, and there were temples to Greek deities. My own city, I was later told, saw itself as the mother-city (*metropolis*) of Naukratis. I have already mentioned the Milesian-founded sanctuary of Apollo where I sought refuge. Merchants from the Ionian island of Samos had also established a precinct sacred to their main goddess, Hera, and some from the island of Aigina, just off Attika in European Greece, had dedicated a cult site to Zeus. But in the southern part of the city there was a large fortified warehouse maintained by the royal government. Since the first Psammetichos, father of the Necho who was king when I arrived in Egypt, had begun hiring Greek mercenaries, he had encouraged trade with Greek cities in order to gain silver with which to pay them.

Quickly, this city, which was about 450 stades upstream from the Kanopic (westernmost) mouth of the Nile, began to attract Greek traders eager both to exchange silver for Egyptian grain (treated as a royal monopoly for purposes of export) and to sell wine and oil to Greek soldiers and other resident Greeks. The king made available plots of land for sacred precincts even to Greeks who did not actually wish to take up residence, although many did. Plans were underway for a large panhellenic temple jointly sponsored by several groups of Greeks who were not present in Naukratis in sufficient numbers to establish the kind of individual sanctuaries my own city and Samos and Aigina had established. The proposed "Hellenion" would be founded by traders and residents from Ionian Chios, Teos, Phokaia, and Klazomenai; Dorian Rhodos, Knidos, Halikarnassos, and Phaselis; and Aiolian Mytilene on Lesbos. During the decades of my residence in Egypt, it would be completed and dedicated. Greek-style pottery was also already being manufactured in Naukratis, to be used by those making votive offerings at the various sanctuaries.[3]

Mentioning the Greek *temene* of Naukratis brings to my mind the various Egyptian sanctuaries around the delta, and some of the rites associated with them.[4] Obviously, my recent employment as a temple-defiler had made me rather sensitive to cult places and practices, and it was a kind of pleasure, during my first days in Egypt, to be able to observe without being expected to destroy. Sais, the capital, which I had already seen briefly, had its temple of Neith ("Athena", Greeks imprecisely tend to say), with a precinct so large that it also contained the tombs of the Saite kings. Behind the main temple was another structure said to be the tomb of Osiris, a peculiar god who rules the underworld and is in the Egyptians' way of thinking somehow connected with deceased Pharaohs. Greeks associate him with Dionysos, but this is even more inexact. There were stone obelisks within the sanctuary as well, and a circular pond that resembled the sacred pool on the island of Delos. Mysteries were enacted by night on this pond. Another night-time observance at Sais, this one an annual event, was called the lamplight festival; it too was connected with mysteries, about which I have no personal knowledge. Very ancient statues within the royal palace at Sais, of a cow with a golden sun between her horns, and of around twenty nude women—described to me but not actually seen by me—may also have been associated with the cult of Osiris, or perhaps his consort Isis.

At Papremis, near the coast of the delta, violent rites were enacted involving the attempt by most of the priests to keep out of the sanctuary the cult statue of a god whom the Greeks equate with Ares (I don't even know his Egyptian name), while the local worshipers opposed them with clubs and sticks in attempting to force them to let the god in. Heads were broken and, I am told, people sometimes actually died in such confrontations, which were purely artificial battles since a few of the priests had only removed the statue from the sanctuary shortly before!

The most honored oracle in the delta region was the one at the place the Greeks called Bouto, north of Sais and near the Sebennytic mouth of the Nile, a city that had been created by combining two originally separate towns. The oracle was dedicated to the Egyptian cobra goddess Wadjet. The Greeks, for no reason I can fathom, identified her with Leto, mother of Apollo and Artemis (both of whom supposedly had sanctuaries there also). The temple of "Leto" had a gateway forty cubits high. Other elements of her precinct included a lake with a supposedly floating island in it, and many palm trees and other trees.

Bousiris, which means "House of Osiris", lay at the very heart of the delta, near the central channel of the river. It was the site of elaborate mourning rituals for Isis and Osiris, attended by tens of thousands of worshipers. Mendes, on its own Mendesian branch of the Nile in the eastern half of the delta, also had rites—which were quite erotic—honoring Osiris, here identified by the Greeks with Pan in his most goat-like aspects. Some Greeks even told me that the rites involved copulation by women with goats or rams! Statuettes of Osiris were made—not just at Mendes, but all over Egypt—which each had a phallus that was as large as the rest of the statue, and was its only moving part.

The wildest rites associated with any deity in the delta region, however, were those dedicated to the goddess Bast or Bastet at Boubastis ("House of Bast", quite analogous to Bousiris, just mentioned). Some Greeks equate her with Artemis, but it seems to me that Aphrodite would be a better analogy. The city, which lay on the Pelousiac (easternmost) branch of the Nile—indeed, it was the very place from which my party and I had set out for Sais by boat, after riding across the desert from Judah—was approached by celebrants on boats (*bareis,* the Egyptians call the particular vessels used in the delta), crowded on, men and women all together. All along their journey, every time they passed a town, they steered the *baris* close to the bank, and some of the women on board stood and pulled up their clothes to expose themselves to the villagers, while others sang and clapped and danced. The sanctuary of Bast, in the middle of the city, was practically an island itself, being surrounded by canals more than thirty cubits wide, drawn from the river, at all points except the entrance. The rest of the city was higher than the sanctuary, so that it was possible to walk around the precinct and look down into it, seeing the temple with its high gateway and elaborate decoration, surrounded by many trees.

Discussion of erotic rites at Egyptian sanctuaries in the delta puts me in mind of the erotic side of the Greek enclave at Naukratis, because that enters very importantly and surprisingly into my story. Naukratis, like many trading centers (such as Korinth in the Peloponnesos), was famous for its prostitutes, including some of the more refined and expensive kind known as *hetairai* ("companions" or "courtesans"). One of the most famous, for example, who operated there not in my youth when I first saw the town, but when I was older and settled on my ex-soldier's farm, was known by the nickname *Rhodopis,* Red Face or, more appropriately, Red Mouth. Her real name, some said, was Doricha or Doriche. She began as a Thrakian slave belonging to a Samian named Iadmon (it was said that one of her fellow slaves was the famous writer of fables, Aisopos), and was sold to another Samian, Xanthes, who brought her to Egypt. The Eresian Charaxos son of Skamandronymos, oldest of three brothers of the famous poetess Sappho, who was in Naukratis on business (he was a wine-seller), bought her freedom and set her up as a *hetaira*. No doubt he received part of her fees as her patron, as well as a generous patron's discount for her services. She became so wealthy plying her trade that there were even stories circulating among the Greeks that she had built one of the gigantic pyramids at Giza from her earnings! That was preposterous, of course (Egyptians knew that the pyramids had been there for more than a thousand years), but she did in fact, I was told, make a very generous offering to Delphoi from a tithe of her fortune. Sappho is supposed to have laughed at her brother's folly for his involvement with the famous courtesan, either because of his infatuation with her (one story even says that Charaxos had children by her), or because he foolishly emancipated a slave who could have made a fortune for her owner.[5]

I was by this time experiencing some personal interest in encountering some of the *hetairai* of Naukratis. It had been more than a year now since I had lost my beloved Tirzah, during which time I had lacked the inclination to pursue other women, initially because of my grief and pain and then because of my preoccupation with finding a way to get out of Judah, while in the meantime avoiding participation in the royally-organized oppressive revolution as much as possible. I was still far from ready for setting up housekeeping with anyone again, or playing father to a new brood of children to replace the ones I had lost. But now that I was breathing more freely, the simple desire for sex, for being with a woman again after so long, was becoming powerful. So I began inquiring among my fellow Greeks, making it clear that I could not afford anyone working in the price-range that would later be exemplified by Rhodopis.

A Samian merchant from whom I had purchased a couple of jugs of wine told me of a clean and peaceable house whose women had an excellent reputation for pleasing and for not cheating their clients. Knowing where I was from, he clinched my interest by telling me he had heard that the proprietress of the house had once lived in Miletos—although she was not a Milesian, indeed not a Greek. Hoping perhaps to satisfy cravings for news from home, in addition to my other cravings, I could hardly wait to set out for this house, as soon as the amused wine-seller gave me directions. The town was not large, and I found the place with minimal trouble. My knock on the door was greeted by a young slave girl, who led me into the cool interior, saying (in pretty good Greek), "The mistress will be in soon". I sat on a comfortable chair and waited.

The woman was talking over her shoulder to one of her ladies as she walked into the room through its rear door, so at first I saw only the back of her head, dark hair streaked with gray. But the *voice* was familiar, the correct though accented Greek with its peculiar gutteral quality, the accent of someone native to the eastern regions. Then she faced me, and I was struck utterly dumb. "Delilah!" I intended to shout, tried to shout, but failed. All I could do—and did—was to race across the room and embrace her, tears streaming from my eyes.

She did not at first recognize me. It had been more than twelve years since she had seen me, then a very young man not much beyond his ephebic training, a neophyte soldier in the early stages of the conflict that had led to her abduction and my father's death. I was a fairly grizzled veteran now, somewhat scarred, more heavily muscled, and no doubt I offered a more serious mien, given the losses I had incurred and the brutalities I had practiced (willingly or unwillingly) since my happy youth under her tutelage.

She was changed as well, of course. From her late thirties to her early fifties, a woman ages more than a man does. But she still stood straight and revealed no noticeable infirmity of age; her waist had thickened only slightly; her complexion was clear, her eyes as bright and intelligent as ever. When she realized who I was, she did not cry; she absolutely laughed with delight. "Archon!" she shouted, "A man and a soldier, a newcomer to Egypt and ready to buy himself a good time tonight with my fine whores!"

When I looked a bit taken aback by her rather bawdy comment, she spoke more quietly, but still with complete frankness: "Do not be disturbed, my beloved boy. None of us exiles here in Egypt need think ourselves among the *aristoi*! You once had such prospects, while I was your father's slave and concubine, though in my earlier days I too had held a respectable station in my own country. Life has rendered us equals. Now I sell the enjoyment of women's bodies, and you sell the damaging of men's. Both of us have been made dealers in human flesh by the fates, and both of us have survived by our own skill and perseverance. To whom shall we apologize? And why should there be any barrier, any lack of honesty, between us?"

With an incredible sense of relief I realized how absolutely right she was! I had spent the last several years of my life enforcing a program of artificial separation—Judahites versus Samaritans, one god versus others (all of them, as far as I could see, mere human devisings), native versus alien. I had always instinctively known that such enforcement was destructive and essentially insane. My Philistine female teacher was telling me again what I had known all along, reaffirmed by the wise Judahite Benaiah and my profound and loving Samaritan bride Tirzah. They had been taken from me, but now she had been miraculously restored. Any response other than delight would be an insult to her, to myself, and to any benevolent fates or gods there might be (just in case such entities existed, which my experience had led me to doubt)!

So I poured out that delight, and my relief at finding her safe and well, and I vowed that we would never lose track of each other again, and that we should be intimate friends and equals for life—a vow I am pleased to say that both of us kept to the letter, as long as she lived. I told her of my service in Judah, even of the worst of it, the part I had most desperately wanted to forget, my slaying of Tirzah's grandfather Machir on the command of the execrable Asaiah. Long-suppressed tears came forth from me in the telling of this. Tirzah and I had tacitly agreed never to mention the painful memory, and there had been no one else with whom I could share my secret (it had been no secret from Benaiah, who had been present at the event, so what more could I have said to him?). Neither of us knew anything of what might have happened to my brother Python.

She told me her story as well, of how the Lydians who had dragged her from my dead father's house had sold her to a slave-trader from the interior of Asia, who in turn sold her to an aging, wealthy landowner who needed an able woman to run his large household and give directions to his many other slaves. Her ability to learn languages and to write had secured her an unusually exalted position, by slave standards, and her age had spared her most of her master's lustful attentions, since he had several younger slave-girls. Upon his death, she had been manumitted and left with a small amount of silver. Her skill at record-keeping and facility with languages had made her a natural businesswoman, but very few businesses welcomed women practicioners, in Asia or elsewhere. So she invested her silver and time and energy and skill in establishing herself in the only trade available; she opened up a house of prostitution. After a few successful years in her inland city, she relocated her operation to the coast, to Tarsos in Kilikia, and there she began to hear from Greek soldiers and sailors and merchants who passed through her house about the opportunities to be found in the new city of Naukratis in Egypt. Selling the house in Tarsos, she had been able to pay for passage on a ship following the coast to Egypt—she told of catching just a fleeting glimpse of her former home, Ashkelon, as she sailed by—and to set up this current house, a couple of years ago.

I began to tell her that I would hire on with Pharaoh's army, save my pay and buy a little farm, and take her away from this life…but she cut me off quite firmly. "No, my friend Archon, that is not what I want from you, or indeed from anyone. I actually enjoy this life. It's the closest thing to freedom a woman is allowed to experience in a world dominated by men. Of course I profit from the sexual services other, younger women provide to men, but my women are slaves or destitute freedwomen who would be subject to considerably worse drudgery than sex, if they did not work for me. I make sure my customers are clean and apparently healthy and not given to brutalizing women—such a person is never welcomed here more than once. And for myself, I live as I wish, beholden to no one. What married woman can say that? What I want from you, as I said, is your friendship and honesty. You live your life, I will live mine. Come visit me when you can, write me letters when you are far away—remember, I can read Greek quite easily. Maybe when I am very old, if you still offer it, I will accept your charity, but as long as I can make my own way, I intend to do it. Do we have a bargain on those terms?"

"Yes, yes, of course, Delilah", I responded enthusiastically. I had always been immensely impressed with her intelligence and ability, but now I was seeing a dazzling independence such as almost no man had ever been privileged to see in a woman. Tirzah had seen through the lies of Josiah's revolution, but Delilah saw through the lies that debilitate every human society—the incredible waste of the talent and intelligence and strength of women. Then I blushed with a remorseful memory: The only reason I had found her was that I had come here to buy sex from some slave prostitute in a house another man had recommended to me! When Delilah asked the reason for my discomfiture, I decided that our newly-sworn vow of friendship and honesty required me to tell her my true thoughts, so I did.

"Why in the world", she asked, "would that bother either you or me? I am certainly not ashamed of the product I sell, and there is nothing unnatural in a young man's wanting it—especially one who has been deprived in the way you have told me you have been. Consider this first visit to my establishment a gift from me to you, in gratitude for seeing you again and for our new pledge of friendship, and you shall have your choice of the very best of my women. I'll tell you the truth, Archon, if I did not know I was too old for you, I might forget about having been your father's concubine and spend the night with you myself! You were always a handsome lad, and you still are".

The same semi-incestuous thought had crossed my mind, but I decided there were more complications there than I needed to confront, so with relief I accepted her offer, and spent a blissful evening with a long-haired Karian named Artemisia.[6] The sun was up before I arose, and I shared a bit of bread, cheese, and wine with Delilah before I departed. She had a regular source of income, but as yet I did not. It was time to seek out the recruiting officer.

13. IN THE ENCAMPMENT OF THE IONIANS

Egypt had been an imperial power for many centuries, and had seen many rival or friendly empires to its north and east come and go. Assyria, the only one that had been strong enough actually to occupy Egypt itself, had now gone the way of its predecessors. A recent period of weakness had included half a century of rule by the Kushites of Nubia—whose culture was so thoroughly Egyptianized through hundreds of years of close contact that they regarded themselves, and were regarded by many Egyptians, as legitimate Pharaohs. Now the Egyptians under the kings from Sais felt they were on the verge of reasserting their power both northeastward and southward.

During this and earlier imperial periods, Egypt has maintained a large standing army, whose soldiers constitute a self-perpetuating military caste; the Greeks call them *machimoi*. Their numbers will seem astounding to Greeks, if the figures told to me can be relied upon at all. I was informed that there are more than 400,000 of them! All of the Egyptian soldiers are expected to devote their entire energy to warfare and training for war, and forbidden from practicing any trade. To provide for their sustenance, each *machimos* is provided, tax-free, with a plot of twelve *arourai* of land, an *aroura* being a square 100 cubits on each side, worked by peasants who rotate from plot to plot year by year. Peloponnesian Greeks tell me that a similar system is used in Lakedaimon, with the Spartan citizen class devoted entirely to war, supported by serfs called Helots. Two thousand picked *machimoi* constitute the king's personal bodyguard, a troop that is changed annually so as to make its perquisites available to more soldiers. These receive, in addition to whatever their plots of land produce, generous daily rations of grain, beef, and wine—at least my Greek informants say "wine", perhaps based on their own practice, although my observation is that Egyptians of all classes prefer a kind of beer made from barley, which they call *zythos*.[1]

In addition to this native military caste, it has been a long-standing custom in Egypt to employ military units made up of soldiers of "foreign tongues"—the Greek term *alloglossoi* presumably translates an Egyptian term I do not even recall, having been recruited and commanded mostly in Greek throughout my service. From very ancient times, Kushite troops had formed contingents within the army of Egypt, a presence that had of course increased during the period when Kushite Pharaohs ruled the country, and plenty of these Nubian troops (or their descendants) remained in Egypt still. Police duties had also, I was informed, often been assigned to groups of Kushites recruited for such purposes. Libyans from west of the delta, just as thoroughly Egyptianized as the Kushites, had also long supplied both military and police units. Some of the Libyan commanders had long ago merged with the ruling families of Egypt, especially in the delta region, and even royal dynasties—including the present Saities—were conscious of Libyan ancestry.[2]

Recruitment of Greeks—and of Karians and others from nearby areas of Asia—was a comparatively recent phenomenon, initiated by the founder of the Saite dynasty, the first Psammetichos. I tend to call him by this name that we Greeks used for him, and for his grandson, under whom I served. It was actually just our version of his Egyptian name, Psamtik. He began claiming the throne of Egypt during the chaotic period when the Assyrians had driven out the last Kushite Pharaohs and then had themselves withdrawn from the country. They had made him their vassal, expecting the same kind of subservience they had received from his father. But he was set on attaining power independently, in a struggle with several other would-be kings in the delta and upriver. For a time the Assyrians even detained him as a suspected traitor, but he satisfied them and was allowed to return and reassert his claims.

Psammetichos was having little success, and it is even said that his enemies had driven him into the marshes at the extreme north of the delta, near the Great Sea, when, in desperation, he sought an oracle from the sanctuary at Bouto. According to the story, he was told that he would get his vengeance when he saw men of bronze coming from the sea. Shortly after, a band of Ionian and Karian freebooters had been forced to land on the coast of the delta, and set out pillaging the nearby plain in their bronze armor. They were duly reported to him by a terrified messenger who referred to them as "men of bronze from the sea". Seizing upon this as the fulfillment of the oracle, Psammetichos immediately offered the men employment as mercenaries, beginning a process he would continue until he built up quite a large force of such foreigners. Some say that King Gyges of Lydia sent him some of his mercenaries. With their help he was able to emerge, after several years, from the struggle with his rivals as the recognized Pharaoh of all Egypt. Even the Assyrians, seeing him as too powerful simply to control, were ultimately content to treat him as an ally rather than as their puppet. Counting his early period of struggle, his reign lasted some fifty-four years, and firmly established the Saite dynasty.[3]

The foreign soldiers never approached in number the native *machimoi*, of course, since it was necessary to pay us in silver, whereas they could essentially be compensated with land grants, except for the extra perquisites provided for the 2000 who served annually as royal bodyguards. But we were quite numerous. In the struggle between Apries and the usurper Amasis that prompted me to begin writing this memoir (since it led to what appears to have been the

Babylonian Nebuchadnezzar's last campaign in the west), Apries was able to call on 30,000 Ionians and Karians.

For his mercenaries, Psammetichos had established the so-called "Encampments", one on either side of the Pelousiac branch of the Nile, downriver from Boubastis, the Karians in one camp and the Ionians in the other.[4] Many served out the time for which they had contracted and then went home, sometimes having gained rich rewards from the king. A good many years after I joined the army of Egypt, a comrade who had recently arrived from Ionia told me of an Egyptian-style statuette that he had seen, somewhat under a cubit in height, dedicated in a temple in Priene. There was a Greek inscription cut on it, describing rewards for bravery, including a gold bracelet, given by "the Egyptian king Psammetichos" to someone called Pedon. He was apparently a mercenary who had brought his trophies home and shared them with the gods: they got the stone statue, while he kept the gold bracelet! Whether he had served the first Psammetichos or the second (Necho's successor, under whom I served), I had no way of knowing; certainly I never met him while on campaign. By the time I had heard of Pedon's dedication, both kings named Psammetichos had already ruled and died.[5]

Other mercenaries stayed on permanently in Egypt. For those the garrison fort and town of Daphnai—called by the Judahites *Tahpanhes*—had been constructed adjacent to the Encampments, east of the river. I would eventually take up residence in Daphnai, and remain there following my retirement. Although the place is smaller than Naukratis, it has some of the same characteristics, including its large fortified storehouse maintained by the Egyptian state.[6] Going back and forth between the two Greek settlements has never been much encouraged—one is for merchants, the other for soldiers—and is not particularly easy, except during the inundation when boat travel becomes less circuitous. But individual soldiers did find it possible occasionally to visit Naukratis, and merchants did sometimes call on Daphnai.

Many mercenaries took wives or concubines, and their sons, who were often given Egyptian names, sometimes succeeded their fathers in the regiments of the *alloglossoi*. Although that term continued to be literally applicable to new recruits such as myself, second-generation and third-generation "foreign-speaking" mercenaries of course spoke Egyptian fluently. They learned it not only (in many cases) from their Egyptian mothers, but from interpreters that the kings provided, who were themselves descended from Egyptian boys who had been assigned to live among, and learn Greek from, the first groups of mercenaries settled at the Encampments. My own commander in an expedition to Nubia about fifteen years after my recruitment would be a second-generation Egyptianized Greek, who bore the same name as the then-reigning second Psammetichos.

All of the background information I have been supplying about the workings of the Egyptian army represents things I discovered later, of course. At the time, all I knew was the general location of the Ionian Encampment and the fact that I needed to get there from Naukratis, after leaving Delilah's house. Travel would have to be by boat and—since, as I have already mentioned, it was *not* inundation season—it would be quite indirect. I would have to go upriver on the western Kanopic branch, perhaps even as far as the head of the delta, where the three main streams of the Nile divide, then downriver on the eastern Pelousiac branch to the Encampment. Perhaps a knowledgeable pilot could shorten the journey somewhat by utilizing various canals and creeks that connected the major river forks, but the speed of my journey would be entirely at the mercy of my pilot, since I could do little more than indicate my destination.

With most of the remaining silver from my Judahite pay, I managed to book passage on a slow-moving *baris* that was being towed upriver from the bank—there was not enough breeze to move the heavy craft by sail. The slow pace, and the fact that this time I was traveling alone, and not distracted by plans for deserting, allowed me to examine the Egyptian boat. What was unique, from a Greek perspective, was Egypt's almost total lack of suitable trees for ship timbers, which necessitated using inferior kinds of wood that could not be cut in long planks but only into short wooden "bricks" from which the sides of the vessel had to be constructed. Seams were stuffed with papyrus prior to caulking. The sail, which was not useful during this particular trip, was made of papyrus rather than cloth. There was a single rudder, but no oars for rowing, and a stone anchor was actually dragged along on the downstream portion of our trip, to help keep the boat straight in the current.[7] The trip, with pauses for unloading goods and loading on others, took a leisurely four days, but I disembarked safe and extremely well rested at the Ionian Encampment.

It was easy getting directions to the recruiting officer's quarters, since everybody I addressed, including the Egyptians in this place, spoke Greek. The officer was a very short, stocky, businesslike man whose father had come to Egypt from Klazomenai in Ionia, but whose mother was Egyptian. I told him of my wish to sign up, long-term rather than just for the current year, and he said my services would be most welcome. This was a sentiment that only increased when I mentioned my long prior service as a mercenary in Judah, since Egyptian plans for increased involvement in the region of Canaan made soldiers knowledgeable in the languages and topography of the area very much in demand. Finally he brought out his scroll with the names of recent recruits, so that he might add mine to the list.

"Name, patronymic, city of origin?" he asked me, perfunctorily, readying himself to write what I replied. But when I said "Archon son of Amoibichos, from Miletos", he seemed not to hear me clearly, saying: "Were you here yesterday or the day before, when I was assigned elsewhere? Your name is already right here on the list". Knowing that was impossible, I protested that I had just arrived, not an hour ago. Then he showed me the scroll. "See", he said, "there's the name you just gave me: Python son of Amoibichos, from Miletos!"

Python! I seized the scroll and brought it close. Yes, my brother was here! Amazingly, he had come to the Encampment and signed up for military service barely a day before my own arrival! Quickly I explained his error to the officer, and expressed my delight at what had caused it. "Please", I entreated, "you must assign me to the same unit, the same barracks. I have not seen, heard from, or heard anything about my brother in thirteen years!" He was happy to oblige, and to give me directions to the barracks. I virtually flew there, down the dirt streets of the camp.

The barracks building was virtually empty when I arrived, occupied only by one other brand-new recruit, who introduced himself as Helesibios from the town of Teos, which I knew was on the southern coast of a long peninsula that juts out from central Ionia toward the island of Chios (Klazomenai, home of the recruiting officer's father, was almost directly across this peninsula on its northern side, actually occupying a small offshore island). Helesibios informed me that the troop stationed in this barracks, including everyone recruited earlier than today, was out doing its customary drills—marching, simulated fighting, etcetera—and should be returning quite soon (it was getting on toward late afternoon). The Teian was considerably younger than I, having come directly to Egypt from home rather than pursuing a roundabout path such as mine—or Python's. He was the one who brought me up to date on some of the events in and around Miletos that I have already reported—the tyrant Thrasyboulos' tricking of the Lydians and the beginning of work on the new temple of Apollo at Didyma, for example.[8]

Sure enough, the sweaty members of the barracks contingent began drifting back shortly afterward, and Python was—mercifully—among the first to arrive. I thought he would collapse when he recognized me, and he just stood for a moment in open-mouthed astonishment. Then he leaped to embrace me, shouting to all the others that here was his long-lost brother Archon—which certainly made for a wonderful introduction and instant acceptance into the group for me. Like myself, Python had aged, and he bore a few scars, but he was likewise essentially physically undamaged. He too had grown to be a man rather than a youth—harder, sturdier, and—I was somewhat chagrined to find—taller. In fact he had bypassed me and was probably now two or three fingers taller than I was, a reversal of our height relationship when we had left Miletos.

We had many adventures to tell each other, and talked far into the night, so that drills the next day were extremely hard on both of us! He had seen more military action, participated in more battles, during his service to various kings and would-be kings on the southern coast of Asia, but he found my stories of Judah and its monotheistic revolution both repellent and fascinating. I told him of Benaiah, expressing a hope that our commanders here would be half so wise and competent. And I told him about Tirzah and her appalling death (along with our daughter), though I did not share even with my brother the things I had told Delilah about the horror that had brought Tirzah and me together. Finally, of course, I told him of finding Delilah, right here in Egypt, in Naukratis!

He was pleased, although not as delirious with joy as I had been, and he seemed to experience some unexpressed distaste when I told him how she earned her living. Python had matured and had seen more of the world; he respected my feelings enough not to contradict me directly. But he remained a more conventional Ionian in his attitudes than I was, or ever had been. He had appreciated Delilah and had been grateful for his upbringing at her hands, but it had always been more significant to him than to me that she was our family's slave. My fascination, infatuation—in fact my love—for her had been the first step in destroying ethnocentric ways of thinking in me, a tendency that Benaiah and Tirzah had furthered, and my revulsion at the murderous xenophobia of Josiah's revolution had confirmed. Delilah had also led me—again abetted by Tirzah—into thinking of women in ways very different from the ways most Ionians thought, indeed almost all men thought.

I had no right to expect my brother to share the mental consequences of experiences that had been mine alone. He had lived these past thirteen years as soldiers usually lived, with brief nights or hours of sex with whores and occasional short shackings-up with camp followers. If he had sired any children, he had no knowledge of it, and the women involved would doubtless have had just as little knowledge of their offspring's paternity. Anyway, despite his reservations, he did in fact want to visit Delilah in Naukratis as soon as we could arrange to do so. Such occasions were fairly numerous in the many years we spent at the Encampment, between campaigns north and south. Artemisia, my first-night "gift" from Delilah, in fact soon became Python's special favorite. I was content with whomever Delilah recommended on any given visit, but was mainly interested in talking with *her*; when she could spare the time, I would sometimes spend my entire evening in that activity, even foregoing sex with any of her lovely employees. Unfortunately, Python did not live to have the chance to visit frequently with the aged Delilah after she took up residence with me and my second wife during my retirement at Daphnai, happily spending her last years in the care of an old man whom she had nurtured as a boy.

But all that was far in the future. Now everything was the joy of reuniting the long-separated sons of Amoibichos. Python had been quick to meet the other members of our troop, mostly Ionians but with some admixture of Aiolians and Dorians from the Asian coast (the Egyptians used "Ionians" as a catch-all term for all Asian Greeks). Pambis was from Kolophon—yet another *polis* on that Ionian peninsula, a bit inland from Teos. Telephos and Anaxanor came from Dorian Ialysos on the island of Rhodos; Krithis, whose specific city I can't recall, was an Aiolian. Most of the names I have forgotten, in the thirty or more years since I joined their band of mercenaries.[9]

Our training, which was intensive and continuous, would not be for nothing. Pharaoh Necho was determined to restore the great-power status of Egypt. He continued with his canal project, hoping to be able to maintain fleets on both the Great Sea and the Red Sea and to be able to move warships freely back and forth. He planned to move into the vacuum in Palaistine and Syria that had opened with the Assyrians' departure, and was contemplating a major invasion. He had already experienced the wrath of the Babylonians during the campaign a year or two ago, and he knew that Nabopolassar had ambitions in the same area as well. But the Chaldaean king was old and infirm, and Necho believed the Babylonians could be beaten, with a really serious effort. We *alloglossoi* were an important part of his plans.

14. CAMPAIGNS AROUND KARCHEMISH

Necho had left a garrison in Karchemish during the expedition that had led to Josiah's death on the way up and the deposing and replacing of his successor on the way back. That garrison was still in place as the second campaigning season since he had installed it was approaching. In the interim, Necho had been preoccupied with his naval projects—the canal to connect the Nile with the Red Sea, the building of warships on both seas, and the dispatch of a group of Phoinikian sailors on an exploratory voyage down the Red Sea coast of "Libya" (a word the Greeks use for the entire continent in which Egypt is located, as well as for the region on its northern coast just west of Egypt). Related to the canal was the constructing of a new fortress on its north bank. It was known in Greek as *Patoumos* and in Hebrew as *Pithom*; its Egyptian name meant "House of Atum" (Atum or Aton being a particular manifestation of the sun god, known in his other aspects by Re and other names).[1]

The Egyptian king had felt free to concentrate his energies in these areas because the Babylonian king Nabopolassar had not brought his army back to the area of the western bend of the Euphrates during this period. Now that the Assyrian Empire was destroyed, perhaps he would be willing to accept a tacit division of spheres of influence with Necho, with the Euphrates, guarded by the Egyptian garrison in the great fortress city of Karchemish, as the boundary between them? The strong-walled fort, I was told (I had never seen it), was located on the west bank of the river at the site of the best ford, its citadel being right at riverside in the town's northeast quadrant. In addition to its strong outer walls—with river, ravines, or steep rockface on several sides, making it very difficult to attack effectively—Karchemish also had an interior wall separating its outer town to the west and south from its higher inner town near the citadel.[2]

Now, however, in the early fall, Nabopolassar at last was moving.[3] Reports reached Egypt that he had crossed the river south of Karchemish and seized and garrisoned a town called Kumukh or Kimukhu, but he had himself returned to Babylon during the winter before any response to his action could be made. Apparently he too thought of Karchemish itself as impregnable, and was planning to cut off its supply-lines from Egypt by occupying places below the fort. In the spring that followed, Necho realized that he had to return to the region, and he called up his army, both Egyptians and *alloglossoi*.

I was almost exhilarated to be on the verge of some genuine military action, as opposed to the bully-boy "police" duties I had mostly performed in Judah, punishing that kingdom's own people for following practices they had always followed. True, I had seen some action at Megiddo, against this very same army of which I was now a part, but that skirmish had been such a mismatch—Judah versus Egypt!—that it was not much of a genuine battle experience, however real the losses I had sustained. We marched in our separate units—Ionians, Karians, Egyptian *machimoi*, other foreign contingents—although all the groups had Egyptians as their chief officers.

Within the native Egyptian contingent marching in front of my troop (naturally we got to eat *their* dust, not they ours!), I could not help noticing one soldier who towered above all the others. My commander, who spoke Greek, told me that he was called Petosiris[4] and came from the region around Thebes. I could see that he was just about as dark as a Kushite, and I would later discover that such complexions became more prevalent the farther upriver one went into Upper Egypt. Certain dynasties of Theban kings, I was later told, claimed Nubian blood within their family lines.[5] Petosiris was described by my commander as a formidable fighter, a match for any two or three heavily-armed enemies. I asked whether he had been involved in the altercation with the forces of Judah at Megiddo. My fears were realized when my commander replied: "Oh, yes. In fact he received a commendation for killing the commander of one of the units of the enemy army—its foreign mercenaries, I believe".

As I had suspected immediately upon seeing him, Petosiris was the slayer of my friend and mentor Benaiah! I realized, however, that there was nothing to be done about it. As I have already said, there had been nothing treacherous about the killing, just one soldier besting another in combat. It was pointless to hate him for the advantage his size and strength gave to him. At this point I might as well just be grateful that such a fearsome fighting machine was on my side, rather than against me! It could have been worse, I later realized, once I had heard about ancient Egyptian battle practices. In the old days, victorious soldiers were expected to demonstrate their success in combat, and thus to earn citations and rewards, by bringing to their commanders the heads or the right hands of their victims. There were even temple relief carvings—interpreters told me, having been shown them by priests—that depicted the body parts collected as *phalloi*![6] Benaiah's body at least had not been mutilated, and I and my mercenary comrades had been able to bury him with proper ceremony.

The long march up the Way of the Sea was made less tedious by the fact that my brother Python and some of my new companions also came along. We camped one evening just north of Gaza, which had been occupied by the Egyptians since around the middle of the long reign of Necho's father Psammetichos. I realized that Ashkelon, Delilah's home, was only about 100 stades farther north and on the coast (Gaza was a few stades inland). With the permission of our commander, I persuaded Python to join me for a quick exploration of the place. Neither of us had ever seen it, and I recalled that Delilah had told me that she had only been able to glimpse it from a ship at sea on her voyage to Egypt. I was eager to be able to describe the town's current appearance to her, once we returned to the delta.

Ashkelon was very large in area, and more or less semicircular in shape. The Sea on its west formed the flat side of the semicircle, with earthworks making an arc probably fourteen or fifteen stades in length around its south, east, and north. A steep plastered *glacis* was topped with mud-brick and stone walls, with the main gate on the north side. As soldiers in an allied army, Python and I were allowed to enter and roam about, although the lateness of the afternoon hour limited our explorations. We spent much of our brief time visiting a winery that was right in the center of the city, tasting a bit of the good local product while we were there. The stone collecting vats for the winepresses reminded me of the vats in the olive presses of Ekron which I had seen during my service in Judah, although pressing the wine grapes here was done by the simple method of stomping them, as opposed to the use of heavily weighted levers to crush the olives. Wine was stored in large, fat-bellied jars with odd spherical clay stoppers that were larger than apples. Within another room of the same building was a shrine that we could clearly see was devoted to Egyptian deities. Around a bronze offering table were several phallic-shaped bronze bottles, each bearing relief sculptures. The most interesting one showed a masturbating figure I later learned was the god Min, contributing his fertility to the world! I did not seek to discover what kind of fluid was in the bottles.

We ended up wandering along a street lined with bazaars that ran directly toward the Sea and the rapidly-setting sun. A butcher's shop displayed sheep and goats, skinned and strung up for carving. Customers came up and selected cuts they liked, which the proprietor hacked away for them from the hanging carcasses, so that alongside whole animals hung others that had disappeared to a greater or lesser degree. Two or three stalls away was a wine shop, operated by a friendly, talkative woman in a blue dress, who was apparently in her mid-thirties. She persuaded us to sample the shop's wares, despite our earlier sipping at the winery. I was pleased to find that I could communicate fairly well with her and with other Philistines I encountered in the town. The language really differed little from the Hebrew I had used during my Judahite-mercenary days. The wine shop was our last stop, since we wanted to be on our way back to camp before nightfall, but we had seen enough to allow us to plan on telling Delilah that her native town was a thriving, prosperous place.[7]

The next morning we set out again, and now we began to enter territory I recognized. Soon came Ashdod, then Eltekeh (where Sennacherib had defeated the Kushite Pharaoh, now almost a hundred years ago). While we were marching between these towns, I did my best not to look westward, toward the Sea, not wanting to see the ruins of the seaside fort where I had spent my happy years with Tirzah before the horror that had ended that period of my life. We continued on, with the Shephelah foothills visible on our right, up the flat coastal plain, through its northern portion known as the Plain of Sharon, and soon reached the pass through the Carmel range that led to Megiddo. Beyond Megiddo, we followed the same route that Necho had used earlier, going inland "behind" the Phoinikian cities on the coast, following the river valleys that paralleled it. We stopped at Riblah, where Necho had put Jehoahaz in chains, and continued down the Orontes valley to Hamath. Leaving the river, but hugging the foothills on our west and then our north, we looped northeastward to Aleppo, and then cut due eastward to Karchemish itself.

Using the huge fortress as our base and source of supplies, Necho besieged the heavily outnumbered Babylonian garrison in Kumukh. Perhaps hoping that Nabopolassar would return and lift the siege, the garrison refused to surrender. As the siege stretched out, ultimately lasting four months, the Pharaoh became more and more angry at the resistance, and probably more and more worried that the rescue might in fact come. When, well into the heat of summer, the walls were finally breached, he ordered the entire garrison put to the sword. "One more atrocity in my military record", I thought, as I attempted to go through the motions while inflicting as little mayhem as possible. Python, who had seen more battle action and been close to dying several times, was more sanguine, but in truth most of the slaughter was carried out by our Egyptian fellow soldiers.

Was Necho trying to intimidate Nabopolassar, serving notice that any Babylonian who crossed the Euphrates would die? Did he hold him in such contempt, or believe that possession of Karchemish made his own position so strong, that he had no fear of indulging in needless bloodshed? True, Nabopolassar was old, and perhaps he had lost some of his vigor, but this was the man who had destroyed Nineveh and Harran, and both within the last five years or so! I feared the consequences of this atrocity, even if my new king and paymaster did not. I was relieved when neither I nor Python—indeed only a few of the foreigners—were left with the mostly native Egyptian replacements for the garrison troops now being relieved at Karchemish. Among the Egyptians who were rotated into garrison duty at the fortress was the giant, Petosiris.

It appeared for a while that Necho's evident contempt for the Chaldaean king was justified. Although Nabopolassar did return to the area in the fall of that same year, he only camped at a place called Qurumati (or Kuramati), which was south of Kumukh and east of the Euphrates, and contented himself with staging a few raids across the river. Then in the winter, although he left his army at Qurumati, he himself returned to Babylon. Was the old king's health failing? That seemed likely enough, although only limited information reached us in the delta. Apparently the commander of the Karchemish garrison sensed weakness, because shortly after the departure of the king, he marched out and descended on the encampment of the Babylonians. Mindful of the fate of their garrison at Kumukh, they fled without a battle, heading southeastward toward the heartland of their empire.

As the main part of campaigning season approached, in the late spring, armies headed for the bend of the Euphrates from both directions. Necho led us out again, apparently hoping this time to finish off any Chaldaean hopes of penetrating beyond the river, and maybe even to seize some territory to the east of it as a buffer zone. The Babylonian forces were led this time not by King Nabopolassar—apparently his health really *was* failing—but by his son, the crown prince, Nebuchadnezzar. He was young, though not a mere stripling, and he had some experience under his father, but of course he was an unknown quantity as commander-in-chief of the army. Necho had reason to be sanguine. He would rendezvous with the garrison at Karchemish and then crush the neophyte!

As the world now knows, it did not turn out that way. The prince had the energy and aggressiveness that his father had lost. Instead of continuing the policy of occupying places near the fortress, seemingly with the intent of cutting off supplies and eventually starving the defenders out, he launched an unexpected attack on Karchemish itself. He crossed the river and struck from the landward side, and did it so quickly that our army from Egypt had not yet arrived to reinforce the garrison. The result was a slaughter, with most of the garrison killed right at the fort. Those who managed to flee reached our advancing forces near Hamath, but they had barely begun to inform us of the disaster when the pursuing troops of Nebuchadnezzar fell on us also. I would hear later, from a Greek in Babylonian service, that the claim made in Babylon was that the *entire* army of Egypt was destroyed, with not a single man left alive to return home! That was an overstatement, one such as is normal in royal annals and national chronicles.[8] Python and I certainly escaped, as did Necho himself and many others, but we definitely fled in disarray with the Chaldaean army in hot pursuit. Many had been killed, either at the fort or during the rout, and among them was the giant Petosiris. How I learned of the particulars of his death I will report in the appropriate place.

Nebuchadnezzar pursued us almost to the border of Egypt, not pausing at this time to deal out much destruction on the cities along the way, in his eagerness to finish off our army. In our disorganized and disoriented situation, he might well have succeeded, but for the fortuitous event of his father's death, of which he was informed some weeks after the confrontation at the Euphrates. In all of these eastern monarchies, the death of a king produces a succession crisis. In this particular case there were no rival claimants—no brother of the crown prince would have been put forward immediately after such impressive victories—but the vassal rulers of subject territories traditionally rose in revolt, or at least withheld tribute, when a new king was on the imperial throne, testing for weakness. Nebuchadnezzar knew he had to return immediately to Babylon for his coronation and to make sure that matters were well in control near home, so he set out as soon as he received news of Nabopolassar's death.

We breathed slightly more easily in Egypt, although not for long, since within a month or two the new Chaldaean king was back in the west, asserting his authority over the region of Syria. He operated right through the winter, very much contrary to normal military practice, until the heavy rains finally forced him to decease and return to Babylon. It was obvious, however, that he would return in the next campaigning season, and would likely work his way farther south, probably assailing cities that he had bypassed in his initial fast pursuit of the fleeing Egyptian army. Although Necho spent the remainder of the winter and early spring recruiting and refurbishing our devastated army, Python and I were able to steal a couple of days for a brief visit to Delilah in Naukratis. Her pleasure in our description of the prospering condition of Ashkelon when we had seen it was severely tempered by her awareness (and ours) that if the local king, Aga, should dare to remain a loyal vassal of Egypt and resist the Chaldaean advance, his city and people might well suffer the fate of Karchemish and its garrison.

In other quarters, as I would later hear, the discomfiture of Egypt was greeted not with dismay but with elation. Jeremiah had rejoiced at the destruction of "the army of Pharaoh Necho king of Egypt, which was at Karchemish on the River Euphrates when Nebuchadnezzar king of Babylon defeated it in the fourth year of Jehoiakim son of Josiah, king of Judah".[9] He then launched into verse, with passages such as:

> Why do I see them
> retreating, panic-stricken?
> Their heroes, beaten back,
> are fleeing headlong,
> with not a look behind.
> Terror on every side,
> Yahweh declares!
> No flight for the swift,
> no escape for the strong!
> Up in the north on the River Euphrates,
> they have collapsed, have fallen.

A little further on (as I later read the oracle in Baruch's transcription) he continued:

> ...Lord Yahweh Sabaoth
> is holding a sacrificial feast

in the land of the north,
on the River Euphrates.
Go up to Gilead and fetch balm,
virgin daughter of Egypt!
You multiply remedies in vain,
nothing can cure you!
The nations have heard of your shame,
your wailing fills the world,
for warrior has stumbled against warrior,
and both have fallen together.[10]

Jeremiah was publicly proclaiming in Jerusalem that Nebuchadnezzar, unwittingly acting as the servant of Yahweh, would soon destroy "Pharaoh king of Egypt, his officials, his chief men and all his people, with the whole conglomeration of peoples there"—I suppose this phrase must have included the thousands of foreign mercenaries—as well as "all the kings of the country of the Philistines: Ashkelon, Gaza, Ekron, and what is still left of Ashdod",[11] plus many other rulers, including those in Phoinikia.[12] The prophet did not flinch at listing Jerusalem and Judah among the fated future victims of the Chaldaean conqueror![13] I would live to see how much of his prophecy proved true, and how much did not.

15. THE SHADOW OF NEBUCHADNEZZAR

As expected, the young Chaldaean king was again in the west just a few months later, in early summer. In the northern part of the area he paused only long enough to collect the tribute of cities and peoples he had already reduced to vassalage during his winter campaign, including the Aramaeans of Damascus and Egypt's traditional allies Tyre and Sidon. It was said in Egypt that Jehoiakim of Judah had also sent his tribute, despite the fact that he held his throne as Necho's appointee. Thus Phoinikia and the inland areas of Palaistine were spared attacks, and Nebuchadzezzar could concentrate on taking control of the Philistine coastal plain and creating a clear path to Egypt.[1]

Egypt's Philistine vassals were terrified. Stationed during this crisis in the various frontier forts, we mercenaries were aware of diplomatic missions passing through on their way to Sais carrying urgent pleas from allies under immediate threat. One soldier had actually managed to get a look at a letter from King Adon of Ekron. He reported its content to me and some of my comrades. After the usual effusive praise of Pharaoh, Adon called down the blessings of his own god, Baalshamayn ("Lord of Heaven") on Necho, and then reported that the forces of the king of Babylon had already reached Aphek, which is located in that part of the Shephelah that is west of the former kingdom of Israel (north of the area I had toured in the service of Josiah). Adon begged Necho to send an army to protect him, stressing his own loyalty as Egypt's ally.[2]

Presumably other Philistine client kings, such as Aga of Ashkelon, sent similar desperate pleas, but Necho was in no position to send an army northward. His fears were for the borders of Egypt itself. Whether Jehoiakim in Jerusalem tried to protect himself in both directions by appealing to Pharaoh at the same time that he was rendering tribute to Nebuchadnezzar, I do not know. I learned later that he had declared a major public fast around this time, though I am not sure whether he declared it in anticipation of, or as a reaction to, the Babylonians' devastation of Philistia. Perhaps Nebuchadnezzar had put Ashkelon under siege, but not yet destroyed it, when the fast was proclaimed.[3]

The same prophetic minority in Jerusalem that had greeted the Egyptian disaster at Karchemish with undisguised glee was equally delighted at the imminent destruction of Egypt's Philistine vassals. Jeremiah, the most fearless and radical of them, did not shrink from predicting also the destruction of his own king, Jehoiakim—and no longer as a conditional threat if the king did not change his ways, but as an inevitable judgment of Yahweh that had already been pronounced. He proclaimed that Yahweh was bringing his "servant" Nebuchadnezzar to wreak ruin on Judah and its neighbors, even offering exactitude in his prediction, saying that "this whole country will be reduced to ruin and desolation, and these nations will be enslaved to the king of Babylon for seventy years"![4] Jeremiah had already been banned from the temple for his earlier prophecies against Jerusalem, but now he instructed the scribe Baruch to write down on a scroll all his prophecies thus far, and to go in Jeremiah's stead and read them out publicly in the area of the temple. This happened about the time of Jehoiakim's proclamation of the fast.[5]

Baruch followed instructions, and his reading was reported to the chief royal officials, who summoned him and had him read the scroll again in their presence. They confiscated the scroll and warned Baruch that he and Jeremiah would both be wise to go into hiding. Then it was brought to the king and, in the presence of many of his officials, he had the scroll read to him. It was winter and a fire was going in the brazier used to warm the room. After every three or four columns of text had been read, the king took a knife and cut them off, throwing them into the fire, so that eventually he burned up the entire scroll. Interestingly, I later heard, one of the handful of courtiers present who had urged the king *not* to burn the scroll was my former commander Elnathan son of Achbor—which confirmed my initial fear that he represented the most zealous faction associated with Josiah's revolution. Jehoiakim ordered the arrest of both Jeremiah and Baruch, but was unable to locate them—"Yahweh had hidden them", their admirers would later say.[6]

Although he did not yet venture to show his face, Jeremiah's reaction was defiance. He countered the loss of the first scroll by dictating from memory a second copy of it for Baruch to write down, adding further prophecies and denunciations, including an explicit prediction of the king's ignominious death without issue—indeed, one might almost describe it as a call for his assassination: "...This is what Yahweh says about Jehoiakim king of Judah: He will have no one to occupy the throne of David, and his corpse will be tossed out to the heat of the day and the frost of the night. I shall punish him, his offspring, and his courtiers for their guilt. On them, on the citizens of Jerusalem, and on the people of Judah I shall bring the total disaster which I have decreed for them but to which they have paid no attention".[7]

Jeremiah was not the only one making such "treasonous" pronouncements in Jerusalem. Somewhere around this time, a prophet known as Habakkuk was said to have had a vision that led him also to counsel non-resistance to Nebuchadnezzar. Yahweh is supposed to have said in this man's vision:

...Look, I am stirring up the Chaldaeans,
that fierce and fiery nation
who march miles across country
to seize the homes of others.
They are dreadful and awesome.
a law and authority to themselves.
Their horses are swifter then leopards,
fiercer than wolves at night;
their horsemen gallop on,
their horsemen advance from afar,
swooping like an eagle anxious to feed.
They are all bent on violence,
their faces scorching like an east wind;
they scoop up prisoners like sand.
They scoff at kings,
they despise princes.
They make light of all fortresses:
they heap up earth and take them.
Then the wind changes and is gone...
Guilty is he who makes his strength his god.[8]

As in the case of Jehoiakim's proclaiming of his fast, whether these events and pronouncements preceded or followed the fall of Ashkelon is impossible now to know. Nor does it much matter, since the fate of Delilah's city was inevitable, lacking the support that Egypt, weakened from the preceding year's devastating double defeats, was at the time unable to provide.

Nebuchadnezzar besieged Ashkelon, and the city fell after a short siege of less than two months. Antimenidas of Mytilene, brother of the poet Alkaios, was serving with the Babylonian army, as already he had been for some years. When I encountered him, a few years later in Judah, he became my chief informant about developments in Babylon—the reason, for example, for my awareness that the Babylonians had claimed that every soldier of

Egypt had been killed at Karchemish and Hamath. From the same official chronicle that had provided him with that information, he also told me that Nebuchadnezzar said he had captured King Aga, deporting him and many others, and had "turned the city into a mound and heaps of ruins".[9] Whether Antimenidas could himself read the wedge-shaped Babylonian script, or had had the chronicle passages about events in which he had been involved translated for him, I do not know. Judging by the few tablets I have seen, the script appears even more difficult to learn than Egyptian hieroglyphics (I have already admitted my inability to read either). Several years later, his brother included a passage about the fall of Ashkelon in a poem written in honor of his return to Lesbos, including a reference to many of the city's inhabitants having been sent to the house of Hades.[10] I did not myself view the ruins of Ashkelon until about four years after its fall; in due course, I will describe some of the things I saw there.[11]

This was becoming another winter campaign, but this time much farther from the Euphrates, so Nebuchadnezzar withdrew to Babylon shortly after taking Ashkelon. But just after the spring rains he was back in the immediate vicinity, bringing siege machinery that this time was clearly intended for Gaza, the last remaining Philistine vassal state of Egypt. A prophecy of Jeremiah I later saw may have been produced during this time, although it could just as easily refer to a period shortly after the fall of Gaza:

> ...The day has come
> for all the Philistines to be destroyed,
> for Tyre and Sidon to be stripped
> to the last of their allies.
> Yes, Yahweh is destroying the Philistines,
> the remnant from the Isle of Kaphtor.
> Baldness has befallen Gaza,
> Ashkelon has been reduced to silence.

You who remain in the valley,
how long will you gash yourselves?[12]

Gaza, closer to Egypt, still containing an Egyptian garrison, and defended with desperation because it was obvious that it was the last redoubt before the kingdom itself would be attacked, held out longer than Ashkelon. Moreover, Nebuchadnezzar was not on the scene all the time, but occasionally had to return home, apparently to deal with problems in the eastern portions of his empire. We in Egypt had only guesswork to guide us at this time, of course, since no member of the Egyptian army was currently either north or east of Gaza, so I can provide no details about the Chaldaean king's activities. Suffice it to say that Gaza did eventually fall, and suffered the same sort of deportations that Ashkelon had suffered, although the city was not destroyed, but was occupied by the Babylonians as a base to use for invading Egypt.

Some three years after the fall of Ashkelon, being now in possession of Gaza and having taken the time to build up his forces to what he judged to be irresistible strength, Nebuchadnezzar appeared once again in the coastal plain of Philistia. His manifest intent was marching directly on Egypt, which was now completely stripped of nearby allies. Some Egyptian-Phoinikian connections continued to exist (Necho still was stronger at sea than the Babylonians were), but our so-called allies on the northern coast were also paying tribute to Nebuchadnezzar.

As long as Gaza had held out, it seems that Jehoiakim of Judah—an Egyptian appointee and vassal, you will recall—had held off paying tribute to Nebuchadnezzar for several years. Now that the king of Judah and everyone else assumed that Egypt itself was doomed, he hastened to make a full obeisance. The conqueror even delayed his planned invasion of Egypt briefly to make a side-trip to Jerusalem to accept his tribute and formally acknowledge his vassalage[13]—perhaps in so doing taking at least minimal precaution against any possible attack from behind by an erstwhile Egyptian ally who had proved generally unreliable. No doubt the Babylonian already had plans for dealing with the worrisome Judahite kingdom, but such plans were to be kept in abeyance until the main foe—Egypt—had been dealt with.

If Jeremiah was gleeful after the fall of Ashkelon, he was positively beside himself, now that Gaza had fallen too. Although he was still working in hiding, Baruch recorded his oracles at the time and they were later made public. I translate, albeit with omissions, from that transcription a passage given the title, "The word that came from Yahweh to the prophet Jeremiah when Nebuchadnezzar king of Babylon advanced to attack Egypt":

> Publish it in Egypt,
> proclaim it in Migdol,
> proclaim it in Noph and Tahpanhes!
> Say, "Stand your ground, be prepared,
> for the sword is devouring all around you!"
> Why has Apis fled?
> Why has your Mighty One not stood firm?
> Why, Yahweh has overturned him,
> he has caused many to fall!
> Falling over one another,
> they say, "Up, and back to our own people,
> away from the devastating sword!"
>
> ....
>
> Get your bundle ready for exile,
> fair inhabitants of Egypt!
> Noph will be reduced to a desert,
> desolate, uninhabited.
> Egypt was a splendid heifer,
> but a gadfly from the north has settled on her.

The mercenaries she had with her, these too
were like fattened calves:
but they too have taken to their heels,
have all run away, not held their ground,
for their day of disaster has overtaken them,
their time for being punished.
Hear her hissing like a snake
as they advance in force
to fall on her with their axes,
like woodcutters,
they will fell her forest, Yahweh declares,
however impenetrable it was,
for they are more numerous than locusts,
there is no counting them.
The daughter of Egypt is put to shame,
handed over to a people from the north.[14]

This fearful outcome—the "Noph" destined for destruction, remember, was none other than the great city of Memphis—certainly looked likely at the time. But I have already described how "true" prophets were sometimes erroneous in their predictions. Jeremiah's words about us mercenaries were decidedly unjustified. We stood and fought, and so did our Egyptian fellow soldiers. Nor was Egypt as defenseless as many believed.

16. FLEETING TRIUMPHS

When the Assyrians had invaded Egypt sixty or seventy years earlier, the delta and the entrances to the valley of the Nile were barely defended. The Kushite kings of that time, based in Nubia and Upper Egypt, especially Thebes (although they had made Memphis their capital), were not themselves particularly strong in the delta region. But the Saites, delta natives, had over the years greatly augmented the fortifications protecting Lower Egypt against attacks from the northeast.

Although the Babylonians now occupied Gaza, just south of it was another Egyptian-held town, which I believe is the place the Greeks call Raphia, or very near to it. There was another town on the sandy strip between the great coastal lake and the Sea, called Ba'al Sapon (its name reveals the influence of the Canaanites who had long formed a major component of the population of the eastern delta). Some 200 stades west of this was the port of Pelousion, which the Saites had established at the easternmost mouth of the Nile. Following the Pelousiac branch upstream another forty-five stades or so would bring an invader to the great fortress of Migdol, a word meaning "tower", the real guardpost of the frontier.

Even that was not the extent of Egypt's defenses, since the very old site of Sile (*Tjel* in Egyptian)—which had been the chief border fort at the time the Assyrians invaded—was still fortified and posed another barrier about 180 stades farther southwest. Anyone who struck directly into the delta beyond this point would find himself in impenetrable marshes, but if he stayed on the road for 180 more stades going westward he would reach Daphnai, the fortified city inhabited mostly by current and demobilized Greek mercenaries! And there was yet another fortified place 225 stades southwest of us, called Weskhupri.

All these defenses would confront an army invading along the coast and down the eastern branch of the Nile, but the defenses could not be circumvented by swinging inland and following the desert route my companions and I had taken from Judah through Kadesh-Barnea. Here a wall stood at the edge of the desert, and then any invader following the valley in which Necho's canal was being dug would come upon his new fortress of Pithom. Beyond that, some 225 stades, was yet another fort at Pi-Sopdu (Per-Soped).[1]

Nebuchadnezzar in fact took the coastal route, and Necho was able to concentrate his forces and meet the Chaldaean in an all-out battle near Migdol. Casualties were heavy on both sides—I saw several of my fellow mercenaries killed and wounded, although Python and I survived with nothing worse than a sword-slash on his left leg that required a bit of recovery time in our camp. In terms of damage inflicted, it could have been called a drawn battle, but in its consequences it was a clear-cut Egyptian victory: Nebuchadnezzar abandoned his plans to invade Egypt and went home to Babylon to rebuild his damaged army. Moreover, we were able to follow up the battle with a retaking of Gaza from the withdrawing Babylonians.[2]

Having participated in this great battle, it was clear to me that a Greek who later told me that Necho had made a dedication to Apollo at Didyma in honor of his victory at "Megiddo" had simply misinterpreted the Hellenic transliteration *Magdolos*, which must have referred in fact to Migdol. This was a great victory over an immensely powerful opponent, infinitely more impressive than the mere skirmish with Josiah at Megiddo. I was certainly able to tell, since I fought in both battles. I even heard it said that Necho chose to make his dedication at the temple near Miletos, in a Greek-Karian area, specifically to honor the valor of his Ionian and Karian soldiers![3]

We camped at the place where we had stopped a few years earlier, north of Gaza. At that time, Python and I had staged our quick reconnaissance of nearby Ashkelon, with the happy intent of describing the appearance of her native city to Delilah. Now I felt I had to go back to see what had been done to the place by the Babylonians, even though the injured Python would not be able to accompany me (he had already been sent back to the Ionian Encampment). Delilah would not be happy this time, but she would want to know what had happened, and how bad it was.

It was very bad indeed. The hill that had once been Ashkelon was hardly recognizable anymore as a city. Its walls had been knocked down; very few towers were left standing. Within the town itself, everything had been pillaged and burned. The fires had been so hot that mud-brick walls had in many places been virtually converted into glass! By its general location facing the Sea, I was able to find the neighborhood that Python and I had visited before, with its winery and shops. All had been destroyed, and not simply burned down, but before the burning the soldiers had apparently entered and smashed everything they could get their hands on—almost every jar and pot was shattered. The roof of one of the places I had visited had fallen in, revealing a small incense altar on its top that I had not noticed before.

But the really disturbing sight confronted me in a room next to the wineshop where the friendly, talkative Philistine woman had greeted us. There, behind a group of broken wine-jars, lay the remains—essentially bare of flesh thanks to the passage of four years—of a woman whose scrap of blue garment appeared to me to have come from the dress our hostess had worn. Seemingly she had tried to hide from the rampaging soldiers, but had been unsuccessful; her skull had been smashed in. I had no time or equipment to give her any kind of burial, and anyway she was only one of hundreds whose remains were lying around the city, so I just left her where she was. In my lifetime, at least—and I am writing more than thirty years later, despite the vividness of my memory of the awful scene—no one ever rebuilt or resettled Ashkelon. Delilah's home town had ceased to exist.[4]

Despite the gloomy effects of my trip to the ruins of Ashkelon, which I dutifully described to a moist-eyed Delilah the next time I was able to visit Naukratis, the ensuing period in Egypt was one of renewed hope and confidence. Nebuchadnezzar did not show his face in the west again for almost two solid years, and even then not in full force. Necho felt safe enough on his northeastern front to lead a naval expedition upriver against the Kushites, who, under their new and energetic king Anlamani, seemed to be contemplating an attempt to recover control of Upper Egypt.[5] I did not participate in this incursion, so I cannot report anything about it in detail. Obviously it did not accomplish too much, since Necho's son Psammetichos would have to organize a similar expedition a few years later—one in which I *did* participate, and on which I shall report in its proper place.

Necho abandoned work on his canal, despite the thousands of workers' lives it had already cost, because, it was said, of an unfavorable prophecy he had heard. On the other hand, he received some utterly amazing news concerning another project he had launched a couple of years earlier. The Phoinikian sailors he had sent down the Red Sea coast to explore for possible trading advantages had been presumed lost at sea, given the passage of time, but now they reappeared—not from the Red Sea, but on the coast of the western delta, having sailed in through what the Greeks call the Pillars of Herakles, after completely circumnavigating Libya! They reported various wonders they had seen, of varying degrees of believability. One thing that made some listeners dubious was their adamant insistence that during a major portion of their journey the sun was on their right as they sailed west![6]

The Egyptians were not the only ones who took heart at the absence of Nebuchadnezzar's forces in the area. Jehoiakim of Judah always had to walk a tightrope between the great powers on both sides of his kingdom, especially now that the cities of Philistia were mostly in ruins. But now he was emboldened to withhold tribute from the Babylonians for three consecutive years, and to draw closer to the Egyptians, whose vassal he had originally been.[7] Perhaps as a result of his saving of resources by not paying tribute, not to mention his employment of forced labor, Jehoiakim built himself an elaborate new palace. Predictably, this was denounced by Jeremiah, who had come out of hiding after the imminent danger from Nebuchadnezzar had passed, relying on the protection of his powerful friends. Baruch wrote down the prophet's words as follows:

> Disaster for the man
> who builds his house without uprightness,
> his upstairs rooms without fair judgment,
> who makes his fellow-man work for nothing,
> without paying him his wages,
> who says, "I shall build myself a spacious palace
> with airy upstairs rooms",
> who makes windows in it,
> panels it with cedar, and paints it vermilion.[8]

Jeremiah went on to compare Jehoiakim unfavorably with his father Josiah, the father being said to have shown concern for the needy, while the son shed innocent blood.[9]

I was told that Jehoiakim's wife, and the mother of his successor, was the daughter of "Elnathan of Jerusalem",[10] whom I was guessing was the same person as Elnathan son of Achbor, my former commander. Perhaps only the support of persons with such high connections could embolden even a prophet as radical as Jeremiah to predict again a disgraceful death for the king, concluding his oracle with these words "of Yahweh":

> No lamenting for him,
> "My poor brother! My poor sister!"
> No lamenting for him,
> "His poor lordship! His poor majesty!"
> He will have a donkey's funeral
> —dragged away and thrown
> out of the gates of Jerusalem.[11]

Finally, Nebuchadnezzar appeared again west of the Euphrates, but he himself came no farther than Syria, only sending out parties to ravage the desert Arabs and returning home within three or four months.[12] Even this trivial activity was enough to prompt Jeremiah, seemingly the Chaldaean's greatest admirer, to inveigh against the Arabs of Kedar and Hazor:

> Up! March on Kedar,
> destroy the sons of the east!
> Let their tents and their flocks be captured,
> their tent-cloths and all their gear;
> let their camels be seized
> and the shout go up, "Terror on every side!"
> Away! Get into hiding as fast as you can,
> inhabitants of Hazor, Yahweh declares,
> for Nebuchadnezzar king of Babylon
> has made a plan against you...[13]

—the reader can see the general tenor of the oracle. When he departed for Babylon, Nebuchadnezzar left small contingents who were assigned to raid the borders of Judah—some Chaldaeans, but mostly his Aramaean, Moabite, and Ammonite allies.[14] Oddly, Jeremiah, who seemed to regard every incursion against Judah or any other kingdom or city by Nebuchadnezzar himself as praiseworthy obedience to the will of Yahweh, nonetheless produced oracles denouncing the Moabites and Ammonites.[15] I am not certain, however, that the raids of this particular year prompted the denunciations of which I later acquired copies; hostility between Judah and its eastern neighbors was endemic.

Although Nebuchadnezzar's renewed activities had thus far been rather limited, there was increasing concern in Egypt. Necho saw no need yet to call up the army in force, but he decided at least to make a show of support for his reinstated vassal Jehoiakim by sending troops to garrison some of the desert fortresses in the Negeb. These forces would establish an Egyptian presence on the fringes of Judah, serve notice to the Babylonians that their incursions were to be discouraged, reassure the Judahites—and could be easily withdrawn if a full-scale invasion from Babylonia should be mounted. Python stayed behind to complete the healing of his wound. Some troops were left at Kadesh-Barnea. I found myself with the contingent sent to the fortress of Arad, south of Hebron.

I had been there before, about fifteen or twenty years earlier, during the days of Josiah's revolution. It was there I had first encountered the vicious, power-mad courtier Asaiah, who initiated the chain of murders that alienated me from service for the state of Judah.[16] I was surprised to find that I recognized the commander of the Judahite garrison. He was Eliashib, the young cavalryman who had been left in charge of making certain arrangements at the fort when Asaiah had led Benaiah's troop of mercenaries deeper into the southern desert, into Edomite territory. I assumed that the expertise in the region that Eliashib had gained in that first assignment had led one of Josiah's sons to appoint him commander at Arad. He had been here for a considerable time already and, as I later observed, would be here—at

least intermittently, whenever the fort was under Judahite control—for quite a bit longer.

Unfortunately, the west's period of comparative tranquility was about to come to an end. Finally, almost two years after the disaster at Migdol had led him to withdraw and begin refurbishing his army, Nebuchadnezzar set out again for the transeuphrates region with that army, now restored to full strength and well-drilled. As he approached the borders of Judah, even the tent-dwelling Rechabites, who had taken a vow in the name of their ancestor Jonadab son of Rechab never to drink wine, build houses, sow seed, or plant vineyards, moved for protection within the walls of Jerusalem. The prophet Jeremiah greeted them with enthusiasm, praising their strict-Yahwist constancy in comparison with the "apostasy" he saw all around him in king, court, and citizenry.[17]

At this most critical moment, King Jehoiakim son of Josiah, having reigned for eleven years, suddenly died—a young man, still in his middle-to-late thirties. Jeremiah, who had practically called for his assassination, certainly did not lament his death, which naturally he attributed to Jehoiakim's lack of zeal for his father's program. Jeremiah's predictions that the king would die sonless and be cast out unburied proved false, however—as in retrospect did about half of his pronouncements, despite his continuing reputation as a great prophet. The deceased king was buried in the royal cemetery, and his young son by the daughter of Elnathan succeeded him in regular fashion.[18]

Exactly *how* young this son was is a bit uncertain, at least for those who, like myself, were not in Jerusalem to see his coronation. I heard it said he was eighteen—which would have made his father barely eighteen when he was born, certainly not impossible but perhaps unlikely—and I also heard it said that he was only eight years old.[19] The reason that I can still be uncertain, so many years later, is that he

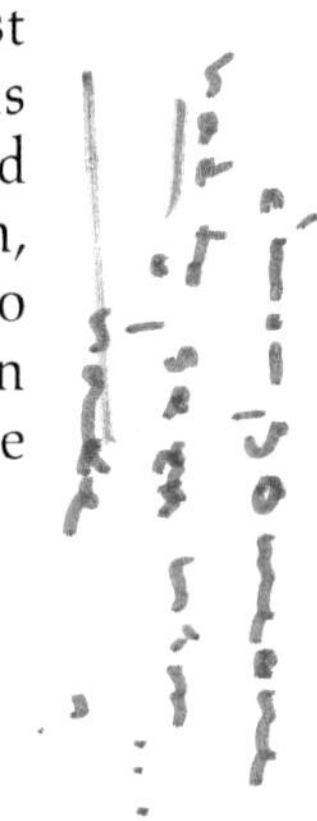

sat on the throne for only three months until he was taken away to Babylon, to remain there for the rest of his life. He is, I am told, still very much alive as I write this memoir, which would put him now in either his late thirties or his late forties.

But I am getting ahead of my story! The new king was called Jehoiachin. Perhaps because his name sounded so much like his father's, he was also known as Jeconiah, and this was even sometimes shortened to Coniah. Within a month of his accession, Nebuchadnezzar had put the city of Jerusalem under siege.[20] At Arad, when he heard of these developments, the commander Eliashib decided there was no advantage in keeping one small troop of soldiers from Egypt around to suffer the Chaldaeans' revenge for Migdol; we were certainly too few to come to the aid of the besieged capital.[21] Eliashib sent us home by the road through the Negeb, before the Babylonian army could approach Arad. With us he sent a letter explaining his decision to the Egyptian authorities, sealed with a *bulla* stamped with the signet he kept on a string around his neck,[22] so that no blame for cowardice might attach to us. I assume that by this kind gesture he saved our lives, and always afterward I held him in great respect—another competent and sensible Judahite commander in the mold of my lamented friend Benaiah.

Joined by the contingent that we had left at Kadesh-Barnea—Eliashib had sent also a letter to their commander requesting that they be allowed to accompany us—we made our way back to the safety of Egypt as quickly as we could. In the Encampment, I was pleased to see that Python was by now pretty much fully recovered. At his insistence, we very soon planned another trip to the house of Delilah. I was always delighted to spend my time in long conversations with her, but Python, frustrated by months of inactivity, was eager to see Artemisia!

I would not see Judah again for another six or seven years, but my experiences there of course made me quite interested in developments within that kingdom. I was able to find out enough to piece together a fairly reliable chronology of events prior to the next time I was sent there, which I will try to report in sequence with events in an around Egypt.

17. FIRST SIEGE OF JERUSALEM

Perhaps the younger age suggested for the new king of Judah, Jehoiachin or Jeconiah or Coniah (whichever we may prefer to call him) was really the correct one, since Jeremiah's denunciations of him, as recorded by Baruch, tended to link him with his mother. Baruch's own prose version of one oracle went as follows: "As I live, Yahweh declares, even if Coniah son of Jehoiakim, king of Judah, were the signet ring on my right hand, I would still wrench you off! I shall hand you over to those determined to kill you, to those you dread, to Nebuchadnezzar king of Babylon, to the Chaldaeans. I shall hurl you and the mother who bore you into another country; you were not born there but you will both die there. They will not return to the country to which they desperately long to return".[1] The same linkage showed up in the prophet's verse:

> Tell the king and queen mother,
> "Sit in a lower place,
> since your glorious crown
> has fallen from your head.
> The towns of the Negeb are shut off
> with no one to give access to them.
> All Judah has been deported,
> deported wholesale".[2]

There was a kind of vicious elation in Jeremiah's crowing over the fate of the hapless boy (or youth) who had found his capital under siege barely a month after his unexpected elevation to the throne. I suspect that the following pronouncement, which in the scroll I saw follows directly after the passage of Baruch's prose quoted a moment ago, was actually delivered some years later, during Jehoiachin's exile, a fate shared with him by several of his sons, who were perhaps born in Babylon:

> Is he a shoddy broken pot,
> this man Coniah,
> a crock that no one wants?
> Why are he and his offspring ejected,
> hurled into a country
> they know nothing of?
> O land, land, land,
> listen to the word of Yahweh!
> Yahweh says this,
> "List this man as: Childless;
> a man who made a failure of his life,
> since none of his offspring will succeed
> in occupying the throne of David,
> or ruling in Judah again".[3]

In any event, despite the much-evoked example of Hezekiah, despite the widespread belief in Jerusalem that "Mount Zion" was protected by Yahweh and hence impregnable,[4] the city was surrendered in the early spring, after a two-month siege. Chronicles maintained in Babylon that refer to the seventh year of Nebuchadnezzar agree entirely, I have been told, with the events as remembered in Jerusalem and as recorded by Baruch in his written account of prophecies and occurrences associated with Jeremiah.[5]

Probably the quick surrender accepted by the young king, whether on his own initiative or at the behest of his advisors, is all that saved the city from destruction—that and the fact that the actual rebel, the disloyal vassal, his father Jehoiakim, was already dead even before the city was besieged. The Chaldaean had no reason to bear the youth any personal enmity, and the brief siege had probably involved few casualties and little expense. Certainly the latter had been amply recouped by carrying off much treasure from the palace and temple. Nebuchadnezzar's chronicle boasted of the "heavy tribute" he took away from Jerusalem.

There were, as prophecies already quoted make clear, deportations. In addition to the young king, his mother, and all his immediate family, numerous courtiers (including the royal eunuchs) and notables, along with craftsmen, especially metalworkers, were taken away to Babylonia. Baruch provides a quite specific and believable figure for the deportations of year seven of Nebuchadnezzar: 3023 persons. Other versions circulating in post-siege Jerusalem were greatly exaggerated; numbers as high as 10,000 were reported to me![6] Among the deportees with Jehoiachin were certain prophets, as is clear from the mutual denunciations in which Jeremiah later engaged with some of them. Likewise there were priests. One exile at this time, Ezekiel son of Buzi, who later became famous among the deportees for the vividness—and eroticism—of his visions, was seemingly *both* a priest and a prophet. Oddly, there is no tradition of any interaction or exchange of messages between him and Jeremiah, though they seemingly worked simultaneously for many years, and each was very much concerned with people and events in the locale where the other operated.

Nebuchadnezzar appointed "a king of his own choice" or "of his liking" (alternate ways the phrase in the Babylonian chronicle was translated for me by my Greek source) in Judah. The new appointee, Mattaniah, was the full brother (that is, they had the same mother) of the former king Jehoahaz. He was thus the uncle of the deposed Jehoiachin. As Necho had once changed the name of his appointee, Shallum, to Jehoiakim, so Nebuchadnezzar gave a new name to Mattaniah. He would henceforth be known as Zedekiah.[7] He became the third son of Josiah to sit on the throne of Judah. During my lifetime at least, and seemingly forever, he was to be the *last* king of the "house of David".

Every vassal, of course, takes an oath of loyalty to his sovereign. It would seem that the oath sworn by Zedekiah was specifically an oath by Yahweh. At least that must be what underlies the story that the exiled prophet Ezekiel later denounced him severely for breaking his oath to the Babylonian king.[8] It is difficult for a Greek like myself to understand the politics of prophets such as Jeremiah and Ezekiel, who seemed to see loyalty to a vassalage imposed by overwhelming power as a higher virtue than loyalty to one's own people or nation. It is obvious that Judahite kings themselves did not share this attitude. *Their* loyalties—and disloyalties—were fully intelligible to Greek political thinkers: they looked to their own, or their country's, interests, and put on or put off loyalties to foreign sovereigns according to what they saw as expediency or advantage.

The prophets' attitudes in such matters once again underline the disparity of worldview between Ionians and easterners. In any Greek city, a man who spoke as Jeremiah did would very swiftly have been executed as a traitor. There were many in Jerusalem, including some who were highly placed, who did in fact urge that the prophet be dealt with in precisely that way. They were even at times powerful enough to force him to go into hiding or (as the reader shall soon see) to have him incarcerated. But he persisted, never silent, rarely conciliatory, and even when the kingdom of Judah was no more, Jeremiah was still standing and still issuing denunciations as fearlessly as ever. His honesty and courage provoked even in me a grudging admiration, but if he had been tried before a Greek *dikasterion,* I would have cast my juror's ballot for his condemnation!

One of the oracles delivered by Jeremiah against Jehoiachin, the reader will recall, had included the verses:

> The towns of the Negeb are shut off
> with no one to give access to them.[9]

I would discover the implication of those lines when I returned to Judah some years after the first siege of Jerusalem. Encouraged by the invading Babylonians, the Edomites across the Arabah had swept westward into the largely undefended southern desert country claimed by Judah. They had seized several towns and fortresses, generally destroying them once it became clear that post-siege Judah, now protected as a vassal state of the Babylonian empire, would be allowed to reclaim them.

Among the places in the Negeb that the Edomite invaders destroyed had been the fortress of Arad. It seemed that the garrison commander Eliashib, by allowing us Egyptian mercenaries to depart at the beginning of hostilities, had saved us not from the Babylonians themselves (who had concentrated their efforts on the capital), but from the Edomites.[10] Who knows? It was even possible that a remembrance of the treatment, some twenty years earlier, of Edomite shrines and Edomite priests by another group of mercenaries—employed by Josiah king of Judah and directed by the unlamented zealot Asaiah—might have encouraged the invaders to take savage reprisals against us. Had that occurred, one at least of the Egyptian-employed mercenaries might reasonably have been considered deserving of his punishment—myself, Archon of Miletos, the only soldier common to both contingents![11]

I know about Arad, and about Eliashib, because I would see both the fort and the commander again. He had not been killed, but had managed to escape. Within the next few years he would be charged with the duty of rebuilding the fortress, and he would once again be its commander when I was stationed there at the time of the *second* Babylonian siege of Jerusalem. For a man who has spent his entire adult life in exile, wandering around large areas of the regions east and south of the Great Sea, I am struck by how often people and places and even closely analogous situations have entered and re-entered my life.

18. LIMBO ON ALL FRONTS

I spent the next few years entirely in Egypt, since the Babylonian presence in the transeuphrates region was not sufficient to warrant bringing Pharaoh's army northward. My knowledge of developments both in Babylonia and in Judah during this period, therefore, is only partial, sketchy, and belatedly acquired.[1] That is, it was mostly acquired only when, almost ten years after the first siege of Jerusalem, I was in Judah again at the time of the second siege and destruction of the city, and in contact with my Greek-mercenary source for events in far-off Mesopotamia.

Antimenidas of Mytilene, the aforementioned source, was not himself fully informed about these years, although he had spent them (in the midst of a long career) as a mercenary in Babylonian service. Matters were sufficiently chaotic, and elements of the Chaldaean armed forces were moved around rapidly and frequently enough, that a soldier involved in one area could be quite ignorant of important developments elsewhere.

In the winter after the deportation of Jehoiachin, he told me, Nebuchadnezzar had spent only a single month in the west, not even venturing beyond Karchemish. Some months after that, the Babylonian monarch had been challenged by an invasion launched by his Elamite neighbors to the east. When Jeremiah, in Jerusalem, heard of the conflict between Babylon and Elam, the ever-vigilant defender of Nebuchadnezzar responded with a few verses of denunciation directed toward the Elamites.[2] The ancient kingdom of Elam had long figured in the interplay between the eastern powers, certainly in the time of Assyrian domination and apparently even earlier. Perhaps trouble had already been brewing, and that may have explained why the Chaldaean army had made such a brief appearance in the west. This became a fierce struggle that preoccupied Nebuchadnezzar for the better part of two years.

Worse, from his standpoint, it seemingly led to an uprising within Babylonia itself, and indeed within the Babylonian army. My informant Antimenidas remained loyal, as did most of the Greek and west-Asian mercenaries, but seemingly some of the native Babylonian commanders had ambitions of their own. The revolt was put down only with difficulty—and with Nebuchadnezzar's customary ferocity. By the winter of the third year after the siege of Jerusalem, the Chaldaean king was able to tour Syria collecting tribute again, but in the west the widespread perception was that he was not as powerful, not as unchallengeable, as he had been a few years earlier.

Also around this time, or slightly later, the priest-prophet Ezekiel, living among the Judahite exiles at a place called Tel Abib beside a large canal known locally as the "River" Chebar, began testifying to visions he attributed to Yahweh. Since there was fairly regular—if slow—communication between the exiles and their countrymen still in Judah, the visions and prophecies of Ezekiel were bandied about Jerusalem as freely as were the pronouncements of the local prophets such as Jeremiah. One reason this was so was probably because Ezekiel's visions were largely about *Jerusalem*! He would see himself somehow miraculously transported by Yahweh to Jerusalem and into various precincts of the temple, where he would report having observed the behavior (usually culticly reprehensible) of specific named individuals within the priestly hierarchy.[3] Like Jeremiah, Ezekiel too found himself beset by false prophets, whom he denounced with comparable vitriol.[4] My contemporary awareness of the pronouncements of Ezekiel has been augmented by a scroll I acquired later, during my retirement, that claimed to contain his oracles. This enables me at times to report his actual words, or at least the scroll's version of them, whether accurate or not.

In Jerusalem, the young king Zedekiah (he had been twenty-one years old at the time of his appointment by Nebuchadnezzar) found himself the nominal head of a nation sharply divided between loyalty to Babylonia, whose tribute-paying vassal he was, and wishes for independence, usually conceived of as necessitating support from Egypt. As was the case with most disagreements that we Greeks would think of as "political", the issues in Judah were posed in religious terms, with prophets proclaiming the will of Yahweh on opposite sides of every issue. If the will, or the help, of any *other* gods was being invoked at this time, I have not heard that fact reported, so perhaps the monotheistic attitude of the reforms instituted by the new king's father was indeed taking hold. Or perhaps those on whom I relied for information were themselves monotheists and had tailored their reportage to give this impression! At any rate, Jeremiah certainly took the position that all the "non-Judahite", "non-Yahwistic" elements of the pre-Josianic religion and cult of Judah had been allowed to come back to the fore under Zedekiah. I assumed that at most the efforts of Josiah, in which I had been an unenthusiastic participant, had succeeded in driving traditional elements of the cult underground, and that only constant governmental and priestly vigilance could keep them there.

Although Jeremiah had been eager to denounce Jehoiachin, now he had for some reason decided that Yahweh was on the side of the deportees and opposed to the king's successor and all those remaining in Jerusalem and Judah! He compared the exiles and the population remaining in Judah to baskets of good and rotten figs, respectively.[5] When, early in his reign, Zedekiah sent as envoys to Nebuchadnezzar the sons of Shaphan and Hilkiah (the two who had "found" the "law of Moses" and reported it to

Josiah), Jeremiah had prevailed on them to take a letter he had written to the exiles. In it he urged them to settle down, raise crops, reproduce, work for the good of Babylon and pray to Yahweh on its behalf, and rely on his (Jeremiah's) prediction that in seventy years they would be allowed to return to Judah. He denounced "those who prophesy lies" in Yahweh's name among the exiles, mentioning a couple of them specifically for denunciation and execution by Nebuchadnezzar. He cursed another man among the exiles for having written a letter to a priest in Jerusalem asking why a "crazy fellow posing as a prophet" such as Jeremiah of Anathoth had not been put in the stocks! Probably the king had not been informed of Jeremiah's letter's contents in advance, since in it was also a strong denunciation of "the king now occupying the throne of David and all the people living in this city", saying that Yahweh would make them like the aforementioned rotten figs.[6]

Baruch's account of events seems to imply that in about the fourth year of his reign, Zedekiah had called together in Jerusalem ambassadors from Edom, Moab, the Ammonites, Tyre, and Sidon. The purpose of the conference is not described, but a reasonable inference would be the forming of a united front to resist the power of Nebuchadnezzar. That certainly appears to have been what Jeremiah assumed, since he made an appearance before the envoys wearing a wooden yoke, telling them to inform their respective kings that each must bend his neck to the yoke of the king of Babylon, as Zedekiah himself must do also. Subsequently, a rival prophet called Hananiah of Gibeon snatched the yoke from Jeremiah's neck and broke it, proclaiming (as quoted by Baruch): "Yahweh Sabaoth, the God of Israel, says this, 'I have broken the yoke of the king of Babylon. In exactly two years' time I shall bring back all the vessels of the temple of Yahweh which Nebuchadnezzar king of Babylon took away from here and carried off to Babylon. And I shall also bring back Jeconiah son of Jehoiakim, king of Judah, and all the exiles of Judah who have gone to Babylon, Yahweh declares, for I shall break the yoke of the king of Babylon'". Jeremiah replied by saying that the broken wooden yoke would only be replaced by an iron yoke, and by predicting Hananiah's death within the year—which Baruch says did indeed occur. We are not told by what agency.[7]

Apparently just after Zedekiah's conference, he had been called to Babylon to explain himself to his overlord. He seems to have been successful, since he returned to Jerusalem and continued to rule. What is most interesting about this journey is another communication sent from Jeremiah to the exiles, that was carried by the lord chamberlain, Seraiah, who accompanied the king to Babylon (he may have been Baruch's brother; at any rate, their fathers had the same name).[8] In this scroll, despite the prophet's constant expressions of support for Babylon to the detriment of his own land, now eventual disaster was called down upon Babylon also, once its duty of chastising Judah in the service of Yahweh had been completed. From the scroll, Seraiah was to read aloud to the assembled exiles the words: "You, Yahweh, have promised to destroy this place, so that no one will live here ever again, neither human nor animal; and it will be desolate forever". Then a stone was to be tied to the scroll and it was to be thrown into the middle of the Euphrates, as Seraiah intoned: "So shall Babylon sink, never to rise again from the disaster which I am going to bring on her".[9] Again, we have to surmise that the prophet's letters were transported without any prior reading by the Judahite authorities; Zedekiah would scarcely have permitted a courtier accompanying him to carry any such message to Babylon when he had been summoned to justify his own conduct and preserve his hold on the throne! No uprising of western vassals occurred at this time; any maneuvering that had been attempted had proved ineffective.[10]

In Egypt itself during this period, concern was less with the Babylonians than with the Kushites. Necho had only recently returned from his upriver expedition, intended to limit the northward encroachments of the aggressive Nubian king Anlamani. Although he had ruled for only about fifteen years, Necho was not young—it must be recalled that his father before him had ruled for over half a century, so he had already been well up in years when he had become king. Now, perhaps weakened by the exertions of the upriver journey, or having acquired some sickness in the unfamiliar Nubian climate, Pharaoh Necho died. He was mummified and buried with the usual elaborate ceremonies in the royal tombs near the temple of the goddess Neith in Sais. He departed his earthly life with three living daughters and only one son. The son, named Psammetichos for his illustrious grandfather, was himself already fairly advanced in years, and was moreover, it was whispered among the foreign mercenaries, of rather frail constitution. Still, he manifestly shared his father's aggressive personality, and was determined to continue his policies of reasserting Egyptian power, both southward and northward. There was no succession crisis; Psammetichos had long commanded units of his father's armies, so these were not years of unrest within the Encampments.[11]

My brother Python and I had been working at learning to speak the Egyptian language, with some success, though neither of us could master the difficult script enough to think of reading or writing it at the time. We managed to travel about a bit within the delta area, and especially to make several trips to Naukratis. There we purchased a certain number of books and some wine from various Greek traders, but primarily we visited the house of Delilah.

Delilah, ever mindful of my needs, told me that she thought that I deserved a bit of long-deferred recreation. She had a new employee, she said, whom I would probably like—a refugee from Judah, seemingly free-born, even aristocratic, but without defenders or resources, and therefore forced to choose between prostitution and starvation.

She had told Delilah that her name was "Gomer", which is what the prophet Hosea had called his unfaithful wife.[12] Delilah had been unable to persuade her to reveal her real name. Her guess was that the young woman had come from a respectable family and did not want to bring infamy on it through her current profession, so Delilah had finally yielded and accepted Gomer as her name. That was how I was introduced to her.

Probably she did not expect a Greek to know the implication of the name she had taken, so I did not bother to let her know that I did, although we conversed more in Hebrew than in Greek, since she had learned but little of the latter. Otherwise, we communicated extremely well! I was quite taken with her, and not merely because of the long period of celibacy I had recently endured. She was lively and enthusiastic and almost as beautiful as my lost Tirzah. I promised to ask for her again on my next visit, and she expressed pleasure at my saying this. Of course I did not know at the time whether this was merely a whore's play-acting (Never alienate a potential regular customer, especially one who treats you with kindness and appreciation!) or genuinely meant. It turned out that it was the latter. Delilah's judgment, as always, was sound.

Our old servant and surrogate mother was beginning to show her age a bit more, as we had all been in Egypt for several years now, but she was still vigorous and very much still her own mistress. Although I continued to spend much time in conversation with her, in subsequent visits I devoted increasing attention to the mysterious Gomer, who persisted in not revealing her real name either to me or to Delilah. Python could hardly be separated from Artemisia during the entirety of any of our visits to Naukratis!

More would happen fairly soon, indeed quite climactic events, in the country of my former paymasters, and I would in fact be back in Judah again to witness developments first-hand. But before that would come an adventure that would provide an entirely new experience for me. I had missed Necho's expedition into Nubia, but both Python and I would participate in his son's. En route, we would also see most of Upper Egypt for the first time, having operated up to this time almost exclusively within the delta and its eastern approaches.

19. EXPEDITION TO NUBIA

Necho's naval foray into Nubia had been directed against the Kushite king Anlamani. Now both those monarchs had died, with their dispute unsettled.[1] The new king of Kush, Anlamani's younger brother Aspelta, had reportedly brought his army north of the second cataract, as far down the Nile as the great riverside temples built by the most famous of the ancient Egyptian Pharaohs, Ramses the Great, centuries ago, at a time when Egypt had firmly controlled Lower Nubia.[2] If Aspelta had encroached so far, it was feared in Sais, he might very well be contemplating a full-scale invasion of Egypt itself, beyond the usually-recognized frontier at the first cataract just above Elephantine. The new Pharaoh resolved to anticipate any such move by launching his own preemptive invasion of Nubia, in the third year of his reign.[3]

A garrison at Elephantine had been maintained since the time of the earlier Psammetichos, whose namesake and grandson led our expedition. Its troops had always been *alloglossoi*, mercenaries of foreign speech, Greeks and others.[4] Their stationing on the southern border of Egypt was analogous to the stationing of my own contingent of foreign mercenaries on the northeastern border. Many of the men with whom I had been serving had rotated in and out of service with the southern garrison, usually for stretches of three years. It was for most of them an unwelcome assignment—isolated in very hot desert country, far less congenial than the comparative lushness of the delta, and much more completely out of touch with our homelands or any travelers who might have brought us news from home. It was safe,

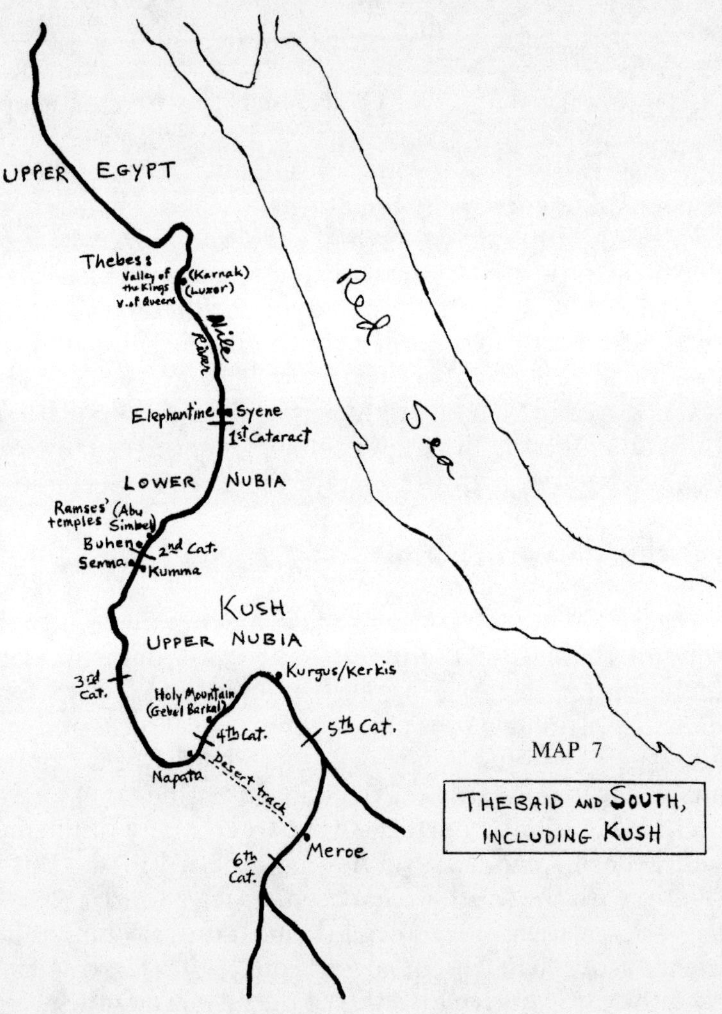
UPPER EGYPT
Thebes:
Valley of the Kings
V. of Queens
(Karnak)
(Luxor)
Nile River
Red Sea
Elephantine
Syene
1st Cataract
LOWER NUBIA
Ramses' temples
(Abu Simbel)
Buhen
2nd Cat.
Semna
Kumma
KUSH
UPPER NUBIA
3rd Cat.
Holy Mountain (Gebel Barkal)
Kurgus/Kerkis
4th Cat.
5th Cat.
Napata
Desert track
Meroe
6th Cat.
THEBAID AND SOUTH, INCLUDING KUSH

MAP 7

at least, from the armies of the ferocious Nebuchadnezzar, but the Kushites were fierce fighters as well.

This, however, was not to be a border raid involving only the southern garrison itself, but a large-scale riverborne invasion by the Egyptian army, considerably bigger than the expedition that Necho had led a few years earlier. Many—though of course not all—of the soldiers normally stationed in the north were to be called up. Never having seen Upper Egypt, much less Nubia itself, I was halfway eager to be involved, and I preferred the idea of an invasion occupying one campaigning season over three years of garrison duty. My brother Python was less eager, not liking the idea of being unable to visit Artemisia for several months, but he, and indeed our whole regular contingent from the Ionian Encampment, went on the expedition.

An Egyptian named Potasimto was in overall command of the contingents of *alloglossoi*, while command of the Egyptian troops was exercised by Amasis—the same man who would later make himself Pharaoh, though no one suspected such ambitions at this point in his career. A second-generation mercenary was in charge of the foreign troops on our particular ship. This man, despite his father's Greek name of Theokles, was called Psammetichos, like the current Pharaoh (presumably named for his grandfather, however, since he had obviously been born before the second Psammetichos became king).[5] The ships from the Encampment sailed up the Pelousiac branch of the Nile. Fortunately the prevailing winds in Egypt, which blow upriver, were blowing at this time (in contrast with an earlier journey I had made within the delta). Otherwise, moving such an army would be virtually impossible. We rendezvoused at the head of the delta with the regular Egyptian troops' ships from the neighborhood of Sais.

We would pick up further contingents as we went, in a slow journey that would require about twenty days to reach

Elephantine.[6] Of course we had to stop and camp along the way, but the commanders chose lightly populated areas for such purposes, not wishing to distract the troops by disembarking at any large towns. I got to see many of the famous old cities of Egypt, but generally all I got was a look at them while slowly sailing by. Actually, on this particular journey upriver, I missed the first such notable place, *Iunu* (Hebrew *On*, Greek Heliopolis), site of the greatest and most reverenced temple of the sun-god Re. It lies somewhat east of the river, connected with it by a canal that comes in very near the head of the delta. In non-military journeys in later years, I would see from the canal that the massive brick double wall around the city and temple was easily more than 2000 cubits long, but I could not see much of what lay behind it. Local legend, I have heard, says that the mysterious bird called the Phoinix makes its infrequent appearances in Egypt here, but no sighting has been reported in a very long time.[7]

Next, on our right, very clearly visible from our ship although some distance west of the river and beyond a smaller stream that parallels and eventually joins the Nile, were the greatest of the several pyramids we would see during our journey. The Egyptians attribute these huge stone structures to kings who ruled more than a thousand years ago (their record-keeping is amazing; we Greeks have nothing remotely comparable). The largest one of all is associated with a king called Khufu, whose name I have seen written by Greeks as Cheops.[8] Nearer the river, in front of the three largest pyramids, was a gigantic stone statue of a sphinx, a mythical creature I had known from Ionian art and had also seen depicted on various artifacts and buildings when I was serving in Judah. Similar creatures called *cherubim* were said to have been depicted in the temple, but of course I never saw them.

Memphis, the Greek place-name, has become so commonly employed outside of Egypt that the Egyptian name of the former capital, *Mennufer,* is little known; in Hebrew (as I believe I have already said) the city is called *Noph.* We passed this ancient city not much beyond the great pyramids, and also on the right-hand (western) side of the river—actually between the Nile and the smaller stream one must cross to reach the pyramid complex. Other smaller, less impressive pyramids lie much closer to the city itself, although all the pyramids and other kinds of elaborate tombs along the western side of the river in this vicinity can be thought of collectively as the necropolis of Memphis. The city was supposedly founded by the legendary Menes himself when he conquered Lower Egypt and annexed it to Upper Egypt, thereby creating the unified Two Lands, more than two millennia ago.[9] The Pharaohs who erected the largest pyramids had ruled from Memphis, and even when the royal residence passed to other locations, Memphis continued to be honored by kings ruling from elsewhere, particularly through additions made to its huge temple precinct dedicated to Ptah—a god whom Greeks rather arbitrarily equate with Hephaistos. The national center for the worship of the Apis bull—called by Greeks Epaphos—is also here.[10] The Kushite Pharaohs who preceded the present Saites had actually made Memphis their capital again, the better to rule the parts of Egypt far downriver from the southern regions firmly under their control.

Many sailing days and many dazzling sites and riverside monuments were passed by the time we reached the territory of the other chief political and religious metropolis of old Egypt, Thebes (I don't know why the Greeks call *Waset* by the name of the chief city of Boiotia, *Thebai*). Whereas Memphis had been a royal center that had also incorporated important cult centers, Thebes was essentially a gigantic cult center that had also functioned as a royal residence and governmental center during certain periods. Really it was *two* large cult centers, both on the eastern bank of the Nile. First we came to a huge complex—easily 2500 cubits or more from end to end—subdivided into several temple precincts dedicated to Amun and other gods. Some seventeen stades farther upstream we reached a smaller precinct, yet it was still well over 500 cubits long. This temple too was devoted to Amun, but in the ithyphallic form the Egyptians name Min.[11] In the fringe of the desert across the river lay the other element of the population center known collectively as Thebes, the royal graves of the Valley of the Kings and Valley of the Queens, the various funerary temples and monuments associated with the tombs, and the villages in which the necropolis workers lived. Statues and structures dedicated by and to the great Ramses are numerous in the area of Thebes, as they are all over Egypt.

Nothing can ever prepare a Greek, or any foreigner, for the magnificence of Thebes. Its temples utterly dwarf anything in the Hellenic world and, as far as I know, anything the barbarians elsewhere have ever built. The priests of Amun, especially those of the northern complex, had often exercised virtually independent power in Upper Egypt, and during times of disunity in the kingdom that power had been not just virtual but quite real. Thebes—also called "City of Amun" both in Greek (*Diospolis*, with the usual equating of Amun and Zeus) and in Hebrew (*No-Amon*)—is often referred to in Egypt simply as "the southern city", as contrasted with "the northern city", i.e., Memphis. Kings both from Nubia and the delta had sought to strengthen their own control in the Thebaid by appointing family members to high positions in the hierarchy of Amun. Even daughters of Pharaohs had held the powerful, though celibate, office of "God's Wife of Amun", and I believe that this position still exists at the time I write my memoirs.[12]

The army finally was allowed a badly needed several days of rest at Elephantine. The name of the place is a direct Greek translation of an Egyptian name (*Yebu*, meaning "Ivory Town") reflecting the fact that this city, on an island in the Nile, had long been the point of importation for elephants' tusks from the interior of Libya, conveyed there during peaceful times by Nubian traders. Both the island and the village called Syene by the Greeks, *Sunu* in Egyptian, which lies opposite it on the east bank of the river, were occupied by garrison soldiers. Since many of them were Greeks, we rank-and-filers could gain our own information about conditions in the area, not to mention rumors about events farther upriver into Nubia, without having simply to rely on official reports handed down to us by our officers.

I was surprised to find that some of the *alloglossoi* stationed here at this southernmost point in Egyptian territory were Judahites who had fled their beleaguered country and sought safety in Egyptian service. They had already become a community of sufficient size to begin construction of a temple dedicated to Yahweh (here referred to as "Yahu"). Interestingly, the sacrifices here—already being conducted at the open-air altars, even though the temple itself was not yet completed—were dedicated (I was told) not only to Yahweh but to other deities of Canaan, a goddess locally called Anath and a god referred to as Bethel.[13] It seems that a pre-Josianic form of traditional non-exclusive Yahwism was preserved at this distant outpost, out of range of the murderous reformers of Jerusalem. Perhaps some of the Judahite soldiers here, with their families living in Syene, were refugees not from the invasion of Nebuchadnezzar but from the depredations of the revolutionaries in Judah itself!

Elephantine was as far as the king himself would accompany our army. He would remain in the fortification on the island and direct the actual invasion of Nubian territory through dispatches carried back and forth by messengers.[14] The land began to climb sharply beyond Elephantine, with the river's channel constricted, lined by (at best) narrow sandy banks in front of steep cliffs. There was virtually no cultivable land on either side, and consequently much of Lower Nubia had almost no inhabitants. At times it was necessary to move the boats upstream by attaching lines to them and towing them from the banks. At other times, we simply had to hoist the boats on our shoulders and portage considerable distances, since immediately above Elephantine began the series of impassible stretches of rapids the Egyptians refer to as "cataracts", numbering them north-to-south, the cataract at Elephantine being called the first.

Our progress was excruciatingly slow as we forged our way upriver, but we encountered no armed resistance between the first and second cataracts, a distance of almost 2000 stades. At about four-fifths of the way between these two cataracts, we sailed through a placid stretch of the river past the great temples built by Ramses, at the base of sandstone cliffs coming almost right down to the water's edge on the west side of the river. We passed first by the queen's temple, facing roughly southeast, with its six large standing figures, two groups of three flanking the central doorway—each group being two statues of Ramses with a statue of his favorite queen, Nefertary, between them (I learned all these particulars only later, by relentlessly quizzing the Egyptian translators who worked with soldiers in the Ionian Encampment).

Just about seventy-five cubits farther along the rock face, and clearly visible from the queen's temple because of the cliff's concave curvature, was the Pharaoh's own temple, featuring four even larger statues of Ramses, seated rather than standing. The upper part of the second one from the left (that is, from the south end of the temple) had broken away and fallen; the fragment was lying in front of the row of seated figures. Of the interior of these great temples we learned nothing on our southbound journey, since we did not stop. Later, on our return from the campaign, we would get the opportunity to explore these monuments at our leisure—and even to leave some evidence of our passing.

As we approached the second cataract, we began observing the remains of abandoned Egyptian fortresses along the banks of the river, built centuries earlier, when all this region had been included in Egyptian-ruled territory. Just before the cataract was the great fort called Buhen, and just beyond it, facing each other across the Nile, were the twin fortresses of Semna (on the west bank) and Kumma (on the east).

In the forbidding rocky region around the third cataract, we finally caught up with the Kushite army, which had apparently been retreating since it had received warning of the scale of our operation. We brought the Nubians to battle within sight of a flat-topped rocky hill called locally the "Holy Mountain" (later I discovered that several temples to Amun were located on and around it, the Kushites having become ardent worshipers of Amun during their centuries of interaction with the Egyptians). Once their army had been routed, we proceeded to sack the nearby town of Napata, which seemingly had been serving the Kushite kings as a royal residence, despite its original status as an Egyptian frontier base.[15] Combining the battle and the pillaging of the city, we netted over 4000 Nubian captives, whom we eventually brought back to Egypt as slaves. Some had been slaves already, notably eunuchs who had served within the royal harem, some of whom had been left behind when the king and his queens and concubines had fled farther upriver in haste with the remnant of the army.

Sending a messenger to announce our victory to Psammetichos at Elephantine and leaving the prisoners under guard, the bulk of our forces pushed on beyond the fourth cataract and got as far as a town called Kurgus or (in Greek) Kerkis before we abandoned the chase. The river going was becoming progressively more difficult, and also we soon discovered that the fleeing Kushites, knowing the geography here in Upper Nubia as we could not possibly know it, had taken advantage of the winding of the Nile by cutting across a great curve on a desert road from Napata to the remote city of Meroe, above the fifth cataract. Not daring to leave the river for fear we would never get back to Egypt, we accepted the fact of the Kushite king's escape.

On our return journey, some vented their disappointment by defacing statues of earlier kings in Napata and on the Holy Mountain—Kushites who had, at least some of them, once been Pharaohs of Egypt![16] I myself took no part in the iconoclasm, having had my fill of that sort of thing while in Judah, and I was displeased to hear later that Psammetichos and his successors made it their policy to deface monuments the Kushite Pharaohs had set up during their reigns within Egypt itself, chiseling away their names and knocking off the distinctive second cobra they had added to traditional royal headdresses in their sculptured images.

The prisoners were apportioned among our troops, so that each ship's contingent had the responsibility of conveying and guarding a group of them. On the boat that carried Python and me and our troop, a particular prisoner intrigued me. He was one of the royal eunuchs, whose Kushite name I was never able to understand (their language is a complete mystery to me and, so far as I know, to all Greeks), so I simply called him "Servant-of-the-King" (*Doulos Basileos*), as if it were a name. Soon he began to recognize how I was using the phrase, and showed this by parroting the Greek phrase while pointing to himself. It turned out that he already knew some Egyptian words, and was a very quick study.

Given my own beginner's vocabulary in Egyptian and the Greek words I was able to teach him, we were more or less able, with lots of hand gestures, to "converse" by the time my comrades and I delivered him to the custody of royal officers at Elephantine. His rapid learning, with my clumsy assistance, had greatly improved his prospects for survival and good treatment, since royal eunuchs are always in demand, especially ones who can speak the languages needed for properly serving whatever court uses their services. I was happy to have been able to give a bit of help to the poor mutilated creature, whose infectious good nature and notable intelligence belied his degraded station in life. I promised myself that I would try to keep track of Servant-of-the-King's future career as a royal slave, and show him kindness if the chance ever arose. In fact, our lives would be linked in ways I never could have imagined.

The trip back downriver was leisurely and easy, moving with the current rather than sailing against it. One place at which we lingered was Ramses' great temple-complex near the second cataract. We were permitted to disembark and spend most of a day exploring both of the amazing temples in the cliffside. We had seen their façades on our upriver journey, but now we discovered from close-up how truly gigantic they were. The southern façade was about eighty cubits wide and some sixty-plus cubits high; the northern one was probably three-fourths as wide, although not as proportionally high. The seated colossal statues of the larger temple were themselves easily more then forty cubits high; I was able to lay my forearm twice along one of the ears of the head that had fallen without covering the full length of the ear.

Moreover, great and complex interiors lay behind those façades, whose temples had been hollowed deep into the solid rock. The larger of the two, the southern one devoted to Ramses himself, was cut some 120 cubits in, from the ornate entry topped by a figure of the sun god through three or four chambers and antechambers filled with statuary and painted carved reliefs on the walls. Everywhere the Pharaoh was depicted with the gods and as a god, even in a couple of places apparently in the act of worshiping himself. He was also shown in battle and leading away gangs of prisoners—by their appearance Nubians and people from the area of Syria or Canaan. The god Min was depicted a couple of times in all his erect glory, quite appropriately being worshiped by Ramses, who, the Egyptians say, had more than a hundred sons and over fifty daughters![17]

While Phoinikians and others carved signatures on other spots within the temple façade, some of the Greek mercenaries were scratching their names on the left leg of the second statue—the one whose head had fallen—to memorialize their participation in the expedition, some adding their patronymics or the names of their native cities: Helesibios of Teos, Telephos of Ialysos, Pambis of Kolophon, Krithis and someone else I can't recall. Even my brother could not resist scratching "Python son of Amoibichos". Anaxanor of Ialysos wrote two whole lines on the left leg of the adjacent statue, the one farthest to the south, going left-to-right and then right-to-left, mentioning both King Psammetichos and Amasis the general.

Finally, I decided that someone should memorialize our exploit in proper "official language", so I elected myself to do the job. I had to stand on Python's shoulders to reach a large clear area of surface on the left side of the left leg of the statue with the fallen head, and I set to work with my trusty axe, an instrument called a *peleqos* by some of my Dorian comrades. In their honor I tried to employ the Dorian dialect, but old habit led me to combine it with the Ionian alphabet used in my native Miletos.[18] Here are the words of my five-line "chronicle" of the expedition:

> King Psammetichos having come to Elephantine,
> these words were written by those who sailed with Psammetichos son of Theokles.
> They came above Kerkis, as far as the river permitted.
> *Alloglossoi* were led by Potasimto, Egyptians by Amasis.

> We words were written by Archon son of Amoibichos and Peleqos son of Nobody.

I couldn't resist that last bit of levity (the last letter wouldn't quite fit on the statue's leg, so I cut it on the wall behind). Let future readers of the inscription puzzle themselves over the odd Dorian name and patronymic of my "co-author"![19]

Once we got north of the cataracts and into Egyptian territory, we progressed easily and pleasantly, drifting with the current and being greeted by the people of every town along the river as glorious conquerors. That was somewhat excessive, since we had not captured the enemy king and certainly had not taken over his kingdom. On the other hand, there had genuinely been a great deal accomplished. The threat of a Kushite invasion of Egypt was seemingly ended forever—at least there have not even been any rumors about such a possibility in the almost thirty years that have elapsed until I write this. With the Nubian threat removed, the kingdom could henceforth concentrate its forces and its energy on stopping the advance of Nebuchadnezzar of Babylon, and encouraging resistance to him by offering alliance and assistance to his potentially rebellious vassals.

The Nubian expedition had greatly augmented the prestige of Psammetichos, and he had no intention of failing to build upon the advantage he had gained. We had barely returned to our barracks in the Encampment (Python had not even visited Artemisia!), when some of us were called up to accompany the king on a "pilgrimage" to the northeast. I was not surprised to be chosen, given my experience in the region. Python and several others of the Greeks who had gone with us to Nubia were also selected. But the military element of Pharaoh's retinue was not large, since the occasion was mainly ceremonial and cultic. Indeed a proclamation was issued calling on the various Egyptian temples to select and send priests to convey appropriate offerings from their shrines to those of the lands to be visited.[20] Philistine and Phoinikian cities (notably Byblos) were on our itinerary, but the most important stop of the entire trip was in Jerusalem. Judah and King Zedekiah were pivotal for any potential anti-Babylonian coalition, and the officially non-military nature of Psammetichos' visit could not alter this fact. The Egyptian king brought with him gifts for Zedekiah—including the recently-acquired royal eunuch whom I had named Servant-of-the-King—and, perhaps tipping his hand in so doing, left behind some troops in the recently rebuilt fortress of Arad. Python and I were among them; again, no surprise. Nor was it a surprise that Zedekiah was soon again contemplating revolt from Chaldaean vassalage.

The surprise came in Egypt, heard about by us at Arad only at second-hand. Psammetichos, at his peak of prestige after successful military and diplomatic expeditions, suddenly fell sick. He proceeded to waste away and die within less than two years of his visit to the region of Canaan, and after only six years of rule. His son *Wahibre,* called by Greeks *Apries,* succeeded him.[21] The Hebrew version of the new Pharaoh's name, *Hophra,* was the form in which I first heard it, stationed as I was in the Negeb of Judah. The young man appeared to be vigorous, and certainly Zedekiah was not dissuaded from his leanings toward revolt by the change in Egyptian rulers. But a new king is always an unknown quantity.

20. SIEGE, SIEGE LIFTED, SIEGE AGAIN

We bided our time at Arad for fully two *more* years before the actual war broke out.[1] The fort had been rebuilt after the destruction associated with Nebuchadnezzar's first siege of Jerusalem, carried out by his Edomite allies as they withdrew. The place was in effect smaller than the earlier fort, since a second set of walls had been built inside and parallel to the standing portions of the former walls, with perpendicular walls between them at intervals for bracing. In one of the series of "rooms" thus created, the commander Eliashib maintained his office. The large fortified gateway on the east had been closed up, replaced by a smaller entryway on the north, merely a passage a couple of cubits wide between two of the short perpendicular walls.[2]

With lots of time on my hands, I explored the area of the fort pretty thoroughly. The instructions that Eliashib had been given, now so long ago, to eliminate all visible traces of the temple and precinct that had once been a feature of the central courtyard of the fortress, had been followed, as I already knew from my second stay at Arad. The recent destruction and rebuilding had not changed that; in Judah there was still, since Josiah's time, only one temple of Yahweh, the one in Jerusalem. Whether the priests there knew about the ongoing construction of a temple at Elephantine in Egypt, I had no idea. At Arad, broken blocks and other debris still lay around the slopes outside the walls, since reinforcing the walls had been a far higher priority than clearing anything away.

Rummaging through the debris on the north side of the fort, close to where the cultic precinct had once been,

I turned up several ostraca with names written on them which I inferred were names of priests who had once officiated in the temple here—I recognized some names as being characteristic of priestly families in Jerusalem, such as Pashhur. The apparently priestly name on one ostracon, Eshiyahu, gave me a clue to explain the unusual duration of the commander Eliashib's connection with Arad. His own father, I knew from seeing the stamp of his official seal on various documents, had been called Eshiyahu. Probably Eliashib was from a priestly family that had lived right here on the site for generations, which would explain both his willingness to be stationed here more or less permanently and the administration in Jerusalem's preference for having him here—his loyalty in defending Arad could not be questioned. Indeed, Eliashib's son (named, as was often done, for his grandfather) was also stationed here, and frequently served as his father's messenger in dealings with other commanders.[3]

Ostraca are used in Judah, as they are in Greece, for everyday documents not important enough to warrant writing them on papyrus, which is expensive and hard to get outside of Egypt (indeed, they are even sometimes used in Egypt, although papyrus is used there far more extensively than anywhere else, of course). We mercenaries wrote our letters to wives, relatives, and friends in Egypt on ostraca, carried there by messengers who were making the trip anyway on official business, or sometimes by soldiers who were for some reason being allowed to return to the delta (an injury incurred in some accident, lingering illness, or something along these lines). I managed to send several letters to Delilah in Naukratis, always with a note added for Gomer, and she found some way to send replies (on papyrus) a couple of times. My brother Python sent and received letters to and from Artemisia on the same occasions. We were both reaching the age when we were contemplating retirement from soldiering, having been at it now for more than thirty years each—he was, the reader will recall, only a year younger than I. Python was in fact trying to persuade Artemisia to join him in retirement at Daphnai, trading the life of a prostitute—for which her age was beginning to disqualify her anyway, despite her only slightly diminished beauty—for that of a farmer's wife. Her responses, he told me, indicated her agreement with his plan; they were planning to marry and set up housekeeping as soon as he returned to Egypt.

I had occasion to see many ostraca on file in Eliashib's office during my years at the fort. The commander was friendly with me, since we had been acquainted now, off and on, for twenty years or so, and he was aware of my interest in his kingdom and its past. He pretty much allowed me to visit him in his office at any time and to peruse his archive at will—it included nothing of a particularly "secret" nature, mostly just receipts for supplies delivered or issued, countersigned by him on the backs and stored as evidence that the transactions had been completed. Some receipts even involved the issuing of wine and bread (or meal for making bread) to us Greek mercenaries, subsumed under the general rubric of *Kittiyim,* a term which probably had originally meant men from the town of Kition on the island of Kypros.[4]

The subject matter of the ostraca passing through Arad would become more sensitive during the crisis brought on by the invasion of Nebuchadnezzar, but by that time my access to Eliashib's files had become so well accepted that I was still permitted to see the documents. One ostracon I saw carried a message from King Zedekiah to the new Pharaoh, Apries, seemingly written just at the time Zedekiah decided to go into open rebellion against Nebuchadnezzar by refusing to pay tribute.[5] I think this ostracon remained at Arad because it was never forwarded—either because Babylonian control of Philistine coastal territory made it impossible to get the message through, or because the message became unnecessary when it was known that Apries had already sent ships to Tyre and Sidon to oppose the Babylonian forces there.[6]

By the autumn of the second year of Apries' reign in Egypt, Nebuchadnezzar had finally come west. He established his headquarters at Riblah in Syria (the same place where Necho, long ago, had deposed Jehoahaz and designated Jehoiakim as his successor on the throne of Judah).[7] From there he sent troops toward the Phoinikian coast to counter the naval moves of Apries, while other divisions advanced southward toward Jerusalem.[8]

Much later I would see written copies of pronouncements said to have been made at this time in Babylonia by the exiled prophet Ezekiel, who seemingly was just as determined to undermine Judah's defense as Jeremiah had always been—despite referring to the Chaldaeans as "the most barbarous of the nations"![9] For Ezekiel, it was an inexcusable crime *against Yahweh* that Zedekiah had broken his oath of loyalty to Nebuchadnezzar,[10] and he denounced the king of Judah's efforts to get help from Egypt. I would learn later that, just before the city was put under siege, Zedekiah had sent a military delegation to Egypt to seek the assistance of Apries' land army, a delegation led by Coniah son of Elnathan. The commander of that troop must have been the son of my own former commander, whom I had eluded in the delta on the occasion of another diplomatic mission to Egypt (extradition of the prophet Uriah), some twenty years earlier, when I had left Judahite service. Elnathan's daughter had borne King Jehoiakim a son named Coniah (the exiled King Jehoiachin), and Elnathan had given his own son the same name.[11]

By the time the year was well into winter, the army of Nebuchadnezzar had surrounded Jerusalem.[12] Communication between the various outlying forts and fortified towns, and between Jerusalem and any of them, had become irregular, unreliable, and dangerous. Simple messages could be conveyed through fire-signals, but anything complicated enough to require a human courier presented the Babylonians with the opportunity to capture and interrogate him, and of course put the messenger's life seriously at risk. Perhaps unfortunately for me, the commander at Arad, Eliashib, not only trusted me but realized that I was particularly valuable as a messenger, since I was able to communicate not only with other foreign troops but also with Judahite contingents as well. Sending me was more efficient than sending two men, or depending on finding a translator. Making several message-bearing forays without getting caught, I was at least able to hear some news of events within the capital since the siege had begun.

Not surprisingly, Jeremiah was still prophesying disaster for the king and the city. Before Jerusalem had been surrounded, he had staged a demonstration outside the walls, in the place called Topheth in the valley of Ben-Hinnom, where Josiah (that time with the willing assistance of his foreign mercenaries, including myself) had abolished the practice of incinerating infants in Molech-worship. Apparently the practice had been reinstituted, since the prophet was said to have announced that, rather than sacrificing their children to Molech, Yahweh now proclaimed: "I shall make them eat the flesh of their own sons and daughters; they will eat one another during the siege", referring to the siege that was about to begin. He had gone from Topheth to the temple, and there continued to proclaim the coming disaster. The priest Pashhur, chief of the temple police, had struck him and had had him put in the stocks overnight, at the Upper Benjamin Gate near the temple. Upon his release the next day, Jeremiah had persisted in his unchanged dire message, adding a prediction of deportation for Pashhur and his family.[13]

After the siege was actually underway, the king had sent a delegation to Jeremiah, consisting of a different man also named Pashhur (obviously a common priestly name;

I have already mentioned seeing it attested also at Arad) and a priest called Zephaniah. This embassy represented a desperate hope of eliciting a miracle from Yahweh to save the city—so respected and feared was the divine inspiration of the prophet, despite his many enemies. Jeremiah, true to the uncompromising line he had been taking, sent back a message to Zedekiah to the effect that Yahweh had said "I will fight against you myself". Not only would the king, Jeremiah stated, be handed over to Nebuchadnezzar, but he proclaimed as the word of Yahweh that anyone who stayed in the city would die, whereas anyone who left and surrendered to the besiegers would live. As for the city itself: "Yahweh declares, It will be handed over to the king of Babylon, and he will burn it down". Despite this clear and unambiguous call for his fellow citizens of Jerusalem to defect to the enemy, Jeremiah remained free to roam the city and undermine morale.[14]

My luck ran out finally during a night-time mission to Hebron. That city was closer to Jerusalem than Arad was, and some of the Babylonian troops besieging the capital had spread their encampment farther to the south than I realized. I was further deceived when, as I approached Hebron, I was challenged by a sentry speaking Greek: "Halt! Who goes there?" Assuming that it was a fellow mercenary in Egyptian or Judahite service, I replied, without alarm, that it was "Archon the Milesian, bringing a message from the commander at Arad to the commander in Hebron". "Come forward, Archon the Milesian", the Aiolic-accented voice answered. Advancing a few more paces, I was surprised to find myself seized by several soldiers armed as hoplites. They were Greek mercenaries all right, but Greek mercenaries in the employ of Nebuchadnezzar of Babylon!

The officer in charge of the squad that had captured me without a struggle, and the one assigned to interrogate me, turned out to be that Antimenidas of Mytilene on Lesbos, brother of the poet Alkaios, of whom I have often spoken in these memoirs. It quickly became evident that I had no information not already known to the Babylonian army. After all, it was they, not we, who were in control of the countryside of Judah, and they had no problems with communication, while their presence interfered with ours and kept us largely ignorant of the situation outside of our own immediate vicinity. Being, like myself, the dispossessed scion of a once-aristocratic family who had for many years made his way in the world through military service to foreign kings, my questioner Antimenidas began quite soon to experience a good bit of fellow-feeling for his captive Milesian exile. What began as an interrogation metamorphosed into an all-night conversation, and at dawn he released me to return to Arad unhurt, confident that I could do his master's cause no harm.

And what a conversation! He was as enthralled to hear about my adventures in Nubia as I was to hear of his participation in the siege of Nineveh, and he imparted much information about Babylon and the region between the rivers in general, in response to my eager questioning. But the charm our stories held for each other was not only in their exoticism, the tales each could tell about places the other had not seen. Even more fascinating—though also much more emotionally painful—were the experiences we had unknowingly shared, or come close to sharing. Our common presence here in the Negeb south of Jerusalem was not the only time our paths had crossed.

I told him of the death of my commander and mentor Benaiah at the hands of the giant Egyptian Petosiris at Megiddo, followed by the strangely mixed emotions I had later felt upon finding myself a fellow-soldier of the same Petosiris in the march to Karchemish, and the sadness combined with relief that I had experienced upon hearing that he had died with the remainder of the garrison we had left there. "You knew the giant's name?" Antimenidas exclaimed, excitedly. Then he stunned me by saying: "I killed him at Karchemish". He went on to explain the circumstances, not denying that his fatal stroke was a lucky blow delivered when the Egyptian was distracted by some other violent action going on just at his side; his momentary sideways glance had given the Mytilenian the opening needed. Years later, in my retirement at Daphnai, I would acquire a scroll of Alkaios' poems, and in it I would read the lines:

> You fought alongside the Babylonians and won
> great fame, and saved them from troubles,
> killing a warrior man
> who lacked only a single span
> from five royal cubits in height.

It's interesting to note that Petosiris' immense size that I described above (the reader will recall) in cubits had expanded in the poet's brotherly hands into an equal number of *royal* cubits—making the giant probably one-fifth again as tall as he was already![15]

Antimenidas commiserated with me, quite sincerely, I believe, when I told of the slaughter of my wife Tirzah and our child at the seaside fort while I was away at Megiddo. But when I described my sadness at the scenes of carnage I had beheld amid the ruins of Delilah's Ashkelon, he was decidedly less sympathetic. He had, in fact, been himself involved in that pillaging, as a member of the Babylonian army. He said he wasted no sympathy on a disloyal, rebel ally and his people (I was not about to contradict him by pointing out that Aga of Ashkelon had been an ally of Egypt!). The like fate awaited Zedekiah and Jerusalem, Antimenidas assured me; Nebuchadnezzar had vowed it before all his officers. If I had any influence, or knew anyone who had any influence, on the commanders of the Egyptian forces in Judah, I would be wise to prevail upon them to get their men out, lest they share the fate of their foolish new allies. I had no such influence, of course, and told him so.

Just before releasing me at dawn, Antimenidas proposed—perhaps motivated by fatigue-induced euphoria—that we should proclaim ourselves Homeric-style *xenoi*, "guest-friends", like Glaukos and Diomedes in the *Iliad*. "Why should we Greeks kill each other, when there are plenty of barbarians for our spears?" he said, loosely paraphrasing Homer.[16] I certainly had no reason to disagree, especially since I was hugely grateful to him for setting me free, when he obviously did not have to do so, and might indeed cause some trouble for himself by freeing me.

Back at Arad, my brother Python, who had given me up for lost when my expected return had been so long delayed—assuming that I would end up deported to Babylonia, if not simply executed—was ecstatic to see me unhurt. He was as amazed as I had been about the coincidences I reported, but the stories made him even more resolute about making this his final campaign, of settling down with Artemisia on a small plot of land around Daphnai and spending a quiet retirement there. He could scarcely wait, he said, for our next letters from Naukratis. I was astounded at the change that had come over my brother in the time he had known Artemisia. One woman had always been pretty much the same as any other to him, as he himself freely admitted, but this Karian had won his heart, and the effect was apparently (to judge by previous letters) mutual. Working as a mercenary—or as a whore—is wonderful tutelage in what is real and what is illusory. If you survive at all, you end up caring about *only* what you *really* care about; all pretense becomes pointless. Either you become utterly hard and callous, or you come to value life and those you love more fervently than others ever value them.

Several months had elapsed since the Babylonians had laid siege to Jerusalem and the surrounding towns. Small bands of soldiers representing the Egyptian army, such as ours, were little more than hostages to assure our allies in Judah that the main army would indeed arrive at some point. Apries, not having gotten underway by the time of the inundation, of necessity had to wait for the waters flooding Egypt to recede, so it was the autumn of the year when he finally set out up the Way of the Sea. His commanders included Potasimto, in charge of the remainder of the *alloglossoi*, and Amasis, now recognized as one of his most important generals.[17]

Ezekiel, far away in Babylonia, did not know, of course, the precise time of "Hophra's" departure or arrival, but he knew (Yahweh told him!) that Judah's relying on Egypt was a disaster. His hatred for the Egyptians was expressed in positively obscene imagery, if the scrolls credited to him that I later saw were in reality his work. Personifying Jerusalem as "Oholibah", a dissolute young woman even worse than her sister "Oholah" (Samaria), Ezekiel produced such passages as this:

> But she began whoring worse than ever, remembering her girlhood, when she had played the whore in Egypt, when she had been in love with their profligates, big-membered as donkeys, ejaculating as violently as stallions. You were hankering for the debauchery of your girlhood, when they used to handle your nipples in Egypt and fondle your young breasts

—and suchlike, at great length![18] In a more poetic vein, he invoked the familiar "broken reed" comparison, addressing the Egyptians in words such as these:

> ...they have given no more support
> than a reed to the house of Israel.
> Whenever they grasped you,
> you broke in their hands
> and cut their hands all over.
> Whenever they leaned on you, you broke,
> making all their limbs give way.[19]

Nebuchadnezzar himself was perhaps more impressed. At any rate, he raised the siege so as to draw together his army to confront the advancing forces of Apries. Hopes rose again in Jerusalem. Zedekiah, despite all the rebuffs he had suffered from the prophet, once more sent envoys to Jeremiah, begging him again to intercede with Yahweh. The effort was in vain, as always. Yahweh's answer, sent back to the king, was:

> Is Pharaoh's army marching to your aid? It will withdraw to its own country, Egypt. The Chaldaeans will return to attack this city; they will capture it and burn it down. Yahweh says this: Do not cheer yourself up by thinking: The Chaldaeans are leaving us for good. They are not leaving.[20]

Yet even Jeremiah himself took advantage of the respite caused by the withdrawal of the Babylonian army to attend to some business in his home village of Anathoth in Benjamin—or he was attempting to do this when he was arrested at the Benjamin Gate and charged with deserting to the Chaldaeans (as he himself had indeed advocated that all the inhabitants of Jerusalem should do).[21]

Jeremiah denied the charge, but was beaten and thrown into an underground vault in the house of the scribe Jonathan. The king, after talking with him and despite receiving no more hopeful prophecy than before, acceded to the prophet's plea for a less unhealthy place of imprisonment (winter was coming on), and confined him in the Court of the Guard, with adequate rations—one loaf of bread a day.[22] While thus confined, incidentally, Jeremiah managed to transact the business at Anathoth, using Baruch as his intermediary. He redeemed some family land and had a careful record of the action witnessed and preserved, thereby symbolizing that he did himself put his trust in his own prophecy that the exiles would eventually return from Babylon and normal activities would resume in Judah.[23]

Yet another indication of the complete sincerity of Jeremiah, however mad his beliefs might sometimes seem, was his attitude in the matter of the freed slaves. Before the appearance of the army of Egypt, when besieged Jerusalem seemed to need every possible fighting man—and perhaps also because no one in the city wanted to be responsible for feeding any extra noncombatant mouths!—Zedekiah had issued a proclamation (he called it a "covenant" with the people of Jerusalem) freeing all "Hebrew" slaves. I assume that phrasing meant all slaves whose native language was Hebrew, in effect slaves who were Judahites by descent and culture, as opposed to foreigners. Yet when Apries was known to be on his way, and the Babylonians lifted their siege in order to go to meet him, the crisis seemed to have passed. Thereupon, led by the king, the citizens of Jerusalem rescinded their manumissions and re-enslaved those who had just been freed!

Jeremiah reacted with utter outrage, denounced the slave-owners for profaning the name of Yahweh with their treacherous deed, and swore to them in the name of Yahweh that they would be made "an object of horror to all the kingdoms of the earth". He promised that Yahweh would treat the covenant-breakers like the calf that is cut in two during the covenant-making ceremony itself, so that those making the treaty can pass between the pieces. And he reiterated that Zedekiah would be handed over by Yahweh "to the army of the king of Babylon which has just withdrawn. Listen, I shall give the order, Yahweh declares, and bring them back to this city to attack it and capture it and burn it down. And I shall make an uninhabited waste of the towns of Judah".[24]

Unfortunately for Zedekiah, it turned out that Jeremiah—and for that matter Ezekiel—had had a better understanding than he had of the mettle of the untried Egyptian monarch. That god-on-earth did not even stay around to fight the army drawn up to confront him, but retreated back across the Egyptian frontier without a battle! Ezekiel gleefully announced hearing yet another word from Yahweh: "Son of man, I have broken the arm of Pharaoh king of Egypt", and went on to report Yahweh's announcement: "I shall scatter Egypt among the nations and disperse it among the countries. I shall strengthen the arms of the king of Babylon and put my sword in his hand".[25] If the Judahites were now rightly fearful, imagine the terror of the troops from Egypt who had been stationed at fortresses in Judah several years earlier, and were now abandoned to the Babylonians' mercy—Python and I and our band at Arad being prominent among these.

Jerusalem was re-besieged, just as Jeremiah had prophesied it would be, though the man who was increasingly proving to be a "true prophet" remained in custody as a would-be defector. The towns of the Shephelah fell one by one, just as they had fallen more than a century earlier to the invading Assyrian king, Sennacherib. Once again, Azekah and Lachish were the last to hold out, and once again the last of all of them was the largest town, Lachish.[26] Finally the only city unconquered was the besieged capital, Jerusalem itself. Isolated desert forts such as Arad and Kadesh-Barnea had not yet come under attack because of their location in the remote south. But we at Arad knew that if—when—Jerusalem fell, our fort would not long survive. Moreover, Apries, by his cowardly retreat, had showed that we could not expect any assistance from Egypt. We were on our own, and we were at the Chaldaeans' mercy.

21. DESTRUCTION OF JERUSALEM

The final siege of Jerusalem that now began in mid-winter would continue through the following winter and well into the summer beyond that, fully a year and a half during which the city was entirely cut off from all assistance and from almost all communication and hope.[1] We soldiers at Arad, whether foreign mercenaries abandoned by our Egyptian master or the Judahite levies under Eliashib trapped here with us, did well to feed ourselves by scavenging the immediate countryside. Intermittently, we were able to communicate with the contingents similarly trapped in smaller nearby forts and at the more distant Kadesh-Barnea. The mercenaries from Egypt at that fortified oasis had decided fairly soon after Jerusalem was re-besieged to take their chances crossing the desert and had fled back to the delta. Judahite forces remained there, of course, as they did at several small forts scattered around the Negeb, such as Qinah and Ramat-Negeb.

Ostraca in the office of Eliashib, commander at Arad—some of them messages received, others copies of messages sent—made me aware of certain communications, and attempts at communication, with Jerusalem and other places during this dark period. As a mere soldier not involved in formulating policy (despite the access to his records that the commander generously allowed me), I could not always fully understand the content of the brief, sometimes cryptic, texts that I saw. One was a reply from someone in Jerusalem to an unspecified message from Eliashib, giving assurances that "everything is fine now: he (unnamed) is staying in the temple of Yahweh". Another was pretty clearly an order issued to Eliashib from some high functionary, demanding in quite threatening tones—"This is an order from the king, a life and death matter for you"—that he must send under the command of Malkiyahu fifty soldiers from Arad, and others from Qinah, to Elisha the commander at Ramat-Negeb, "lest the Edomites go there".[2]

Otherwise, only the sketchiest of verbal reports reached us from Jerusalem, brought by occasional fugitives who had managed to get over the walls and through the besieging army by night. It seems that for a long while Nebuchadnezzar had been willing to let famine and the influence of surrender advocates such as Jeremiah do his work for him. Conditions had become very nearly as horrible as Jeremiah had predicted they would. Whether parents actually ate their children I cannot say. Such stories are always told about cities under long sieges, but how do the story-tellers acquire such knowledge? I do not suppose that such cannibalism would be indulged in in the street, where others could watch! That conditions were extremely severe we could not doubt, since we ourselves at Arad, although few in number and not yet under siege, were experiencing considerable deprivation.

Finally, more than a year after his forces had encamped around the capital, Nebuchadnezzar lost patience with slow and indirect measures, and began his efforts actually to break down Jerusalem's defenses and take the city. His engineers began raising mounds against the walls. Such mounds were certainly built up on the north side, where the temple district constituted the beginning of what was essentially a walled-off extension of the plateau that terminated in the "peninsula" (between valleys) known as the City of David. It is also possible that similar mounds were raised on the west side, where the slope of the gentle hill lately called "Mount Zion", incorporated into the city back in King Hezekiah's time, was less steep than the sides of the Ben-Hinnom and Kidron valleys to the south and east. It was hard to be certain of this, however, since our reports were scanty and often confused, and usually received from persons who had fled southward or eastward at night. Later I would read, not knowing whether I could believe it or not, that Ezekiel, far off in Babylonia, had been given two signs on the very day the assault on Jerusalem began: his wife suddenly died and he was himself struck dumb, unable to speak. Yahweh had told him (the scroll attributed to him said) that the death of his wife was to be paralleled by the destruction of the temple, and that on the day he (Ezekiel) received news from a refugee of the fall of the temple, his ability to speak would be restored.[3]

Within a month or two of the initiation of serious efforts to take the city by the Babylonians, around mid-summer, they succeeded in breaching the walls.[4] We heard vague rumors (substantiated later) that King Zedekiah had fled on the night of the day when the walls were breached, but had been captured and taken to Nebuchadnezzar at his headquarters at Riblah. The Babylonians occupied the city, but, very much to our surprise, they did not immediately sack or destroy it. Just about an entire month passed, and we at Arad lay frozen in uncertainty—if I may use that metaphor for our mental state in the blistering Negeb summer. The few refugees and stragglers who reached us during this month of trepidation did not provide us with much useful information, none of them being very highly connected with temple or court. We did hear that the man set over the occupied city by Nebuchadnezzar was named Nebuzaradan, who held the rank of commander of the king's guard; the king himself stayed at Riblah and issued his orders from there.

Finally arrived a refugee who *had* had access to the highest levels of the Judahite establishment, and whose identity was a great—and pleasant—surprise to Python and me. The reader will recall that among the prisoners we had escorted back from our expedition to Nubia was a eunuch who had once served the royal court of Kush, to whom I had become a sort of patron, because of his good nature and amazing facility with languages, and whom I had given the name Servant-of-the-King. Psammetichos, as I have also reported, had subsequently presented the eunuch as a courtesy-gift to his ally Zedekiah, at which point—now some five or six years ago—I had lost track of him. Hearing it noised about the fort that a pudgy, beardless Kushite fugitive from Jerusalem had arrived begging for refuge, I immediately guessed that it must be my former protégé, and I rushed to see him and confirm my suspicion. I was correct, and the eunuch instantly recognized me as well. He greeted me effusively in Greek: "Archon, *philos kai euergetes mou*!" (my friend and benefactor). He had continued, he told me, to call himself by the name I had given him, which was obviously very appropriate to his profession of royal eunuch. But now Servant-of-the-King was rendered in Hebrew, a direct translation: Ebed-Melech.

Ebed-Melech was able to bring me and my comrades up to date on what had transpired within the city during the past year and a half of virtual non-communication. He was also able to discuss in surprising detail a matter of continuing interest to me, a fascination I found impossible to shake, namely the adventures and vicissitudes of the prophet Jeremiah. This was because the eunuch's good nature and kind heart, qualities I had observed in him long ago, had led him to use his standing with the king to alleviate the harsh conditions that had been imposed on the imprisoned prophet. I will try to report the tale as he told it to me, aiding my memory with the written account of Baruch, of which the eunuch was no doubt also the main source.[5]

Jeremiah had been confined, as I have said, in the court of the guard by Zedekiah after their initial interview following the prophet's arrest. But a delegation of courtiers—including two of the men who had earlier approached Jeremiah on Zedekiah's behalf—complained to the king that the prophet's confinement was insufficient punishment for the damage his advocacy of surrender was doing in the city. Zedekiah, irresolute as ever, allowed them to remove the prisoner from his fairly comfortable cell and put him in a cistern beneath the court of the guard, out of use but still having mud on the bottom—obviously expecting him to perish there from cold (it was still winter when this happened) and starvation (his rations were sharply reduced).

As the king was sitting dispensing justice in the Benjamin Gate, he was surprised to find among the petitioners one of his own palace eunuchs, Ebed-Melech, who had heard of the relocation of Jeremiah. "My lord king", the eunuch had said, summoning up all the courage he could muster, "these men have done a wicked thing by treating the prophet Jeremiah like this".[6] Here I pause to point out that Ebed-Melech told me (this information does not appear in Baruch's account) that whereas the imprisoned prophet had spoken kindly to him, some of the aristocratic accusers had treated him with the contempt and minor violence that arrogant men often manifest toward the unfortunate and the powerless. I infer that his motives were a combination of generosity and resentment, but I do not think that the latter negates the former.

Returning to the eunuch's conversation with the king: he went on to stress that the prophet would starve to death, given the conditions of scarcity within the city. Zedekiah relented, sent Ebed-Melech himself to lead a gang of workmen to haul Jeremiah up out of the cistern, and restored him to his former cell and former rations, which conditions prevailed until the fall of the city. Later, Ebed-Melech, said, he received a message from the prophet, addressed to him by name:

> Yahweh, God of Israel says this: Look, I am about to perform my words about this city for its ruin and not for its prosperity. That day they will come true before your eyes. But I shall rescue you that day, Yahweh declares, and you will not be handed over to the hands of the men

> you fear. Yes, I will certainly rescue you: you will not fall to the sword; you will escape with your life, because you have put your trust in me, Yahweh declares.[7]

Whether the eunuch, in putting on his Hebrew name, had also become a worshiper of Yahweh—of the monotheistic kind Jeremiah represented—I cannot say. The brilliant linguist was nothing if not adaptable; having lost his manhood, he had no intention of losing his life for some abstraction. I never heard him speak ill of any god—Judahite, Egyptian, Greek, or Kushite. So I prefer to think that he helped Jeremiah not out of zealotry but out of human kindness, regardless of any interpretation put on his actions by the prophet himself. If I could, I intended to make Jeremiah's prophecy come true for him, and for the same kind of motives.

Ebed-Melech told of a further—secret—conversation between the king and the prisoner. He did not say which of the two had revealed it to him; my guess is the prophet, since he had more reason for gratitude, that is assuming the conversation was real, and not just the eunuch's invention. If this story can be believed—it is inconsistent with the prophet's repeated message of Yahweh's unrelenting, already-decided intention of destroying the city, so there is at least some reason for being suspicious—the prophet, in response to the king's promises not to have him killed or put him again in the custody of his enemies, softened his predictions of inevitable disaster. Jeremiah supposedly at this time told Zedekiah, claiming that he spoke Yahweh's own words:

> If you go out and surrender to the king of Babylon's generals, your life will be safe and this city will not be burnt down; you and your family will survive. But if you do not go out and surrender to the king of Babylon's generals, this city will be handed over to the Chaldaeans

> and they will burn it down; nor will you yourself escape their clutches.

The king responded (the eunuch's story continued) by expressing his fear of the harsh treatment he would receive from the Judahites who had already defected to the Babylonians, and Jeremiah was unable to reassure him. The interview was said to have ended with the king swearing the prophet to secrecy about what had been discussed.[8]

The Kushite also provided me belatedly with details about the flight and fate of the king, although he knew of these matters only by report, since most of the events had taken place outside the city. Once the walls had been breached, Nebuchadnezzar's highest-ranking courtiers (even his chief astrologer) occupied the Middle Gate, in effect proclaiming themselves the provisional government of the conquered city. Zedekiah, the disloyal vassal, did not dare even appear before them. By now it was night, and he fled from the city under the cover of darkness, accompanied by his military escort, going out by way of the King's Garden and the gate between the inner and outer walls on the east side of the city. He was heading for the Jordan valley, presumably hoping to cross the river and seek the protection of the king of the Ammonites. In the open country near Jericho, the pursuing Chaldaean troops captured him, delivering him to Nebuchadnezzar at Riblah.

Probably Zedekiah's punishment was not administered immediately, since it was necessary first to round up the remainder of the royal family and as many courtiers as could be caught, and to bring these also to Riblah. Once that was done, Nebuchadnezzar compelled the rebel to look on as all of his sons were slaughtered, followed by most of his close advisors. Having registered these horrific sights, Zedekiah's eyes were then put out, and he was loaded down with chains. He was taken away, presumably to Babylon, but nobody whom I was ever able to consult knew whether he even arrived there.[9] He was never heard from again, although the presence of his earlier-deposed nephew Jehoiachin in Babylon is well-known, and continues to this day.

If a certain prediction recorded in the scroll of Ezekiel is either a true prophecy or (as I suspect) something written afterwards so as to look like a true prophecy, Zedekiah may in fact have reached Babylon. Supposedly, before the fall of Jerusalem, Yahweh had given the prophet the message that the "House of Israel" would be deported and that the king would try to escape through the wall. But, says Yahweh, "I shall throw my net over him and catch him in my mesh; I shall take him to Babylon, to the land of the Chaldaeans, though he will not see it"—I assume that that phrase is a reference to Zedekiah's blinding—"and there he will die".[10] It will not surprise my reader to learn that Ezekiel also reported that on the very evening before a fugitive arrived to tell him in Babylonia that Jerusalem had fallen—remember that Judahites count their days as beginning at sunset, so in effect this is saying "on the same day"—Yahweh had restored his ability to speak.[11]

I return now to the point I had reached in my narrative before the arrival of Ebed-Melech made it possible for me to reconstruct events in Jerusalem that had occurred during the months in which we had received little news. Almost another month had now passed,[12] with the Babylonian army still encamped around the defeated city, the Chaldaean king still at Riblah, and no direct moves yet made against Arad and the other far-south desert fortresses—beyond the increasingly-visible presence of bands of Edomites, edging closer ever more menacingly, but seemingly waiting for permission from their Babylonian overlord before they launched any overt attacks.

Finally, a written message put at least the Greek mercenaries at Arad into motion. Eliashib called us together and announced to us that another fugitive from Jerusalem had delivered an ostracon to him, the messenger claiming that he had received it from a scribe in the service of the handful of remaining royal courtiers still in hiding in the city. These now-powerless administrators wished, as an act of mercy they hoped would be pleasing to Yahweh, to permit the foreign troops at Arad to depart for Kadesh-Barnea and thence to Egypt, and they instructed the commander to give us supplies for the first leg of our trip. The commander showed me, and any of the others who could read Hebrew, the potsherd. In a conventional scribal hand, like that of other ostraca I had examined, it was addressed to Eliashib, and it instructed him to "give to the *Kittiyim*" enough wine and bread "for the four days"—the normal travel time to Kadesh-Barnea—and it included the admonition "Send them out tomorrow. Do not wait".[13] He issued the order, and we began making our preparations to depart. I asked for and received Eliashib's permission to take Ebed-Melech back with us; the eunuch certainly had nothing further to do in Judah, and would doubtless end up in Babylonia if he did not come with us. He was extremely happy to join our flight.

Our journey was hurried but mostly uneventful. We got out just before the Babylonians pillaged the capital and just before the Edomites were unleashed against the Negeb forts. All along the way, however, and even after I was back in the safety of the Ionian Encampment on the Pelousiac branch of the Nile, I was puzzled by the mysterious nature of the document that had authorized and facilitated our flight from grave danger. Eliashib had spoken of a messenger or a refugee who had delivered the potsherd, but no one else claimed to have seen such a man, although none of us had thought to ask about this matter at the time. And who were the mysterious "authorities" left in Jerusalem, whom a fortress commander still felt it necessary to obey? Was the ostracon a forgery designed to save us? If so, a forgery by whom?

Eliashib himself was the obvious suspect. His order had saved my troop of *alloglossoi* once before, during the siege of Jerusalem that had led to the deportation of Jehoiachin. Then too he must have known that the Edomites would be permitted to destroy the fort he commanded. Fortunately, on that occasion the damage to Jerusalem and the disruption of the kingdom had been temporary and limited. Zedekiah had been appointed to rule as a Babylonian vassal, the fortress had been reclaimed from the Edomites (although it had to be rebuilt, after the damage they had done to it), and Eliashib himself had survived to command there again. An intelligent man, he knew that the outcome this time would be much harsher. The kingdom would not survive and he, as a high-ranking military officer, probably would not either; deportation was the best fate for which he could hope, but execution was just as likely. Of course the fort, and anyone left in it, would soon be destroyed again by the Edomites. So perhaps he had composed an "order" to himself to do something that his Judahite troops—who were going to have to stay and fight and probably die with him—might have questioned, if he had done it openly on his own authority. Why not at least save the mercenaries' lives, if he could not save his own or those of his native soldiers? This scenario still seems probably the most plausible to me, and because of it, I have always held the memory of Eliashib in the highest honor—even higher than I had already held it for his earlier kindness.

But another possibility exists, one that did not occur to me until much later—too late to verify or refute it. One other candidate for the forger is available, someone to whom in a long night of all-revealing conversation I had told about the archive of ostraca in Eliashib's office, along with everything else—and someone in a better position even than Eliashib to know how imminent was the danger threatening his recently-sworn *xenos*. I refer of course to Antimenidas of Mytilene, lamentably among the dead as I write this in old age. He could not have himself forged the Hebrew text, of course, but he knew (thanks to me) of the general form and content of such documents and the name of the commander at Arad. He could have captured a scribe and have forced him to compose an appropriate order to Eliashib, drawing on the scribe's own knowledge of proper form and phrasing. Then he could have seized someone from the captured city—either a fugitive intercepted in the countryside or just someone selected at random in the street—and have induced the man by threats or promises or cash payment (or some combination of these) to deliver the ostracon to the commander at Arad, providing him safe-conduct through the Babylonian lines to get there, as well as the chance to escape from Judah once he had gotten that far away from Jerusalem.

I will never know, and perhaps the ostracon was the genuine order it purported to be.[14] But it does no harm, and it makes me feel good, to think myself indebted to either or both of my possible benefactors, the Judahite or the Mytilenian. Let my praise for them in this memoir be my humble monument to their kindness. If either or both of them does not actually deserve praise for this particular benevolent deed, each of them had showed me enough generosity and regard already that I do not begrudge a bit of over-praise.

Of the actual destruction of Jerusalem by the Babylonians I have only the reports that afterward reached me in Egypt, stories told by various refugees, supplemented by Baruch's account in his collection of oracles and narratives associated with Jeremiah.[15] Apparently, Nebuzaradan, the commander of Nebuchadnezzar's guard, ordered the burning down of the palace, temple, and houses of Jerusalem, as well as the demolition of the city's walls, within days of our departure from Arad. Before burning the temple, he had ordered the breaking up of the two eighteen-cubit-high bronze pillars that had stood in front of it and of the huge bronze sea and the twelve bronze oxen on which it was mounted. These, in addition to all the other bronze instruments and furnishings that had been employed in the cultic activities of the temple—and of course all the silver and gold ones—were transported to Babylon as spoils of war.

In addition to the courtiers who had already been killed along with the king's sons, Nebuzaradan now rounded up and sent to Riblah for execution the two highest-ranking priests, certain military officers, a handful of high-ranking courtiers ("friends of the king"), and some sixty other notables still in the city whom he was able to locate. There were also deportations. Baruch says that they included all of the population left in the city, the deserters who had gone over to the Babylonians during the siege, and the remaining artisans. These groups must not by now have been numerous, since he reports 832 persons as the total number of deportees in the eighteenth year of Nebuchadnezzar—not much more than a quarter of the number that he reports for the earlier deportation which had included King Jehoiachin.

The non-aristocratic portion of the population—in Judah, as everywhere, the great majority—was of course left in place.[16] Nor were all those who remained in Judah simply poor people and farmers. Nebuchadnezzar put in charge of the conquered kingdom a high-ranking Judahite named Gedaliah son of Ahikam, grandson of that Shaphan who had been the secretary of King Josiah to whom the priest Hilkiah had—more than thirty-five years earlier, at this time—delivered the scroll of the "law of Moses" that had supposedly been found in the temple. In a real sense, the grandiose ambitions that that "discovery" had inaugurated had been the first step in the development that had now, under the last of Josiah's sons, led to the extermination of the Davidic dynasty and had reduced the kingdom of Judah to a ravaged and desolated province under the Babylonians. Gedaliah set up his headquarters (now that Jerusalem was in ruins) at Mizpah in the region of Benjamin. Certain military leaders who had been in the field when the capital was taken escaped deportation as well, and were reassured by Gedaliah's promises that the Chaldaeans would take no further reprisals against them, if they did not resist Babylonian rule. Soon, even some Judahites who had fled, during the long siege, into nearby kingdoms across the Jordan began filtering back and resettling the devastated coutryside. Before long, agriculture began to return to something approximating normal.

Among those staying in Judah was the prophet Jeremiah.[17] He had originally been among the designated deportees, and was at Ramah among them, in chains, when he was located on the explicit orders of Nebuchadnezzar himself. Nebuzaradan presented to him the king's offer, reported by Baruch as follows: "If you like to come with me to Babylon, come: I shall look after you. If you do not want to go with me to Babylon, do not. Look, you have the whole country before you: go wherever you think it best and most suitable to go". Then he added, before dismissing him with both provisions and a present, that the prophet's options included going to Gedaliah. Rewarded thus for what many of his countrymen would doubtless have described as his treason, Jeremiah journeyed to Mizpah and joined Gedaliah, whose father Ahikam had protected the prophet at the time of his trial, in the early days of the reign of Jehoiakim.

The attack by the Edomites on Arad and other outposts in the Negeb, in fear of which my troop of mercenaries had fled back to Egypt, was not long in coming, although information about it was even slower in reaching me than information about Jerusalem had been. The fortress was again destroyed—this time I do not believe it has ever been rebuilt—and the garrison there, including its commander Eliashib, seems to have been slaughtered. May Yahweh, or any less vindictive god, bless his memory! Considering the enthusiasm with which they had greeted the Babylonians' destruction of Jerusalem, describing the Chaldaeans as Yahweh's divine agents, I could not be very favorably impressed by the denunciations against the Edomites indulged in by several prophets—Jeremiah and Ezekiel, of course, plus someone of whom I had not heard before, named Obadiah.[18]

22. RETIREMENT AND REMINDERS

As soon as we had reached the safety of the Ionian Encampment, my brother Python was insistent that we should immediately make a journey to Naukratis. He was concerned that it had been some while since we had heard anything from Artemisia or any member of Delilah's establishment. We both realized, of course, that the Babylonians' occupation of much of Judah during the time when we had been stationed there had made all forms of communication with the outside world difficult and chancy. Python was determined to marry Artemisia immediately, and to settle with her in Daphnai among the many retired foreign mercenaries there. I was almost equally eager to see Gomer, and of course our beloved Delilah herself, so I was more than willing to accompany him.

When we arrived, we discovered the real reason our letters from Naukratis had ceased. Some sort of deadly, contagious fever had struck the town—probably brought in by recently-arrived Greek traders—and the house of Delilah was one of many places that had lost someone. It had lost three or four of its women, in fact, one of whom had been the beautiful Artemisia. Python was devastated, inconsolable, despite all my best efforts, and Delilah's.

His tragic news threw a pall over my own reunion with Gomer, but it also led us into unprecedentedly serious discussion of our own hopes and plans. She did not want to run out on Delilah in the wake of the hard times that had struck the house, but she did agree that once I had actually retired from service and acquired a plot of land around Daphnai, she would come there and join me—even marry me, if that was my wish, though ceremonies were meaningless to her. We also agreed to ask Delilah to join us and live out her old age in our care. Gomer had seen that Delilah's usual toughness and resilience had been diminished by the recent losses, and I told her of the conversation I had had with Delilah some years earlier about just this eventuality. When we broached the subject with her, she was happy to assent. If I was eager to retire, the eagerness of Delilah, nearly twenty years my senior, was even greater. She recalled our earlier discussion, and agreed that the time indeed had now come.

On our voyage back down the Pelousiac branch of the Nile, I earnestly entreated Python to join us in the household we planned to set up. Ebed-Melech, the Kushite eunuch we had rescued from Judah, who had been eking out a living doing occasional menial jobs around the Encampment, could be expected to join us and help out. In time, I told my brother, he could find someone to aid him in forgetting Artemisia. Maybe even another of Delilah's girls would be interested in coming to Daphnai with us—we could count on Delilah to recommend one who would be to his liking, and to speak well to her on his behalf. The distraught Python would hear none of it. "Just plan your idyllic garden", he shouted at me, "I will live and die a soldier—and my death can't happen soon enough!"

At the Encampment, we were told that a serious mutiny had arisen among the mercenaries stationed at Elephantine, who were actually threatening to desert to the Kushites, and thus to imperil the entire southern frontier of Egypt, canceling the effects of the invasions that both Necho and Psammetichos had recently led. Volunteers were being sought, especially among those who had had experience fighting in Nubia, to travel southward and augment the forces there under Nesuhor, Overseer of the Gate of the Southern Foreign Lands (the elaborate title given to the Egyptian commander at the Nubian border).[1] It seemed probable that Apries' recent ignominious retreat from Judah had undermined confidence in him among many elements of the army, and those "sentenced" to the virtual three-year exile of garrison duty at Elephantine had the further motivation of their unwelcome assignment. Python could not wait to volunteer, and could not wait to sail upriver. I parted from him with an expression of hope that he would return somewhat recovered in spirits, and with reassurances that he would always be welcome in the household I was on the verge of establishing. I never saw my brother again.

I was not far short of sixty years old, and had been working as a soldier for almost forty of those years, a mercenary either of Yahweh of Judah or Amun-Re of Egypt, with very little personal regard for either god. Now I was eager to become a humble farmer, though I would never be the aristocratic landowner I had expected to become during the distant days of my youth in Miletos. But sharing a household again with my "mother" Delilah would be a consolation, and it was time for me to take a new wife and finally put the memory of Tirzah to rest. In general I cared as little for ceremony as Gomer did, but the wedding would for me symbolize that ending as well as our new beginning, so I decided that indeed I did want to go through with it.

One factor inhibited me. I did not want to bind myself in marriage to someone I knew only through an obviously false name, indeed one apparently adopted as a sort of self-insult. Gomer had been the name of the prostitute Yahweh had supposedly ordered the prophet Hosea to marry, but if my Gomer was no longer going to be a prostitute, I did not want her to carry a prostitute's name into our marriage. Now, for the first time, I insisted on knowing her real name, and parentage. She was reluctant, but finally yielded to my importunings, and to Delilah's, probably because now she really did want to relocate to Daphnai with us and give up the life of whoring—and perhaps because she agreed with my reasoning, that the name would no longer be appropriate.

"I am Miriam daughter of Ahab, son of Kolaiah", she finally confessed, ceasing her tears when she saw that I seemed to attach no significance to the connection. "I was left behind in Jerusalem", she explained, "when my father was taken away to Babylon in the first deportation, with the group that accompanied King Jehoiachin. At first I struggled to earn my living in chaste ways, working as a servant, although my family had been well-to-do. Then word reached me that Nebuchadnezzar had executed my father by roasting him alive, on a charge of committing adultery with his neighbors' wives".

"Why was I trying to preserve the family's honor, I then asked myself", Gomer-Miriam continued, "if my hypocrite father—he had even claimed to be a prophet of Yahweh!—had already forfeited it, irrecoverably? A whore's life would be easier and better-paying than the life of a starving servant, so I took a prostitute's name and paid my way to the booming new town of Naukratis by selling my favors to several merchants and shipmasters I encountered on the way. But good fortune, or some god, put me under Delilah's protection, and the years with her have softened my anger and lessened my shame. She has taught me that it is pointless to see my profession as degrading, when practicing it is necessary for staying alive and it does no one any harm. But now I'm tired of it, and ready for a different life. I shall henceforth be Miriam wife of Archon, of Daphnai".

Later, I would recall that Ahab had been one of the "false prophets" denounced by Jeremiah in a letter he had sent to the first group of deportees, a letter to which I have already referred in its appropriate place in my narrative.[2] When I checked my recollection with Miriam, she icily confirmed it, cursing the prophet with several Hebrew words I do not know quite how to translate into Greek—probably they are just as well omitted. I did not share with her any of the expressions of grudging admiration for at least the courage and honesty of Jeremiah that I have offered to my readers.

Since neither she nor I had any prospect of ever entering Judah, or indeed leaving Egypt, again, I anticipated no difficulty in sheltering Miriam from any future references to the prophet. I reminded myself to admonish Ebed-Melech to observe the same reticence, when he moved into our household.

I will not waste the reader's time with details on my demobilization (there was no objection, given my age), the negotiations whereby my meager savings were converted into a small farm with a run-down but fairly spacious house on it, and the arrangements that had to be made to sell Delilah's establishment in Naukratis and to transport her and Miriam (and some of their possessions) to Daphnai.[3] Ebed-Melech, being a refugee without possessions, had only to bring himself, and was able to do that simply by walking the 200 stades or so from the Ionian Encampment. He had been a servant to kings—indeed to kings of three nations: Kush, Egypt, and Judah—but his status in our household was more ambivalent, since I had neither captured nor purchased him in Judah, but had in effect liberated him in the process of rescuing him. Suffice it to say that he willingly helped with the work on the farm, but that I—and the older and younger women—worked equally hard as well. There were no oppressed and no parasites in our home. The labor was difficult at first, none of us being either skilled or experienced at it. The silver Delilah had acquired in exchange for her house in Naukratis was vital in getting us through the first year, since the purchase price of the farm alone had already taken everything I had accumulated.

One thing that kept us hard at work during that early period was our hope, even expectation, that fairly soon Python would return from Upper Egypt, and would be persuaded to join his efforts with ours. As I have indicated already, this was not to be. Nesuhor was successful in suppressing the rebellion and in bringing its leaders downriver for execution. I heard later that he even boasted on a stele he set up at Syene that he had won over the rebels by convincing them with reasonable arguments.[4] But in fact there had been some fighting, and one of the front-line casualties—no doubt he had placed himself in the front line out of reckless disregard for his survival—was my brother. The notice I received from the army informed me that Python son of Amoibichos of Miletos had died heroically in defense of the king and the gods of Egypt. Yes, of course—just as Benaiah son of Elhanan had died for Josiah and Yahweh! A soldier dies when somebody kills him. Any further reasons provided are usually lies.

Surprisingly, however, I was belatedly made aware of a kind of reason for my brother's death, in addition to his grief over Artemisia, because a month or so after the official notice just described, I received a posthumous letter from him, one he had written (on papyrus) just before his last battle (since he fully expected not to survive it), a report of a sort of parting act of hard kindness. Among those recruited for the campaign on short notice, he said in his letter, had been many Greeks and other *alloglossoi* who had been stationed in the *western* delta, soldiers that neither he nor I had encountered during our service in Egypt. Sitting up nights, drinking and bragging around the campfire, he had struck up a few shallow friendships with some of these men.

One of the most talkative—and hard-drinking—had been an Ionian (Python did not supply his city) named Eukles. A couple of nights before the writing of the letter, Eukles had gotten even drunker and more boastful than usual, and had told anyone who would listen about a particular act of "heroism" that had led him, he said, to leave a votive offering in the temple of Aphrodite in Naukratis.[5] "Why would a soldier give thanks to the goddess of love?" he had asked rhetorically. Because, he smirkingly explained, his victory had come not in war, but in sexual conquest! Then he told of serving long ago, almost twenty-five years ago (Eukles was a grizzled veteran), in the army that had marched with Necho and crushed the forces of the king of Judah at Megiddo on its way to the Euphrates. His "victory in love" had come, he said, on the way north, along the coast, when the army had come upon a completely undefended fortress, occupied only by the women and children of a group of mercenaries in Judahite service who had been called to join the king's army at Megiddo.

He laughed as he described how he and some of his comrades (most of them dead by now, he said) had had their way with the women, before killing them and burning their houses. One particular little dark-haired, dark-eyed spitfire, he said, had fought him so furiously that he had decided to kill her young daughter before her eyes as a preliminary to raping the woman and killing her. "Oh, she was a sweet one!" he had exclaimed, "So beautiful I almost hated to finish her off, but there was no way to take her along, with a campaign to be fought up the road, so I gave her a rough ride to remember me by as she died!"

Python, who had heard from me of the fates of my wife Tirzah and our daughter Mahlah, had instantly recognized the scene whose aftermath I had described. Eukles had even provided enough detail to make it more than likely that his specific victims had indeed been my womenfolk, rather than one of my comrades'. In either case, the beast and butcher deserved to die like the animal he was. With great difficulty, Python wrote, he had managed not to say anything in reaction to Eukles' story, but had soon after made his excuses to the group around the campfire and, he told them, headed for his sleeping mat. In reality, he picked a secluded spot and lay in wait for the drunken rapist-murderer, who finally obligingly staggered into dagger range. Not offering such a creature an honorable fair fight, my brother had slipped up behind him and slit his throat. Nor did he even provide any explanation when the dying man gurgled out "Why…?" Python wrote: "I thought, let him have all the explanation my brother Archon ever had!"

He had certainly felt no regret the next day when the body was found and an inquiry was begun to find Eukles' killer. At this point he was indifferent, he said, as to whether he should be found out or not, since he had come on this expedition with the intent to die, anyway. "I expect to accomplish my goal in a battle very soon", he said in the last paragraph of his letter, "but I want you to know, Archon, that at least your family has been avenged. Farewell. Your loving brother, Python son of Amoibichos, Milesian". The letter reached me by the hand of a member of Python's troop who had returned from Nubia. It was, I suppose, some consolation after all these years finally to know who had destroyed my loved ones, and even to know that their killer had met the fate he deserved. But the information had not brought Tirzah back, and the letter itself rekindled my grief for my just-recently-departed brother, so it prompted in me tears of wretched sadness rather than of satisfaction.

If my brother, who had been expected to show up at Daphnai, did not, someone who was absolutely and completely *un*expected *did* show up! To explain this unanticipated appearance, some background must be provided—things I learned about during and after the visit I will describe.

Gedaliah son of Ahikam had been put in charge of the remaining territory and population of Judah by the Babylonians, governing from Mizpah, as I have already reported, and I have already told of developments tending toward recovery—returning refugees from nearby kingdoms, renewed planting of crops, and other positive signs. This situation persisted for four or five years. But one of the military commanders who had sworn an oath of loyalty to Gedaliah, Ishmael son of Nethaniah, had claims of his own—an asserted connection with the deposed royal family, I do not know whether valid or spurious—to be the ruler of Judah. Working in collusion, it was said, with Baalis, king of the Ammonites (the neighbor to whom Zedekiah had been trying to flee when he was captured), Ishmael plotted to murder Gedaliah and make himself king.

Although warned of Ishmael's intentions by another commander, Johanan son of Kareah, Gedaliah did not believe him. At a formal dinner party, Ishmael and his companions turned on and murdered Gedaliah and his Judahite associates who were nearby, as well as the guard of Chaldaean soldiers present. Further murders ensued in support of the coup, and several hostages were taken. Johanan and others managed to free the hostages, but Ishmael escaped to the protection of his Ammonite ally. Now Johanan and the others remaining in Judah had to decide what to do, and what the Chaldaean king was likely to do in response to the murder of his appointee. Would he now deport everybody? Or simply kill everyone? Would he be able to see that those who had pursued Ishmael had remained loyal, and spare them? There were, in fact, ultimately further deportations. Baruch's scroll says that 745 Judahites were deported in Nebuchadnezzar's twenty-third year, a figure that brings Baruch's totals for all three deportations to exactly 4600 persons.[6]

Before that, and not yet knowing what would happen, Johanon and his companions had decided to seek an oracle of Yahweh from—who else?—Jeremiah. Contemptuous of the suppliants, and divining their real hopes in order to dash them, Jeremiah—after keeping them waiting for ten entire days—responded by saying that Yahweh wished them to remain in the country and, above all, not to seek refuge in Egypt. The words attributed to the prophet in Baruch's text warned the questioners, in Yahweh's name: "If you are determined to go to Egypt, and if you do go and settle there, the sword you fear will overtake you there in Egypt, and there you will die".[7]

Not only did Johanan and the others reject the prophet's advice, they forcibly seized and took along Jeremiah—and Baruch—with them on their journey to Egypt, planning to settle there. As Baruch tells it, they stopped in Egypt at Tahpanhes. Tahpanhes is *Daphnai,* the very settlement in which I and my household were now living! Thus, utterly unexpectedly, did Miriam (seething) again look upon the denouncer of her errant father, thus did the eunuch Ebed-Melech see again the prisoner he had rescued, and thus did I see close at hand the inspired madman I had long studied with interest from afar.

The recognition was at first in only one direction, since the Kushite stayed in the background, and since Jeremiah had never seen the daughter of his deportee victim Ahab, nor would he have been able to pick me out among the numerous foreign mercenaries at whom he might have glanced on the street in Jerusalem. Restraining the eunuch from approaching the newcomers, I insisted on first listening in on some of the conversation between them, profiting by their apparent assumption that a Greek retired from Egyptian service would not understand Hebrew.

Referring erroneously to the large fortified storehouse that the Egyptian government maintains in Daphnai, as it does in every city of any size, Jeremiah announced to the assembled refugees that he was burying certain large stones in the terrace outside "Pharaoh's palace in Tahpanhes", saying that Nebuchadnezzar king of Babylon would soon arrive and place his throne over those stones, preparatory to conquering and pillaging Egypt. He then proceeded to denounce Judahites who had already settled in Egypt—there were some in Daphnai, and others in nearby towns, many of whom had gathered to see the newcomers, as word of their arrival had spread. His fiercest denunciation was for their "offering incense to other gods", besides Yahweh, in Egypt—accusing especially the women of this "offense".

Baruch records accurately the unrepentant response of one of the accused women, so I use his text to fill in gaps in my memory of the confrontation:

> We have no intention of listening to the word you have just spoken to us in Yahweh's name, but intend to go on doing all we have vowed to do: offering incense to the Queen of Heaven and pouring libations in her honor, as we used to do, we and our ancestors, our kings and our chief men, in the towns of Judah and the streets of Jerusalem; we had food in plenty then, we lived well, we suffered no disasters. But since we gave up offering incense to the Queen of Heaven and pouring libations in her honor, we have been destitute and have perished either by sword or by famine. Besides, when we offer incense to the Queen of Heaven and pour libations in her honor, do you think we make cakes for her with her features on them, and pour libations to her, without our husbands' knowledge?

Where could one find better evidence that the monotheistic worship of Yahweh, imposed by Josiah on Judah through the use of force (I should know; I was part of that force!), was regarded by the population in general as a betrayal of ancient traditions—and indeed as the *cause* of the disasters that subsequently befell Judah?

Jeremiah, of course, responded with further denunciations, and with a prediction (in Baruch's phrasing) that Yahweh would hand over Hophra king of Egypt "to his enemies and to those determined to kill him" just as he had handed Zedekiah king of Judah over to Nebuchadnezzar.[8]

After the crowd had finally cleared, I approached the prophet and his scribe, who were momentarily left alone, bringing the eunuch with me. Miriam had been quite pleased with the woman's defiance of Jeremiah. But now she categorically refused to have anything to do with the man whom she had such good reason to hate. She went into our house, seemingly somewhat hurt that I was willing to associate with him. Later, I tried to explain to her that my interest was merely an aspect of the "research" (*historia*)[9] that events since the time of Josiah had aroused me to conduct, because of my fascination with the effects of the revolution her nation had undergone. Although herself a victim of these developments, she was not very sympathetic to my argument. She would have preferred simply to forget the events that had brought her to Egypt.

Jeremiah immediately recognized the Kushite, of course, and greeted him enthusiastically, in remembrance of his former kindness. Baruch knew him also, having previously been introduced by his master. I let the three of them talk amiably for a while before introducing myself and reporting (without comment either way) that I had—long ago, before taking service in Egypt—been one of the mercenaries who had helped King Josiah enforce his reforms in the countryside of Judah. Conversing with the prophet himself was difficult. I had the constant feeling that his piercing eyes could see right through my vague and misleading show of sympathy for his cause. I was sure that he could barely restrain himself from denouncing me to my face as a foreign idolator, enemy of the one true god, Yahweh. Probably only his gratitude to the eunuch, who obviously appeared here as my friend and supporter, led him to bite his fiery tongue.

Mercifully, the prophet and the eunuch walked a bit apart as they talked, and I was briefly left alone with the scribe Baruch son of Neraiah. Although he too was a convinced supporter of the monotheistic revolution, he was at least a person of ordinary objective speech in most matters. He admired Jeremiah, and stood in awe of him as a being possessed and inspired by Yahweh, but he knew—better than anyone, since the prophet totally eschewed family and friendships, as part of his understanding of his duty to Yahweh—how difficult his master could be in dealings with normal, uninspired mortals. Without describing my skepticism, I made bold to tell Baruch of my interest in his nation's ancient and recent past, and particularly in the fascinating movement (that description was true enough, whatever attitude one took toward it) in which his mentor was such an important participant.

Perhaps flattered by the efforts a foreigner was making to understand the events we had been discussing, Baruch surprised me with an astoundingly generous offer. He, in his role as Jeremiah's personal scribe, had for a long time been compiling not only a collection of the oracles his master dictated to him, but also a narrative about the prophet's activities and encounters. With his master now effectively retired, exiled to Egypt with the kingdom of Judah in ruins, he believed that he should be able to draw together in some coherent form all the oracles and narratives within the next few months. Would it aid me in my studies if he had a copy of his scroll made and sent to me within the next year or so?

I was stunned, and incredibly appreciative. I accepted Baruch's offer with profuse thanks. Now I thought to myself how fortunate it had been that I had not let myself be swayed by my wife's very understandable hostility so as to have avoided meeting these men. I salved my conscience with the thought that she had, anyway, nothing against *Baruch*, only against Jeremiah, and it was Baruch with whom I was dealing in a friendly manner.

Soon our visitors went on their way, seemingly heading upriver to make stops at other settlements of Judahites, which I already know by personal observation to extend at least as far as Elephantine. I wondered if the temple there had yet been completed, and what Jeremiah might have to say when he discovered gods in addition to Yahweh being worshiped in it, and receiving sacrifices? I never saw either the prophet or the scribe again, but Baruch was true to his promise: about a year later, a mercenary returning from duty in Upper Egypt dropped off with me in Daphnai a packet containing a large papyrus roll, sealed with a blob of dried clay on which a signet had stamped a brief text in three lines: "Belonging to Berekyahu son of Neriyahu, the scribe". This papyrus roll is the "scroll of Baruch" which I repeatedly cite in my narrative, and which enables me to reproduce many of the pronouncements of Jeremiah with an exactness that might otherwise seem suspect to the reader.[10]

My narrative could easily end here: no need to strain the reader's patience with the tale of a man growing old on his farm, as others grow old around him. Delilah enjoyed only a few years of quiet retirement, since she had already been very advanced in years by the time we settled at Daphnai. Miriam, considerably younger than myself, is still very much alive, though we have never been blessed with children, so it is a mystery what will happen to the farm when we die. Ebed-Melech, with our blessing, set out to return to his native Nubia shortly after Delilah's death. I was able to persuade an old fellow-soldier (not as old as I, obviously!) to take him aboard ship as a servant, with the understanding that he would be dropped off at Elephantine and left to find his own way from there. I believe he reached Napata safely, since he managed to send me a letter—in his odd combination of Greek, Hebrew, Egyptian, and Kushite—telling me he had seen the gravestone of my brother Python at Syene. He also reported stopping at the great riverside temples of Ramses the Great again, and even rubbing his hand over the inscriptions Python and I had carved there.

Yet my account does not end here. As my reader knows from the opening lines, the very thing that finally galvanized me to write down in some coherent form information from all the notes and scrolls I had been accumulating for many years was the unexpected reappearance in the west of the now-aged Nebuchadnezzar. Describing events surrounding that appearance will suffice to make me consider my story complete.

23. ONE FINAL CRISIS

My narrative of Nebuchadnezzar's last western campaign must necessarily begin sometime before his appearance and extend somewhat beyond his departure.[1] Both the reasons for his invitation to intervene and the consequences of his intervention must be discovered within Egypt itself. Although the brief skirmish in which his army was involved occurred in the region east of the delta, close to where I have been living in retirement, the significant events both leading to and following that encounter took place in the western delta, or even farther west,[2] so I know about those events only from second-hand and perhaps unreliable accounts. Indeed, some of the reports I have heard *must* be unreliable, since the stories disagree very greatly.

All informants agree that Apries' troubles began with his intervention in strife involving Kyrene. That city is a Greek colony on the Libyan coast, many stades west of the delta, which had been founded somewhere around the time when I was serving as a mercenary under King Josiah in Judah.[3] The Greeks there, Dorians from the island of Thera, had coexisted fairly peacefully with the Libyan tribes of the area until recently. But then they had issued an invitation to other Greek colonists to come and join them, offering as inducement more land to be taken over from the Libyans. The most important of the Libyan chiefs, called Adikran, had asked Apries for help in resisting the new influx of Greeks, and Apries had agreed to provide it.

Since the enemy was to be the Greeks of Kyrene, the Pharaoh had marched out with only his native Egyptian soldiers, not his Greek mercenaries (this fact alone tends to limit the reliability of my account, since fellow Greek mercenaries were usually my primary sources for military information). Unfortunately. Apries had greatly underestimated the Kyrenians and their new colonists, and his army was decisively defeated at a place near Kyrene called Irasa, with a great many Egyptian soldiers killed. The ineptitude in command that had been evident in the early days of Apries' reign, during his futile invasion and ignominious retreat from Judah, continued to the end.

This time, however, the Egyptian soldiers had had enough. Blaming him for the heavy casualties the Kyrenian campaign had brought, they rose in revolt. Apries sent his leading general, Amasis, with orders to quell the uprising, but—as everyone now knows—Amasis instead accepted the rebels' offer to take over the leadership of their movement and claim the throne for himself. Colorful stories are told about Amasis; they are still being told, now that he is firmly in power as king. Having seen Amasis at close hand during the Nubian invasion and on other campaigns, I find many of these stories believable—including the one about how he responded to Apries' emissary seeking peace. This man, an eminent courtier, delivered Apries' summons to Amasis and asked for his reply. It is said that Amasis, who was sitting on horseback during the conference, lifted his leg and loudly farted, bidding the courtier to take that reply back to Apries![4]

The wordless answer was clear enough, and preparations for battle ensued. Since the Egyptian regulars were solidly behind the usurper—the reader may recall that Amasis had commanded the Egyptian troops during the Nubian campaign many years earlier—Apries had no choice but to pin his hopes on the *alloglossoi*, his Greek and Karian mercenaries. These were of course the very troops whom he had left behind when making war on the Greeks of Kyrene, distrustful of their loyalty in that conflict! They were a formidable force, as many as 30,000 strong, but the numbers supporting Amasis were even larger. All informants agree that the battle took place at the western edge of the delta, some of them specifying the town the Greeks call Momemphis, and everybody agrees that Amasis was victorious.

Agreement ends there, however. Some—obviously wrong!—used to say that Apries was killed in that first battle. Others assert that the defeated Apries immediately fled abroad, to the island of Kypros. Wherever he went at first, Apries clearly was not dead, since he ended up taking refuge in Babylon with Nebuchadnezzar, and persuading that king to assist him in trying to reclaim his crown.

The Chaldaean was not motivated by generosity, of course. He had long coveted Egypt, and his inability to conquer it during the period of his frequent western campaigns had been his one conspicuously unsuccessful military undertaking. He still lacked the ability to conquer the Two Lands directly, but having it in the control of a grateful ally whom he had reinstalled as king would proclaim his power to the whole world, a fitting capstone to his long and successful reign.

Amasis, meanwhile, had made his peace with the foreign mercenaries whom Apries had led against him. They certainly had no loyalty to a king in exile, and their services were too valuable for the new king to hold a grudge against them. So the Egyptian army that confronted Nebuchadnezzar and Apries included both of its traditional elements. Not surprisingly, it won in the encounter. I did not get close enough to the battle-site to bring myself into personal danger (my old legs are not so good at running anymore, if that should have proved necessary!), and that is why I once again have to rely only on conflicting reports of what happened to Apries during the battle.

Some say he was killed in the skirmish and Amasis brought his body back to Sais, others that he was captured and taken back to Sais alive.[5] In either case, Nebuchadnezzar's project had aborted, and he took his army back to Babylonia, presumably never to return to the frontiers of Egypt again.

Those prophets—notably Jeremiah and Ezekiel—who had crowingly predicted his conquest of Egypt, in punishment for the broken reed's encouragement to the kings of Judah in resisting the will of Yahweh, have proved false prophets in this particular, at least.[6]

Whether Apries arrived in the capital as a corpse, or survived there for a while as a prisoner, it is generally agreed that the clever Amasis granted to his predecessor an opulent state funeral and all the traditional burial rites and post-burial reverence due to a King of Upper and Lower Egypt. This he did in his own interest, to establish his own legitimacy. In the few years that have passed since his usurpation of the position of Apries, he appears to have been successful. There seems to be no challenge to the power of the second Pharaoh Ahmose. That is his actual Egyptian name, shared with the founder of what is called the "New Kingdom", who ruled almost a thousand years ago,[7] even though I have consistently referred to him by the name the Greeks give to him. I expect him to be ruling Egypt long after I am gone.

It is said that many Egyptians, recalling Apries' use of Greek troops against their own soldiers, would like to see the Greek presence in Egypt restricted, if not eliminated. Some say that the politically astute Amasis is considering restricting Greek trading activities entirely to Naukratis, and nowhere else in the kingdom. Rumors also suggest that he is contemplating moving the base of the *alloglossoi* from the Encampments on the Pelousiac branch of the Nile to Memphis. Even if he ends up making those concessions to ethnocentric sentiment, I don't think it will have any really deleterious effects on Greeks already in Egypt, such as myself. The great majority of Greek trading has always taken place in Naukratis, and we retired soldiers tending our farms at Daphnai and elsewhere are surely not classified as "traders" or "merchants".

In fact, Amasis, despite his rise as the champion of the native Egyptians against the Greek mercenaries, shows some tendencies toward philhellenism. He realizes that he cannot do without his foreign troops (wherever they are stationed), and he continues, like his predecessors among the Saite kings, to recruit at the Greek festivals and games, maintaining good will at the Greek sanctuaries with generous votive offerings. Although many mercenaries have always taken their pay and gone home, those of us who have stayed on in Egypt have not been bothered, anymore under Amasis than under the preceding kings.[8] I expect to die here in peace, doubtless fairly soon!

EPILOGUE

During the few years that have passed since Nebuchadnezzar's final withdrawal from the Egyptian frontier, I have been able to acquire other scrolls, or pieces of scrolls, thanks to a few lingering army contacts both in Egypt and in Judah. Thus I have come into possession of numerous texts attributed—I do not know how accurately—to Ezekiel and other Judahite prophets, and what appear to be early drafts of some kind of narrative treatment of the story of the kingdoms of Israel and Judah. Myths and legends about earlier times, too, long transmitted orally, were beginning to be written down during my lifetime, both before and after the fall of Jerusalem, both in Judah and among the deportees in Babylonia, although I personally have seen few of these texts.

It is hard to guess where all this literary productivity will go, or whether anyone will ever gather it into some kind of coherent collection. When and if that happens, it is a safe bet that stories will be rewritten and events will be reinterpreted. I thought I already saw the beginning of that process in the way the partisans of Josiah interpreted the events of the time of Hezekiah—making the rebel against the Assyrian Sennacherib into a proto-Josiah in all respects, political and cultic. My own forays into the Judahite countryside had caused me to doubt such assertions at the time. Subsequently, of course, Josiah too had to be reinterpreted, since he cannot have been both Yahweh's most favored king and an insignificant petty ruler just tossed aside by Pharaoh Necho on his way to deal with serious opponents. Will Baruch's collection of texts relating to Jeremiah be revised by later editors if his predictions—the utter destruction of

Egypt, then of Babylon, and the return of the deportees to Judah, for example—turn out to be inaccurate?[1]

With such considerations in mind, I resolved to compile my memoirs of the eventful years of my life, as a potential corrective to the kind of culticly-slanted accounts of these years that I expect will be written among the Judahites. At least my narrative will have the virtue of being essentially an eyewitness account, not re-thought and updated a generation or a century or more later. I write of what I experienced or saw or heard about, and I try to say which is which.

It seems to me that the kind of intolerant monotheism that Josiah's revolution had advocated and practiced is extremely dangerous. What if some descendant of Josiah's people should someday decide to detach the religion's intolerance and violence from its ethnic roots in Judah, and preach a form of intolerant and repressive monotheism that could be adopted by some larger, more powerful kingdom or empire? What if such a movement should spread—horrifying thought!—to the entire Greek-speaking world, for example? Even worse, what if *rival* prophets should establish intolerant, violent monotheisms in two or more great powers, and each should decide that *its* version of monotheism must triumph over any or all others, by violence and murder? The slaughter that could ensue would be unimaginable and potentially interminable.

Surely I am worrying excessively, in expressing such thoughts and imagining such terrifying phantasms. Most of those who were closely associated with Josiah's monotheistic revolution are either dead or in exile in Babylonia. Despite Jeremiah's prophecy of their eventual return, there seems to be little likelihood of it ever happening, any more than the deportees from Samaria ever returned there. Even if some of the Babylonian exiles should ever make their way back to the neighborhood of destroyed Jerusalem, it seems unlikely that they, or their particular interpretation of divine will and human events, would be able to take over from the great majority of their countrymen who had been left behind when the elite of court and temple were deported. The Yahweh-worshipers of the Babylonian western province that was once the kingdom of Judah practice their cult in much the same old-fashioned way that the ones who have taken up residence in Egypt do—treating Yahweh as their chief god, but as one god among several.[2]

Nonetheless, I am eager to have my counter-version of the events of this period preserved, and I have some hopes of accomplishing this. I have earlier spoken of the interpreters who worked among the soldiers of foreign speech in the Encampments in the eastern delta, and mentioned how helpful some of them had been to me in learning about Egyptian customs and the Egyptian past. One of these young men, indeed one who took a genuine interest in my inquiries and became quite friendly with me, later moved on to a position in the household of a high-ranking Egyptian official near Memphis. We maintained our friendship through correspondence over many years, into my old age and his middle years.

Among the many Egyptian customs he described to me was the practice of enclosing within the sarcophagus of a mummified Egyptian noble a large scroll of papyrus covered with all kinds of spells to assist the deceased in his afterlife, rendered in ink in a version of the Egyptian sacred writing. Such a scroll is called a "Book of the Dead".[3] His own employer has ordered the writing of such a Book to be buried with him. My Egyptian friend is certain, thanks to his contacts with other servants of this aging nobleman, that when the time comes to put him in his tomb, it will be possible to arrange to have a second scroll—my manuscript—put in the sarcophagus along with his master's copy of the Book of the Dead. As the only member of the household able to read Greek, he has been able to convince his fellow servants that the scroll he is asking them to inter is just another kind of Book of the Dead, one invoking the blessings of foreign gods on the deceased!

So I conclude my narrative here, lest I should die before handing it over to my Egyptian co-conspirator, and lest his employer should die before he has the chance to add the manuscript to the grave-goods. Where the grave will be I do not know; it is a closely-guarded secret, because of the very legitimate fear Egyptians have of grave-robbers. Even the tombs of Pharaohs have not been exempt from their irreligious greed, so I know that it is only a matter of chance whether the tomb in which my text is to be buried will escape robbery, or for how long. But if a manuscript will endure anywhere, it will endure in the arid climate of Egypt's desert, in whose fringes nobles' tombs are usually located.

I hereby sign this long manuscript, produced with a different instrument than the *peleqos* with which I once scratched my "report" of the Nubian expedition on the leg of Ramses' statue:

> We words were written by Archon son of Amoibichos and Reed-Pen son of Nobody.[4]

Editorial Materials

CHRONOLOGY OF ATTESTED EVENTS

Every item below has at least ancient documentation that is not demonstrably unreliable, although some dates may be approximate or controversial. All years are BCE.

Late 13C	Inscription of Merneptah (son of Ramses II) lists entity called "Israel" among defeated foes
Late 10C	Itinerary of Sheshonq I (=biblical Shishak of Rehoboam's reign?) lists cities in regions of Judah and Israel taken during invasion (not mentioning either kingdom by name)
853	Battle of Qarqar (Assyria vs. Aramaic-organized coalition including Ahab of Israel), first mention of Israel or Judah in Assyrian documents
9C	"House of David" mentioned in Aramaic inscription from Tel Dan, maybe also in Moabite Stone
ca. 750-710	Prophets Amos and Hosea active in Israel, Micah in Judah
740s-720s	Tiglath-pileser III (invited by Ahaz) begins Assyrian dominance of Canaan-Palestine
ca. 740-700	Prophet Isaiah active in Jerusalem
722-721	Assyrians take Samaria, reducing Israel to an Assyrian province, deporting and soon replacing part of population
by 716	Kushites in control in Egypt; Piye's invasion some years earlier, but apparently withdraws
713-712	Yamani (=Yawani?) seizes power in Philistine city of Ashdod, is driven out by Sargon, flees to Shabako, but is sent back to Sargon
ca. 705	Hezekiah deposes Assyrian vassal Padi in Ekron, is also involved in Ashkelon

701	Sennacherib invades Judah, takes many cities (especially Lachish), defeats (at Eltekeh on coast road) Egyptian force sent to aid Judah, deports thousands, menaces Jerusalem (newly enlarged, strengthened, and given improved water supply by Hezekiah), departs on receipt of huge tribute, gives much Judahite territory to Philistine allies
680s-640s	Manasseh is generally loyal vassal to Assyria; some territory apparently restored
Reign of Manasseh?	Achish son of Padi of Ekron dedicates temple to goddess
671-mid-660s	Assyrian invasions of Egypt, driving out Taharqa, then Tantamani, setting up Saite kings as Assyrian vassals in delta, who are left in control when Assyrians withdraw
656	Psammetichos I effectively king of united Egypt from this date
Reign of Psammetichos I	Judahite mercenaries established at Elephantine; Skythians (who have plundered temple at Ashkelon) bribed not to invade Egypt
652	Kimmerians sack Sardis in Lydia, Magnesia on Maiander in Ionia; Ephesos and Miletos escape damage
640s-on	Saite Egyptians, now independent but in alliance with Assyria, assume nominal control of vassals west of Euphrates, as Assyrians are increasingly preoccupied with troubles in eastern parts of empire, especially secession of Babylon, from ca. 631
by 633	Josiah is asserting independence from Assyrian-Egyptian alliance, working with Babylonians
ca. 627	Beginning of Jeremiah's prophetic activity
Late 620s-late 610s?	Lydian kings Sadyattes and Alyattes ravage territory of Miletos, until Thrasyboulos negotiates alliance
622	Book of Law of Moses reportedly found in Jerusalem temple by priestly and governmental

	officials, taken to Josiah, who, after consulting prophetess Huldah, begins—or intensifies—major cultic reforms, involving complete centralization of cult in Jerusalem temple and destruction of all other shrines to Yahweh and other gods throughout Judah
621 and beyond	Josiah celebrates national Passover ceremony in Jerusalem, extends cultic changes to some parts of former kingdom of Israel, including northern royal shine at Bethel
Reign of Josiah	Greek mercenaries and Judahite laborers apparently stationed at fort Mesad Hashavyahu, on coast north of Ashdod
616	Assyrian and Egyptian forces repel incursion into Assyrian territory by Nabopolassar
615	Babylonian siege of city of Asshur fails
614	Medes take Asshur, then make alliance with Babylonians
612	Nineveh falls to Babylonian-Median coalition; rump Assyrian kingdom established in Harran in western Mesopotamia
610	Harran falls to Babylonians and Medes
Reign of Necho II	Accomplishments include beginning canal from Red Sea to Nile and sending Phoinikian naval squadron to circumnavigate Africa (clockwise from Red Sea)
609	Necho unsuccessfully tries to re-take Harran for Assyrian remnants, encounters and kills Josiah on his way north, at Megiddo; on his way back south, he deposes Jehoahaz and sets up another son of Josiah, Jehoiakim, as his vassal king in Judah
605	Chaldaean crown prince Nebuchadnezzar defeats Necho at Karchemish and Hamath, interrupts follow-up campaign to return to Babylon for coronation upon father's death
604	Nebuchadnezzar returns to west, takes and destroys Ashkelon, occupies Gaza

ca. 604-3	Egyptian vassals in area fearful, including letter-writer Adon of Ekron
601	Nebuchadnezzar advances on Egypt, but is stopped at Migdol; Egyptians reoccupy Gaza
600	Jehoiakim withholds tribute from Nebuchadnezzar
599	Nebuchadnezzar busy with Arab tribes, only sends minimal forces vs. Judah
598-597	Nebuchadnezzar besieges Jerusalem; Jehoiakim dies during siege and is replaced by son Jehoiachin (=Jeconiah=Coniah); Jehoiachin, his family, courtiers, and others (including the prophet Ezekiel) deported to Babylon after surrender
Now or during later siege	Ostraca at Arad in Judah show provisions distributed to *Kittiyim* (Greeks and other western mercenaries)
597	Zedekiah, uncle of Jehoiachin and son of Josiah, designated king in Judah by Babylonians
593	Expedition to Nubia led by Psammetichos II, one of his commanders being Amasis; graffiti carved at Abu Simbel in Lower Nubia by Greek mercenary Archon son of Amoibichos and others; among soldiers scratching their names is Python son of Amoibichos
591	Psammetichos makes religious pilgrimage to Palaistine area, invites Egyptian priests
589-588	Zedekiah rebels from Babylonian vassalage, contrary to advice of Jeremiah, who is imprisoned but aided by Kushite eunuch Ebed-Melech; Jerusalem besieged by Nebuchadnezzar
588	Apries brings army up from Egypt, causing Babylonians to lift siege of Jerusalem temporarily, but returns to Egypt without a battle
587-586	Jerusalem re-besieged, wall breached, city and temple destroyed, king caught and blinded, further deportations; Gedaliah appointed to govern those left behind, including Jeremiah (released and favorably treated for having encouraged sur-

	render to Babylonians); Nebuchadnezzar begins 13-year(?) siege of Tyre
580s?	Mercenaries at Elephantine attempt to desert to Nubia; Nesuhor suppresses the revolt
ca. 582 or 581	Gedaliah assassinated; many in Judah flee to Egypt, forcibly taking Jeremiah with them to Tahpanhes (Daphnai); further deportations
6C	Charaxos, brother of poet Sappho, is smitten with the courtesan Rhodopis, in Naukratis; Alkaios writes of his brother Antimenidas, mercenary with the Babylonian army
570	General Amasis seizes Egyptian throne; Apries flees, ultimately to Nebuchadnezzar
567	Nebuchadnezzar approaches Egypt in attempt to restore Apries, but is driven off; Apries, killed in or after the battle, is given royal funeral by Amasis
561	Exiled Judahite king Jehoiachin freed from imprisonment, allowed to dine daily at table with Amel-Marduk
Reign of Amaisis	Greek traders restricted to Naukratis and mercenary camps moved from delta to Memphis, but Amasis cultivates good relations with Greeks, gaining reputation as philhellene
550-525	Persians conquer Medes, Lydians, Ionians, Babylonians, Egyptians, establish huge empire
539	Persian capture of Babylon is followed by release of deportees from Judah
520-515	Temple in Jerusalem rebuilt
From 5C	Cultic practices such as those advocated by Josiah become the norm around Jerusalem

King			
GREEK TYRANTS	LYDIA & *MEDIA*	EGYPT	NUBIA
		Menes=Narmer? c.3100s	
		Khufu=Cheops 2500s	
		Ahmose (I) c.1552-1527	
		Tuthmosis III c.1490-1436	
		Ramses II the Great c.1290-1224	
		Merneptah 1224-1204(?)	
		Sheshonq I 945-924	
			Kushites:
			Piye 746-716
			Shabako 716-702
			Shebitku 702-690
			Taharqa 690-664
			Tantamani 664-656
	Gyges c.680-c.652		
	Ardys c.652-c.630		
	Sadyattes c.630-610	**Saites:**	Anlamani c.623-568
Pittakos of Mytilene	*Cyaxares* *625-585*	Psammetichos I 664-610	
Periandros of Korinth	Alyattes c.610-c.560	Necho II 610-595	
Thrasyboulos of Miletos			
			Aspelta c.593-568
		Psammetichos II 595-589	
	Astyages *585-550*	Apries 589-570	
	Kroisos (Croesus) c.560-540s	Amasis 570-526	
		Psammetichos III 526-525	

LISTS

PHILISTINE CITIES	ISRAEL	JUDAH	ASSYRIA & *BABYLONIA*
	Saul? 11-10C?		
		David? 10C?	
		Solomon? 10C?	
	Jeroboam (I)	Rehoboam	
	922-901	922-915	
	Omri 876-869		
	Ahab 868-850		Shalmaneser III
			858-824
			Tiglath-pileser III
	Hoshea	Ahaz (Jehoahaz I)	744-727
	732-722	735-715	Shalmaneser V
"Yamani" of			726-722
Ashdod		Hezekiah	Sargon II
Sillibel of		715-687	721-705
Gaza			Sennacherib
Padi of Ekron		Manasseh	704-681
Mitinti of		687-642	Esarhaddon
Ashdod			680-669
Achish of		Amon	Ashurbanipal
Ekron		642-640	668-c.631
		Josiah	*Nabopolassar*
		640-609	*626-605*
		Jehoahaz (II)	Ashur-uballit II
		609	611-609
		Jehoiakim	
		609-598	*Nebuchadnezzar II*
Aga of		Jehoiachin	*604-562*
Ashkelon		598-597	
Adon of Ekron		Zedekiah	
		597-587	
		Gedaliah?	
		586-582?	
			Amel-Marduk
			561-560
			Nabonidus
			555-539

CONTROVERSIES, CONVENTIONS, SOURCES, ABBREVIATIONS

CURRENT BIBLICAL HISTORY CONTROVERSIES

My primary field in Ph.D. studies, and the area in which I have published scholarly books, is Classical Greece, so my grasp of ancient Greek is far superior to my very minimal knowledge of biblical Hebrew and my virtually nonexistent exposure to Egyptian writing. But I had some graduate-level training in biblical studies many years ago, I have long taught my department's survey course in the ancient Near East, and I have lately tried my hand at teaching a seminar dealing with Egyptian history. In doing the research for my article, "Ancient Israel in Western Civ Textbooks", *History Teacher* 34 (2001) 297-326, I became conversant with much of the recent scholarly literature in English concerning the history of the later decades of the kingdom of Judah and the development of the Hebrew Bible. Intensive reading begun then has continued, so that I am now aware of several important more recent studies, and I have also belatedly consulted some key works that I had missed. Important collections of essays not cited by me in *HT* include S.W. Holloway and L.K. Handy (eds.), *The Pitcher Is Broken* (Sheffield 1995) and two volumes edited by Lester L. Grabbe, *Can a 'History of Israel' Be Written?* (Sheffield 1997) and *Did Moses Speak Attic?* (Sheffield 2001).

Treating Archon's memoir as essentially reflecting historical reality would tend to put anyone at a fairly definable point along the spectrum of current scholarly controversies about the writing of the Hebrew Bible and its constituent parts. Archon claims awareness of collections of oracles circulating, at least partly in written form, that are attributed to prophets working in the eighth century BCE, in the time of King Hezekiah and even somewhat earlier. With respect to his own time, from the reign of Josiah in Judah to the early years of the reign of Amasis in Egypt, Archon asserts a rather thorough knowledge of the prophecies of Jeremiah and the narratives about that prophet attributed to the scribe Baruch. He claims a lesser level of knowledge about pronouncements of the deportee Ezekiel, and says that he has seen at least some of that prophet's oracles in written form also. Archon is more vague about what other prophecies and narratives from Judah he has seen and/or heard about, but he says enough to lead the reader to think that at least parts of what modern commentators call the Pentateuch and the Deuteronomistic History were being written in his day. Certainly he accepts that some written document relating primarily to cultic law was "found" in the temple in Jerusalem shortly before his own arrival in the city, although he explicitly denies having actually seen it.

Given such claims, no one who accepts Archon's narrative as basically historical can take a hard-core "minimalist" position in the contemporary debate about biblical composition. It would be impossible to answer an unqualified "yes" to the question in the title of Niels Peter Lemche's celebrated article of 1993, "The Old Testament—A Hellenistic Book?" (reprinted, "slightly revised", in *Did Moses Speak Attic?*

287-318). Archon claims to provide independent testimony that the so-called Deuteronomic Reformation of Josiah did in fact occur, at least in outline, pretty much as described in 2 Kings 22-23, minus the theological editorializing. It is otherwise a logically valid objection that the linchpin of the entire "documentary hypothesis"—acceptance that the law "found" in Josiah's time is in some sense to be identified with the biblical book of Deuteronomy—is merely the formulating of a theory of biblical composition whose only source is the biblical text itself, an unverifiable and circular process. Thus, e.g., Donald H. Akenson, *Surpassing Wonder* (New York 1998, pb Chicago 2001) sees very clearly the centrality of the book of Deuteronomy for the structure of Genesis-Kings (26-27), yet finds it impossible—and unimportant—to decide whether the "finding" of the law under Josiah was a deception perpetrated by Josiah or the literary invention of a mid-6th-century "writer-editor" among the deportees in Babylonia (51-52). For other suggestions of late invention of the whole story, see *HT* nn. 22 and 59.

Archon also generally accepts the various chronological indicators and biographical details supplied in the biblical Book of Jeremiah, a position which would necessarily discount the brilliantly deconstructionist treatment of that book in Robert P. Carroll's monumental 874-page *Jeremiah: A Commentary* (Philadelphia 1986) and subsequently in, e.g., the three chapters he contributes to A.R.P. Diamond, K.M. O'Connor, and L. Stulman (eds.), *Troubling Jeremiah* (Sheffield 1999) 73-86, 220-243, 423-443. One would have, instead, to favor something closer to Carroll's earlier orientation as presented in *From Chaos to Covenant: Prophecy in the Book of Jeremiah* (New York 1981), which granted the biblical book a considerably larger historical kernel.

On the other hand, Archon's narrative provides little comfort to "maximalists" who believe in the existence of extensive pre-biblical Hebrew documents dating from the reign of Solomon and produced more-or-less continuously thereafter, or even to those who simply accept the historicity of Solomon and the united monarchy in general. Nor does Archon lend any support at all to fundamentalists and crypto-fundamentalists who assert the reliability of the patriarchal narratives, the exodus, the conquest of Canaan, etc. To him these are mere stories, about which he is openly skeptical. Nor is Archon compatible with essentially fundamentalist commentaries on Jeremiah, such as the two-volume opus of William L. Holladay (Philadelphia 1986 and 1989).

Following Archon would place the reader in the camp of someone like Israel Finkelstein (see F&S in FREQUENTLY-CITED MODERN WORKS..., below), who views the reign of Josiah as the decisive moment marking the beginning of the creation of what ultimately became the biblical text. A clear description of Finkelstein's views appears in Haim Watzman, *Archaeology* 54.5 (2001) 30-33, while a detailed interview of Finkelstein by Hershel Shanks in *Biblical Archaeology Review* 28.6 (2002) 38ff clarifies his position in the spectrum of archaeologists and biblical historians; see also the reasoned critique of his position by Amihai Mazar, *BAR* 29.2 (2003) 60-61. Baruch Halpern's observations on the nature and consequences of Josiah's revolution are largely compatible with Finkelstein's. See citations and descriptions of his brilliant, fundamental article "Sybil" (1996) at *HT* n. 71 and in my notes to ch. 3 below. Views in that article build upon those expressed in his chapter in J. Neusner, B.A. Levine, & E.S. Frerichs (eds.), *Judaic Perspectives on Ancient Israel* (Philadelphia 1987) 77-115.

Halpern and Finkelstein work together on the excavations at Megiddo: *BAR* 29.5 (2003) 19-20 shows them both at a celebration marking the 100th anniversary of the beginning of digging there. They clearly agree on many issues; it is noteworthy that a letter critical of arguments offered in Finkelstein's interview (above) is answered by Halpern at *BAR* 29.2 (2003) 16. Halpern is more inclined than Finkelstein is, however, to accept the antiquity and usefulness of sources underlying earlier periods of the history of Judah and Israel as described in the biblical narrative. See his *The First Historians: The Hebrew Bible and History* (San Francisco 1988), his chapter on "The State of Israelite History" in G.N. Knoppers and J.G. McConville (eds.), *Reconsidering Israel and Judah* (Winona Lake 2000) 540-565, and his defense of the earliness of numerous biblical passages at *BAR* 29.5 (2003) 50-57. Presumably his history of Israel (forthcoming 2004) will defend his position in detail.

William G. Dever, for all the demons of crypto-fundamentalism that clearly tempt him, and contribute to the excessive and *ad hominem* attacks on "minimalists" in his recent book (see Dever, *W&W* in FREQUENTLY-CITED MODERN WORKS..., below) and many articles, does not differ fundamentally from the position of Halpern, and is closer to Finkelstein than he probably would like to admit. See Shanks, *BAR* 28.6 (2002) 6 and 71 for a brief account of the bad blood between Dever and Finkelstein; obviously by prior arrangement, the interview of Finkelstein by Shanks, which mentions dozens of archaeologists and biblical historians, omits any reference at all to the very prominent Dever.

Archon is a skeptical or even hostile witness to what appear, from his account, to be the beginnings of biblical monotheism. He is turned off, appalled, horrified—even if also strangely fascinated—by the religious revolution that so many have found so positive and admirable in its implications. His jaundiced Ionian eye is the critical historian's eye, whether that of Herodotos a century later or of Halpern or Finkelstein or the "minimalists" of today. Perhaps personalizing the horrors and cruelties of religious developments that have been viewed favorably and admiringly by most readers—whether readers of traditional "biblical histories" or of Bible-friendly "inspirational" novels—is an exercise worth performing.

CONVENTIONS ADOPTED IN THE TEXT

When Archon quotes directly from collections of prophecies that have ended up within the Hebrew Bible, I have plugged in the appropriate passages from the *New Jerusalem Bible* (NJB). This is a translation that I favor (despite its imperfections) because, unlike any other in-print English-language Bible of which I am aware, it says "Yahweh" when the consonants YHWH appear in the Hebrew. The online WEB version (http://worldenglishbible.org/bible/web) shares this virtue, but all other printed and online translations seem to follow the late pious synagogue tradition of substituting "The Lord", based on the "Adonai" that was pronounced instead of the divine name when reading the Hebrew text aloud. Very obviously, no such convoluted usage was practiced by the biblical prophets, whose only claim to legitimacy was the assertion "Yahweh says this". Sometimes I slightly modify punctuation or capitalization, and I "Americanize" the NJB's British spelling ("honor" instead of "honour", etc.). Biblical names and places (including names of Assyrian and Babylonian kings mentioned in the Bible) are spelled in the traditional Latinized-Anglicized ways, for ease of recognition (thus, e.g., I use the biblical "Nebuchadnezzar" rather than the more correct "Nebuchadrezzar" of scholarly histories of Babylon). Invariably, however, I employ "Judahites" in referring to natives of the kingdom of Judah, rather than the commonly-used but anachronistic and Latinized "Judaeans", based on the Latin name of the later Roman province of Judaea, or the even more anachronistic and primarily religious term "Jews".

Greek names and toponyms—including Greek versions of Egyptian names and toponyms—are directly transliterated, not Latinized. Thus I use Miletos and Naukratis, not Miletus and Naucratis; Alkaios and Psammetichos, not Alcaeus and Psammetichus; etc. A few very familiar toponyms, e.g., Athens and Thebes, are simply Anglicized. Transliterated Greek spellings in my text generally follow the classical Attic versions of the words, since these should be less exotic for the reader than Archon's archaic Ionic spellings would be. I have let him give his distances in *stadia*, Anglicizing the term itself to "stades", rather than using modern units of distance or even anachronistic ancient ones employed by the Persians (see Herodotus 2.6 for several), Hellenistic Greeks, or Romans. The reader may think of a stade as being approximately 600 feet or 200 yards or.18 kilometer; thus about nine stades equal a mile, and some 5.63 stades equal a kilometer. Archon's cubit (the distance from the elbow to the tips of the fingers) is approximately a foot and a half, or a bit under half a meter.

FREQUENTLY-CITED ANCIENT WORKS OR COLLECTIONS OF WORKS IN TRANSLATION, WITH ABBREVIATED CITATION FORMS

Books of the canonical Hebrew Bible ("Old Testament" in Christian terminology), are cited by the chapter(s) and verse(s), of the *New Jerusalem Bible* translation, with names of books abbreviated in traditional or obvious ways. Examples: Jer. 52.28-30; 2 Kgs. 24.3; Ezek. 16.12.

Non-biblical Ancient Near Eastern works are frequently cited in the translations of James B. Pritchard (ed.), *The Ancient Near East*, 2 vols. (Princeton 1958, 1975), handy selections—Egyptian, Assyrian, Babylonian, Aramaic, and non-biblical Hebrew documents—derived from the much larger *Ancient Near Eastern Texts*, which is usually cited by Near Eastern specialists. Citations are by volume and page number(s), thus: Prit. 2.122A and fig. 38 = the first of three ostraca from Arad translated on p. 122 of Pritchard's vol. 2 and a photograph (actually two photographs) of this ostracon at the back of the same volume.

These particular ostraca are accessible via Yohanon Aharoni *et al.*, *Arad Inscriptions* (Jerusalem 1981, including some annotations and additions by W.F. Rainey after Aharoni's death), with black-and-white photographs, drawings, unpointed and pointed typeset Hebrew texts, English translations, and commentaries, plus a general introduction, conclusion, etc. Texts in this, the most important collection of non-biblical Hebrew documents for the notes on Archon's chapters, are cited as "*AI* #__".

W.W. Hallo and K.L. Younger (eds.), *The Context of Scripture*, 3 vols. (Leiden 1997-2002) include versions (often fuller) of many texts in the Pritchard volumes, as well as many texts not found in them. The new collection cannot, however, truly be regarded as having superseded Pritchard, since some of his texts are omitted and others are presented in *less* complete versions; in saying this I disagree with the review of *COS* vol. 3 by A. Millard, *BAR* 30.1 (2004) 62: "Now that it is complete, this major publication project will clearly replace James B. Pritchard's long-standard *ANET*". Hallo & Younger are cited by volume and item (not page) numbers, e.g., *COS* 1.137, *COS* 2.113A, *COS* 3.95.

Greek literary sources are generally cited in the dual-language Loeb Classical Library versions, unless another text or translation is specified. The most important, of course, is Hdt. = Herodotos, *Histories* (a.k.a. *Persian Wars*), which I have consulted not only in the Loeb Greek and English, but also in the Greek of the Oxford Classical Text and various other English translations, especially that of Robin Waterfield (Oxford World's Classics 1998), with introduction and notes by Carolyn Dewald. Hdt.'s text itself is cited by book and chapter (thus Hdt. 2.161-163, 169), whereas comments *ad loc.* by translators, editors, etc. are cited by surname and passage discussed (Dewald re Hdt. 2.160-161, for example). The same applies to separate commentaries, such as the older one by How and Wells, 2 vols. (Oxford 1912), which would yield a citation such as H&W re Hdt. 4.159, and the more recent 3-vol. commentary just on Hdt. Book 2, by Alan B. Lloyd (vol. 1: *Introduction*, Leiden 1975, cited by page; vol. 2, 1976, and vol. 3, 1988, cited by passages discussed).

Other frequently cited Greek authors include commentators on Egypt such as Diodoros Sikeliotes (Diod.) and Strabon (Str.); poets whose extant poems and fragments appear in the Loeb *Greek Lyric* volumes; writers of miscellanies such as Athenaios (Athen.); and such well-known authors as Thucydides (Thuc.) and Plutarch (Plut.).

Greek inscriptions, both original texts and translations, are cited whenever possible by standard collections or, if necessary, by specific journal publication of a text's *editio princeps*. Greek collections cited include *Supplementum Epigraphicum Graecum* (*SEG*); Tod, *Greek Historical Inscriptions* (Tod); Meiggs & Lewis, *GHI*[2] (M&L); Jeffery, *Local Scripts of Archaic Greece*[2] (*LSAG*[2]); and H. Collitz, *Sammlung der griechischen Dialekt-Inschriften* (*SGDI*). Collections of translations include C. Fornara, *Archaic Times to the End of the Peloponnesian War*[2] (Fornara) and M. Crawford & D. Whitehead, *Archaic and Classical Greece* (C&W).

Archon's inscription at Abu Simbel, for example, is Tod 4a; M&L 7a; *SEG* 8.870, 26.1812, and subsequent discussions; *LSAG*[2] plate 69 no. 48a; and Fornara 24a. Its most useful edition (although not its *ed. prin.*), with facsimile, Greek text, and French translation, appears at A. Bernand & O. Masson, *Revue des Études Grecques* 70 (1957) 5 (insc. no. 1).

FREQUENTLY-CITED MODERN WORKS ON ARCHAIC GREECE, THE ANCIENT NEAR EAST, EGYPT, AND ISRAEL/JUDAH

HT = Jack Cargill, "Ancient Israel in Western Civ Textbooks", *History Teacher* 34 (2001) 297-326, cited by page and (usually) note number(s), is primarily cited as a shorthand way to make reference to the extensive bibliography to be found in its notes.

Kuhrt = Amélie Kuhrt, *The Ancient Near East* c. *3000-330 BC*, 2 vols. (London 1995), cited simply by Kuhrt and page(s), since pages are numbered continuously through both volumes, is my main reference work for general historical information—the source, for example, of the great majority of years of reigns in my King Lists and for many items in the Chronology of Attested Events. Kuhrt quotes many documents not in Pritchard's volumes, so I sometimes cite her page(s) for the most accessible translated version of some ancient source, or I cite her versions in addition to those of Prit., *COS*, etc.

Murray, *EG* = Oswyn Murray, *Early Greece*[2] (Cambridge, MA 1993) deals with many elements of Archaic Greece, including connections with the Near East; it is cited by page(s).

F&S = Israel Finkelstein and Neil Asher Silberman, *The Bible Unearthed* (New York 2001), cited by page(s), is a very up-to-date and reader-friendly treatment of the history of Israel and Judah from a primarily archaeological perspective, treating the biblical narratives as late and secondary works not to be preferred to the physical evidence when conflict between them is apparent.

Dever, *W&W* = William G. Dever, *What Did the Biblical Writers Know and When Did They Know It?* (Grand Rapids 2001) has much valuable commentary (cited by pages) on archaeological evidence relating to ancient Israel and Judah, when Dever is not bogged down in diatribes against authors he calls "minimalists" (and several less friendly terms).

Redford, *ECI* = Donald B. Redford, *Egypt, Canaan, and Israel in Ancient Times* (Princeton 1992), cited by page number(s), is valuable for emphasizing the interactions of Egypt and Israel/Judah over centuries, and for its critical perspective; it is also sometimes cited for translations of ancient documents.

OHAE = Ian Shaw (ed.), *The Oxford History of Ancient Egypt* (Oxford 2000), cited by chapter author and page number(s), is a scholarly textbook that discusses Egypt from prehistoric times through the Roman period, its fifteen chapters being written by specialists in their respective periods; although not footnoted, it incorporates much very recent scholarship and includes extensive bibliographies for all periods.

M&H = J. Maxwell Miller and John H. Hayes, *A History of Ancient Israel and Judah* (Philadelphia 1986), cited by page(s), is the most accessible of several moderately-critical detailed histories of the ancient kingdoms. M&H, like Kuhrt and Redford, sometimes quote documents not in Pritchard or *COS*, or provide somewhat different translations of documents that also appear there.

Soggin, *Intro.* and Ahlström, *History* = J. Alberto Soggin, *An Introduction to the History of Israel and Judah*, tr. John Bowden (Valley Forge, PA 1993, rev. of 1984 *History of Israel*) and Gösta W. Ahlström, *The History of Ancient Palestine*, with a contribution by Gary O. Rollefson and posthumously ed. Diana Edelman (Minneapolis 1993, 1994) are reasonably critical historical treatments comparable to M&H, and more recent, but somewhat less reader-friendly and therefore less frequently cited.

Popular reference works consulted frequently and cited occasionally, primarily for the illustrations they provide, without presuppositions about their scholarly quality, include: Tyndale's *Illustrated Bible Dictionary*, 3 vols. (Sydney 1980), references *sub verbum* (*IBD*, s.v. "__"); Facts on File's *Atlas of Ancient Egypt* (New York 1980), not specifically referenced but maps consulted; and the (London) Times' *Atlas of the Bible* (1996 reprint), used similarly.

BAR = *Biblical Archaeology Review*, cited by article author's initial and surname, volume, issue, year, and page(s), is, I find, the most accessible guide to the archaeology of biblical Israel and Judah for non-specialists such as myself, and thus is by far the most frequently cited periodical in these notes. Its articles are profusely illustrated with photographs, drawings, and maps. References to specific page(s) within an article are by number or range of numbers; references to entire articles (whose pages tend to be discontinuous) take a form such as the following: R. Cohen & Y. Yisrael, *BAR* 22.4 (1996) 40ff.

BR = *Bible Review*, sister publication of *BAR*, is less frequently interested in physical remains, but can be occasionally useful; it is cited in the same manner.

Less-frequently Cited Works

These, both ancient and modern, are cited initially in full form and thereafter by obvious or standard abbreviations.

NOTES

PROLOGUE

[1] The manuscript's beginning date is 567 BCE, within the thirty-seventh year of Nebuchadnezzar II. In general, for dates of all events mentioned, see Chronology of Attested Events. I will not simply repeat in the Notes dates provided there, or reign lengths from the King Lists, unless such repetition seems necessary for clarification. When dating that is more precise is relevant and available, such dates will be provided, and disagreements about dating will be discussed.

[2] 2 Kgs. 18.21; Isa. 36.6; Ezek. 29.6-7.

[3] Archon shows no awareness, here or elsewhere, of the "freeing" of Jehoiachin in the first year of Nebuchadnezzar's son and successor Amel-Marduk (561), mentioned at 2 Kgs. 25.27-30 and Jer. 52.31-34. Therefore the completion date of his MS—and the death of the aged Archon—is to be set within the period 567-561 BCE.

[4] The eclipse predicted by Thales is generally dated to 585 (some say 582), and is said to have halted a battle between the Lydians and the Medes (Hdt. 1.74). One of the negotiators of the peace made after the eclipse is called "Labynetos the Babylonian" by Hdt., and scholarly disagreement exists as to his identification (Nebuchadnezzar? Nabonidus? Hdt. 1.77 and 188 compound the confusion).

[5] Famous Milesian thinkers include Thales, Anaximandros, Anaximenes, and Hekataios (mentioned in the Preface). See Murray, *EG* 248-251 for a discussion of these thinkers and a defense of the essential rationalism of archaic Ionian philosophy, against other modern commentators who see the movement as merely a different slant on basically religious ideas. Lloyd, *Intro.* 112, 157, 160, 168 characterizes Ionian rationalism much as Murray does, in the process of putting Hdt. firmly in the tradition; he cites ancient (not Hdt.) and modern authors who suggest that Thales visited Egypt, dismissing the idea (ib. 50-55).

[6] Archon returns to his reasons for writing, and sources in his possession, in ch. 23 and the Epilogue. His description of what he is and is not attempting to do with his narrative looks like a prefiguring of the famous disclaimer of Thuc. 1.22, where the historian admits to an "absence of romance", but hopes that his work will "be judged useful" by those wishing to learn from the past.

Chapter I
MILETOS

[1]The silting up of the Maiandros River has turned the port city into an abandoned site several miles inland, and the island of Lade is now a hill on the mainland (cf. Hdt. 2.10 and Lloyd *ad loc.*). See Vanessa B. Gorman, *Miletos, the Ornament of Ionia* (Ann Arbor 2001) and Ekrem Akurgal, *Ancient Civilizations and Ruins of Turkey* (Istanbul 1983) 206-231. Most of the visible remains of the city appear to be of Roman date, and the large and impressive ruins of the great temple of Apollo at Didyma are Hellenistic, with few traces to be seen of the archaic structure that was completed ca. 560 or 550, then destroyed by Dareios I of Persia when he destroyed Miletos itself in 494 BCE (Hdt. 6.19). Photos of the Didyma temple are accessible at Peter Green, *Alexander to Actium* (Berkeley 1990) 99 and at *BAR* 28.2 (2002) 24. Murray, *EG* 242 describes widespread Greek "competition" in temple building in the 6th century BCE, specifically mentioning the temples of Ephesos and Samos, among others. I saw Alan M. Greaves, *Miletos: A History* (London 2002) too late to use it.

[2]Archon is referring to Homer, *Iliad* 2.867-869 (Karians ruling Miletos) and 2.647 (Miletos on Krete). Hdt. 1.146-147 and 9.97 shows awareness of Milesian foundation legends, although the fullest extant version is to be found in the very late Pausanias 7.2.

[3] Hdt. 1.15 describes the Kimmerians' capture of the lower parts of Sardis. A fragment of Kallinos appears to be connected by Murray, *EG* 246 with the plague Artemis sent upon the Kimmerians, although the fragment (Bergk no. 3 in E. Diehl, *Anthologia Lyrica* [1922], Part 1, p. 2) says nothing about either the plague or Artemis, nor does the reference to the Kallinos passage at Str. 14.1.40, so I am unaware of Murray's basis for the connection, though I assume there must be some.

[4] Amoibichos was active in the council, not the assembly. Although it doubtless had some kind of assembly, neither Miletos nor any Greek city—nor any city in the world—was a "democracy" in the late seventh century. The first democracy established in Greece or anywhere began operating in Athens in the very late *sixth* century. Still, many archaic Greek cities had fairly broadly based constitutions, at least among property-holders; monarchy was a rarity, except in the temporary form of tyranny, which was generally seen as extralegal. The contrast with the hereditary and culticly-reinforced monarchies Archon would later encounter is extreme, and he can never repress his Greek distrust for them.

[5] "Delilah" may be a Philistine feminine name, although the biblical evidence in Judges 14-16 is ambiguous. The legendary Samson is said to have married an unnamed Philistine wife, and later to have visited an unnamed (perhaps Philistine) prostitute in Gaza. His nemesis Delilah is called "a woman of the vale of Sorek" (see ch. 5), but is never explicitly called a Philistine, although she works with Philistine chiefs against him.

[6] The Skythian raid that led to the capture of Archon's Delilah is described in Hdt. 1.105, with further details; see also a brief reference at 7.20.

[7] That a woman in the late seventh century should acquire literacy in two very different languages and scripts certainly strains belief, especially given her status as a slave from young adulthood. Uniquely talented individuals do exist, however, in every time, place, and culture. It would appear that Archon inherited his extreme openmindedness from his father.

[8] The Greeks were quite conscious that they had borrowed their letters from the Phoinikians (Hdt. 5.58). Hdt. claims personally to have seen examples of "Kadmaian" writing (named for Kadmos, the legendary Phoinikian colonizer of Boiotia), and describes it as "basically similar to Ionian script" (5.59).

[9] "Canaan" is the traditional English spelling for biblical Hebrew *K^e^na'an*, which in turn is apparently derived from Egyptian *Kinahni*, a term already in use in the 14th-century Amarna Letters: see index to William L. Moran, *The Amarna Letters* (Baltimore 1992) 389, but note discussion of problems with derivations at Redford, *ECI* 167-168 and nn. 191-192.

[10] See Murray, *EG* 93-95 for a clear discussion of the Greeks' adoption and adaptation of the Phoinikian writing system. Although the Greeks' switch from right-to-left to left-to-right was indeed well underway in the time of Archon, the transition was still incomplete. Some inscriptions were still cut *boustrophedon*, i.e., with lines going in alternating directions—even one of the texts scratched on the monuments at Abu Simbel by one of Archon's fellow soldiers was written *boustrophedon* (see ch. 19).

[11] Kaphtor (or Caphtor) is described as the former home of the Philistines in several biblical passages. Amos 9.7 has Yahweh say: "Did I not bring Israel up from Egypt and the Philistines from Kaphtor...?" Deuteronomy 2.23 does not use the ethnic "Philistines", but "the Kaphtorim, coming from Kaphtor" who are said to have exterminated the previous inhabitants and settled in Gaza obviously can be nobody

else. For Jer. 47.4 see ch. 15. Finkelstein, *JSOT* 27 (2002) *passim* suggests reasons to question the Bible's Kretan origins for the Philistines. He thinks that the presence in the region of *Greek* mercenaries (some of them perhaps from Krete) in the late monarchic period may have contributed to the biblical picture of the Philistines in earlier centuries (Goliath's seemingly Greek-hoplite armor, etc.).

[12] Early Philistine pottery does indeed closely resemble late Mycenaean pottery, although tests on its clay have shown that it was manufactured locally. See a couple of handy photos at *BAR* 29.2 (2003) 31, in the midst of two articles (totaling 19 pages) on the Philistines in Canaan, with additional responses at 29.6 (2003) 22ff, and another very nice Philistine jug photo on p. 34. Akurgal, *Ancient...Turkey* 206 confirms discovery by excavators of "an abundance" of Mycenaean pottery at Miletos; Gorman, *Miletos* 26-27 agrees.

[13] The story of "Yamani" of Ashdod is to be found in documents of Sargon II; Prit. 1.196-198 has three versions of the story, one of them having an editorial date (Sargon's eleventh year). The rebel is called [Ya]dna at *COS* 2.118A, but Yamani at 2.118E,F,J. M&H 352 date the beginning of Sargon's troubles in Ashdod in 713 and the flight of Yamani to Shabako in 712; Lloyd, *Intro.* 12-13 seems to put the entire process in 712, and real complexities in the chronology are raised in the discussion of Robert G. Morkot, *The Black Pharaohs* (London 2000) 200-204.

[14] Greek *hebe* is the time just before, or just having arrived at, manhood; youths at (*epi*) this stage (usually around age eighteen) were *epi-hebe*, and were called *epheboi* (noun) or *ephebikoi* (adjective).

[15] Samaria was besieged in 722 by Shalmaneser V, but the siege was completed by Sargon II, followed by destruction of the town and deportations. Prit. 1.195 has three reports of these events from Sargonic documents, one of them dated to his first year (721); another passage dated to his seventh year (p. 196) tells of Sargon's settling of certain defeated Arab tribes in Samaria (for the biblical version, see notes to ch. 8). *COS* 2.118A,D-H and M&H 338 offer other translations of some of Sargon's documents. Three Assyrian texts from Til Barsip, on the Euphrates near Karchemish, all dated 644 BCE, attest to a man called Ishar-duri "the Samarian"; one of these texts appears as *COS* 3.114 (see line 21 and intro.). Marc Van De Mieroop, *A History of the Ancient Near East ca. 3000-323 BC* (Blackwell 2004) 202 says that in 647, after Ashurbanipal had ransacked the Elamite capital Susa, "The population was deported wholesale to Samaria"; his (uncited) source appears to be *COS* 1.99, known as "The Aramaic Text in Demotic Script" (see its intro.).

[16] On Sennacherib versus Hezekiah in 701 see ch. 5.

[17] The chronology of the Lydian invasions of Milesian territory, described in Hdt. 1.17-22 with most of the same details provided by Archon, is somewhat problematic (Hdt. certainly can be, and has been, doubted on chronological points), as the differing dates in Kuhrt's Lydian king list (p. 568), Murray, *EG* 246, and Gorman, *Miletos* 67 show. Such inconsistencies and disagreements tend to justify my own Chronology's vague "Late 620s-late 610s?" as the dating for these invasions. Archon would have to have left Miletos by sometime in 622 to have reached Judah in that year, the year of Josiah's reformation.

[18] Concerning conflicts on Lesbos, especially at Mytilene, see Murray, *EG* 155-158. For the encounters referred to at the end, see chs. 12 and 20.

CHAPTER 2.
JOURNEY TO JERUSALEM

[1] For the notorious pirates of Kilikia, see Plutarch, *Pompey* 24-28; *Caesar* 1-2. As for Phoinikian seamanship, see Hdt. 7.44: when Xerxes in 480 BCE, in the Hellespont area just prior to the invasion of Greece, had all his naval contingents race, the winners were the Phoinikians from Sidon (see also 7.100, 128; 8.67). A Hellenistic inscription honoring a Sidonian chariot-race winner at the Nemean Games refers in passing to how Sidon excels in its ships (M.M. Austin, *Hellenistic World* [Cambridge 1981] #121).

[2] Hdt. 4.38 calls the bay the *Myriandikos kolpos*; it is otherwise known as the bay of Issos, whose plain was the site of Alexander the Great's first encounter with Dareios III, in 333 BCE. Perhaps the ruins included those of the Bronze Age city of Ugarit, destroyed around 1200 BCE.

[3] For Byblos' early connections with Egypt, see entry "Gubla" in Moran's *Amarna Letters* index, pp. 389-390. The late-2nd-millennium story of Wenamun (Wen-Amon) describes at length an Egyptian emissary's efforts to bring timber home from Byblos; see *COS* 1.41; Prit. 1.16-24.

[4] A. Flinders, *BAR* 15.4 (1989) 40 has drawings of several Phoinikian ports that incorporate offshore islands, including Arvad, Sidon, and Tyre.

[5] Ezek. 29.18 says that the siege failed; a thirteen-year duration for the siege is asserted at Josephus, *Antiquities* 10.228 and *Apion* 1.156.

Alexander's ultimately successful siege of 332 BCE was not much easier; see A.B. Bosworth, *Conquest and Empire* (Cambridge 1988) 65-67 for description and sources.

[6] On Jezebel and Ahab, see 1 Kgs. 16-2 Kgs. 9, *passim*.

[7] The biblical text does not say that Josiah hired soldiers from among the *goyim*, and Finkelstein, *JSOT* 27 (2002) 145 considers the presence of Greek mercenaries in Josiah's Judahite army "highly unlikely, as Judah was economically poor and politically (and probably militarily) dominated by Assyria and Egypt" during his time. On the other hand, the various contemporary inscriptional references to the presence of *Kittiyim* in and near Judah cannot all be shown to refer *only* to Egyptian-employed mercenaries, to the exclusion of the hiring of some of them by Judah.

[8] General histories of Israel and Judah tend to devote part of an early chapter to the topography, climate, and roads of the region; see, e.g., M&H 40-52 (including the maps on pp. 41-42 and 131); Soggin, *Intro.* 8-12; Ahlström, *History* 61-69. See *IBD*, s.v. "Kishon" for a very clear map of the northwest end of the Jezreel Valley.

[9] The best-documented ancient battle at Megiddo was fought by Tuthmosis III, as described in his Annals at Karnak; see *COS* 2.2A and Prit. 2.175-182. For the site in general, see I. Finkelstein & D. Ussishkin, *BAR* 20.1 (1994) 26ff (with a detailed map of Tuthmosis' campaign, p. 32); 29.6 (2003) 28ff is a well-illustrated cover story on Megiddo.

[10] Akrokorinth's position made it the chief of what the Greeks' Hellenistic Makedonian overlords called the "fetters of Greece"; see citations s.v. in the index to Green, *Alex. to Act.* 947.

[11] On the biblical "replacement" of the deported Israelites by the "Samaritans", see ch. 8 below.

[12] 1 Kgs. 16.23-24.

[13] See L. Stager, *BAR* 29.4 (2003) 26ff (cover story).

[14] On the topography of ancient Jerusalem, see H. Shanks, *BAR* 25.6 (1999) 20ff, with photos, drawings, maps, and plans.

[15] V. Hurowitz, *BR* 10.2 (1994) 24ff has drawings, plans, and a detailed discussion of the temple.

[16] Josiah's destruction of "the horses which the kings of Judah had dedicated to the sun" and his burning of "the solar chariot" are described at 2 Kgs. 23.11.

CHAPTER 3.

JOSIAH'S REVOLUTION

[1] Foreign mercenaries employed by David are mentioned at 2 Samuel 15.18-22 and 23.35-39; see also citations for Benaiah (below).

[2] The question of whether *any* kings of Judah were actually descended from David is raised by Halpern, *David's Secret Demons* (Grand Rapids 2001) 92-94, 391-406, who suggests that even David's immediate successor Solomon may have been the son of Bathsheba by her first husband, Uriah the Hittite!

[3] On Josiah as a "second David", see Soggin, *Intro.* 256: "According to the biblical sources, Josiah not only presided over a religious reform but also sought to restore the Davidic empire...". See also the comment of R. H. Lowery, *The Reforming Kings* (Sheffield 1990) 208, to the effect that Josiah "might have had a reunited kingdom in mind"; cf. also F&S 275, 279.

[4] See 2 Sam. 8.18; 20.23 for the command of Benaiah son of Jehoiada.

[5] Events described here of what scholars call the "Deuteronomic Reformation", because of its apparent connection with at least the core (called D) of the canonical book of Deuteronomy, are reported at 2 Kgs. 22.3-23.4, 6-7, 11-12, and with slight variations in 2 Chron. 34-35 (see later chapters for other events of the Reformation).

[6] Josiah's elevation by the *am ha-aretz* is described at 2 Kgs. 21.24; see ch. 10, below.

[7] The reader can appreciate the unintended irony in Archon's term *Proteronomia* (Anglicized as Proteronomy), since it is clear to him, as it would have been to any contemporary observer, that Judah had never, before the time of Josiah, had a written law code. The current Hebrew title of the book of Deuteronomy, *Devorim*, meaning the "words" or "speeches" of Moses, is simply taken from the opening line. According to Everett Fox, *The Five Books of Moses* (New York 1995) 841, already in ancient times a name for the book was *Mishne Tora*, literally "copy of the Torah", but sometimes understood as "Second Torah", i.e., the equivalent of the Greek title Deuteronomy, "*second* system of laws". Presumably such a title, whether in Hebrew or in Greek, is used for the canonical book because it appears in the biblical text *after* the elaborate system of laws depicted and described in the books of Exodus, Leviticus, and Numbers. Yet these appear mostly within the "Priestly document" (P), which many critical scholars believe was written down much *later*

than the original version of Deuteronomy, even if small portions (such as some version of the Ten Commandments) may have existed earlier in oral form. But compare the complex interrelationship between the "documents" D and P suggested by Alexander Rofé, *Introduction to the Composition of the Pentateuch* (Sheffield 1999) 128-129 and the argument by Richard E. Friedman, *Who Wrote the Bible?*[2] (San Francisco 1997) 161-187 supporting the priority of P over D. A position that is accepted by so formidable a scholar as Baruch Halpern—see *BAR* 29.5 (2003) 52 ("P was written in the seventh century…")—cannot simply be dismissed. But even if it had been *written* within some out-of-power priestly circle (Friedman's position, p. 214), P had certainly *not* been promulgated and published as national law prior to Josiah's "finding" of D. Halpern (same page of same article) quite explicitly dates the language of Deuteronomy to the 7th century and says "Its laws also square with Josiah's religious reforms". He reiterates the linguistic point in replying to a letter at *BAR* 30.1 (2004) 12 and 66.

[8] One of the main reasons, beyond the general similarities in cultic attitudes and practices advocated, why scholars for more than a century have associated the book of Deuteronomy with Josiah's reforms, as reported in Kings, is its reference to the centralization of cultic activities in one spot only. The speaker is Moses:

> You must completely destroy all the places where the nations you dispossess have served their gods, on high mountains, on hills, under any spreading tree; you must tear down their altars, smash their sacred stones, burn their sacred poles, hack to bits the statues of their gods, and obliterate their name from that place.
>
> Not so must you behave towards Yahweh your God. You must seek Yahweh your God in the place which he will choose from all your tribes, there to set his name and give it a home: that is where you must go. That is where you must bring your burnt offerings and your sacrifices, your tithes and offerings held high, your votive offerings and your voluntary offerings, and the first-born of your herd and flock; and that is where you must eat in the presence of Yahweh your God, rejoicing over your labors, you and your households, because Yahweh your God has blessed you….
>
> To the place chosen by Yahweh your God as a home for his name, to that place you must bring all the things that I am laying down for you....
>
> Take care you do not offer your burnt offerings in all the sacred places you see; only in the place that Yahweh chooses in one of your

> tribes may you offer your burnt offerings and do all the things which I have commanded you. (Deut. 12.2-7, 11, 13)

Josiah and his allies obviously designated the Jerusalem temple of Yahweh as the single permitted place for sacrifice, but of course the creator(s) of the recently-found "Law of Moses" could not explicitly name a building that would not yet have existed in the time of the legendary Moses. It is to be noted that 2 Kgs. associates the scroll with *Moses* only at v. 23.25, in a summary passage at the end of the description of Josiah's reform. The much later 2 Chron. 34.14 makes the Moses connection immediately in describing the finding of the scroll, and repeats it at 35.12.

[9] Morton Smith calls the "Deuteronomic" law code possibly "the most influential forgery in the history of the world"; see *HT* 309 and n. 59 for citation of his views and others along similar lines.

[10] See Morton Smith's seminal 1952 article, "The Common Theology of the Ancient Near East", which is reprinted in his posthumous (ed. S.J.D. Cohen) *Studies in the Cult of Yahweh* (Leiden 1996) 1.15-27.

[11] The uniquely-evil Manasseh appears in 2 Kgs. 21.2-9, 16; 24.3. *BAR* 29.5 (2003) 35 provides color photos of a red signet seal inscribed "Belonging to Manasseh son of Hezekiah king of Judah" and of its gold setting, both once offered for sale by a suspected forger of antiquities, but turned down by the prospective buyer precisely because he feared they might be forged (p. 37). The caption next to the photos concludes with the observation that "these two objects have dropped from sight and may have been smuggled out of Israel".

[12] See Ephraim Stern on what he calls "Pagan Yahwism", *BAR* 27.3 (2001) 20ff; cf. Smith's "syncretistic Yahwism" in his *Palestinian Parties and Politics That Shaped the Old Testament,* 2nd corr. ed. (London 1987). For a detailed treatment of Josiah's revolution as virtually a war on the religion and culture of Judah, see Halpern, "Sybil, or the Two Nations?" in J.S. Cooper and G.M. Schwartz, *The Study of the Ancient Near East in the Twenty-First Century* (Winona Lake, IN 1996) 291-338. In a comparable vein, see also F&S 240-264, 275-292. Less passionate, but in essential agreement, is Mark S. Smith, *The Origins of Biblical Monotheism* (Oxford 2001) 149-166.

[13] Hezekiah's reforms(?) are described at 2 Kgs. 18.1-8, his consultations with Isaiah at 2 Kgs. 19.1-7, 20-34; 20.1-11, 14-19 (cf. Isa. 37-39). The differences in the programs of Hezekiah and Josiah are pointed out by Halpern, "Sybil" 317, 328-329, 332 and by Lowery, *Ref. Kings* 147-149, 158-161, 168, 206-209.

CHAPTER 4
ISRAEL AND JUDAH

[1] F&S discuss the size of Josiah's kingdom in App. F, pp. 347-353; their map (p. 258) shows its limits pretty much as Archon describes them. The map at Dever, *W&W* 130 is similar.

[2] The phrase "house of David", meaning the royal dynasty of Judah, appears in a ninth-century Aramaic inscription discovered at Tel Dan, near the headwaters of the Jordan; see Shanks, *BAR* 20.2 (1994) 27 and 38-39; discovery of an additional fragment is briefly reported at *BAR* 20.5 (1994) 22. Now see *BAR* 23.4 (1997) 34 and Dever, *W&W* 129 for clear photos of both fragments. *COS* 2.39 provides a conservative translated text; for reasonable restorations and discussion see F&S 128-129, 201-202 and William H. Stiebing, *Ancient Near Eastern History and Culture* (New York 2003) 231-232, 251. This fairly unambiguous reading "house of David" (despite some quibbles cited at *HT* 313 and n. 69) encourages A. Lemaire, *BAR* 20.3 (1994) 30ff and 20.6 (1994) 72 to suggest a similar reading (not made earlier) in the long-known "Moabite Stone" or Mesha Stele (Prit. 1.209-210=*COS* 2.23=Kuhrt 469-470). Perhaps considerably more suspect is an *emendation* by Kenneth Kitchen that produces a reference to David in an Egyptian hieroglyphic text, reported by Shanks at *BAR* 25.1 (1999) 34-35.

[3] As to Omri, the Assyrian texts translated at Prit. 1.188-198 refer to his kingdom by a variety of names, including "land of Omri" (p. 193), and to his dynasty as the "house of Omri" (194-196; cf. *COS* 2.113E, 117C,F-G, 118G-H). Surprisingly, the biblical slayer of the last members of the Omride family, Jehu, is called "son of Omri" in some texts (Prit. 1.191-192, although *COS* 2.113F translates the second of these passages, from Shalmaneser III's "Black Obelisk", as calling Jehu "[the man] of Bit-Humri" [diacritical marks omitted—JC]). The biblical treatment of Ahab appears at 1 Kgs. 16.29-22.40.

[4] On the currently much-discussed issue of whether the biblical "united monarchy" ever actually existed, see literature cited at *HT* 302 and n. 26; for a negative argument, see F&S App. D, pp. 340-344. J. Taylor at *OHAE* 333 is conventional in accepting the biblical account of Solomon's marriage to the daughter of an unnamed Egyptian Pharaoh (1 Kgs. 3.1; 7.8; 11.1), and in suggesting Siamun as the king referred to; cf. Van De Mieroop, *Hist. of the ANE* 209-210, whose comments emphasize the separateness of the histories of Israel and Judah and include the following summary: "[M]any believe in the existence of a large kingdom under David and Solomon, but this cannot be ascertained

and seems unlikely in a setting where all Syro-Palestinian states were very small" (p. 210).

[5] For Herakleidai among the Spartans, see Hdt. 7.208; 8.114; 9.26-27, 33.

[6] The fall of Samaria and associated deportations are described at 2 Kgs. 17.5-6; 18.9-11; for Assyrian sources, see notes on ch. 1, above.

[7] For boundary stones of precincts on the Ionian island of Samos dedicated to *Athena Athenon Medeouses* see Cargill, *Athenian Settlements of the Fourth Century B.C.* (Leiden 1995) 7 n. 29 and 187-188 n. 3.

[8] Covenants with Abraham appear at Genesis 15.18-21 and all of 17; for David's covenant see 2 Samuel 7.

[9] On Sennacherib's invasion see ch. 5.

[10] 2 Kgs. 22.14-20.

[11] Various Israelite/Judahite settlement "models" are cited and discussed at *HT* 306 and n. 51, to which may be added F&S 329-339 (App. C). M. Bietak, *BAR* 29.5 (2003) 40ff claims to have found evidence for the presence of a four-room "Israelite house" (see ch. 5 for the house type), apparently built by "workmen, perhaps slaves" (p. 46) at Medinet Habu in western Thebes, in a context datable to the middle-to-late 12th century. The dating of these remains leads him to conclude that the Israelites' settlement in Canaan *preceded* the exodus ("the order of the Biblical tradition should be reversed", p. 49). Depending on how late and uniquely Israelite this type of house is, it may be relevant that B.M. Bryan at *OHAE* 258 says that Thutmosis IV (dated 1400-1390 in the book's chronology) had "taken punitive action against Gezer; ...some of the population of this town were transported to Thebes" (no source citation).

[12] For the Egyptian Empire in Syria and Palestine, see Kuhrt 317-329 and Redford, *ECI* 192-213, as well as C. Higginbotham, *BAR* 24.3 (1998) 36ff.

[13] Deut. 14.8 does indeed proscribe the eating of pork. For Homer's very favorable treatment of the swineherd Eumaios, see his hospitality for the unrecognized Odysseus in *Odyssey* bk.14 and his invited participation in his master's battles against aristocratic enemies in bks. 21-22. Hdt. 2.47-48 indicates that Egyptians thought of pigs as unclean, but the presence of pigs—and swineherds—in their society is also clearly attested (ib. and 2.14, 164). See Lloyd re Hdt. 2.47 for further ambiguous ancient evidence on this matter. Hdt. adds the Skythians (4.63) and the coastal Libyans and the women of (Greek) Barka (4.186) to the list of anti-pig ancient peoples.

[14] Archon's list of circumcised Near Eastern peoples parallels the list at Jer. 9.24-25, and his comment about Egypt—or possibly Nubia—as the ultimate source of the practice finds support in Hdt. 2.36-37, 104. Diod. 1.28.2-3 cites "the Egyptians" as saying that the *ethnos* of the *Ioudaioi* was among nations founded by emigrants from Egypt, which is why such peoples circumcise their male children, "the custom having been brought over from Egypt" (Loeb trans.); a similar statement occurs at 1.58.5. Str. 17.2.5 says that the Egyptians circumcise (*peritemnein*) males and "excise" (*ektemnein*) females, "as also is a custom for the *Ioudaioi*"—who are "Egyptians in origin"; see also 16.2.34. For a detailed discussion of Egyptian circumcision and related issues, see Lloyd re Hdt. 2.36. On dress, ib. re 77 says: "The light linen clothing—sometimes nakedness—of antiquity was admirably suited to the climatic conditions of Egypt whereas modern dress, whether European or Arab, is not"; see also re 85.

Chapter 5.
IN THE STEPS OF SENNACHERIB

[1] On the Shephelah in general, see H. Brodsky, *BR* 3.4 (1987) 48ff.

[2] The primary biblical version of the conflict between Hezekiah and Sennacherib is presented in 2 Kgs. 18-19 (much of which reappears verbatim in Isaiah 36-37) and 20.20; the much longer account in 2 Chron. 29-32 may actually in this case contain a believable element from some independent source, in its slightly greater detail on Hezekiah's improvements in the water supply of Jerusalem at 32.30. *BAR* 29.6 (2003) 18 reports that carbon-14 and isotopic tests have now conclusively verified that the "Siloam tunnel" dates to the time of Hezekiah. Sennacherib's own account of the campaign on his prism (Prit. 1.199-201; see other trans. at *COS* 2.119B and M&H 360-361) and the captioned relief carvings in his great palace at Nineveh (e.g., *COS* 2.119C=Prit. 1.201 and fig. 102, cross-referenced incorrectly in the margin as "*Fig. 121*") provide much greater detail. Another inscription, combining two fragments formerly associated with Tiglath-pileser III and Sargon II, respectively, has become *COS* 2.119D, whose editors now ascribe it to Sennacherib and see it as his report about taking the city of Azekah and other places during his campaign in Judah. In general Archon's comments are consistent with what Sennacherib says. For a succinct description of Sennacherib's destruction, see F&S 259-264,

ending with this uncompromising summary:

> For all the Bible's talk of Hezekiah's piety and YHWH's saving intervention, Assyria was the only victor. Sennacherib fully achieved his goals: he broke the resistance of Judah and subjugated it. Hezekiah had inherited a prosperous state, and Sennacherib destroyed it.

On Sennacherib vs. Hezekiah in general, see Morkot, *Black Phar.* 210-217, 225-226 and Dever, *W&W* 167-172.

[3] Sennacherib's boast of victory in the plain of Eltekeh over the "kings" of Egypt and Kush (which should refer to Shabako, who held both titles at the time) becomes in the biblical account a mere alarm on Sennacherib's part that "Tirhakah (i.e., Taharqa) king of Kush" was on his way to attack him, with no reference to any actual battle (2 Kgs. 19.9 = Isa. 37.9). It *appears* in the biblical account—it is not explicitly *said*—that Sennacherib was engaged in besieging Jerusalem, i.e., had already left the Shephelah, when "the angel of Yahweh" struck down 185,000 men in the Assyrian camp overnight, which seemingly prompted the invaders to withdraw. Sennacherib mentions no such disaster, implying that he withdrew simply because Hezekiah, trapped in his capital city "like a bird in a cage", had paid him a huge tribute; his numbers are not out of scale with the tribute the biblical account says Hezekiah had earlier agreed to pay (2 Kgs. 18.14-16). Some scholars debate whether the confusing sources warrant a two-invasion theory: W. Shea, *BAR* 25.6 (1999) 36ff is countered by M. Cogan, 27.1 (2001) 40ff; see also Morkot, *Black Phar.* 210-212, 226, 260.

[4] A. Maeir & C. Ehrlich, *BAR* 27.6 (2001) 22f argue that Philistine Gath was located at the present site of Tell es-Safi (see map, p. 24), six miles south of Tel Miqne, itself only recently definitely identified with Ekron. These would have been the two Philistine cities closest to the heartland of Judah, whereas Gaza was the most distant. Since Sennacherib says that Hezekiah was holding the king of Ekron, Padi, as a prisoner in Jerusalem, and also reports on dealing with disloyalty in Ashkelon, incorporation of Gath into Judah at this time (or, probably, earlier) seems believable, and should be implied in the statement that Hezekiah "beat the Philistines back to Gaza" (2 Kgs. 18.8). See Finkelstein, *JSOT* 27 (2002) 137-142 for a suggestion that no-longer-independent Gath is a phantom member of the Philistine "pentapolis" in biblical passages describing periods later than the time of Hezekiah.

[5] The Assyrian king's claim to have given many conquered Judahite towns to his Philistine vassals is undisputed and believable. The hated Manasseh receives no biblical credit for regaining any of the lost territories (2 Kgs. 21.1-18 is all theology, no geography), and F&S 264-

274 and (App. E) 345-346 can only argue for this development on the basis of likelihood.

[6] Sennacherib claims to have besieged and conquered forty-six cities, a datum the biblical accounts conveniently overlook; Lachish is mentioned a couple of times, and Libnah once, in the biblical narrative, though neither is said to have fallen. See Micah 1.10-15 for the names of many towns of the Shephelah. No biblical figure for deportees from the countryside of Judah is offered in preference to Sennacherib's 200,150; indeed there is no implication that any deportations occurred at all.

[7] For the topography of Timnah, see G. Kelm & A. Mazar, *BAR* 15.1 (1989) 36ff; for the adventures of Samson, see Judges 13-16 (ch. 14 is devoted to his stormy marriage to the Philistine woman from Timnah).

[8] On Ekron, see T. Dothan, *BAR* 16.1 (1990) 266ff and 29.6 (2003) 46-49; S. Gitin, 16.2 (1990) 33ff.

[9] In *The Prince*, chap. 7, Machiavelli praises the statecraft of Cesare Borgia in employing "a cruel, efficient man" to pacify the Romagna, then winning the favor of the people by killing the man he had used as his instrument (Penguin trans. by George Bull, pp. 57-58).

[10] For *lamelech* stamps specifically associated with Hezekiah and bearing images of winged scarabs, see the discussion at *COS* 2.77 (no texts included) and articles by F.M. Cross, *BAR* 25.2 (1999) 42ff and M. Lubetski, 27.4 (2001) 44ff, both with photos and drawings. Even more strikingly, R. Deutsch, 28.4 (2002) 42ff publishes a *bulla* of Hezekiah (with large color photos of it on cover and p. 42) that features a winged sun-disk between twin *ankhs* (the Egyptian life-symbol)!

[11] Beth-Shemesh and its surprising cistern are discussed by S. Bunimovitz & Z. Lederman, *BAR* 23.1 (1997) 42ff, with a map (p. 44) and drawings (pp. 46). For the grudging return of a disputed site in a destroyed condition, cf. the Boiotians' dismantling of the border fortress of Panakton, which was to be ceded to Athens under the terms of the Peace of Nikias of 421 BCE, negotiated between Athens and Boiotia's hegemon Sparta (Thuc. 5.39-42).

[12] A house very much like the one described by Archon, although located in Transjordan, is described and depicted by L. Herr & D. Clark, *BAR* 27.2 (2000) 36ff; especially see drawings (p. 40). An example of a four-room house in the Shephelah itself (at Izbet Sartah, perhaps biblical Ebenezer, less than two miles from Aphek) is described by Shanks, 28.3 (2002) 40ff, with a good post-excavation photo (p. 42). Two more articles about the four-room house, by V. Fritz and by S. Bunimovitz & A. Faust respectively, appear in 28.4 (2002) 28ff and 33ff; for a clear photo of a

four-room house in Samaria, see 29.5 (2003) 49.

[13] The incredible "Underground Metropolis" (the article's title) of Mareshah (or Maresha) is celebrated, and illustrated, in the cover story by A. Kloner, *BAR* 23.2 (1997) 24ff.

[14] Lachish, with its huge, impressive ruins, has probably been more discussed—and certainly more illustrated—in the pages of *BAR* than any other spot in the territory of biblical Israel and Judah, with the possible exceptions of Jerusalem and, maybe, Megiddo. This is partly because of the fantastic reliefs relating to the fall of Lachish that were found at Nineveh, which give the viewer good reason to suspect that Sennacherib saw the conquest of the chief city of the Shephelah as his greatest achievement. The excavator of the site, David Ussishkin, has penned the following articles in *BAR*: cover story in 5.6 (1979) 16ff, with a large picture (p. 21) of the mound at an early stage in the excavations and several photos and drawings from the palace reliefs at Nineveh; 10.2 (1984) 66ff, following a profusely illustrated review of Ussishkin's book about the reliefs, by H. Shanks, pp. 48ff (26 solid pages devoted exclusively to Lachish); 13.1 (1987) 18ff (see plan, p. 22); and 14.2 (1988) 42ff. S. Feldman, 28.3 (2002) 46ff describes a re-visit of the mound of Lachish with Ussishkin as his guide. So impressive, and photogenically documented, is the siege of Lachish that even articles supposedly about Jerusalem (and with "Jerusalem" in their titles) are sometimes illustrated largely with photos of the reliefs about Lachish; see, e.g., both the Shea and Cogan articles cited above, especially Shea.

[15] For Archon's informant on the Nineveh reliefs and all things Mesopotamian, see ch. 15 and subsequent chapters.

CHAPTER 6
CONSOLIDATION IN THE CAPITAL

[1] Modern scholars seem to disagree about whether Zephaniah 1.1 indicates descent from the king; see comments ad loc. in, e.g., *IBD* saying probably yes, but Otto Eissfeldt's Old Testament *Introduction* calling the ancestor only "a certain Hezekiah".

[2] Concerning social damage in Judah from Hezekiah to Josiah, see Halpern, "Sybil" 293-307, 311-312, 319-329, 331-332.

[3] Amos 5.10-12.

[4] On the death of Sargon II, Kuhrt 499 quotes a very terse notice of 705 BCE, saying that the king was killed (apparently in battle), but

not saying by whom.

[5] On Hezekiah's improvements in Jerusalem's water system, see D. Gill, *BAR* 20.4 (1994) 20ff and a related article by S. Parker on the famous "Siloam inscription" (Prit. 1.212=*COS* 2.28) found in his water tunnel, ib. 36ff. Shanks, 25.6 (1999) 20ff follows up Gill, while a collection of short discussions by several authors in 23.2 (1997) 41ff deals with issues associated with the inscription; see also 29.6 (2003) 18.

[6] The analogy of Hezekiah's strategy of 701 with the "island Attika" strategy enunciated by Perikles at Thuc. 1.143 is noticed by Halpern, "Sybil" 317.

[7] For towns captured north of Jerusalem, see Isa. 10.28-32.

[8] Stripping of gold from the temple doors is described at 2 Kgs. 18.16.

[9] The biblical summary of 2 Kgs. 23.11 and 12 attributes the horses of the sun and the altars on the temple roof only to unnamed "kings of Judah", but the plural noun indicates more kings than Manasseh alone.

[10] 2 Kgs. 19.35.

[11] See the aetiological legend reported at Hdt. 2.141. Morkot, *Black Phar.* 216 connects the Hdt. passage with the Bible's apparent plague. See also the very full discussion of Lloyd re Hdt. 2.141. I can find no passages in Homer associating Apollo with mice, although the arrows of the "shooter from afar" were clearly seen as bringing plague. It would have been very natural both for the Assyrian to omit the disaster and for the Judahites to "remember" (and later write down) that the blow struck by "the angel of Yahweh" had broken the siege of Jerusalem, rather than preventing the invasion of Egypt.

[12] For changes in agriculture in Judah after the devastation of Sennacherib see F&S 264-274. The Philistine kings' names (doubtless remembered and hated in Judah eighty years later, and thus available to Archon) all appear in the report of the campaign in Sennacherib's prism, as does the story of the removal and restoration of Padi.

[13] The inscription described by Archon was unearthed at Ekron, and excavators have had the same kind of trouble with the epithet of the goddess. See A. Gitin, T. Dothan, & J. Naveh, *Archaeology* 51.1 (1998) 30-31, with photo and trans., and especially A. Demsky, *BAR* 24.5 (1998) 53ff, with plan of the temple complex (p. 55), large photo plus facsimile and translation of the inscription (56) and illustrated discussion of the problematic letter (57). A trans. appears at *COS* 2.42; see n. 6 there for discussion of the goddess' name and n. 3 for another local inscription mentioning Padi.

[14] For divine sanctions behind Near Eastern lawcodes, consider, e.g., the Code of Hammurabi, whose Epilogue (omitted from the trans. of Prit. 1.138-167, but quoted in part at Kuhrt 112 and much more fully in *COS* 2.131) derives the king's laws from the sun-god Shamash (depicted giving the laws to Hammurabi in a relief at the top of the stele) and the Babylonian national god Marduk.

[15] 2 Kgs. 23.8-9.

[16] 2 Kgs. 23.13-14.

[17] 2 Kgs. 23.10.

[18] For Manasseh, see 2 Kgs. 21.6; the only other Judahite king specifically described in the Bible as having indulged in such practices is Ahaz, at 2 Kgs. 16.3.

[19] Archon is unaware of the irony in his description of sacrificing exclusively at the Jerusalem temple as no hardship, given the smallness of the state of Judah, although even in his own lifetime occurred the Babylonian exile and the settlement of numerous Judahites in Egypt. He is describing his feelings at the time of Josiah's revolution, which predated such dispersions. Later in antiquity, after the Near Eastern incursions of the Macedonians and especially of the Romans, the "Jewish Diaspora" became what would have been considered at the time "worldwide". It has been argued, in fact, that it was precisely the (second) destruction of the temple by the Romans in 70 CE that led to the development of a Judaism not tied to sacrifice or to location, and thus capable of being practiced anywhere.

CHAPTER 7
INTO THE SOUTHERN DESERT

[1] The gravestone Archon describes was discovered at a place known as Khirbet el-Kom. The very large photo and facsimile of A. Lemaire, *BAR* 10.6 (1984) 42-43 is reproduced in subsequent *BAR* articles: 20.3 (1994) 55; 22.5 (1996) 37; 27.3 (2001) 28. The trans. at *COS* 2.52 differs slightly from the one used here. See also Dever, *W&W* 186-187 and (for other objects and inscriptions on the site) 214, 216-218.

[2] 2 Kgs. 23.24.

[3] Photos of pillar figurines appear at *BAR* 10.6 (1984) 47; 17.2 (1991) 65; 22.3 (1996) 24; 22.5 (1996) 36; 27.3 (2001) 29; see also Dever, *W&W* 192-194.

[4] Discussions by Dever of Asherah appear at *W&W* 192-198 and

BAR 10.6 (1984) 42; 17.2 (1991) 64-65; *BAR* discussions by other authors include R. Hestrin, 17.5 (1991) 50; Shanks(?), 18.3 (1992) 42; J.G. Taylor, 20.3 (1994) 52; Shanks(?), ib. 56.

[5] For Yahweh(?) as mounted warrior, see E. Stern, *BAR* 27.3 (2001) 29.

[6] Aharoni, *AI* p. 142 says that Beersheba was destroyed by Sennacherib; other scholars' treatments do not seem to infer this.

[7] The Beersheba altar figures prominently in the discussion of the meaning of "high place" by B. Nakhai, *BAR* 20.3 (1994) 18ff (photo on p. 28); see also M. Coogan, 21.3 (1995) 44.

[8] Archon's location matches that of M&H 399; the phrasing at 2 Kgs. 23.8 could seem to imply that the gate was at Jerusalem.

[9] Discussions and/or photos of cult-stands may be seen at Dever, *W&W* 188; the cover of *BAR* 17.5 (1991); *BAR* articles by Nakhai, 20.3 (1994) 18ff; Taylor, ib. 52ff; Stern, 27.3 (2001) 20ff.

[10] The definitive treatment of Arad is to be found in three consecutive articles, by a total of six authors, in *BAR* 13.2 (1987) 16ff, 36ff (this article relates to ostraca found there, relevant in later chapters, not here), 40ff (map of area p. 19, plans of fort phases pp. 26-27, section with cistern pp. 28-29, illustrations of temple pp. 20 and 30-34). Other photos, plans, etc. of Arad appear in other articles in *BAR*: Nakhai, 20.3 (1994) 26; Stern, 27.3 (2001) 24-25; U. Avner, ib. 34. Avner 37 says that the destruction of the Arad temple was not done under Josiah but was done later by either the Babylonians or the Edomites. The dating of Arad's temple, its construction, shutting down, and then building-over, as presented in most current scholarship is consistent with Archon's narrative, but note the doubts about the site's stratigraphy in general that are expressed by Dever, *W&W* 181 and the scholarly argument that the temple was built only *after* Hezekiah, in the seventh century, cited by F&S 250 and note. For further developments involving Archon at Arad, see ch. 16-17, 19-21 and notes.

[11] Asaiah's seal (although not the complete ring) has turned up on the antiquities market (find-spot unknown), and it is exactly as described by Archon; its text appears at *COS* 2.79, where the comm. identifies its owner as he is identified here. See Shanks, *BAR* 22.2 (1996) 38 for a color photo and drawing of the seal; Shanks comments on the irony of the depiction of a horse on the seal of an official in an aniconic movement. Asaiah's participation in the embassy to Huldah is reported at 2 Kgs. 22.14. Obviously, I have given the briefly-attested Asaiah a personality here, to present an individualized face for the murderous behavior associated with the reform that is described dispassionately

in 2 Kings.

[12] Biblical denunciations of the Edomites are found at Amos 1.1-12; Isa. 21.11-12; 34; Jer. 49.7-22; Ezek. 25.12-14; 35; Obadiah 1.

[13] For later conflicts with the Idumaeans, seen as descendants of the Edomites, see 1 Maccabees 5.1-3, 25; 2 Macc. 10.15-23; 12.32-37.

[14] On Jacob and Esau, see Gen. 25.21-34; 26.34-28.9; 32.4-22; 33.1-17; 36.1-37.1.

[15] For standing stones in the southern Negeb, see ch. 11.

[16] The abandoned Edomite site is modern Qitmit (or Horvat Qitmit). See two articles by I. Beit-Arieh, *BAR* 14.2 (1988) 28ff and 22.6 (1996) 28ff, for very full treatments of the site, with maps, plans, and numerous photos.

[17] Gen. 14.7; 1 Kgs. 9.18; Ezek. 47.18-19; 48.28.

[18] Asaiah's Tamar is the place now called Haseva or 'En Hatseva or Ein Haseva, etc. R. Cohen & Y. Yisrael, *BAR* 22.4 (1996) 40ff describe and illustrate it very fully. The vessels laid in a pit and then smashed by stones are now completely restored; a large photo and drawing of the beautiful ring stone appear on p. 50. Recent excavations at a manifestly *Moabite* wayside shrine in Transjordan surprised the excavators, who report: "[O]ur finds have their closest affinities with the supposedly Edomite finds from Horvat Qitmit and 'En Hatzeva"; see P.M.M. Daviau and P.-E. Dion, *BAR* 28.1 (2002) 38ff (quote from p. 63, map. p. 41, photo of shrine p. 46).

[19] Zeph. 2.4-5.

[20] Zeph. 2.12-15.

CHAPTER 8.
BETHEL AND BEYOND

[1] For the biblical line on the Samaritans and their priests, see 2 Kgs. 17.24-41; Ezra 4.1-2, 9-10.

[2] See M&H 131 for a map of roads around Bethel. The destruction of Ai by Joshua is reported at Josh. 8.1-28 (v. 28 indicates the basis for its name). The topography of the supposed battle and problems with acceptance of the biblical account are discussed by Z. Zevit, *BAR* 11.2 (1985) 58ff and J. Callaway, ib. 68-69; on p. 63 appears a photo of the modern village of Beitin, located on the site of ancient Bethel.

[3] Abraham's altar at Bethel is reported at Gen. 12.8. The biblical

tradition is uniformly hostile toward Jeroboam I's altars and priests at Bethel and Dan, with much greater emphasis on the former place. See, e.g, 1 Kgs. 12.26-13.34; 2 Chron. 11.13-17; Amos 3.14; 4.4; 5.5; 7.9-13; 9.1; Hosea (who sometimes refers to Bethel as "Beth-Aven", House of Evil) 4.15; 5.8; 6.10; 8.5; 10.5, 8, 15; 12.5. F&S 287-288 report that the royal altar at Bethel has not been located by archaeologists.

[4] Dever, *W&W* 152, 175 discusses bulls in Canaanite cults; see also A. Mazar, *BAR* 9.5 (1983) 34ff (and cover photo).

[5] The southward flight of the Levites is reported biblically only at 2 Chron. 11.13-16, a passage obviously written long after Archon's time, but apparently such stories were already being told in the days of Josiah. This must also be true of the "bull and seven rams" story of 2 Chron. 13.9, supposedly from words directed against the Israelites by the Judahite king Abijah (Abijam in Kings), son of Rehoboam.

[6] The biblical story of Josiah at Bethel appears at 2 Kgs. 23.15-18. Archon reports the same events, adding his interpretations and suspicions. The supposed prophecy delivered to Jeroboam I and specifying the future king Josiah by name, with all the elaborate details reported by Archon as the current sycophant's invention, is described at 1 Kgs. 13.1-32. Presumably both passages, both within the "Deuteronomistic history", were written at the same time, i.e., during or after the reign of Josiah (as F&S 166 conclude), so it was easy enough for the biblical writers to make the "prophecy come true".

[7] For the site of the Israelite capital, Samaria, see F&S 180-183 (p. 181 has a drawing of a "proto-Aeolic" capital found there) and Dever, *W&W* 164-165.

[8] Archon's likening of the slain Asaiah to "a slaughtered calf" is a bitter play on the reputation of the northern kingdom as a hotbed of calf-worship!

[9] All the family names mentioned by Tirzah occur in a family among the clans of Manasseh (subsequently a tribe of the northern kingdom of Israel) at the time of a census supposedly taken by Moses at Numbers 27.1-8. Interestingly, the orphaned daughters of Zelophehad (whose great-grandfather is named Machir) in that story, two of whom are called Tirzah and Mahlah (see ch. 9), petition successfully to be recognized as their father's heirs, since they have no brothers. Tirzah as capital of Israel is well attested: 1 Kgs. 14.17; 15.21, 33; 16.6, 8-9, 15, 17, 23; see Dever *W&W* 176-177 for description and plan of the site.

[10] F&S 220-222 say that the believable number of about 40,000 deportees derived from Assyrian sources "comprises no more than a fifth of the estimated population" of the area (p. 221). K.L. Younger,

BAR 29.6 (2003) 36ff seems to imply larger deportations from Israel by Assyria, stretched over the years from Tiglath-pileser III to Sargon II, although the only actual *numbers* provided (13,520 and 27,290) add up to approximately the 40,000 of F&S; the article cites extensive evidence for the deported Israelites' roles in Assyrian society.

[11] Josiah's supposed deeds within the province of Samaria other than at Bethel are reported at 2 Kgs. 23.19-20. The territory impacted is expanded in 2 Chron. 34.6 to include the towns and open spaces of "Manasseh, Ephraim, and Simeon, as far as Naphtali" (cf. similar phrasing at 34.9). The phrase "from Geba to Beersheba" appears in the general description of the scope of Josiah's reform at 2 Kgs. 23.8. Archon is apparently correct in characterizing the phrase as an intentionally misleading reference to "Geba of Benjamin", which is mentioned at 1 Kgs. 15.22. M&H 401 conclude that Josiah's expansion of control in a northward direction did not extend beyond Bethel itself. A reader familiar with the main biblical description of Josiah's reformation will observe that Archon's version of events seems more geographically logical—the reforms beginning in and near Jerusalem, then expanding to affect all of Judah, and only at that point extending into the north. M&H 398-399, 401 suggest a similar sequence, asserting (p. 398): "Close analysis of the account in Kings...suggests that the reform occurred in stages which the compilers have telescoped".

[12] Archon is not exaggerating the murders involved. See 2 Kgs. 23.20: "All the priests of the high places who were there [in the towns of Samaria] he slaughtered on the altars...".

[13] The slaughter of high-place priests in Judah is asserted at 2 Kgs. 23.5.

CHAPTER 9.
ON THE EDGE OF EVENTS

[1] The site Archon describes is Mesad (or Metsad) Hashavyahu, otherwise known as Yahveh-Yam; *mesad* means "fort". For its location see the map at G. Kelm & A. Mazar, *BAR* 15.1 (1989) 39.

[2] The peculiar combination of remains at the site—Greek pottery and Hebrew ostraca—has led to various speculations about precisely who occupied the fort. Interpretations (none of which exactly matches the situation described by Archon) range from seeing the site as evidence that Josiah had established control on the coast and stationed Greek mercenaries in his army there, to seeing the Greeks and Hebrew-

speakers both as elements of Judah's army, but stationed at the fort on Egypt's orders, because Judah was an Egyptian vassal, to seeing both the Greeks and the Judahites as mercenaries in the Egyptian army. See the discussions of Ahlström, *History* 752-753, 767-768; F&S 286-287, 348, 350-351; M&H 389; Redford, *ECI* 444; M.M. Austin, *Greece and Egypt in the Archaic Age* (Cambridge 1970) 16; Lloyd, *Intro.* 21.

[3] In contrast with the rather dense preceding chapters (and most of the chapters that follow), this chapter covers, or rather skips over, several years of the life of Archon, beginning in 621 and ending at some point within 609 BCE.

[4] The pottery of Mesad Hashavyahu is said by Kelm & Mazar, *BAR* 15.1 (1989) 49 to have reached Timnah (see ch. 5). F&S 350, more inclusively but less specifically, say that its pottery is known from "a number of sites in the southern coastal plain and the Beersheba valley".

[5] For Josiah's Passover, see 2 Kgs. 23.21-23; cf. the greatly expanded account in 2 Chron. 35.1-19. For the legend of the first Passover, see Exodus 12. The combining of Passover and unleavened bread occurs in Exo. 12 and 13, though the passages may come from different "documents" or "strands" identified by most scholars; the canonical book of Deuteronomy also combines them, while prescribing the observation of other annual feasts (Deut. 16.1-17).

[6] See trans. of the ostracon from Mesad Hashavyahu at Prit. 2.121 (photo, fig. 39), *COS* 3.41, M&H 390, and F&S 287, and discussions by Dever, *W&W* 215-216 (biblio. n. 65, drawing p. 216) and F&S 286-287. Dever compares the legal principle with complaints made in Amos 2.8; F&S make a connection with Deut. (unspecified); the actual relevant law seems to appear in Deut. 24.14-15.

[7] Ahaz's calling on Tiglath-Pileser III is reported at 2 Kgs. 16.5-18. Ahab's Israel as a key element in an anti-Assyrian coalition is attested by the so-called "Monolith Inscription" of Shalmaneser III; see relevant passage at Prit. 1.190, *COS* 2.113A, or M&H 259. For Omride building projects, see F&S 180-190 and (App. D) 340-344; Dever, *W&W* 131-135 and 269 more conventionally attributes some of the architecture to Solomon. Finkelstein and Halpern, who agree on much, consistently disagree about the "Solomonic" remains at Megiddo, Gezer, and Hazor; see, e.g., *BAR* 29.5 (2003) 20.

[8] The international developments summarized as background for what will follow in Archon's narrative begin in the ninth century, with the Neo-Assyrian Empire's first extensive campaigns west of the Euphrates, especially those involving Shalmaneser III, Tiglath-pileser

III, Sargon II, Sennacherib, Esarhaddon, and Ashurbanipal. In Egypt, the kings of the 25th (Kushite) dynasty and the early 26th (Saite) dynasty are relevant. See the surveys of the general period in M&H 250-401; Redford, *ECI* 338-364, 430-469; Kuhrt 483-501, 540-546, 576-590, 623-638; and Morkot, *Black Phar.* 197-228, 259-304.

[9] Sennacherib's destruction of Babylon is strongly asserted by one of his inscriptions (see trans. at Kuhrt 585=second half of *COS* 2.119E). Scholars doubt that the destruction was anywhere nearly as total as he claimed, since his son Esarhaddon is said to have rebuilt the city; see Kuhrt 583-587 and *COS* 2.120; Morkot, *Black Phar.* 259, 262. The assassination of Sennacherib is firmly dated to 681 BCE (see *COS* 3.95 for the event, though not the date), despite the apparent immediacy of his "divine punishment" as described in 2 Kgs. 19.37.

[10] On "Yamani", see ch. 1 and notes.

[11] Concerning Psammetichos I's efforts to aid the disintegrating Assyrian Empire, see Redford, *ECI* 446-447, who points out that the Babylonian Chronicle for the years 615-610 mentions no Egyptian army in Mesopotamia, and speculates that the campaign of 616 may have damaged the health of the aging Pharaoh. The same Chronicle describes Chaldaean and Median campaigns against the chief cities of Assyria from 615 through 610; see translation at Prit. 1.202-203; cf. the much longer selections, ranging from 626 through 597, at M&H 380-381, which overlap the selections of *COS* 1.137.

[12] Jer. 2.18.

CHAPTER 10.
ARMAGEDDON AND AFTER

[1] Discussions of Necho II's encounter with Josiah and his dealings with Josiah's sons may be found at M&H 387, 402-405; Ahlström, *History* 765-767, 780-781; Kuhrt 543; Redford, *ECI* 448-452. For the topography of Megiddo, see the photos, plans, and maps of I. Finkelstein & D. Ussishkin, *BAR* 20.1 (1994) 26ff (site photo pp. 26-27) and of A. Malamat, 25.4 (1999) 34ff (site photo pp. 34-35, map relating to Josiah's battle p. 36). These articles also discuss the motives of Josiah and Necho, the former article briefly (p. 43), the latter at greater length (pp. 36-38). Malamat associates Josiah's resistance with a bizarre interpretation of a fragmentary ostracon from Arad, whereby "I", the speaker, is interpreted as being Yahweh, calling on all Judahites to resist the king of Egypt, a summons answered by Josiah! Archon would be amused

to learn that Eliạshib, the commander at Arad (ch. 20) had received a letter from Yahweh. See further theories about this ostracon (*AI* #88) in ch. 20 notes.

[2] Biblical versions of the encounter appear at 2 Kgs. 23.29-30 and 2 Chron. 35.20-24. Perhaps the written warning from Necho, read out to the Judahite commanders, was preserved and somehow made its way into the text of 2 Chron. 35.21, in another of the rare cases where Chronicles seems to show independent sources not reported in Kings. Josiah's cry when shot also appears only there (verse 23). The biblical book of Lamentations is certainly in no way a lament for Josiah, whoever its author may be; it laments the destruction of Jerusalem, which took place almost twenty-five years after the death of Josiah.

[3] 2 Sam. 23.21.

[4] Shallum as the original name of Jehoahaz is attested at Jer. 22.11 and 1 Chron. 3.15. The latter verse in fact lists four sons of Josiah, explicitly in birth order: Johanon (who must have predeceased the king), Jehoiakim, Zedekiah, and Shallum. If the accuracy of this list be accepted, it appears that the fourth son (called by his birth name) was jumped ahead of not one, but two, living older brothers, both of whom are listed by their throne names. But scholars, e.g., Redford, *ECI* 449, deny the sequence and see Zedekiah (born Mattaniah) as the youngest.

[5] See 2 Kgs. 22.12 for Archon's new commander's father, Achbor son of Micaiah. On the son himself, see below.

[6] The brief reign, deposition, and deportation of Shallum/Jehoahaz are described at 2 Kgs. 23.30-34 and 2 Chron. 36.1-4.

[7] Jer. 22.10; see similar sentiments at Ezek. 19.1-4.

[8] 2 Kgs. 23.34-35; 2 Chron. 36.4-5.

[9] Redford, *ECI* 449 stresses not the new king's mother but the idea that "his grandfather from Galilee, Pediah, had borne a quasi-Egyptian name"; the inferred consequence is the same—pro-Egyptian policies.

[10] 2 Kgs. 23.35.

[11] Nothing in canonical Deuteronomy stipulates how national taxes are to be collected. Archon, who explicitly admits never having actually seen the "scroll of the law", is being influenced here by his general sense of its principles of benevolence toward the poor, as exemplified by such biblical passages as Deut. 17.17; 24.6, 10-15, 17-22; 26.12-13. Redford, *ECI* 449 suggests that perhaps Necho loaned Egyptian troops to his vassal to help with the collection of the tax.

[12] The speech or sermon of Jeremiah that led to his trial is reported at Jer. 7 and again at 26.1-6, immediately before the description of the

trial itself at 26.7-24. The prose quotations are Jer. 26.4-6 and 26.12-14, respectively.

[13] Uriah's flight and the diplomatic mission given to Elnathan son of Achbor (depicted here as Archon's new commander) are described at Jer. 26.20-23.

CHAPTER II.
THROUGH THE DESERT TO THE DELTA

[1] Maps relevant to Archon's journey may be found at Dever, *W&W* 185 and in R. Cohen, *BAR* 7.3 (1981) 20ff (map on p. 22). M&H 46 describe Kadesh-Barnea as "an oasis that marks the southernmost limit of Palestine". The site figures very prominently in biblical narratives about the Israelites' supposed forty years of 'wandering in the wilderness' after leaving Egypt and before conquering Canaan; see, e.g., Numbers 10.11-12; 12.16; 13.26; 14.25; 20.1, 22; 33.36-37; Deut. 1.2-3, 19, 46; 2.14; 8.2; 9.23. The Cohen article (*BAR*'s cover story) argues convincingly that Ein el-Qudeirat is Kadesh and provides many photos and plans. An interesting ostracon found at the site has symbols in both Egyptian hieratic script and Hebrew (pp. 26-27). Remains of fortresses of three periods have also been found (p. 30). Cohen dates these forts 10th-9th century, 8th-7th, and 7th-6th, arguing that the last one, destroyed by Nebuchadnezzar, was probably built by Josiah. He is puzzled over one "question":

> But, where are the remains from the time of Moses (and of Abraham), from the period of the Exodus, and from the era of the Judges, which we would expect to find if this site is, indeed, Kadesh-Barnea? Thus far our excavations have yielded nothing earlier than the tenth century B.C....,

and this prompts him to mention the almost unthinkable:

> A final possibility, which some scholars urge, is that the Biblical references are not historical, that they are aetiological stories to explain later events and were in fact composed during the period of the Israelite monarchy (both quotes from p. 33).

F&S 42 accept Cohen's site identification and occupation dates, and do in fact use these to give a late date to the Patriarchal narrative in Gen. 14.7 that mentions Kadesh. Citing Cohen on the Josianic building-date for the third fortress (p. 349), F&S appear to prefer "a no less appealing alternative" proposed by Nadav Na'aman, that the fort was built "under Assyrian auspices with the assistance of the local vassal", i.e., Manasseh; they seem also to accept Na'aman's suggestion that the hieratic-Hebrew ostracon apparently indicates a late-seventh-century takeover of the fort by the Egyptians (pp. 351-352).

[2] Concerning standing stones in the southern Negeb and Sinai, see the discussions and numerous photos in V. Hurowitz, *BAR* 23.3 (1997) 46ff and U. Avner, 27.3 (2001) 30ff (cover story).

[3] The place south of Kadesh that Archon encountered is today known as Kuntillet Ajrud (or 'Ajrud).

[4] The jar has prompted much scholarly discussion. See especially Dever, *W&W* 183-186, 213 and several items in *BAR*: Z. Meshel, 5.2 (1979) 24ff; A. Lemaire, 10.6 (1984) 42ff; B. Margalit letter, 15.6 (1989) 12, 14; R. Hestrin, 17.5 (1991) 50ff; H. Shanks, 20.2 (1994) 52-53; J.G. Taylor, 20.3 (1994) 52ff; U. Avner addendum, 27.3 (2001) 37. Dever, writing in 2001, complains that the excavations, done in 1978 (Hestrin says 1975-76), have thus far led only to the publication of preliminary reports. Shanks' comments may suggest part of the problem, in that the artifacts from the site were to be ceded to Egyptian control (along with the Sinai peninsula itself, returned to Egyptian sovereignty) by the Israeli archaeologists who discovered them. Lemaire's half-page color photo of the storage jar Archon describes, and the large drawing of the figures on it (done by Pirhiya Beck), are simply reproduced, reduced in size (with the photo sometimes slightly cropped), in the articles of Hestrin, Shanks, and Taylor, and in Dever's book. So are the identifications of the figures suggested by Lemaire: two depictions of the Egyptian god Bes and, on their right, a nameless human female lyre-player. Thus the graffito above the figures that mentions Yahweh and his Asherah is taken as being unrelated to the persons (or gods) depicted immediately below it. Among dissidents is Margalit, who, in his letter to *BAR* (p. 15), denies that Bes is shown and asserts that the clearly bovine figures at left and center are "Yahweh himself, accompanied by his consort designated 'asherah', an archaic Canaanite-Hebrew common-noun meaning wife"; he promises subsequent publication on the issue (which I have not seen). Even Margalit's letter is accompanied by the Beck drawing, presumably supplied by the editor. The disagreement by Avner is truly fundamental. He says (as editorially reported, presumably by Shanks, in a note appended to his *BAR* article on standing stones) that Beck's drawing is inaccurate, that "the middle figure in the drawing has been erroneously portrayed as male", i.e., has been given an apparent 'penis' like that of the larger figure on its left, despite "her obviously female breasts" (much like those on the universally-admitted female

lyre-player, I might add). A revised version of the Beck drawing, with the 'penis' removed, is appended to the summary of Avner's comments, which conclude with:

> That middle figure is the goddess Asherah,...wearing a cow mask that resembles the bull mask of the Yahweh figure on the left. [Moreover,] the position of the male to the left of the female corresponds to the usual positioning of a taller *massebah* to the left of a shorter and wider *massebah* in pairs of *masseboth* found in the desert.

It appears that P.K. McCarter, who edits the inscription on this "Pithos 1" at *COS* 2.47A, has been won over by arguments such as those of Margalit and Avner, although their names are not among those cited in his introduction or references. *COS* 2.47B-D are other inscriptions from Kuntillet Ajrud (not including the inscription on the bowl, quoted here).

[5] Biblical assertions of about forty years of wandering in the desert are to be found at Exo. 16.35; Deut. 2.14; 8.2; 29.4. For the divinely-sent "manna" and quails, see Exo. 16; Num. 11.4-32. Compare the observations of F&S 61-63 and 326-328 (App. B), including the following:

> Some archaeological traces of their generation-long wandering in the Sinai should be apparent. However, ...not a single campsite or sign of occupation from [the relevant period] has ever been identified in Sinai. And it has not been for lack of trying. Repeated archaeological surveys in all regions of the peninsula...have yielded only negative evidence: not even a single sherd, no structure, not a single house, no trace of an ancient encampment. ...But modern archaeological techniques are quite capable of tracing even the very meager remains of hunter-gatherers and pastoral nomads all over the world. Indeed, the archaeological record for the Sinai peninsula discloses evidence for pastoral activity in such eras as the third millennium BCE and the Hellenistic and Byzantine periods. There is simply no such evidence at the supposed time of the Exodus... (pp. 62-63).

What was intuitively obvious to Archon (not under the spell of a biblical tradition that was only barely nascent in his time) is confirmed by modern archaeology.

[6] The "valley or dry river bed" to which Archon refers is the Wady Tumilat. Redford, *ECI* 359 says: "Bedu from the Negeb and Sinai had frequented this route from time immemorial...", and quotes Egyptian documents referring to the traffic (203, 228, the latter including the document *COS* 3.5=Prit. 1.183-184, from the time of Merneptah).

Redford also refers specifically to Necho's canal (434), whose digging he says (451) began in the period autumn 609 to spring 606, i.e., just after Archon's arrival in Egypt. For the canal and its problems, see Hdt. 2.158; Diod. 1.33.8-12 discusses Necho's work on it and subsequent work by Dareios I and Ptolemy II; Str. 17.1.25 says that work on the canal was begun by "Sesostris", though some say it was "the son of Psammitichos" [*sic!*], and also adds Dareios and "the Ptolemaic kings". See Lloyd re Hdt. 2.158 for detailed discussion of all issues associated with Necho's canal. Hdt. 4.39 shows that Dareios completed it. D. Peacock at *OHAE* 433 points out that even the refurbished canal of Ptolemaic and Roman times "was not extensively used, ...largely because of the severe northerly wind that blows down the Red Sea for 80 per cent of the year"; therefore cargoes from Asia were usually unloaded at Ptolemaic-built ports far south along the Egyptian side of the Red Sea and carried overland to the Nile! Further references to the canal in Archon's memoir occur in chs. 13, 14, and 16.

[7] Diod. 1.33.5-8 surveys the Nile mouths and their associated fortified cites, from east to west; the survey of Str. 17.1.18-21 goes west to east. Lloyd re Hdt. 2.17 shows that the exact courses of the Nile's branches are irrecoverable, saying that "both number and position clearly varied from date to date".

[8] On the word *Aigyptos* and its history, see Lloyd re Hdt. 2.1; *KMT* means "the black land" (ib. re 2.12) fertilized by the Nile silt, as opposed to "the red land", the desert. *Pathros* in the Bible (Gen. 10.14; Isa. 11.11; Jer. 44.1, 15; Ezek. 29.14; 30.14; 1 Chron. 1.2) corresponds to Psammetichos I's political subdivision of *Ptores*, "the Southern Land", extending from Memphis to Syene; see Lloyd at B.G. Trigger *et al.*, *Ancient Egypt: A Social History* (Cambridge 1983) 335. On the Egyptian name(s) of Memphis, see Lloyd re Hdt. 2.99 (where the Hebrew variant *Moph* is preferred to NJB's *Noph*). In this and succeeding chapters (and their associated notes) that deal with events in Egypt, I am grateful for the useful Anglicizations of Kushite-period Egyptian toponyms in Morkot, *Black Phar.*, even though I occasionally borrow a variant from elsewhere. Lloyd's 3-vol. commentary on Hdt. 2, though indispensable at many points, transliterates Egyptian terms into symbols that only specialists can understand—or pronounce. It is doubtless true, as Lloyd says re Hdt. 2.79, that "We are far from well informed on the principles of transliteration from Eg[yptian] into G[ree]k", but for my purposes it is better to be pronounceable than demonstrably exact.

[9] On the equating of the names of Egyptian and Greek gods, see Hdt. 2.42-43, 144.

[10] For the effects of the inundation, with cities compared to islands

in the Aegean, see Hdt. 2.97; cf. Str. 17.1.4. The geographical relationship between Sais and Naukratis is described at Str. 17.1.23.

[11] The Milesian temple to Apollo in Naukratis is mentioned at Hdt. 2.178.

[12] Jer. 26.22-23.

[13] For Jeremiah in Egypt, see ch. 22.

CHAPTER 12.
NAUKRATIS

[1] Archon's wish was fulfilled by Hekataios, whose work is unfortunately lost except for fragments; see Murray, *EG* 21-22, 24, 260. Hdt. refers to him at 2.143; 5.36, 125-126; 6.137; cf. the simple dismissal of Diod. 1.37.3. It was of course Herodotos, from Dorian-Karian Halikarnassos (although writing in the Ionian dialect), who most thoroughly fulfilled Archon's hopes. Lloyd, *Intro*. 68 puts Hdt.'s visit between ca. 459 and 430 BCE.

[2] On Naukratis, said to have been established ca. 620 BCE, see Murray, *EG* 228-231, including quotation (p. 229) of Hdt. 2.178-179; Murray describes the site's location (ca. fifty miles upstream from the Kanopic mouth and about ten miles from Sais) and its excavation history. Lloyd, *Intro*. 25 shows that literary sources imply an earlier date for the establishment of Naukratis than the date suggested here, which is derived from archaeological remains; some of these points are reiterated at ib. re 2.178, where Lloyd, apparently disagreeing with Petrie, puts the city on the *east* bank of the Kanopic branch (consistent with his map). A site plan, seemingly putting the town east of the Nile branch, may be seen at *OHAE* 375, with discussion by Lloyd on preceding page. Str. 17.1.18 preserves a story that "in the time of Psammitichos" certain Milesians founded Naukratis. Gorman, *Miletos* 56 denies the ancient tradition that Miletos founded Naukratis, saying that "it is completely unsupported by the archaeological evidence and...almost certainly false".

[3] According to H. Collitz, *SGDI* 3.2 (Göttingen 1905), excavations at Naukratis turned up a Milesian's gravestone (#5513) and dedications to Apollo, Aphrodite, the Dioskouroi, and Hera from Ionians (5756-5770), including obvious or apparent Milesians (5757, 5759).

[4] Archon's statements about the delta cities are essentially consistent with those of Hdt. on Sais (2.59, 62, 129-132, 169-171,

175-176), Papremis (2.59, 63, 71), Bouto (2.59, 63, 83, 133, 151-152, 155-156; 3.64), Bousiris (2.59, 61), Mendes (2.42, 46), and Boubastis (2.59-60, 137-138). Str. 17.1.19 quotes a passage from Pindar about goats having intercourse with women at Mendes. Lloyd re Hdt. 2.46 cites archaeological evidence for such practices there. Concerning the women's self-exposure at Boubastis, see ib. re 60. On the boat called a *baris*, see ch. 13 and notes.

[5] For Rhodopis/Doricha, Charaxos, the supposed pyramid connection, etc. see Hdt. 2.134-135; Str. 17.1.33; Diod. 1.64.14; Athen. 13.596b-d; testimonia on Sappho in *Greek Lyric*, vol. 1 (Loeb) items 1, 2, 9 (Hdt.), 14, 15 (Athen.), 16; and frag. 202 among her poems there (quoting passages from Hdt., Str., Athen., and other works). Lloyd's discussion of Rhodopis re Hdt. 2.134-135 is very full, including citation of her apparent inscribed dedication at Delphoi; ib. re 100 suggests that her fame even influenced traditions about Queen Nitokris, perhaps the last ruler of the Old Kingdom. Nicolas Grimal, *A History of Ancient Egypt* (New York 1992, French ed. 1988) 89 makes the same Nitokris-Rhodopis connection.

[6] Artemisia is a well attested name in Karia, borne by, e.g., the "tyrant", naval commander, and advisor (all one person) to Xerxes (Hdt. 7.99; 8.68-69, 87-88, 93, 101-103, 107) and by the wife, sister, and successor (all one person) of the fourth-century Karian satrap Mausolos (see Demosthenes 15.27 and Tod 155). Her statue is displayed near his in the British Museum, both being from the famous Mausoleion of Halikarnassos (Green, *Alex. to Act.* 97 has a photo of the statues).

Chapter 13.

IN THE ENCAMPMENT OF THE IONIANS

[1] On the Egyptian *machimoi* and subsets within them, see Hdt. 2.164-168 and the detailed discussion of Lloyd re 164; ib. re 165 finds the huge numbers of Hdt. believable. Diod. 1.34.10 calls *zythos* "little inferior to wine in fragrance" (trans. of Murphy, whose note says: "Zythos is, of course, beer"); see also Str. 17.2.5.

[2] Kushites were recruited into Egyptian service as early as the Old Kingdom's 6th dynasty (S. Seidlmayer at *OHAE* 130) or the Middle Kingdom (Kuhrt 171), Libyans by some point during the New Kingdom (ib. 623).

[3] The story of Psammetichos I's rise is told along similar lines in Hdt. 2.151-152; Diod. 1.66.8-12 dismisses much of Hdt.'s story as fanciful.

Lloyd, *Intro.* 14-15 (cf. ib. re Hdt. 2.152) cites Assyrian evidence for the initiative being taken by Gyges of Lydia in opposition to Ashurbanipal, rather than by Psammetichos, suggesting that Hdt. was misled by Egyptian informants; presumably Archon was also. Morkot, *Black Phar.* 297-298 suggests that the alliance of Psammetichos and Gyges was directed against the last Kushite king of Egypt, Tantamani.

[4] For the establishment of the Encampments, see Hdt. 2.154; Diod. 1.67.1. The 30,000 mercenaries of Apries are attested at Hdt. 2.163. On archaeological traces of the Encampments, see Murray, *EG* 231-233.

[5] Pedon's inscribed statuette, lacking its head, was found in a cave near Priene; the discovery was published in 1987. The most accessible discussions of the artifact, its fully-preserved nine-line *boustrophedon* text, and associated problems (*which* Psammetichos, the nominative-case spelling of the name of Pedon's father, what the additional award of "a city" to Pedon means, etc.) are to be found in *SEG* 37 (1987) 994 and subsequent volumes. S.M. Burstein, in his contribution to *Current Issues and the Study of Ancient History* (Claremont, CA 2001 = *Pubs. of the Assoc. of Ancient Historians* 7) 26 provides an English translation of the inscription and suggests that Pedon was not simply a successful mercenary, but that he and certain other 7th-6th-century Greeks were "government officials, who were fully integrated into Egyptian society and culture". Archon, of course, is only basing his interpretation on a second-hand report of a dedication in Ionia, and has no personal knowledge about Pedon. *LSAG*^{2} and other literature cited in *SEG* and elsewhere about Pedon—and about Archon *et al.*—mention various other archaic-period Greeks attested in Egypt.

[6] Hdt. 2.30 refers to a garrison posted in "Pelousian Daphnai"; H&W re Hdt. 2.30.2 summarize the findings of Petrie on Daphnai (Tell Defenneh) and assert that the town was immediately contiguous with one of the Encampments. Minor adjustments in this picture are suggested by R.M. Cook, *JHS* 57 (1937) 227-237. Austin, *Greece and Egypt* 15 puts the capacity of the fort at Tell Defenneh at ca. 20,000; see also *LSAG*^{2} 354-355. Lloyd re Hdt. 2.154 seems to *equate* Daphnai and Migdol with the Ionian and Karian Encampments, respectively, putting Daphnai *west* of the Pelousiac branch of the Nile (shown there on his map at the end of vol. 2, though Migdol is not shown anywhere). This argument appears to conflate places that Hdt. differentiates, so I prefer the location indicated by Archon. The map of *IBD*, s.v. "Tahpanhes" puts Tahpanhes/Daphnai east of the easternmost branch of the Nile, as does the plan of "Tell Defenna"—illustrating a chapter written by Lloyd himself—at *OHAE* 373.

[7] On *baris* construction see Hdt. 2.96; Lloyd *ad loc.* illustrates his

discussion with drawings. Str. 17.1.4 says that during the inundation people even use "earthenware ferry-boats" in the delta.

[8] For Miletos events, see ch. 1.

[9] See Archon's comrades' names again, in connection with inscriptions, in ch. 19 and notes.

Chapter 14.
CAMPAIGNS AROUND KARCHEMISH

[1] On the Phoinikians' voyage and the general complex of fortifications limiting entry to Egypt from the northeast see ch. 16 and notes. Redford, *ECI* 451 and n. 92 points out that although Pithom "was later identified as one of the cities built by the Israelites in bondage" prior to their rescue by Moses (Exo. 1.11), the fact "that Pithom's foundation dates from the early years of Necho II is now certain, thanks to the recent excavations…". Redford's comm. is only relevant, however, if the Exo. passage refers to Necho's Pithom and not to the Pithom mentioned in a 19th dynasty papyrus (*COS* 3.5=Prit. 1.183).

[2] A large, clear plan of Karchemish (almost a full page) is provided by *IBD*, s.v. "Carchemish".

[3] Archon's account of these campaigns of 606-605 BCE is generally consistent with the narrative of Redford, *ECI* 451-454; see also M&H 403.

[4] Lloyd re Hdt. 2.81 does not supply a date for the Petosiris whose tomb is mentioned in literature he cites, but certainly the name Petosiris is attested later, e.g., it belongs to the high priest of Thoth at Hermopolis under Ptolemy I, according to G. Hölbl, *A History of the Ptolemaic Empire* (London 2001) 27, 90. Lloyd says at *OHAE* 391 that "the tomb of Petosiris at Tuna el-Gebel contained burials of five generations of his family running from the 30th Dynasty into the Ptolemaic Period", and a color photo of Petosiris' inner coffin appears on the unnumbered plate facing p. 385.

[5] The so-called Prophecy of Nefer-Rohu (or Neferty or Neferti), assertedly of the 4th dynasty but apparently an *ex eventu* "prediction" of the rise of Amenemhat (Amenemhet, Ammenemes) I of the 12th dynasty, includes a passage translated by Pritchard as follows: "…a king will come, belonging to the south, Ameni, the triumphant, his name. He is the son of a woman of the land of Nubia; he is one born in Upper Egypt"

(Prit. 1.256=*COS* 1.45, where the king is called Imeny). The translation of the king's mother's native land is one possible interpretation of the expression Ta-Sety (Kuhrt 163) or Ta-Seti (Morkot, *Black Phar.* 53), which literally means "Bow-Land". Morkot, though recognizing the ambiguity of the term, finds in the passage "a strong suggestion that Amenemhat may have had some Kushite blood"; cf. B.J. Kemp at Trigger *et al., Anc.Egy.: Soc.Hist.* 79, citing G. Posener and saying "this deduction is no longer necessary".

[6] An easily-accessible photo of an Egyptian relief showing the collection of hands after a battle (with the Hittites) may be found at Prit. 1 fig. 93. The reference of Joyce Tyldesley, *Ramesses: Egypt's Greatest Pharaoh* (London 2000, Penguin pb 2001) 197 to the "piles of Meshwesh hands and penises" on the walls at Medinet Habu, celebrating Ramses III's victory over the Libyans, seems to match two piles of body parts in the less clearly labeled photo of the Medinet Habu relief in L. Casson, *Ancient Egypt* (New York 1965) 68-69.

[7] L.E. Stager, *BAR* 17.2 (1991) 24ff provides photos, drawings, and a vivid description of Ashkelon prior to its destruction by the Babylonians. The city covered an area of some 150 acres (photo, p. 27).

[8] Redford, *ECI* 453-454 quotes the Babylonian Chronicle passage from Nabopolassar's 21st year that describes his son's great victories, concluding with the claim that not one man returned (to Egypt); *COS* 1.137 (605 BCE passage) is slightly fuller.

[9] Jer. 46.2.

[10] Jer. 46.5-6 and 10-12.

[11] Jer. 25.19-20.

[12] The oracle concludes in Jer. 25.21-26 (Phoinikians in v. 22), summing up (v. 26) with "in short, all the kingdoms of the earth".

[13] Jer. 25.2, 9-11.

CHAPTER 15.
THE SHADOW OF NEBUCHADNEZZAR

[1] The events Archon describes in this chapter span the period from summer 604 through late 601 BCE; see the accounts of Redford, *ECI* 455-457 and M&H 405-406.

[2] Adon of Ekron's letter is quoted at M&H 386; the translation of Kuhrt 591 lacks the place-name, but recent archaeological work has made Ekron a certainty, as is clear from the entry at *COS* 3.54.

[3] Jehoiakim's fast was proclaimed in the ninth month of his fifth year, says Jer. 36.9.

[4] Jer. 25.11.

[5] Jer. 36.1-8.

[6] Jer. 36.10-26.

[7] Jer. 36.27-32 (quoted passage corresponds to vv. 30-31).

[8] Habakkuk 1.6-11.

[9] The destruction of Ashkelon took place around December of 604; the Babylonian Chronicle passage that includes the "heap of ruins" quote is accessible at M&H 381.

[10] A fragment of Alkaios' poem appears as frag. no. 48 in *Greek Lyric*, vol. 1 (Loeb); among the few extant words are *Babylonos, Askalona*, and *Aidao doma*.

[11] For the effects of the siege, see ch. 16 and notes.

[12] The Gaza oracle is Jer. 47.1-7 (vv. 4-5 are quoted).

[13] Jehoiakim's submission at the next appearance of the Chaldaean king in the area after the fall of Gaza may be referred to in 2 Kgs. 24.1's statement that Nebuchadnezzar invaded and Jehoiakim "became his vassal for three years".

[14] Jer. 46.13-16, 19-24.

Chapter 16
FLEETING TRIUMPHS

[1] Fortified places blocking the entry to Egypt from the northeast are described at Redford, *ECI* 457-458, with distances in kilometers that correspond to Archon's stades. Is Redford's "Pahsay" the same as "Repeh" (Raphia) in Morkot, *Black Phar.*? Diod. 1.57.4 refers to the wall Archon mentions; although Murphy's note says "There is no archaeological evidence of such a defensive wall", he cites a "Wall of the Prince" mentioned in the 12th-dynasty Story of Sinuhe (the trans. of Sinuhe at Prit. 1.7 calls it the "Wall-of-the-Ruler"). These citations and reservations are paralleled in the discussion of G. Callander at *OHAE* 158-159, though I. Shaw appears to accept the "Walls of the Ruler" at ib. 318. A 19th dynasty model letter for scribes (*COS* 3.2) seems to include a "Conclusion" that lists fortified places from Per-Ramesses to Raphia in geographical order.

[2] The Babylonian Chronicle's report of this campaign is surprisingly

honest: "In open battle they smote the breast (of) each other and inflicted great havoc on each other. The king of Akkad [i.e., Nebuchadnezzar] and his troops turned back and returned to Babylon" (M&H 381, 4th year passage, essentially the same as the *ANET* version quoted on p. 407 and the trans. of Redford, *ECI* 458). Judging from the caption (I cannot read the inscription), the tablet bearing this passage from the Chronicle appears in a photo at *BAR* 25.4 (1999) 41.

[3] Hdt. 2.159 has Necho defeating the "Syrians" at *Magdolos*, then taking the "Syrian" city of *Kadytis* afterward. The translations of both Waterfield and David Grene (Chicago 1987) simply transliterate (and Latinize) "Magdolus" with no clarificatory note. Grene, A.D. Godley (Loeb edition 1920), and H&W all identify Kadytis (correctly) with Gaza, and the Loeb note says Magdolos is Migdol. H&W, however, say that "The battle was really fought at Megiddo", but that Hdt. "confuses" it with Migdol! Gorman, *Miletos* 188 dodges the main issue, citing the Hdt. passage and commenting only that Necho made his dedication "when he defeated Gaza in Syria in 608", without discussing Hdt.'s Magdolos at all. The treatment of Lloyd re Hdt. 2.159 is very detailed (he informs us, e.g., that some have even seen "Kadytis" as being Kadesh on the Orontes River) and strongly supports Migdol and Gaza as the places mentioned. Lloyd reports the publication of recently-discovered evidence for other dedications by Necho at the temple of Athena Polias in Ialysos. The rumor that Archon heard seems consistent with the speculation of Redford, *ECI* 459 (see also Lloyd at Trigger *et al., Anc.Egy.: Soc.Hist.* 342) about the dedication perhaps reflecting the key role played in the battle by Necho's Greek auxiliaries. Compare the dedication by Amasis of "a remarkable linen breastplate" to Athena of Lindos (Hdt. 2.182, Waterfield trans.), also discussed in detail by Lloyd *ad loc.*

[4] On the destruction of Ashkelon, see the detailed sixteen-page treatment of Stager, *BAR* 22.1 (1996) 56ff, with photos illustrating many of the very streets, shops, and artifacts Archon describes, including one of the skeleton of the woman in the blue dress (p. 69), which is reprinted within a more general treatment of Judah caught between the great powers at 25.4 (1999) 39. Stager cites a Babylonian ration list of 592 BCE that includes the names of several deportees from Ashkelon, including two sons of King Aga (p. 69 and n. 15). Excavators say that Ashkelon remained uninhabited for 75 to 80 years after the Babylonian destruction.

[5] Redford, *ECI* 462 and n. 159.

[6] Necho's abandonment of his canal is described at Hdt. 2.158, the surprising success of his Phoinikian explorers at 4.42 (where the launching of their expedition is dated—contrary to Archon's narrative—

after the abandonment of the canal project). Lloyd re Hdt. 2.158 suggests that only Necho's death stopped work on his canal (which is drawn as complete on Lloyd's map), but says that "the alleged circumnavigation of Africa...is best explained as a pseudo-historical fabrication...". Lloyd's skepticism, somewhat muted in his contributions to Trigger *et al., Anc. Egy.: Soc.Hist.* 285 and 362 (cf. D. O'Connor's acceptance at p. 252), is strongly reasserted at *OHAE* 376. Str. 17.3.3, without citing Hdt.'s story directly, dismisses circumnavigation-of-Africa stories in general as fabrications. Hdt., like Archon, does not believe the explorers' story about the sun's position—which is of course the very datum that (contrary to both the ancient and modern opinions just mentioned) makes it certain the story is true, i.e., it proves that they were sailing west in the southern hemisphere; DeWald's note agrees.

[7] Jehoiakim, having paid Nebuchadnezzar's tribute for three years after the destruction of Ashkelon (see ch. 15 notes), now apparently withholds it for a like period after the battle of Migdol (2 Kgs. 24.1).

[8] Jer. 22.13-14.

[9] Jer. 22.15-17.

[10] 2 Kgs. 24.8; her own name was Nehushta.

[11] Jer. 22.18-19.

[12] Redford, *ECI* 459 and n. 137.

[13] Jer. 49.28-30.

[14] 2 Kgs. 24.2.

[15] Jer. 48.1-49.5.

[16] See Archon's earlier experiences at Arad in ch. 7; see also ch. 17, 19-21.

[17] See Jer. 35.

[18] It is said at 2 Kgs. 24.6 that Jehoiakim died (the date would be ca. December of 598 BCE); cf. 2 Chron. 36.6, which says that Nebuchadnezzar "loaded him with chains and took him to Babylon".

[19] Archon's uncertainty about the age of Jehoiachin at his accession is paralleled by the uncertainty of the biblical tradition. 2 Kgs. 24.8 says that he was eighteen, but most Hebrew MSS of 2 Chron. 36.9 say that he was only eight. NJB, the translation I normally use for biblical passages, is deceptive in *emending* Chron.'s eight to eighteen (without even a note to say this has been done, in the Reader's Edition I consulted). The account of Redford, *ECI* 459 and n. 141 accepts the age of eight, based on Chron.; M&H 408, however, describe the king as being eighteen.

[20] Jerusalem came under siege probably very early in 597. See ch. 17 notes for sources.

[21] The fact that no army from Egypt came to Jerusalem's assistance, implicit in Archon's narrative, is emphasized at 2 Kgs. 24.7: "The king of Egypt did not leave his own country again, because the king of Babylon had conquered everywhere belonging to the king of Egypt, from the Torrent of Egypt to the River Euphrates".

[22] Three of Eliashib's seals have been found at Arad, two of which had remnants of string through them; see A.F. Rainey, *BAR* 13.2 (1987) 36-7 for photos of all three. The seals are among the 112 Hebrew texts (plus 52 later Aramaic, Greek, and Arabic texts) published very fully in Aharoni, *AI*, specifically #105-107. Accessible selections of translated texts of the Arad ostraca include thirteen at *COS* 3.43, six at M&H 418-419 (via the collection in *Handbook of Ancient Hebrew Letters*), and three at Prit. 2.122.

CHAPTER 17.
FIRST SIEGE OF JERUSALEM

[1] Jer. 22.24-27.

[2] Jer. 13.18-19.

[3] Jer. 22.28-30.

[4] For "Zion theology", see various passages in Psalms (difficult to date, but the idea presumably was current in the days of the kingdom of Judah), notably Ps. 46.5: "God is in the city, it cannot fall; / At break of day God comes to its rescue"; see also Pss. 48 and 76.

[5] The first Babylonian siege of Jerusalem and its surrender in early 597 BCE are described succinctly by Redford, *ECI* 459-460 and M&H 408. On the besieging and surrender of Jerusalem, see 2 Kgs. 24.10-12, with looting of the treasury and temple at v. 13. The Babylonian Chronicle, 7th year passage, is translated at *COS* 1.137, M&H 381, Prit. 1.203 (where fig. 58 shows the actual tablet), Kuhrt 591, and Redford, *ECI* 460.

[6] The numbers Archon mentions correspond to the reports of Jer. 52.28 and 2 Kgs. 24.12, 14-16, respectively; Redford, *ECI* 460 seems to prefer "the more judicious records of Jeremiah".

[7] Zedekiah is called Jehoiachin's paternal uncle at 2 Kgs. 24.17, whereas 2 Chron. 36.13 calls him his predecessor's brother.

[8] Ezek. 17.12-20; cf. 2 Chron. 36.13; see also ch. 20.

[9] Jer. 13.19.

[10] Aharoni, *AI* p. 149 argues, based on one ostracon (#34) written

in hieratic, that the 7th-century fort at Arad (Stratum VII) fell in 609, at the time of Necho's killing of Josiah; he asserts (p. 129) that from that point Judah was "ruled by Egypt for four to five years". This dating is rejected by Aharoni's colleagues in the excavation (including his wife), writing after his death: Z. Herzog, M. Aharoni, & A.F. Rainey, *BAR* 13.2 (1987) 25 say that "fortress VII was probably destroyed in a softening-up operation by Nebuchadnezzar in preparation for th[e] campaign of 597 B.C." In a separate but related article, Rainey, ib. 37-38, dates Stratum VII to ca. 620-597, specifically refutes the argument based on the hieratic ostracon, and repeats the "softening up operation" in 598/597 suggestion. Archon's suggestion that the Edomites, not the Babylonian army, destroyed the fortifications at Arad in 597 seems plausible. Nothing in the literature seems to provide a clear basis for deciding between destroyers. In any case, Dever, *W&W* 181 points out of Arad in general that "The dating and interpretation of the various 10th-6th-century phases remain controversial because of faulty excavation methods and the lack of final reports".

[11] See ch. 7, above.

Chapter 18.
LIMBO ON ALL FRONTS

[1] For events of the period described in this chapter (ca. 597-594 BCE), see Redford, *ECI* 460-462, M&H 408-411, and Kuhrt 592.

[2] Jer. 49.34-38.

[3] Ezek. 8-11.

[4] Ezek. 13 denounces false prophets—and prophetesses ("the women...who make up prophecies out of their own heads", v. 17).

[5] Jer. 24.

[6] The letter is described in Jer. 29: those said to be prophesying lies are Ahab son of Kolaiah (see ch. 22) and Zedekiah son of Maaseiah (vv. 21-23, including details of their crimes and punishment); the letter writer referred to is Shemaiah son of Nehelam (vv. 24-32); denunciation of the king *et al.*, compared to rotten figs (vv. 16-17).

[7] Zedekiah's conference and the attendant confrontation between Jeremiah and Hananiah are described in Jer. 27-28; the 4th-year date is provided only at 28.1 in the Hebrew text, with these events otherwise only said to have occurred "at the beginning of the reign of Zedekiah" (ib. and 27.1), though the conference and confrontation are explicitly

put in the same year. M&H 409-410 reject the 4th-year statement and put the conference and confrontation in 597, saying that the ambassadors discussed "prospects of a united revolt to take place two years later"—perhaps (this is only my guess) taking their cue from Hananiah's prediction that Nebuchadnezzar's "yoke" would be broken and the exiles and temple treasures returned "in exactly two years' time" (Jer. 28.3; phrase again in v. 11). Redford, *ECI* 461-462 and n. 153, relying on the Septuagint's reading of Zedekiah's 4th year in Jer. 27.1 (I assume in addition to 28.1), dates the conference "[p]robably in the autumn of 594".

[8] The summoning of Zedekiah to Babylon and the letter of Jeremiah conveyed by Seraiah are described at Jer. 51.59-64. Seraiah is called "son of Neriah, son of Mahseiah" (v. 59); Baruch's homonymous father, but no grandfather, is named at Jer. 36.4. *IBD*, s.v. "Baruch" describes Baruch and Seraiah as brothers. Although dating the conference earlier, M&H 410-411 put Zedekiah's trip and Jeremiah's letter in 594-593; Redford, *ECI* 465 provides no date for Zedekiah's "interrogation in Babylon".

[9] Quotes from Jer. 51.62 and 64.

[10] I note in passing that Aharoni, *AI*, comm. on #20 (pp. 40-41) and "Summary: Historical Information" (p. 150), argues—based entirely on this ostracon, whose extant text says *only* "In the 3rd year" plus the name of a month—that the last Judahite level at Arad (Stratum VI) was *destroyed* in Zedekiah's 3rd or 4th regnal year (equated with 596/5) as a consequence of his failure in organizing a rebellion. The editorial introduction at Prit. 2.122 to the translated texts of three Arad ostraca (all from Stratum VI) dates the archive from which they came to probably shortly before the first surrender of Jerusalem in winter 598/7. Yet even the final editor of *AI* itself, Rainey, finds Aharoni's chronological argument far-fetched (see bracketed editorial addition, p. 41). Rainey and Aharoni's other colleagues, *BAR* 13.2 (1987) 25, suggest rather that the fort of Stratum VI was probably *built* in Zedekiah's 4th year (594 or 593, they say), and probably destroyed by the Edomites "at the time of the Babylonian conquest of Judah" (p. 28, an event dated on p. 26 to 587). A confusion probably injected by the *BAR* editor is the providing of the dates 605-595 for Stratum VI in a photo caption in Rainey's associated article (p. 36), a dating clearly inconsistent with Rainey's views at the time. *COS* 3.43's introduction to its selection of thirteen ostraca is appropriately imprecise, dating most of them "end of the seventh/beginning of the sixth centuries".

[11] On Necho vs. Anlamani, Necho's death, and the accession of Psammetichos II, see Redford, *ECI* 462.

[12] Hos. 1.2-3: "Yahweh said to Hosea, 'Go, marry a whore, and get children with a whore...'. So he went and married Gomer daughter of Diblaim, who conceived and bore him a son". More unpleasantries follow.

Chapter 19.
EXPEDITION TO NUBIA

[1] These events, from the years 593-589 BCE, are described in varying detail in Redford, *ECI* 462-465; Kuhrt 640-642; M&H 411-412; Murray, *EG* 233-234; and T.G.H. James, *Cambridge Ancient History*[2] 3:2 (1991) 726-729. For useful maps, see Morkot, *Black Phar.* 4 and 6; John H. Taylor, *Egypt and Nubia* (Cambridge 1991) 4 and 39. "Nubia", wherever it appears in my text, is an anachronism employed for stylistic variety; Morkot 2 says that the term is unattested prior to the third century BCE, but it is less confusing for a modern reader than the Greek "Ethiopia", whose meaning has changed since antiquity. Hdt. 2.161 provides only the bare fact that Psammetichos invaded "Ethiopia"; that the expedition dates to his third year is based on Egyptian inscriptions (Lloyd re Hdt. 2.161). Compare the bizarre statement of Diod. 1.37.5 to the effect that no Greeks had ever entered "Ethiopia" before the time of Ptolemy II!

[2] The "great riverside temples" built by Ramses (II) the Great are of course those at Abu Simbel, which are almost always illustrated in any picture book about Egypt. For detailed discussion and many photos, see William MacQuitty, *Abu Simbel* (New York 1965).

[3] Psammetichos II's third regnal year is still dated to 591 by some scholars (including some cited in these notes), but a consensus for 593 appears to be growing; Lloyd re Hdt. 2.161 (anticipated by his comment at Trigger *et al., Anc.Egy.: Soc.Hist.* 281) says that the other date arose from an error about the king's *first* year.

[4] No extant source indicates the presence of Greeks in the garrison at Elephantine at this early date. G. Callender at *OHAE* 151 says that Mentuhotep II (11th dynasty, 2055-2004 BCE) established a garrison (presumably of Egyptian troops) at Elephantine. For Judahite troops there, see below.

[5] For Potasimto, Amasis, and Psammetichos son of Theokles, see Archon's inscription (below).

[6] Hdt. 2.175 says that from Sais to Elephantine was twenty days'

sailing; Lloyd re 2.4 and 175 accepts the estimate as substantially accurate (ca. 35-36 miles per day).

[7] Lloyd, *Intro.* 70 says that Heliopolis was six kilometers east of the Nile, connected by a canal, citing Str. 17.1.27, which seems to permit (if not require) this interpretation. Hdt. 2.73 says that he was told in Heliopolis that the Phoinix appears at 500-year intervals, and admits that he has "not actually seen" one.

[8] On the pyramid builders, see Hdt. 2.124-134 (a passage famously out of chronological sequence). Mark Rose, *Archaeology* 55.4 (2002) 9 reports the recent discovery of a small pyramid five miles north of Giza; this is said to have brought the total number of pyramids discovered in Egypt to 110.

[9] Menes is called Min at Hdt. 2.4 and 99, a name generally given to the ithyphallic god mentioned below in connection with Luxor and Abu Simbel.

[10] For Apis/Epaphos, see Hdt. 2.153.

[11] The large temple complexes at Thebes are, respectively, Karnak, called by the Egyptians *Ipet-Sut* (which Morkot, *Black Phar.* 239 translates as "the most select of places"), and Luxor, *Ipet-Resyt.*

[12] Psammetichos I had facilitated the Saite takeover from the Kushite Pharaohs by sending in 656 his daughter Neitiqert (Greek Nitokris, not to be confused with the sixth dynasty[?] queen of Hdt. 2.100) to be adopted as her successor as God's Wife of Amun by the Kushite-princess incumbent. Morkot, *Black Phar.* 299-302 provides full details, including a passage from an inscribed stele about Nitokris' departure and a drawing of a relief showing the flotilla of boats greeting her arrival. She would eventually hold the office until her death seventy years later, in 586 (year 4 of Apries); see also Kuhrt 638; Redford, *ECI* 432.

[13] Archon visits Elephantine prior to the building of any temple, and explicitly relies on hearsay in reporting that other deities of Canaan are worshiped in the area, along with Yahweh. Persian-era (i.e., much later) Aramaic documents from garrison soldiers seemingly of Judahite heritage indicate that their ancestors had been at the site prior to the Persian conquest of Egypt. Selections of such documents are to be found at *COS* 3.46-53 and 59-81; Prit. 1.170-172, 278-282, and 2.83-86, 193-194. See especially Prit. 1.280=*COS* 3.51: "Now, our forefathers built this temple in the fortress of Elephantine back in the days of the kingdom of Egypt, and when Cambyses came to Egypt he found it built". Neither *COS*'s nor Pritchard's selections mention any gods other than "Yaho the God of Heaven", nor (obviously) do the

three of Prit. 1's six texts presented at M&H 466-467. But *COS* 3.46 and 49 invoke "the gods", and *COS* 3.47 invokes the blessing of "the gods, all (of them)". Although Morton Smith, *Pal. Parties*[2] 67; M&H 435-436; Ahlström, *History* 869-872; and Soggin, *Intro*. 297-298 all conclude that the "Judaeans" (Smith), "Jews" (M&H), "Jewish military colony" (Soggin), or "Palestinians"—perhaps "many...descendants of Israelites and Samarians" (Ahlström) worshiped gods in addition to Yahweh in their temple at Elephantine, and although each of them cites and/or lists among associated bibliographical references Bezalel Porten, *Archives from Elephantine* (1968), Porten himself–at least in more recent writings (I have not looked at the 1968 book)–takes a different position. In his general discussion at *BAR* 21.3 (1995) 54ff, Porten says (p. 61): "The Aramean soldiers on the mainland at Aswan [=Syene] were also allowed to erect temples to their gods—Banit, Bethel, Nabu and the Queen of Heaven". This position is maintained and supported both in *The Elephantine Papyri in English* (Leiden 1996) and in Porten's editing of the Elephantine papyri selections of *COS*. Archives of "Makkibanit Letters" and "Miscellaneous Letters" from Elephantine, included in Porten's *E.Pap.in Eng.* 89-124, which do seem to mention such other gods, are *not* included among *COS*'s selections. I do not know whether these latter letters always refer to separate temples in Syene, or whether Porten infers this because of a presupposition that the Elephantine temple of Yahweh could not have been shared with other gods. What is obvious to any reader of the present work, however, is that even in Jerusalem, Yahweh did indeed share his temple with other gods, up to the time of Josiah's revolution.

[14] That Psammetichos remained in the Elephantine area is clear both from the phrasing of Archon's inscription (below) and from stelai set up at Karnak and Aswan, one of which is translated at Kuhrt 642 (and partially at Redford, *ECI* 463); it mentions, e.g., the report reaching the king there that 4200 captives had been taken (see below).

[15] The "Holy Mountain" referred to by Archon, like "The Hill" mentioned in a stele at Tanis cited at James, *CAH* 728, must have been the major Nubian archaeological site near Napata and the fourth cataract known now as Gebel Barkal. See Morkot, *Black Phar.* 137-138, including a photo of a nineteenth-century painting of the 300-feet-high "mesa"; Taylor, *E&N* 31 has a color photo.

[16] Morkot, *Black Phar.* 303-304 says that the destruction of Nubian royal statues at Napata and Gebel Barkal by the returning soldiers of Psammetichos II is the usually accepted interpretation of the condition of remains found there. *OHAE* 353 has a photo of the famous triumphal stele of the Nubian king Piye at Gebel Barkal, in which the figure of

Piye himself has been chiseled out of the relief.

[17] Archon's description of the Abu Simbel temples corresponds to the narrative, photos, and drawings of MacQuitty's guidebook (above); see also the full description and historical discussion of Tyldesley, *Ramesses* 104-109.

[18] All the inscriptions mentioned (including Anaxanor's *boustrophedon* text) are extant; facsimiles and texts of each are provided by Bernand & Masson, *REG* 70 (1957) 1-20. Tyldesley 107 says that enough sand would have accumulated at the long-abandoned temple to have made it possible for the Greeks to have "left their graffiti at the new ground level, just under the knee". Archon's five-line text is clearly legible in the two-page center spread color photo (pp. 98-99) of MacQuitty. Although both Archon and his brother Python supply their patronymic (*Amoibichou*), neither adds an ethnic. Jeffery, *LSAG*[2] 355 asks whether those omitting ethnics in this collection of inscriptions might be, like Psammetichos son of Theokles, second-generation Egyptian mercenaries.

[19] Archon's "future readers"—at least some of the pedantic scholars among them—have indeed puzzled themselves over his "Dorian co-author", *Peleqos Oudamou*. Bernand & Masson 10 say that it is likely that the "authors" of the longest of the inscriptions (Archon and Peleqos!) were mercenaries from (Dorian) Rhodos, like the others from Rhodian Ialysos. Hopefully, such stodgy seriousness has been put finally to rest by M.P.J. Dillon, *ZPE* 118 (1997) 128-130, who concludes: "This is clearly intended as a joke", and describes it as "a pun which is probably the first instance of humour in a Greek inscription", adding moreover that Archon may have been inspired by remembering Odysseus' famous joke at the expense of the Kyklops Polyphemos, identifying himself as *Outis*, "Nobody" (Homer, *Odyssey* 9.366-460). Murray, *EG* 233 ends his translation of the inscription with "Archon son of Amoibichos and Axe son of Nobody (or for those without humour, 'Pelechos son of Eudamos')"! See also Epilogue.

[20] M&H 411 provide a translation of a passage from a papyrus inviting Egyptian priests to join in Psammetichos' "victory tour of Palestine" in 591; see also James, *CAH* 729; Redford, *ECI* 464; Kuhrt 644. Lloyd at Trigger *et al., Anc.Egy.: Soc.Hist.* 285 puts Psammetichos' "ceremonial progress" in 592.

[21] Hdt. 2.161's entire treatment of Psammetichos II (whom he calls "Psammis") consists of reporting that he ruled only six years, died shortly after invading "Ethiopia", and was succeeded by his son Apries.

Chapter 20.
SIEGE, SIEGE LIFTED, SIEGE AGAIN

[1] For events of ca. 589 through early 587, see Redford, *ECI* 465-467 and M&H 412-414.

[2] For the rebuilding, see the color-coded plans of *BAR* 13.2 (1987) 26-27, with Stratum VI in blue and the location of the "house of Eliashib" indicated.

[3] Ostraca bearing priestly names from the pre-Josianic Stratum VIII include *AI* #54 (Pashhur) and #51 (Eshiyahu); the Eshiyahu of #40, from this same stratum, is not necessarily a priest. I invite the reader to identify the priest Eshiyahu of the fictional interrogation of ch. 7 with Eliashib's attested father of that name; Eliashib's son Eshiyahu is fictional, although names do recur in families, and the pattern suggested is normal.

[4] See also *COS* 3.43A n. 3 for discussion of the term; for biblical uses of it, see *IBD*, s.v. "Kittim". The ostraca of *AI* repeatedly refer to supplies given to groups of *Kittiyim* (#1, 2, 4, 5, 7, 8, 10, 11, 14, 17), but Aharoni (p. 13, re #1) concludes: "There are no indications that the Kittiyîm lived at Arad. Rather, ...here at Arad they were given provisions for their journeys to more distant places". This obviously directly contradicts Archon's opening statement of this chapter; my plot-line requires him to be resident as an observer, but this convention has no impact on the historical events he describes.

[5] The letter Archon says was written from Zedekiah to Apries is the fragmentarily preserved #88 ("I have come to reign in all[?]... / Take strength and... / King of Egypt to..."). The *AI* eds. say that its script appears to date this ostracon to Stratum VII, i.e., too early. On the other hand, the note at *COS* 3.43M expresses doubt as to this text's "literary genre...date and historical significance". The ostracon was found out of context by a visitor to the excavation site, and speculations of scholars about its partial text vary greatly. Aharoni says that Jehoahaz is writing Eliashib to prepare for war with Necho; he also infers from the partially-preserved phrase "in all" that Josiah had indeed conquered the former territory of Israel and ruled it in addition to Judah, which leads his son to claim the same enlarged territory. Yigael Yadin sees the ostracon as an announcement from the last *Assyrian* king, Ashur-uballit, that he is ruling *in Karchemish* [*sic!*]; Rainey properly dismisses this as an "idle fancy" (see Aharoni, *AI* p. 104 and notes for all these views). A. Malamat,

BAR 25.4 (1991) 37-38, calling the reconstructions of Aharoni and Yadin both "at best dubious", offers one seemingly even more bizarre (already mentioned in ch. 10 notes): the speaker is *God*, who proclaims his rule over "all the nations"!

[6] Apries' ships to Tyre and Sidon are referred to in a chronologically-vague context at Hdt. 2.161; Redford, *ECI* 465 sees spring or summer 589 as appropriate. Diod. 1.68.1 says that Apries "took Sidon by storm, and so terrified the other cities of Phoinikia that he secured their submission" (Loeb trans., spelling Hellenized).

[7] Jer. 39.5 puts Nebuchadnezzar's headquarters at Riblah, but only in the context of Jerusalem having already fallen.

[8] Ezek. 21.23-27 depicts Nebuchadnezzar at a cross-roads, casting lots to decide whether to invade the territory of the Ammonites or to besiege Jerusalem—predicting the latter. The Chaldaeans' siege of Tyre is described, with attendant oracles, at Ezek. 26.1-28.19, followed by vv. 20-23 against Sidon.

[9] The phrase appears at Ezek. 28.7.

[10] Ezek. 17.15-21.

[11] An ostracon found at Lachish and dated close to this year (all scholars agree) refers to Coniah's mission (Lachish Ostracon III, translations at *COS* 3.42B, Prit. 1.213, and M&H 418, 1st Lachish text). See ch. 11 and notes for the expedition led by Elnathan. *AI* #119 refers to someone whom Rainey calls the "squire of Elnatha[n...]"; his comm. (p. 123) seems to equate this Elnathan with the high official Elnathan son of Achbor mentioned at Jer. 36.12, 25 (see ch. 15 and 16 and notes), and perhaps also with the father of Nehushta, Jehoiachin's mother (2 Kgs. 24.8), but he calls Coniah's father in the Lachish ostracon "[a]nother Elnathan". Archon's guess seems just as plausible.

[12] Ezek. 24.1-2 claims to give a precise date (9th year, 10th month, 10th day) for the beginning of Nebuchadnezzar's "attack" on Jerusalem. Since this date matches the date of 2 Kgs. 25.1, where it is clearly applied to the initial laying of the siege, I assume the Ezek. passage means that too.

[13] Jeremiah's activities immediately before the siege are described at Jer. 19.1-20.6, the quotation corresponding to 19.9. For Archon with Josiah at Topheth, see ch. 6.

[14] The embassy from the king and Jeremiah's response to it are described at Jer. 21.1-10 (quotations are from vv. 5 and 10).

[15] For Antimenidas, see ch. 15. The lines quoted are from the trans. of Murray, *EG* 232 of Alkaios frag. 350; cf. *Greek Lyric* I (Loeb) p. 387 and Str. 13.2.3. Archon's description of the Egyptian giant appears in ch. 10. Murray, *EG* 232 says: "The height is that of a real Goliath, 8′

4″." I assume exaggeration, as Archon's comment about regular and royal cubits indicates. Hdt. 7.117 tells of a Persian—a member of the royal family—who was "only four fingers short of five royal cubits" and who in addition "had the loudest voice in the world". He further tells of scavengers after the battle of Plataia in 479 finding "the skeleton of a man who was five cubits tall" (9.83).

[16] For Glaukos and Diomedes, see Homer, *Iliad* 6.212-231, including lines 226-229: "So let us shun one another's spears even amid the throng; full many there be for me to slay, both Trojans and famed allies, whomsoever a god shall grant me and my feet overtake; and many Achaeans again for thee to slay whomsoever thou canst" (Loeb trans.).

[17] The departure of Apries from Egypt, "probably in the fall of 588", is described and documented by Redford, *ECI* 466.

[18] Ezek. 16.26 accuses Jerusalem of fornicating with her "big-membered neighbors, the Egyptians", a theme to which the prophet obviously returns in the quoted passage from ch. 23 (vv. 19-21 here are but a small sample of the imagery!).

[19] Ezek. 29.6-7.

[20] Zedekiah's desperate appeal to Jeremiah is described at Jer. 37.3-10; the passage quoted is vv. 7-9.

[21] Jer. 37.11-16.

[22] Jer. 37.17-21.

[23] Jer. 32.

[24] The slaves' manumission and re-enslavement, etc. are described at Jer. 34.8-22 (quoted phrases are parts of vv. 17 and 21-22).

[25] Ezek. 30.21-24.

[26] The re-besieging of Jerusalem seems to be referred to at Jer. 34.7, which names Lachish and Azekah as the only other towns of Judah still holding out. The biblical passage is strikingly supported by Lachich Ostracon IV, which concludes with the ominous report: "[W]e are watching for the signals of Lachish, ...for we cannot see Azekah" (Prit. 1.213, with photo and drawing in fig. 80; cf. M&H 418, 2nd text, and *COS* 3.42C).

CHAPTER 21.
DESTRUCTION OF JERUSALEM

[1] The eighteen months of renewed siege (early 587 to mid-586 BCE) and the destruction, executions, and deportations that follow are described in M&H 414-420 and Redford, *ECI* 467-469. Biblical accounts appear at 2 Kgs. 25.1-21 and Jer. 39.1-10; 52.1-27.

[2] The two ostraca partially quoted by Archon are *AI* #18 (=*COS* 3.43I=Prit. 2.122A & fig. 38=M&H 419, 2nd text) and #24 (=*COS* 3.43K=M&H 419, 5th text). See a vivid color photo of the former at *BAR* 27.3 (2001) 25, although the comment there refers the phrase to the temple at Arad itself, which most scholars (e.g., *COS* 3.43I n. 26) see as having long been suppressed at this time; cf. 13.2 (1987) 35. Dever, *W&W* 212 (with drawing) says that the reference actually could be to either temple, Jerusalem's or Arad's. This argument might be conceivable if the stratigraphy of the site is as hopelessly wrong as Dever says, but I would suggest that writing the commander at Arad to tell him that someone is in the temple in his own small fort would be rather pointless. Admittedly, in Dever's translation (which differs fundamentally from all others I have seen), the writer is not describing the location or condition of any person, but saying that "the house (i.e., temple) of Yahweh is well; it endures". The same sort of objection would apply, however: surely the commander at Arad would already know whether his fort's own temple was "enduring". A photo of #24 appears at *BAR* 22.6 (1996) 35. *AI* p. 147 provides a map of the immediate vicinity of Arad, showing probable subsidiary fortresses (using their modern, rather than ancient names, however).

[3] Ezek. 24.15-27.

[4] 2 Kgs. 25.3-4; Jer. 39.2; 52.6-7.

[5] For Ebed-Melech (Servant-of-the-King) see ch. 19. His dealings with Jeremiah and Zedekiah are described at Jer. 38.1-13. P.K. McCarter, *BAR* 28.2 (2002) 46ff discusses recent evidence about Nathan-Melech in the time of Josiah (2 Kgs. 23.11), seeing him as another attested royal eunuch.

[6] Jer. 38.9.

[7] Jer. 39.16-18.

[8] Jer. 38.14-24 (quoted prediction in vv. 17-18).

[9] Jer. 39.3-7; 52.7-11; 2 Kgs. 25.4-7 (all three passages do indeed say that the blinded Zedekiah was taken to Babylon).

[10] Ezek. 12.12-13.

[11] Ezek. 33.21-22.

[12] To show the Babylonians' pause while deciding on the fate of Jerusalem, compare Jer. 52.6 = 2 Kgs. 25.3-4 (4th month, 9th day: wall breached) with Jer. 52.12 (5th month, 10th day: Nebuzaradan enters the city to burn it, etc.), from which 2 Kgs. 25.8 differs only by indicating the 7th day rather than the 10th.

[13] The ostracon is *AI* #2=*COS* 3.43B=M&H 418, 2nd Arad text. See Aharoni's comm. (p. 15) and the fuller discussion in his summary chapter (p. 145) on the distance, which he estimates at ca. 110 km. from Arad to Kadesh-Barnea, with three nightly stops at small forts (identified) about 25-30 km. apart.

[14] My narrative is, of course, dealing playfully with these cryptic ostraca; the reader is not meant to accept "Archon's guesses" as historical truth. Note, however, that supposedly serious scholarship can come up with interpretations of these texts that are as bizarre as—or more bizarre than—my admittedly fictional ones; see ch. 10 n. 1 and ch. 20 n. 5.

[15] On pillage, destruction, executions, and deportations, see 2 Kgs. 25.9-21; Jer. 39.8-9; 52.13-29.

[16] On non-deportees, Gedaliah, and some recovery, see 2 Kgs. 25.22-24; Jer. 39.10; 40.7-12. See also ch. 22, below.

[17] On the treatment of Jeremiah, see Jer. 39.11-14; 40.1-6 (quotation from 40.4).

[18] Jer. 49.7-22 (date and context uncertain); Ezek. 25.12-14; 35; Obadiah 1.1-18; cf. Ps. 137.7. See also ch. 7 notes.

Chapter 22.
RETIREMENT AND REMINDERS

[1] The mutiny at Elephantine by "the mercenaries, Libyans, Greeks, Asiatics and foreigners" is described in a stele of Nesuhor at Aswan (Syene); the quoted phrase is from a passage of the inscription translated at Kuhrt 642. Both Kuhrt and James, *CAH* 727, 729-730 seem to imply—if not to state with absolute clarity—that this mutiny of the reign of Apries is confusedly referred to at Hdt. 2.30, where a very large-scale desertion of Egyptian troops is set in the reign of Psammetichos I (Lloyd makes no such suggestion *ad loc.*).

[2] See Jer. 29.21-23, where the punishment of this Aḥab (obviously not to be confused with the 9th-century king of Israel) is reported; this is discussed in ch. 18 and notes.

[3] Archon chose to retire to Daphnai for reasons of convenience. Apparently other *alloglossoi* retired elsewhere: Dillon, *ZPE* 118 (1997) 128 suggests that a settlement of Greeks (Hdt. 3.26 actually describes them specifically as "Samians") at an oasis seven days west across the desert from Thebes "may well have been made up of retired mercenaries".

[4] Nesuhor's stele says: "I re-established their heart in reason by advice, not permitting them to go to Nubia, but bringing them to the place where his majesty was; and his majesty executed their punishment" (Kuhrt 642).

[5] There was in fact a white glazed vase discovered in this temple with an Ionic-alphabet inscription bearing the name Eukles (*SGDI* 5762), although of course this incident is fictional—as is the brutalized personality I have foisted upon the otherwise-unknown Eukles.

[6] Archon is as imprecise about the actual title of Gedaliah as the canonical biblical Hebrew texts are, although the NJB translations of the relevant passages of 2 Kgs. 25 and Jer. 39 and 40 inferentially supply the word "governor" seven times. M&H 421-424 make at least a plausible argument that Gedaliah might have been appointed *king*, but that this datum has been deleted and concealed by biblical editors committed to the inviolability of the Davidic succession. For Gedaliah's capital Mizpah (Tell en-Nasbeh), see J. Zorn, *BAR* 23.5 (1997) 28ff (with many photos and plans). This and subsequent articles by E. Stern, 26.6 (2000) 45ff; J. Blenkinsopp, 28.3 (2002) 37ff; and Stern again, ib. 39ff discuss, with some heat, whether there is a "Babylonian gap" in the archaeological history of the territory of the former kingdom of Judah; see further letters from Blenkinsopp and Zorn in 28.5 (2002) 13-14. Archon's "four or five years" for the administration (reign?) of Gedaliah is consistent with the statement in Jer. 52.30 that a third deportation from Judah (namely the 745 people Archon reports, citing Baruch) occurred in Nebuchadnezzar's 23rd year, i.e., 582-581 BCE. For the assassination of Gedaliah, see Jer. 40.7-41.18; cf. the terse 2 Kgs. 25.25. Although both Jer. 41.1 and 2 Kgs. 25.25 say only that Gedaliah was assassinated "in the seventh month", implying by omission that he was in his *first* year of control, it seems surprising that Nebuchadnezzar's vengeance, in a province so recently and thoroughly crushed, would be so slow in coming, especially since Chaldaean troops were among those murdered. Nor could much of the recovery described in Jer. 40.11-12 have taken place in such a short period. Van De Mieroop, *Hist. of the ANE* 259 puts the assassination of "the Babylonian governor" and the additional deportations in 582. *COS* 2.70D, found at Lachish, may be a seal of Gedaliah from an earlier year (see intro. there). R. Deutsch, *BAR* 25.2

(1999) 46ff reports the finding of what purports to be the seal of the Ammonite king Baalis (large color photo on cover). *COS* 2.71 seems to be the seal of a minister of Baalis (see n. 49 there); see photo and drawing at *BAR* 19.6 (1993) 32.

[7] Some scholars (notably Lloyd at Trigger *et al., Anc.Egy.: Soc.Hist.* 339, citing no source) associate the third deportation with a supposed invasion of Egypt by Nebuchadnezzar in 582 or 581, but the only evidence for such an invasion is the *predictions* of it at Jer. 42.7-22 (quote from vv. 15-16) and (after he was taken to Egypt himself) at Jer. 43.8-13; 44.11-14, 26-30. It is not surprising to see the prophet's predictions turned into historical reality by Josephus, *Antiquities* 10.180-183, but modern historians should be less gullible. The discussion of these issues at M&H 425 is sensible and judicious.

[8] The Hebrew name for Daphnai, Tahpanhes, may reflect an Egyptian original meaning "Mansion of the Nubian" (*IBD*, s.v. "Tahpanhes"). Jeremiah's and Baruch's abduction to Egypt is reported at Jer. 43.1-7, Jeremiah's prophecy about the stones at 43.8-13, his colloquy with the woman at 44.15-28 (including the quotation from the woman in vv. 16-19), and his prediction about "Hophra" at 44.30.

[9] Archon's explanation to his second wife employs *historia* in exactly the same way that Hdt. uses the term in his introductory chapter (1.1): "Here are set forth the results of the research (*historiês*, Ionic genitive) of Herodotos of Halikarnassos...".

[10] Shanks, *BAR* 22.2 (1996) 36-37 reports the finding of not one, but two, clay lumps (*bullae*) bearing a seal impression exactly like the one Archon describes (=*COS* 2.70A, referred to as two bullae stamped by the same seal). The one shown in a large color photo on the cover seems to bear a partial fingerprint of the person who impressed it on the clay, leading Shanks to state as a fact, both in his article title and in the cover photo's caption, that here we have the "Fingerprint of Jeremiah's Scribe". Friedman, *Who Wrote the Bible?*[2] (1997) 147-148 reports that in the first ed. (1987) the author had suggested Jeremiah himself as the identity of the "Deuteronomistic historian", i.e., the author-editor who had put together a version of Deut.-2 Kgs. in the time of Josiah, then re-edited this collection, with additions, after the destruction of Jerusalem and its temple. Reconsidering, Friedman in his second ed. prefers Baruch for this role, calling him "the recorder—and possibly the author/editor—of eight books [Deut.-2 Kgs. plus Jer.] of the Bible". The scroll to which Archon refers, of course, would contain only portions of the biblical Book of Jeremiah.

CHAPTER 23.
ONE FINAL CRISIS

[1] For the political and military events of ca. 571-567 BCE, see Kuhrt 644-645; M&H 427-428; Lloyd re Hdt. 2.163.

[2] Hdt. 2.6-7 supplies a distance along the coast of the delta that amounts to about 400 miles, although in fact the distance is a bit under 300 (Lloyd re 2.6). Judging from Lloyd's map, the distance between Daphnai, near the easternmost Nile branch, and Momemphis, the western-delta site of the battle between Apries and Amasis, would seem to be roughly half of that. Kyrene, again to judge from various maps, appears to have been farther west of the delta than the north-south distance between Sais and Thebes.

[3] For the foundation of Kyrene, see Hdt. 4.150-158 and M&L 5 (both handily translated at C&W 16; see also Fornara 17-18).

[4] Apries' failure at Kyrene is described at Hdt. 4.159, ending with a brief allusion to the Egyptians' uprising that refers the reader back to the story of Apries vs. Amasis at 2.161-163, 169. The flatulent reply of Amasis to Apries' envoy appears at 2.162. For other "colorful" details about Amasis, see Hdt. 2.172-174 and a demotic story translated at Kuhrt 645.

[5] Lloyd re Hdt. 2.163 seems to provide a sensible reconstruction of the conflict between Apries and Amasis, correcting some obvious errors in Hdt.'s account. Citing a 4th-year stele of Amasis (which he says was misdated by earlier scholars), Lloyd puts Amasis' initial victory in his year 1 (570 BCE) and the repulse of Nebuchadnezzar's forces supporting the return of Apries in year 4. Also cited as relevant is a fragmentary Babylonian text that tells of Nebuchadnezzar's intervention in his 37th year, accessible at Prit. 1.205(2) and M&H 427. The convolutions produced by trying to reconcile Hdt.'s account with the other sources can be seen, e.g., in H&W re Hdt. 2.169.

[6] Predictions of Nebuchadnezzar's conquest of Egypt by Jeremiah are cited in ch. 22 and notes. The prediction at Ezek. 29.17-20 is internally dated to (Nebuchadnezzar's) 27th year, which should be ten years *earlier* than the 37th-year date of the Babylonian text just cited, yet M&H 427 for some reason call the Ezekiel passage "an oracle dated to April 571 B.C.E."—which would in any case be irrelevant to a campaign of 567. Both prophets were simply wrong in predicting the Babylonians' conquest of Egypt. Whenever they predicted it, however many times they predicted it, it never happened!

[7] Ahmose (I) was credited with driving out the hated Hyksos rulers; see *COS* 2.1, which is fuller than Prit. 1.173-174.

[8] For an unrealistically rosy picture of Amasis' dealings with Greeks, see Hdt. 2.178-182, some of which extends to periods later than the end of Archon's narrative.

EPILOGUE

[1] Obviously, Archon could not have seen the complete canonical Book of Jeremiah. Since Nebuchadnezzar was still king when Archon completed his narrative, for example, he could not have seen the passage that became Jer. 52.31-34 (=2 Kgs. 25.27-30), which tells of Amel-Marduk's release of Jehoiachin from confinement. It is to be assumed that many other passages that appear in the biblical book were also added or modified later. The editors did not bother to eliminate Jeremiah's incorrect prophecies about the imminent destruction of Egypt and Babylon, presumably seeing these as insignificant in comparison with his "accurate" predictions of the deportees' "return from exile". It is in fact quite possible that editorial tinkering has occurred at Jer. 44.30, where "Yahweh" says that "Hophra" will be handed over "to his enemies and to those determined to kill him"—not to Nebuchadnezzar by name, although other oracles specify him as the agent of Egypt's and Apries' punishment. The imprecise phrase may reflect knowledge that Apries in fact died at the hands of Amasis, not Nebuchadnezzar.

[2] There is a heavy, if unintended, irony in Archon's own dire "prophecies" of the possible ultimate consequences of the spread of Josianic-style intolerant monotheism. Archon can be seen as predicting the rise of both crusading Christianity and *jihad*-waging Islam. All the probability-based reassurances Archon gives himself turn out to be illusory. The "exiles" *did* return, *did* push aside the numerically-larger but less single-minded holdover population of the subprovince of Yehud, and *did* impose their sectarian vision on their own and future generations. The concluding chapter of Norman K. Gottwald, *The Politics of Ancient Israel* (Louisville 2001) 250-251 is very much to the point:

> In conclusion, I would point to the religious dimension of ancient Israel as both a persistent source of "utopian" or "eschatological" hope in the achievement of peace and justice in human affairs and as an equally enduring source of impediments to the realization of peace and justice. What I have to say on this point, I believe, applies in principle to the three scriptured

> monotheistic religions of Judaism, Christianity, and Islam. In my estimation, it is the conjunction of scripture and monotheism that has generated both high hopes for peace and justice and constant frustrations of those hopes.
>
> ...[M]onotheism has encouraged a worldwide vision of peace and justice, while simultaneously nurturing the belief that "we" monotheists—of a particular type—are the sole or superior carriers of that peace and justice, all too easily dividing the world into "us" and "them".

I am grateful to my former student, William Abbott, for reminding me of a vivid passage I had read long ago in G.E.M. de Ste. Croix, *The Class Struggle in the Ancient Greek World* (Ithaca 1981) 331-332, which describes the enthusiasm expressed for exterminating both non-Israelite populations and insufficiently-zealous Israelites in the Torah and the Deuteronomistic history, even though Ste. Croix doubts the factuality of many of the stories, saying (p. 618, n. 10): "...I am concerned here not so much with what actually happened as with what the Israelites wished to believe about their own past and the role played by their God". See also Regina M. Schwartz, *The Curse of Cain: The Violent Legacy of Monotheism* (Chicago 1997). Johathan Kirsch, *God Against the Gods: The History of the War Between Monotheism and Polytheism* (New York 2004) 70-74, except for Kirsch's questionable acceptance that the Torah's law codes other than Deuteronomy were already known and revered before the "discovery" of the scroll in Josiah's time (p. 71) and his thoroughly erroneous supposition that Josiah opposed Necho in "the land of the Jews" because "Josiah sided with the Assyrians" (p. 73), presents a description of the reign and accomplishments of Josiah that is quite consistent with Archon's; the subtitle (p. 69) of his section about Josiah is "The Man Who Invented Biblical Israel".

[3] Numerous copies of Egyptian Books of the Dead (e.g., *COS* 1.118, 120; 2.11, 12) have been found. Photos of portions of such scrolls are to be seen at Prit. 1 figs. 71, 158, 161 (all captioned as such and/or listed as such in the index), and apparently 157 (which appears to be the same kind of photo).

[4] Archon's concluding word-play recalls, of course, his inscription's "co-author", Peleqos (Axe) son of Nobody; see ch. 19 and notes.